Just a Stage

A continuation of
No Small Parts

MARILYN LUDWIG

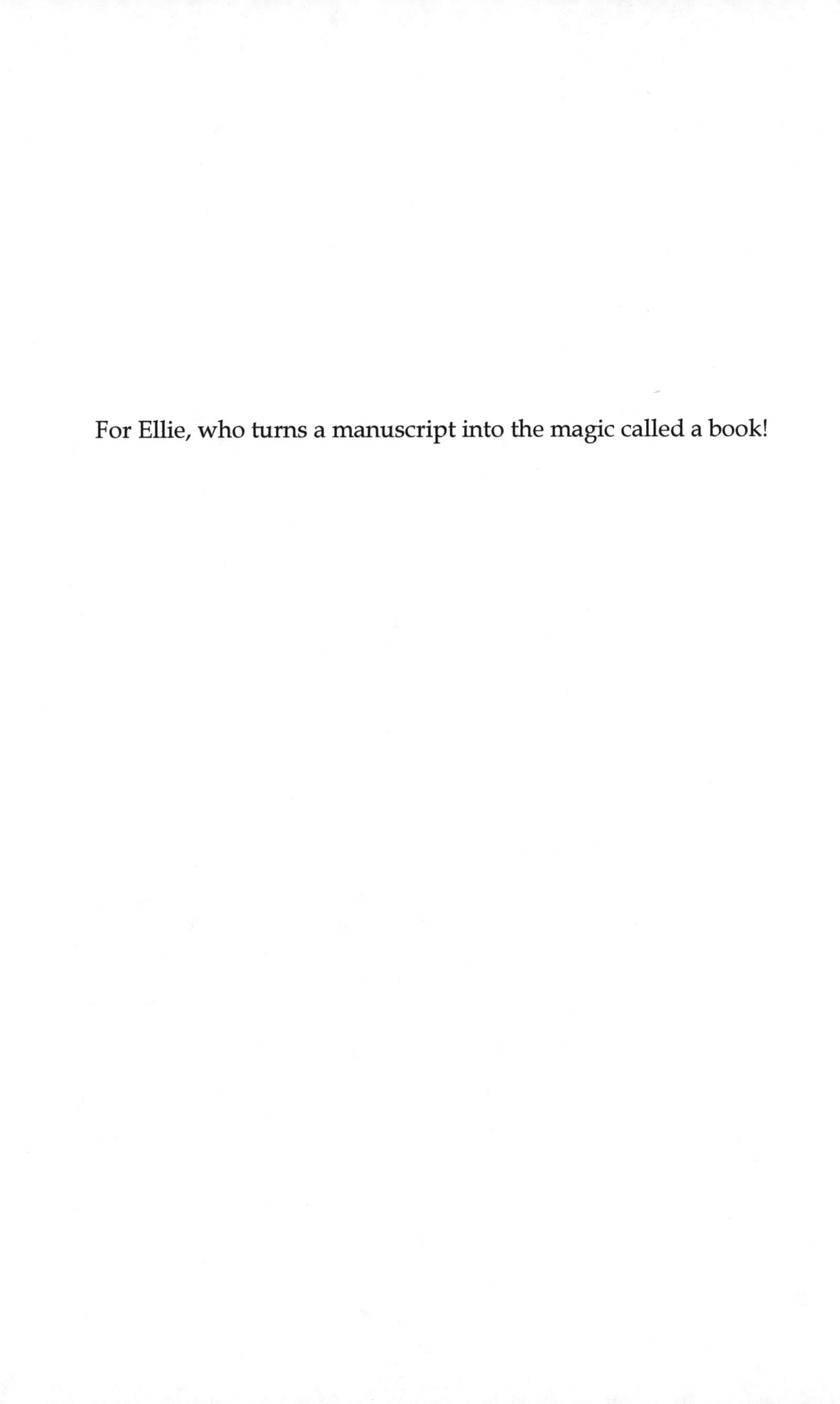

For Ellie, who turns a manuscript into the magic called a book!

LATE AUGUST IN THE SMALL village of Castle Bluff, Illinois. Ceaseless sounds of drilling, crashing, yammering, and hammering fill the air, while large trucks and machinery clog the narrow streets. At the construction site, workers turn up their radios, and then shout to be heard. "Noise pollution!" citizens complain. "How much longer will it last?"

Smithy's Ice Cream Parlor and Grill is largely empty these days, except for its die-hard fans, Castle Bluff's ever-loyal teens. Smithy handles the noise problem by removing his hearing aids, although his financial problem remains acute. The beloved restaurant he has owned for over forty years will close for good if the construction continues much longer.

Althea Grainger, or Gee, as she is fondly known, fearful of her sudden rise in blood pressure, has decided she needs new items for her many collections and heads to Chicago for an extended shopping trip. Her grandson, Kurt Brockway, has started his freshman year at Croft's School of Performing Arts, fortunately a few miles from the construction site. He is too busy to visit Gee for cookies and donut holes.

And out on an imposing bluff over Lake Michigan, all is blissfully quiet at Markey Castle, now that the installation of an elevator is complete. The many bedrooms of the castle are almost full now that Leland Duncan and his bride, the former Janet Armstrong, and her nieces Anna and Roberta Armstrong are in residence. Old Mr. Markey is delighted by the presence of his new live-in companions.

Schools should be in session, of course, but the School Board was indecisive, as were the residents. They agreed that an addition to the middle school was needed and that having it consist of only two grades, ridiculous. In most towns middle school is for grades six through eight or seventh through ninth. Which direction will Castle Bluff go? Arguments on both sides are rancorous, almost as loud as the hammering itself. Even family members have differing opinions, and many parents have imposed a no-talking-about-it-at-the-dinner-table rule.

Beth Walters has mixed emotions. Sometimes she thinks it would be terrific if her ninth-grade friends, especially Kylie and Marla, could stay with her in middle school. Then she remembers that would mean she wouldn't graduate until the following June and that ninth graders would lord it over the younger classes once again. But if sixth graders joined them, one would be her brother, Porter. Would she like that? Beth's parents, overly protective after her frightening experience last year, preferred that their daughter avoid growing up for as long as possible. Better to stay in middle school another two years, they think. When asked his opinion, Porter shrugs. "I'm neutral," he says, "just call me Switzerland."

The Kennedy family members, too, are not in full agreement. Danny Kennedy, a new sixth-grader, hopes for middle school. "Because of the sports." He would drop the childish name of Danny. Not Daniel, which did not sound like a sports hero. He'd be Dan— much more grownup. When Mom points out that Dan is his father's name, he snaps, "Why didn't you give me my own name? Why am I stuck with a stupid little kid's name?" Mom sighs. Just a stage he's going through, she says privately. Just part of maturing—they'd live through it. His sister, Kylie, is in total agreement with Danny about school. She had graduated from eighth grade and was ready for the next big adventure. Besides, Castle Bluff Middle School would not be the same without Roe, her best friend.

Danny and Kylie's mom, Jane, thinks the family should remain loyal to Saint Joseph's. "They've given our kids good educations. It seems wrong to desert them when they're in such a bad way financially." Dad keeps quiet. Although working again, he is aware of his family's own financial straits. It would be a relief not to pay Saint Joe's tuition, especially since Kylie's high school fees are so high. Close to a grand for a public school! He shudders but is grateful she no longer wants to go to Crofts.

Next door, in Roe's old house, the residents are too new to form an opinion. Hannah Rendina will be a seventh grader, no matter the board's decision. She'd rather not attend any school, of course. The kids will know everyone, and she'll be the unwelcome stranger. If she had stayed with her mom, she'd know a few people, even if she didn't like them very much. She was too unfriendly, most people said. Hannah didn't disagree. Here in Castle Bluff, instead of walking around the neighborhood looking for kids her age, Hannah spends most of her time perched up high in an old maple tree. With Uncle Martin's help, she's managed to rest some planks on a few branches so she can relax while reading or spying on the boy next door. Her own private tree fort! Keep out, everyone!

September comes, but the racket continues. Public schools remain closed. "It all depends," residents say. "It all depends on time."

ACT ONE

Two rules:
1. Anything can happen
and
2. Something must happen.

—Peter Brook

SCENE 1 – HANDWRITING ON THE WALL

"THE HANDWRITING IS ON THE wall!" Beth's dad flung the newspaper onto the dining room table, narrowly missing the urn of homemade vegetable soup.

"John!" his wife scolded.

"Sorry, a bit more dramatic than I intended."

Beth grabbed the paper. "They're no longer offering sixth grade at Saint Joseph's? That's the handwriting on the wall? They've been talking about it for years. No big deal, unless it's cursive handwriting."

"Can we at least eat while we talk?" Mrs. Walters asked. "John, ladle out the soup. Beth, please bring out the garlic bread and relish tray." They followed orders, knowing Mom would not allow arguing to ruin their supper.

"Okay, now we can talk," Mom announced, once the whole family, including Porter and Kelly, with baby Zoe in a highchair next to Dad, was eating. "Why should Saint Joseph's eliminating sixth grade affect us? Porter goes to East. Beth is right. It's no big deal."

Dad and Porter exchanged glances, and then shook their heads. "Wrong, Mom," Porter said. "It's huge. East is too crowded already — especially my grade. We can't handle any more kids. There's no room for more desks, even if we had some."

"Porter is correct, Sue. The addition is on the middle school, not East Elementary, although we may decide we should have voted for both. My guess is that at tonight's Board meeting, they'll decide that sixth grade will be part of middle school. There's really no alternative now."

"Then I'll be in the graduating class," Beth said, only a little disappointed.

"And Danny and I will go to the same school," Porter said. "We'll like that."

Beth wondered. All-sports Danny and brainy, academic Porter? It never seemed to matter before—when they went to different schools.

"We'll see," Mom said. "Your father and I are going to the meeting tonight, and I, for one, will have things to say."

Beth wanted to assure Mom she'd be fine whatever decision was made. "I've learned a lot since my stupid crush on Mr. Carroll," she wanted to say. "I'll never make a mistake like that again." But she was afraid to bring up the topic in case Mom brought up other mistakes Beth might make. Honestly! Mom treated Porter with more respect, even though he was two whole years younger. Beth could be nine-year-old Kelly, or even Baby Zoe, the way Mom acted. Well, this year Beth would prove she was responsible and mature. Starting now. She cleared the table. "I'll do the dishes," she announced.

"Go get it, Bingo!" The little dog happily retrieved the ball. Playing with Danny in the backyard was Bingo's favorite thing—even more fun than stealing the family's slippers.

Everything was going to be perfect, Danny thought, once the construction ended. Then, as soon as the inside rooms were cleaned and furnished, school would open at last. True, they might have to go through mid-June next summer, and there would be plenty of complaints made then, but finally everything would be settled. Sixth graders would go to middle school, where he would be Dan—not Danny or Daniel, neither of which sounded like an award-winning Cross Country team runner or soccer player. He'd remain Danny at home, of course.

And it would be terrific to go to the same school as Porter, his best friend. Good thing East School was crowded, so Danny wouldn't end up there, where the sports possibilities were even worse than at Saint Joe's. Cross Country and soccer—just the beginning, Danny decided, before becoming aware of Bingo's frantic yapping.

"Bingo! What is it boy? What's wrong?"

Bingo was jumping against the neighbor's tree. "Did you tree a squirrel?" Most people thought squirrels were cute, but Danny considered them a darned nuisance when they teased his dog. His sister Kylie always defended the squirrels. "It's instinct. They can't help being squirrels any more than Bingo can help being a dog."

"Hey, turn that thing off!" Surely that didn't come from a squirrel.

"Hush, Bingo," Danny commanded, looking high up into the branches. "Is someone up there?"

"Well, I'm not a squirrel," the voice said angrily. "This is my property. You're trespassing, and I don't need a mangy mutt barking at me."

A mangy mutt? He'd skip that for now. No sense in fighting with a stranger. "I can't see you. Come on down."

"Won't." But at last a face looked down at Danny. A girl.

"Hey, cool! You built a tree house in Roe's old yard. I'll bet you can see for miles up there."

"Far enough that I'd like you to go home," she said. "And it's a tree fort."

Danny, not used to unpleasant people, tried again. "I'm your next-door neighbor, Danny Kennedy. I wondered who moved in. We were good friends with Roe, the girl who lived there."

"Roe. Stupid name."

He would not let her get to him. "It's short for Rosita. She lives in Spain now. What's your name?"

"Hannah."

"How old are you, Hannah?" No answer, but Danny waited.

Finally, after a long pause, "I'm twelve. Seventh grade, once school opens."

Name, rank, and serial number only, Danny thought, remembering war movies he and Dad watched on Netflix. "I'll only be in sixth, but we'll both be in middle school. I can't wait. I'm going to try out for a bunch of sports."

Hannah shrugged. "Not my thing. I want to go inside, so call off your dog."

"Oh, he won't hurt you. He's just a puppy. I'm sorry you don't like dogs."

Cautiously, Hannah climbed down. "I don't know if I like them or not. I've never known any." Bingo ran over to her, and she took a step back. But Bingo sat expectantly and smiled. He was used to people loving him.

Perhaps Hannah could tell, for she smiled back and gave Bingo a tentative scratch. Her reward was a full-face bath. "Eww," she said. "Yucky!" But she grinned. "See ya!" She ran toward the back door.

"See you around, Hannah," Danny said. "Time to go inside, Bingo." He doubted he and Hannah would be friends, but he could tell she needed one.

He wasn't so bad, Hannah reflected as she started supper. It wouldn't hurt to have someone to talk to occasionally. Maybe not at school, depending on whether seventh graders got along with sixth. They sure didn't at her old school. Sixth grade was hell. She didn't mind being unpopular, but she did not like to be bullied or teased. She'd be fine in Castle Bluff — until people found out about Dad and Uncle Martin. They planned to be discreet — Dad's word — but they knew it might not be long before they had to move. "The world is changing," they always said, and that someday having two Dads would seem normal. Well, maybe in cities, but what about in this poky town?

Dad and Uncle Martin planned to be late, so supper would be sub sandwiches again. No matter. They all liked them. Hannah set the kitchen table with paper plates and plastic utensils. Playing with Bingo could be fun, she thought. A nice little friend who wouldn't care about her personal life. She had a hunch Danny might be that way, too. She'd be friendlier next time, and—"Darn! I should have asked him!" Maybe Danny had also noticed the creepy man who had been hanging around their houses. "I'll say he was carrying knives and a gun. That'll get Danny's attention."

SCENE 2 – TOTALLY UNFAIR!

"NO FALL PLAY!" BETH MOANED to her good friend, Imani Jones. "It's not fair!"

"It is totally unfair," Imani agreed. "Especially since they've figured out how to have sports."

"Maybe it wouldn't be so bad if eighth graders could go to Community, too, but no, we've got to be the guinea pigs. Remote learning at home! I'm sick of my computer already!"

"I agree." Imani put her arm through Beth's, as they walked in silence toward Markey Castle this October Saturday. They hadn't visited Mr. Markey in ages. Fall seemed to be coming early, and the village's many maple trees were putting on a splendid show, but the girls barely noticed the crimson and gold leaves. Beth and her friends had assumed all would be settled once the School Board and Saint Joseph's had made their decision to send sixth grade to middle school, but that was not the end of their difficulties.

Sure, the hammering had ended, and the builders had gone on to other projects. The problems were inside now: electricity, heat, water—"You name it," Beth's father said.

Then, just to add to the fun, Saint Joseph's announced it was closing its school permanently. East Elementary couldn't handle the influx of all of St. Joe's students and would go double-session, kindergarten through fifth. West Elementary was too far away for east side students, and also full. What a mess! Everyone agreed on that. More than one set of parents expressed regret that the more inclusive referendum hadn't passed. "But taxes!" they'd said back then.

Beth stopped. "Well, we're here. Time to put on our happy faces for Mr. Markey."

Imani giggled. "I can't wait to find out how marriage has changed Mr. Leland Duncan."

"You mean if." Beth grabbed the nose of the troll-shaped doorknocker, remembering the first time Kylie, on a self-dare, had rapped it. That had been the beginning of so many splendid happenings for their friends: the cast party, Cinderella play, and friendship with Marla. Her horrible experience with the teacher, Mr. Carroll, had also taken place at that time. She whisked away the thought—definitely ancient history.

"Leland?" Beth exclaimed at the sight of the handsome stranger who opened the door. He looked years younger, wearing black jeans and a casual blue pullover. The biggest difference, though, was his happy smile. No one would mistake him for a butler now.

Grinning, he bowed from the waist, feigning formality. "What can I do for you, ladies?" he asked.

A thin voice in the background called out, "Do we have company?"

"Yes, sir, a couple of middle school youngsters, no doubt wanting something utterly impossible and impractical."

The only things utterly impossible, Beth thought, were Leland's twinkling eyes. "I'm almost experiencing deja vu," she said. "Almost."

"Well, for heaven's sake, let them in, Leland." A female voice this time.

"Yes, dear," Leland said, winking at the girls.

This time, Leland led them into a sitting room, newly furnished with comfortable couches and chairs, sunlight streaming through the sparkling, clean windows.

"Wow!" Imani said, once Leland had introduced the girls to his wife Janet, and Mr. Markey had given them delighted hugs. "What a difference! This room is amazing, Mrs. Duncan."

"You call my husband Leland, so you might as well call me Janet. I don't think I've met Beth before, but I saw you, Imani, when you played the fairy godmother. I thought you were wonderful!"

"Thanks. It was so much fun."

Leland returned to his familiar role. "I do believe refreshments are in order. I'll fetch the donuts and cider."

"Let me help you, dear."

It was Beth's turn to say, "Wow! I don't believe it. I've never seen such a change in anyone!"

Mr. Markey laughed. "Leland is happy. He's also in love. Janet and he were a couple many years ago but separated because of a foolish quarrel neither of them can quite remember. A lot of what's happened here is due to you and your friends."

Kylie mainly, Beth reflected.

Imani patted Mr. Markey's hand. "You look in good spirits, yourself."

Mr. Markey nodded. "I normally am, but this has been a fine development. Janet has brought us into the present century. We even have an elevator and telephones." He pointed to his shirt pocket. "Believe it or not, I own a cellphone."

Leland and Janet brought in the treats. Beth remembered when they balanced china precariously on their laps. Now each of them had a table tray on which to place sturdy paper plates. "Pumpkin donuts, my favorite," Imani said.

Soon they were telling Mr. Markey and the Duncans about the situation at the middle school. "Our high school friends started immediately once the school decided where ninth graders would go," Beth said, "and Kurt started ages ago at Crofts. But the rest of us are stuck waiting for school to open."

"The play?" Leland asked.

Imani shook her head. "No play. Not even Drama Club. And they say that once school opens, we might have to go until five every day, so there won't be any clubs."

"But they always figure out how to do sports," Beth added glumly.

Silence while they drank their cider and polished off the donuts.

"How about coming here?" Leland asked suddenly.

Beth was grateful she'd finished her cider; she would have been certain to spill it. "Here?" she sputtered. "How? When?"

"Saturdays," Leland continued. "You might not have time to do a play, but you could do your club. As long as you have an adult in charge, I don't see why anyone would object."

"I'd love to help," Janet said. "Maybe Anna, your Miss Armstrong, could, too, if she's free."

"Or Gee," Mr. Markey added. "She's used to all of you. But isn't there a new theater teacher? Who would have directed your fall play?"

Beth shook her head. "Well, they really haven't hired anyone yet. My seventh-grade English and social studies teacher said she'd give it a try. She said she needed to learn more about it, though."

"A Saturday Drama Club would be wonderful," Imani said. "It would be great to have something to look forward to again. We could have skits and theater games and just be together—especially eighth graders tied to a computer all day. And Mrs. Hunt could learn at the same time."

"If she's willing to come on Saturdays," Beth said doubtfully.

"Even if she only came sometimes, it would work," Janet said. "I'm sure we can fill in on adult chaperones."

Mr. Markey grew excited, as he always did when the students had a plan. "Maybe Kylie and Brad and some of the other ninth graders could join you."

"It would be good to see them again," Leland, who was particularly fond of Brad, added.

Beth and Imani looked at each other. They liked that idea—and didn't. Yes, having the gang back together was sort of appealing, but they were the upper class now. They did not want the ninth graders to come back and take over. If this new Drama Club at the castle happened, it should be their baby.

Danny raced around the outdoor track, wondering whether to pause so Porter could catch up. No, he'd keep on going; Porter would understand. Danny was proud of his friend for giving Cross Country a try, even though sports really wasn't his thing.

Even though Danny didn't like the thought of going to school through June, everything was working out well for him. The campus of Community College was impressive, and Danny felt important. He was the best runner on the sixth-grade team and was certain to win a medal at the final meet in November. Then, on to indoor soccer! Community was terrific. Maybe he'd go to college there someday, after middle school and high school, of course. Or maybe he'd do professional sports, if his parents allowed him to skip college. Hockey would be his choice. For now, running was as good as flying. Danny had never felt so free.

Sixth grade at Community wasn't awful, even though the classes were way too crowded. Sixth and seventh graders met in one dilapidated building that had been empty because the college planned to tear it down. Administrators were happy to wait on that, eager for the elementary district's rent. Conditions weren't great, but Danny thought they were luckier than the eighth graders, working on their computers at home. He would not have enough self-discipline for that! All classes had gobs of homework, of course, and the teachers were strict about students turning it in on time. Porter was a much better student, but Danny was better at sports, so it all worked out. Porter and Kylie would help if he had trouble, but so far he was handling it.

Uh-oh! Porter was down. Danny raced back to help him up. Just a skinned knee, Porter told him. What a good sport his friend was!

"Ready, get set, go!" Hannah knew she would never win a race against Bingo—unless a squirrel distracted him. She couldn't tell whether Bingo hated squirrels or loved them. She asked Danny once the race was over.

"Both, I think," Danny said. "Chasing them is his favorite sport, next to playing with you and me, of course."

Hannah smiled. Deciding that she and Danny could be friends was the best decision she'd made in Castle Bluff. His parents were nice, too, and appreciated Dad's offer of driving both of them to Community for their classes. Dad's new job was teaching art there. After school, Danny stayed for sports, so Hannah waited for Dad to bring them both home.

"You're a good runner," Danny said. "You should join Cross Country, too."

Hannah shook her head. "I'm not much of a joiner. I get my homework done in the library, so I can do whatever I want at night." Not that there was much to do, but she didn't share that.

"Danny, supper!"

Kylie, Danny's big sister—Hannah hadn't decided how she felt about her. She was awfully pretty but not very friendly. Hannah admitted that she hadn't been exactly friendly, either, to the high school freshman. She shrugged. Didn't matter. Danny was her friend; she didn't need more than one.

"Come on, Bingo. See ya tomorrow, Hannah."

"Bye."

Dad was supposed to fix dinner, but he was all wrapped up in his new painting. She'd fix something. Maybe warm up the leftover spaghetti. Then Dad would join her before he left to pick up Uncle Martin in the city. He'd probably make her go with him. Those trips were getting boring. He was trying to find someone to stay with her when he couldn't be there, especially once school started, but it was hard being brand new in the community and not knowing anyone. Besides, it would have to be someone who wasn't nosy and wouldn't care that two men had a daughter. Hannah would rather be alone, even if it meant that sometimes she was lonely. Maybe if she promised to stay inside and lock the door, Dad would agree. Then she'd just do her own thing.

She should tell Dad and Uncle Martin, of course, about the strange man still lurking around. She'd seen him again last night, peeking from behind the garage. A couple of times she'd seen him walking toward the Kennedy's house as if he were planning to ring the doorbell, but he changed his mind and dashed away.

Hannah couldn't decide if he was a young man or an old kid. Whatever, he wasn't in great shape. Maybe he was homeless and needed help. Whatever, he was creepy. She didn't want to worry Dad or Uncle Martin. She'd get around to telling Danny someday.

SCENE 3 — WE'LL START A CLUB!

"Y OU'RE KIDDING! SOME GUY IS hanging around here?" Danny said, appalled. "Do you think he's dangerous?"

"I don't know. Probably. I think he was carrying knives and a gun." Now, why had she said that? Why did she lie when it wasn't necessary? The truth was worrisome enough. It was the following day—Sunday afternoon. Hannah had joined Danny and Bingo for a walk in the park. They had stopped to rest at a picnic table while Bingo scouted out squirrels. "The man could be homeless, I guess. He looks pretty shabby." And maybe hungry, she thought.

"So what does he look like?"

"Well, it's always dark, so I can't see clearly. His clothes are black—maybe gray—and he wears a dark hoodie. His skin is darkish, too. I don't think he's African American, but he's darker than you or me."

Danny laughed. "That's not saying much."

Hannah wished she could laugh at herself the way Danny did. He was comfortable in his own skin while she hated being so pale and washed-out looking. "What do you think I should do about it? The man, I mean."

"We could tell our parents—that would be the smart thing to do."

Hannah could tell Danny didn't want to, either. She wondered why. "My dad and uncle have their own problems. I don't want to make things worse."

"My parents are just plain busy. But I think it would be more fun if we figured it out for ourselves."

"Fun?" How could a nighttime prowler be fun?

Instead of answering, Danny jumped to his feet so suddenly that Bingo ran toward him, barking, deciding it was an invitation to play.

"Danny?"

"I've got it! We'll start a club, the kind that figures out weird things—like mysteries. I helped solve one last summer." Danny explained his involvement with the pollution mystery at Camp Shimmer Lake, embellishing on his own contributions, of course.

"An odd kind of club," Hannah said, "with only two members. Do you have time with all your sports? When would we meet?"

"Oh, Saturday or Sunday afternoons, when our families don't have plans. We'll figure out what's up with that man, and then find other mysteries."

"Well, okay—"

"We do need more members. You're right; only two is lame. I'll ask my friend, Porter. You'll like him, Hannah. You need more friends."

"No, I don't," Hannah wanted to say, but she didn't want Danny to get mad at her. Castle Bluff was turning out better than she'd expected, and she didn't want to ruin it. "Okay, I guess," she said softly.

"Great! Let's go home and call him. Maybe he can come right over. He's smart. He'll have great ideas."

Porter didn't let them down. He was a super friend, Danny thought for the millionth time. And he was quiet and serious. Hannah didn't seem spooked by him at all.

"Well, we should tell our parents, of course," Porter said, "although it could be interesting to solve it ourselves. But if it starts looking dangerous, we'll tell someone."

"Like Kylie or Beth," Danny suggested, not willing to involve adults.

"Or parents," Porter said, "but Kylie and Beth could be a start. Hannah, what do you think?"

Hannah nodded slowly. "Okay."

"Maybe Beth should join our club." She and Danny had become good friends over the summer.

Porter shook his head. "She's too busy getting Drama Club started again and taking art lessons. I don't think she's interested in much else right now."

"Just us three," Hannah said. "That would be best."

Danny beamed. "So we've got a club. If Hannah sees the man, she'll let us know at once, and we'll try to meet every weekend. Shouldn't the club have a name?"

Porter nodded. "The whole thing sounds corny, like something little kids do, but I've never been in a club before. How about the Super Sleuths Club?"

"Definitely corny," Hannah said, "but we could use an acronym. The SSC. No one but us will know what it means."

"The SSC," Danny breathed. "Perfect." It was sophisticated— important. He'd keep his eyes open for more mysteries, so they could keep the club going, even after they'd solved the mystery of the lurking man. He wasn't sure Hannah was telling the truth. She might have made up the whole thing just for attention. The club would still be fun, though.

First, Beth got permission from her parents, who thought that Drama Club at the castle was a fine idea, as long as Beth understood that family activities might take priority some weekends. "How kind of Mr. Markey to offer," Mom said.

"Actually, it was Leland's idea." Beth related how marriage had changed the rigid man they'd all known.

"I thought art was more important to you," Dad said.

"It is, but I don't think I could start an art club."

Next, Beth called Mrs. Hunt, who agreed as long as she wasn't required to be there every Saturday. Beth assured her they had a few willing substitutes. That wasn't exactly the truth. Beth had not contacted Gee, but Janet had sounded eager. Beth wondered why she hesitated calling Gee or Miss Armstrong, or even her friends in ninth grade. They were the big shots last year, she thought. Now it's our turn. Yes, she might be selfish, but that's how she felt. "I'll talk it over with Priyanka, Imani, and Gabrielle," she said softly. "Maybe they won't agree. Maybe it's just me."

Mrs. Hunt gave her some interesting information. "We will definitely have a spring play," she said. "The chorus director is willing to switch with us. The musical will be during Drama Club's usual November time slot."

"That is good news, but will they have time?"

"Music classes are taking place at Community. They'll rehearse there. They chose a fairly simple show — *School House Rock Live*. It should work out fine. Your Drama Club plan will give me time to decide on a play and the opportunity to learn more about directing."

Beth and Mrs. Hunt agreed that the new club would start the following Saturday at ten and last until noon. Then Beth called eighth graders who were in Drama Club last year. They needed to meet, she said. "Tomorrow at seven at my house." After checking with their parents, most of them said they could come. All girls! They had to find boys. That could be tough — most of the Drama Club boys from last year had graduated. So many things to do, but at least she felt alive again.

Before turning out the light, Beth heard a knock on her bedroom door. "Come in."

A worried-looking Porter came into the room.

"Porter, what's wrong?"

He sat on the edge of her bed. "I guess I need some advice."

That wasn't unusual. Beth and her brother were used to bouncing ideas off each other. "Okay."

"The problem is Cross Country. Danny really wants me to do it, and Mom and Dad think it's a great idea, too. But Beth, I hate running. I'm no good at it. And I don't want to do soccer and hockey and everything else that Danny thinks is so important we do together. We didn't go to the same school before, so it was no big deal, but now —"

"But now you're worried about losing your best friend." He's absolutely miserable, she thought.

Porter nodded.

"Just tell him," Beth said. "I don't think he'll ever stop being your friend. Tell him how you feel. He'll understand."

"Maybe, but maybe he'll say that I won't have anything else to do."

Drama Club needed boys. "Here's an idea." And she told him her plan.

"At the castle? That's cool. I'm not sure if I'd fit in, but I'll think about it. Thanks."

Beth would tell him more throughout the week, as their actual plans formed. If Porter joined, maybe other boys would, too. So how did she feel about having her brother in the same club? Good, she thought. She'd like it a lot.

AFTER EMAILING, TEXTING, AND CALLING everyone they knew, the newly formed Drama Club met in the grand ballroom of Markey Castle, with its director, Mrs. Hunt. It was Saturday once more.

Beth looked around the spacious room that seemed even larger than usual. "Eleven? Only eleven? We must have contacted at least fifty!"

"Plus we're all girls!" Priyanka wailed. "No boys!"

"We knew that would be a problem," Imani added, "but this is ridiculous!"

"Let's give it a few more minutes," Mrs. Hunt cautioned. "It's just ten now."

By 10:15, five seventh graders arrived, apologizing because they got confused about where they should go, and three sixth graders. Again, all girls.

"I guess we should get started," Mrs. Hunt said. "My name is Carol Hunt, and I teach English and social studies at Community — I mean, CBMT." She smiled in a jokey way and was rewarded with a few chuckles. "I know some of you from last year, and I'm getting to know you seventh graders who are in my classes now. I did some theater in college, but that was years ago, and I'm very rusty. Since I am learning, too, I'm going to turn this first meeting over to the eighth graders."

All eyes turned to Beth, who felt herself turning beet red. They saw her as the leader. That had not been her plan at all. Well, here goes nothing, she thought. "Welcome to all of you," she said. "It was so nice of Mr. Markey to allow us to meet at the castle. I know we're going to have a lot of fun. I brought along a thank you note for us to sign before we leave today." That had been a late idea when she couldn't sleep. "I was a little worried about not having any boys, but I think it will be okay—especially when we're back in our own building."

Imani gave support. "A lot of the kids are in Cross Country, which is practically a religion at CBMT. We're sure to have more members as soon as the season ends in November."

"My brother, Porter, plans to join," Beth said. "He couldn't be here today because he had to work some things out. I think he'll come next week, especially if we can get another boy."

A couple of the seventh graders nodded as if they knew a few they might ask.

Beth was aware they ran the risk of losing the new girls if they didn't have a good time today, but she didn't really know what to say next.

Mrs. Hunt came to the rescue. "Sometimes it comes in waves," she said. "Last year the eighth-grade class was very strong, especially the boys, and seventh wasn't. You'll see more members once they learn about us. Maybe we can use our imaginations to figure out ways to rope them in."

Beth could tell that everyone liked Mrs. Hunt. She was going to work out just fine, at least as their sponsor, if not as a director. "I think a lot of kids would love to see the castle," she said. "Maybe even a tour if we can get permission. A tour, followed by refreshments. I know someone who makes terrific homemade donuts and would love to help." Was she really planning to involve Gee, after her determination not to? Suddenly she had another idea—one that she had resisted before. "One of my best friends is an acting student at Crofts. I'll bet many of you have heard of him. Kurt Brockway. He's terrific at improvisation. I could ask him to come and demonstrate."

Everyone perked up noticeably. Kurt was popular throughout Castle Bluff.

One of the seventh graders, shaking with excitement, leaped to her feet. "A Halloween party," she shrieked. "We could have the most amazing haunted Halloween party and invite all three classes." Loud chattering and buzzing filled the room, which no longer seemed too large.

Beth smiled. "That's a great idea. We'll need Mr. Markey's permission first, but I bet he'll agree. Maybe not invite everyone, though."

Mrs. Hunt raised her hand to stop the din. "In the meantime, though, you girls will have a chance to improve your acting skills and have a better chance at getting roles once we're able to have shows again."

The girls grew serious, although still enthusiastic. They knew that girls had a harder time getting parts because of their sheer numbers. Mrs. Hunt pulled folders out of her briefcase. "I brought along scenes and monologues that Miss Armstrong left behind. These folders are just for girls. Perhaps we could start by choosing parts and rehearsing. Then we'll rehearse for a few weeks and, if you like, have a simple program for your parents."

"What's a monologue?" one of the sixth graders asked.

Priyanka explained that it was a scene for only one person. "Monologues are a good option if you don't think you can come to every meeting. You can rehearse at home without letting a scene partner down."

Mrs. Hunt nodded. "Thank you. I hadn't thought of that."

"And," Beth added, "if you take a scene or monologue home, be sure to bring it back—in case we don't have extras."

Mrs. Hunt laid out the materials and the girls were about to read and choose partners when Beth had another thought. "I think we eighth graders shouldn't just pick our friends as partners. Let's get to know the new kids."

The girls were happily claiming parts when the main door to the ballroom opened. In came Janet, followed by Mr. Markey, with a platter of cookies. Mr. Markey beamed. "Elevator," he said. "Makes all the difference." The girls cheered!

"You're awfully quiet tonight, son," Mr. Kennedy said at dinner Monday. "Anything wrong?"

Danny answered quickly before Mom could say the dreaded words, "he's just going through a stage." He hated that expression, although he wasn't quite sure what it meant.

"I'm a little down," he said, "but it will be okay."

"Anything in particular?" Kylie asked. Danny was glad she did, although he'd rather they talk in private. They hardly saw each other lately, and he missed her.

"Yeah, it's about Porter. He doesn't really like sports all that much. He's trying, but he can't keep up with me. Actually, he slows me down. I feel guilty about that, so I keep slowing down to help him. He's fallen a couple of times. He told me today that he wants to quit."

Mom shrugged. "So what's the problem? It's not like he gets a grade for it. He should quit if he doesn't like it."

"I know, but—"

Kylie nodded. "I get it. I'm going through that with a few of my friends who don't want to do theater anymore. Like Brad," she admitted.

Danny stared at her. He had no idea that Kylie was having problems with her long-time boyfriend.

"You're wondering," Kylie continued, "whether or not you and Porter will stay friends."

Danny nodded but remained quiet. Kylie had hit it on the head. That was exactly what he was worried about.

Mom snorted. "You've been friends with Porter all your life, and you've always gone to different schools."

Dad stood. "I agree. It will work out fine. Now, if you'll excuse me I've got another Board meeting. Wish I'd never run for the fool thing. Nothing but squabbling."

"Take care of the dishes," Mom said to Danny and Kylie. "I'm going to attend that meeting, too. This construction delay is affecting all of us."

Arguing once again, they left, with Dad explaining to Mom that it no longer had anything to do with construction.

Danny stacked plates and sighed. "I guess we're all going through a stage," he said.

Kylie burst out laughing. "I'm getting that in my face lately, too. Look, Danny, I'm having trouble with math, and I have a ton of homework. I should have worked over the weekend, but—well, you know. I'll pay you if you take care of the dishes."

"That's okay, Kyle. I'll do it for free this time. I don't have anything else to do."

"Except worry. Tell you what. If I finish before you go to bed, we can talk more. Maybe we can dream up some things you and Porter can do together."

Danny agreed, although he didn't think it would be much of a problem after all. Before this year, he and Porter had lots in common, and he was sort of relieved Porter was quitting. He just didn't like feeling guilty.

Later that evening, there was a knock on Danny's door, and Kylie peeked in. "All done," she said. "Want to fix a snack? Mom and Dad aren't home yet. That must be some meeting!"

"I think they were going to the Walters afterward. A snack sounds good." Danny turned off his light and followed Kylie downstairs.

Leftover chocolate cake and milk hit the spot. It was different talking with Kylie now, Danny thought. It was more serious, mature. She wasn't treating him like a little kid anymore, although they always got along. And he had to admit he was more interested in her as a person now. Perhaps he was finally growing into Dan.

"I thought about what you said, Kylie. You're right. Porter and I will be fine. What about you and Brad? Have you broken up?"

"Maybe. I'm not sure. He's different, and he's not telling me what's going on. Kurt invited me to the fall dance at Crofts, but Brad doesn't seem to care."

Danny shook his head. "That's weird, but what about Beth? I'll bet she minds plenty."

"She says she doesn't—that they're just friends. Well, Kurt and I are just friends, too, but she may not believe me. Everything is different, even worse than last year. Marla and Eric are dating, and Roe . . . " Kylie sighed.

"I miss Roe," Danny said.

"Everyone does."

"You don't get many letters from her, Kylie."

"Beth gets a lot. I wonder why. Sometimes she passes them on to me."

Danny laughed, just a little because he didn't want to hurt Kylie's feelings. "Probably Beth gets letters because she writes them."

Kylie gave a reluctant grin. "I always get caught up in what I'm doing and let other things slide. What about you, little brother? Any potential girlfriends? Like Hannah next door?"

Danny shook his head vehemently. "Hardly. She's in love with Bingo. Occasionally she's pleasant to me."

"She doesn't seem friendly."

"She isn't." Then he and Kylie looked at each other and smiled. This was the first time ever they had talked about boy and girlfriends. It was the most adult conversation they'd ever had. He almost wanted to tell her about the secret club. Almost.

Hannah. He needed to talk with her. They'd never had another SSC meeting. Had the strange man stopped prowling around? Danny thought the three of them—he, Porter, and Hannah just might need their secret club right now. For friendship's sake, if nothing more.

Hannah had spent hours in her tree fort, hoping Danny would come outside. Soon it would grow dark—time change soon—but she was afraid to use her flashlight. She had heard a rustling noise, coming from the Kennedy's garage. She couldn't see anyone, but she thought he was there. Probably up to no good, she thought. She shivered. She should have worn a hoodie or brought out a blanket. Well, she needed to go inside, but it would be too dangerous to go down the tree with so little light. She couldn't take a chance of bumping into the man.

"I've got it," she whispered. She'd pretend to talk on her cellphone to someone in the house. She'd talk loudly. The man wouldn't know that Dad and Uncle Martin weren't home—she hoped. "Okay, Dad. Yes, I'll come in now. I'm getting cold. We can make some hot chocolate. I've got a flashlight, so I won't have any problem. If I'm not inside in three minutes, come and check." Following the steady beam of light, Hannah climbed down and raced into the house. "I've got to convince Dad I need a cellphone. Tomorrow I'll grab Danny and insist we have a meeting." She'd call right now, but the light in Danny's bedroom had been turned off.

SCENE 5 – COMMUNICATION IS THE KEY

"I'M SURE SOMEONE WAS IN your garage," Hannah told Bingo, because the little dog was the only one listening to her. Danny and Porter were having an intense conversation about sports versus Drama Club.

Before school that morning they had agreed upon this emergency SSC meeting. Danny, pleading that he needed Porter's help on homework, managed to get his parents to approve Porter coming over. Straight-A student Porter didn't have any problem getting his parents to agree. "Just call when you're ready to come home," his dad said.

Actually, Danny had already received the help he needed—from Hannah. He'd been fumbling to find a subject for his composition. "It's supposed to be about something we care about a lot. I care about lots of things. Couldn't I write about that?"

Hannah shook her head. "Nope. Stick to one thing and make each paragraph something about that." She tried to explain five-paragraph essays, but Danny didn't understand her any more than he did his teacher. "Write about Bingo," Hannah said. "Talk about how you always wanted a dog. Then you could say how you got him, why you named him Bingo, and all the goofy things he does. When you're done, I'll help you make sure it's in good order. I like writing."

Well, thanks to her, Danny's composition was great and ready to be turned in. At least that was Hannah's opinion. Porter would look it over, too, just so Danny wasn't a total liar."

"Woof," Bingo announced.

"I agree, Bingo. You and I will have a good run, and—" Hannah got into the boys' faces—"when I return, the meeting *will* come to order. Come on, Bingo!"

Meetings were going to be harder once winter came, but Hannah thought it unlikely they'd still have a club if the boys didn't start taking more of an interest.

"Are you certain you didn't hear a stray cat?" Porter asked.

"Or a bear?" Danny growled, pretending to attack Porter.

Hannah got up from the grass. "If you're going to be like that, I'm going inside. It wasn't a cat, and I was really scared."

Danny pulled her back down. "I'm sorry," he said. And he was, but he was mainly glad everything had been sorted out with Porter. "You're right. Whatever it was, we should take it seriously, especially since you saw a man before. Why didn't you call me?"

"I can see your room from my window. It was dark. My dad and uncle weren't home, so I wanted to call you. Dad has your phone number on our kitchen bulletin board, but I don't have your cellphone number."

"Cause I don't have a cellphone," Danny said, frowning. It was a sore point with him. His mom couldn't see any reason why a sixth grader should have one. Dad said maybe Christmas. The truth was the Kennedys still weren't back in shape financially. "You could have called our landline. My folks weren't home either. I was in the kitchen talking with my sister."

"I'll give you our number," Porter said. "Although it might not do much good; I live too far away to help."

"But Porter could call me," Danny said. "Mom and Dad wouldn't think that was weird. Then I could sneak out and join Hannah in the backyard, or just keep watch from my window."

"Communication is the key," Porter said. "Maybe you and Hannah can come up with an emergency signal from your bedroom windows. Lights flashing or something."

That was more like it, Danny thought. Signals, for real or pretend, were exciting. Hannah could be making the whole thing up, but they'd still have fun. He hoped it was real. A mysterious prowler was cool!

Porter stood. "I should call home. It's starting to get cold."

"And dark," Hannah said. "Come inside first. You can have a Coke while we're exchanging phone numbers."

Danny hadn't been in the house since his mother had fixed it up for Roe's dad to sell. It looked almost as sterile as it had then. There was no warmth as there was in the Kennedy's kitchen, always messy with books and stacks of papers on counters, plus the smells of yummy baking. Porter wrote down his phone number and asked if he could use the bathroom.

"Sure." Hannah pointed the way.

Danny then regretted his Coke and said he needed to go, too, and didn't think he could wait. "Could I go upstairs?"

Giggling, Hannah pointed upward. "You know the way," she said.

Normally, Danny wasn't the nosy type. But after talking with Kylie, he realized how much he missed Roe and her dad, whom he called Uncle Carl. He was curious about the house—that's all. After using the bathroom, he peeked into the open bedroom doors. Yes, Hannah could look across into his bedroom and the backyard. She had Roe's brother Mateo's old bedroom. Danny remembered him; he hadn't been very nice. What about Roe's room? Probably her Uncle Martin slept there. No, it was furnished with office supplies—two desks, lots of bookcases, and a photocopy machine. No bed. A small bedside light was on in the master bedroom—a huge king-sized bed for Hannah's parents. Wait a minute. Hannah's mom didn't live there. On a large dresser was a framed photo. Danny knew he shouldn't, but he was curious to see if Hannah's mom looked like her, so he crept cautiously to the dresser. How strange. It was a photo of Mr. Rendina and a man. Uncle Martin, maybe? Strange that Hannah's dad had a framed picture of himself and his brother. He shrugged. Uncle Martin must sleep in one of the rooms downstairs.

"Danny, are you coming?"

He got out of the room fast. "Coming!" he yelled.

Downstairs, Hannah and Porter seemed to be having an argument but paused when Danny reappeared. "It's about time," Hannah said, looking at him suspiciously.

"I called for Dad to come," Porter said. "He was wrapping things up and said he'd be here in fifteen minutes."

Danny sat on a kitchen chair and grabbed a handful of pretzels. "I could hear you on the stairs. What's wrong?"

"Porter wants to tell Kylie and Beth what's going on. I disagree."

Danny thought about it. If Hannah were making the whole thing up to get attention, she would not want to tell. Time to call her bluff. "Porter might be right," he said slowly. "If we were just little kids with a secret club, it would make sense not to say anything. But a stranger with weapons is dangerous. Someone else needs to know."

"Kylie and Beth wouldn't say anything," Porter said. "It sounds strange to say, but Beth is my good friend as well as a sister."

Danny nodded. "She's mine, too, and the best artist I know."

Hannah snorted. "Oh, right. An eighth-grade artist."

"She is! If she saw the man, she'd draw a sketch of him."

Hannah still looked skeptical.

"Just think about it, Hannah, and remind me to show you the sketchbook Beth gave me. It's full of her drawings."

They heard a car horn. "That will be my dad," Porter said. "See you tomorrow. Thanks for the Coke, Hannah."

"And the pretzels. I'd better go home, too." Danny left the house that still housed a lonely and alone girl. *What's going on there? Is she telling the truth or not?* he wondered.

The SSC members weren't the only ones worrying about communication. Beth had called Kurt, asking if they could meet. "I need your help with Drama Club," she said. Kurt seemed flattered and suggested Smithy's after school the next day. Beth hadn't been to the ice cream parlor in ages—not since the end of summer—and she hadn't seen Kurt since Crofts started. She'd pretended not to be hurt that he and Kylie were going to the dance—just as friends—but doubted she'd fooled anyone. *He could have asked me,* she thought. *We're friends, too. Closer friends.*

Beth arrived first. She waved at a few people she knew but found a back booth where, hopefully, they could talk quietly. She supposed it would depend on what kind of reception popular Kurt received. Beth wondered if the reason he wanted to meet there was to receive an ego boost. That wasn't a very nice thought, but it was honest. It was the way Kurt was. It felt weird being there alone. She'd always come as a hanger-on with a large group of more popular friends. She hoped she wasn't going to be stood up.

"Kurt! Great to see you!"

"What's up?"

Smithy's was filled with shouts and noisy buzzes. The great man himself had arrived. Beth stood and waved until Kurt noticed her. Then she sat and waited while Kurt made his way back. His huge smile that seemed just for her was puzzling. He was happy to see her, so why hadn't he invited her to the dance?

"Beth, hi! Look, I thought this would make a good meeting place, but it's too loud. Let's grab a couple of shakes and walk to the park. We can talk there."

Beth nodded. "The weather is perfect, but it won't last long."

"Just three weeks till Halloween."

They didn't say much on their way to the park. Too busy sipping shakes or too uncomfortable to talk? Beth wasn't sure about Kurt, but she was plenty nervous. It's to help Drama Club, she thought. Just stick to that subject and don't bring up anything personal.

"This looks good," Kurt said, pointing out a picnic table far enough away from a group of elementary school kids playing softball and farther away from young children on the playground, supervised by moms. Castle Bluff was proud of its three lovely parks, especially now that numerous maples and oaks were staging a splendid show. This park, named after the early settler, Herman Hope, was only a block from the lake. "Maybe we can walk to the lake when we finish talking."

"Sounds good," Beth said, before noisily sucking the rest of her chocolate shake.

"Okay, you start. Something about Drama Club?"

Beth explained the problems with the fledgling group. "It's great that we can use the castle, since we can't get into the school. But it's hard that eighth graders are doing remote learning while the sixth and seventh graders are meeting at Community. We had a decent turnout last Saturday, about nineteen if everyone comes again. But the thing is—they're all girls!"

Kurt whistled. "Saturday morning during Cross Country season. I see your problem, even with the enticement of being at the castle. Not enough boys is often a problem, even at Crofts. It seems to come in waves."

"That's exactly what Mrs. Hunt said, but I'm not sure what she meant."

"Because this is the first time you've noticed it. My class was really active in everything—not just theater. When I was in seventh grade, there weren't many eighth graders in Drama Club, period— boys or girls. That's why our group got such great parts. Your class wasn't so hot. Last year, the only seventh graders in *Mouse* were girls, and the parts were small. Gabrielle and Imani were the only seventh graders in *Cinderella*."

"I see what you mean," Beth said. "And this year, maybe eighth won't be strong, but we can't tell about sixth and seventh graders because we're not with them. Most of them are new to us."

"It's a problem, all right, but how can I help?"

"Well, we've started out okay. We picked scenes and monologues to practice for a mini-show, and we came up with some ideas for getting more members. Someone, I'm not sure who, mentioned you." Beth knew darned well that she had, but that was her secret. "Even kids who don't know you have heard about you—because of Crofts and stuff." She thought he might be the most popular boy in town. "I thought if you could come to one of our meetings and lead us in various theater games, a lot of people would come. We could put up signs in the classrooms at Community and at Smithy's. I'll bet we could put something on the school's email bulletin, too."

"Oh, I'd love to," Kurt said, finally turning back into his old enthusiastic self. "That would be so much fun!"

"I'm not sure when—we haven't decided when the scenes and monologues show will be. We've only met once."

"Hmmm . . . I know something about that, I'm afraid. It won't be as easy as you think. I've learned this already at Crofts. You'll have kids not showing up and leaving their partners in a lurch. All kinds of things can happen. You'll have your show, but it will take awhile. Give it a few months. How about I come the Saturday after this? That will give us time to get the word out, and for me to plan."

Then Kurt said something totally out of character. "Thank you, Beth. This means a lot to me."

"Kurt?" Was something wrong? But Kurt shied away.

"And I will work on finding you some boys," he said. "Not everyone is doing sports."

"Porter is going to join," Beth said proudly. "He promised, even if he's the only boy."

"Courage and loyalty—what a great kid. Unlike me," Kurt whispered. Then he put his hand on Beth's. "Beth, I need to tell you something. I've been such a coward."

Beth laughed nervously. "You? I find that hard to believe."

"You know I asked Kylie to the dance."

"Yes, she told me."

"I want you to know why I didn't ask you."

"It's okay." Beth tried to sound indifferent.

"No, it's not. Do you remember what Roe told us about Crofts? She wasn't going to take the scholarship, even if she stayed in Castle Bluff."

"Yes, Roe said the kids were mean snobs."

"She was right, although she had a worse time than I'm having. At least I'm in ninth grade, and everyone knows I got a scholarship. But they are full of themselves, and if I asked an eighth grader to the dance, I'd be teased something terrible. And Kylie is a good friend and I knew she was confused about Brad, and—well, I should have done what I knew was right and I'm sorry."

"Slow down, Kurt. It's okay. I understand—really—but I am glad you told me. I was a little hurt." She was massively hurt, but she'd keep that to herself. In a way, she was glad she wasn't going. She would have been out of place at Crofts, but as an eighth grader in middle school, she was starting to feel important. She changed the subject. "I don't know what's up with Brad, do you? Kylie's unhappy because he's not doing theater at CBHS."

"I'll tell you, but please don't tell Kylie. Brad needs to."

Beth nodded. "I won't tell."

"Brad's parents are getting a divorce, and he might be moving away. Everything is up in the air, so he doesn't want to get involved in anything until he knows for sure."

"Oh, no! That's terrible! All those younger brothers and sisters! But he could tell Kylie. She'd understand."

"That's what I keep telling him. And I'll keep on trying."

Beth stood suddenly and shivered. In spite of the nice day, she was getting cold. "Let's go now. All of us need to talk more—to communicate. Even if we're in different schools."

"Yes," Kurt said eagerly. "Maybe we can have monthly reunions or something. Then I won't feel like I'm losing my old friends as well as not making new ones."

"And when we meet, we could call Roe in Spain."

"Good idea," Kurt said. "I was just thinking about what Roe said at your birthday party in August—that no matter where we were in the world, we'd always be best friends."

Wanting to lighten the mood, Beth burst into an almost-forgotten song she'd learned in Girl Scouts. "Make new friends, but keep the old; one is silver but the other's gold."

Kurt laughed. "Now I know why you never tried out for the musical."

"Oh, you." Beth gave him a good-natured punch. It felt like old times again.

And she suddenly remembered the vow she, Kylie, and Roe had made almost a whole year ago. *We promise that we will always share our problems and help each other the best we can.* That's what they had promised. Now they needed a reminder.

SCENE 6 – TO HAVE A FRIEND

"IT'S AFTER SCHOOL TODAY," Danny told Hannah in Mr. Rendina's car the next morning. "Will you come?"

"To what and where?" Hannah asked crossly. She had gone to bed before Dad and Uncle Martin came home but hadn't fallen asleep until long after she'd finally heard their bedroom door close. She knew they'd be late—but not that late!

"My first meet, and I'm determined to win. The band will perform, and Band Boosters is going to sell refreshments. Will you come? Please?"

"I don't know," Hannah said. "It doesn't interest me very much."

Hannah's dad pulled into the parking lot, where Danny jumped out as soon as the car stopped. "Whatever," he said, before rushing into the building.

Dad stopped her from following. "Why did you do that?"

Hannah shrugged. "Do what?"

Dad sighed. "Why were you so unpleasant to Danny? You can tell he really wants you to see him run."

"I'm going to do homework in the library, just like always."

"I have work to do, too, but I think I'll skip it and go over to the stands. Then I'll go straight to the city and pick up Martin."

"I'll need a ride home first."

"Hannah Banana—" Hannah cringed. The only time he called her that childish name was when he planned to give her a gentle scolding. Sometimes she wished he'd just yell at her, so she could yell back. "Do you want Danny to be your friend?"

"Sure—I guess. It's handy. He's right next door."

"To have a friend, you must be a friend. I know you've had a rough time since your mother and I called it quits. We're all adjusting, but whether or not things get better depends on you. If you don't make peace with yourself and knock that chip off your shoulder, you're going to continue being a lonely, unhappy girl."

"I'm going to be late." Hannah bolted out of the car before Dad could see her tearing up.

In social studies, they had a movie on the Industrial Revolution. Big yawn! Hannah thought she might get away with only sort of watching it. Frowning, she thought about what Dad had said. Like he wasn't responsible for the hermit she'd become? He and Uncle Martin were seldom home. Dad drove her home from school and sometimes stayed for supper, but normally he'd leave right away for the city to pick up Uncle Martin from work. Uncle Martin had an incredible job as a cellist for the Chicago Symphony. Hannah was proud of him, but he didn't have a car, and train transportation at the end of the day was expensive and long. Lugging a valuable cello around wasn't easy, either. They were saving for a second car, but it would take time. Hannah wished she could tell people about her family, but was it safe? Dad wasn't sure and couldn't risk losing his teaching job at Community.

In fairness, though, she'd always been kind of grumpy. But did she want to lose Danny as a friend? No, she thought. For one thing, she loved Bingo. She wasn't sure about Porter, but he seemed nice enough. Their club, the SSC, was the only exciting thing in her life at the moment. "I'll go to Danny's stupid meet," she whispered as the film came to an end and the teacher handed out a worksheet due the next day. She skimmed through the questions. I'll find the answers on Google, she thought, not worried.

Beth sat hunched over her computer, longing for the school day to end. I'm doing okay, she thought, but this is a rotten way to learn stuff. Teachers sent assignments out on Monday, and everything for the week needed to be completed by end of day Friday. If students had questions, they emailed teachers. It took forever for things to be graded, but Beth imagined having so many things to correct was awful for teachers. She sighed. They didn't deserve this either. Everyone just wanted to be back at school. The sixth and seventh graders were lucky stiffs, attending classes at Community.

"I'll finish social studies and then take a break." A YouTube video on the Industrial Revolution. "Didn't we cover that last year? In fact, I think that's the same film we saw in class." Honestly, she couldn't believe she'd once thought YouTube was so great.

Time for a quick snack. Carrot and celery sticks were the only things allowed today. Mom was on a health kick. "Well, we won't have those at our Halloween Party." She'd forgotten to mention the possibility to Kurt. Maybe it was just as well. They still needed Mr. Markey's and Leland's permission, so she'd better ask soon. Maybe she and Imani could go together. They should talk with Mrs. Hunt, too. It probably wasn't a great idea to invite everyone. Most kids wouldn't be interested in Drama Club but would go just to see the castle. Some might even want to cause trouble. Too risky. Their party must serve its purpose — to attract new members, and also be safe and fun.

Back to work. She should at least start her essay for English. Her phone gave an urgent beep. Saved by the text, Beth thought, peering down. Hmmm, from Kylie, but it was a group text, so it wouldn't have anything to do with Kylie's date with Kurt. "Hoping all of you can join me to see Danny in his first Cross Country race, Community track at 4:00. We'll sit together and cheer. Danny doesn't know. Huge surprise!"

Beth checked to see who else had been included: all of her ninth-grade friends—even Roe. "I'll be there," she responded. "Porter is running, too." At breakfast Porter said he would participate in this one meet before leaving the team. The final meet would come soon after Halloween, and he knew he wouldn't be picked for that. Only the top five runners from each class would. "I'll text Imani and Priyanka." Soon, Beth's phone pinged each time someone replied. It was a little annoying to be interrupted but also gratifying to see that everyone who could was going.

An answer also came from Roe. "I'll be there in spirit. Please give Dan a big hug from me. I'm sure he'll be a winner!"

It would be a real reunion. Now for the essay—write about something personal. Beth wished teachers would stop giving that assignment. Why should she want to share something personal with a teacher she didn't even know? Think of something personal that's not too personal. Beth wished she'd thought about this a few days earlier. She couldn't write about last year's experience with the pedophile teacher, Mr. Carroll—way too personal—or the adventure at Camp Shining Lake when they were in danger from Mrs. Crofts-Baker's family. They'd kept quiet about that because of Crofts Performing Arts' reputation in Castle Bluff. Her essay should be about something happening to her right now. How she felt about her former boyfriend asking one of her best friends to a dance? No way! Maybe she could write about friendship, though. About how growing up changes friendships and how hard it is to adjust when you're separated from long-time friends. Without stopping once, Beth knocked off the rough draft.

Danny did his stretching exercises before running in place. If he was careful and consistent, he had a good chance of being one of the best runners on the sixth-grade team. He might even be better than some of the seventh graders. Because of school being so messed up, the eighth graders were running with the ninth at CBHS. Danny doubted he'd have a chance against them. The season should be over by now, but the school's schedule had changed everything. They were lucky Cross Country was being offered at all.

"All set, Porter?" he asked, as Porter joined him.

"I guess," Porter said nervously. "I don't think I'm going to be very good, though."

"Doesn't matter," Danny said. "You're the best sport I know."

Each team, starting with seventh-grade girls, would run around the track for a 3K (1.8 miles) race. It shouldn't take more than 20 minutes, but the time to beat was 10. Danny thought he could make it, but Porter—probably not. CBMT had a no-cuts system, so anyone who wanted on the team was welcome. "Do you have your inhaler?" he asked.

Porter patted his shorts pocket. "Got it."

Normally, there were many meets before the final conference of just the very best against other athletes in surrounding communities. Next year, Danny vowed, if it didn't happen today.

The head coach reached into a can and drew the order of racing. He showed it to an assistant, who raced with flags, printed with the name of each runner. The flags, posted at the starting mark, showed where each runner was to stand. Danny's team was last. He hoped Mom and Dad came in time to take a photo of the Kennedy flag. Being last was okay. He'd be able to see how everyone scored.

In good spirits, everyone cheered everyone else. After all, they were from the same school. Some of the seventh-grade girls were especially good, Danny thought. Most of them came in with a score of at least 10. He thought he could run better than the seventh-grade boys.

Finally, it was time for Danny's team. He took his place next to the Kennedy flag. Then he looked up at the stands and saw Mom and

Dad waving. He mimed taking a picture. Dad held up his camera and Mom her cellphone. They understood. He wondered if Kylie had come. Suddenly, he heard a loud shout from another part of the bleachers. "Dan Kennedy! Go, go, go!"

A large crowd of friends sat together—Kylie, Beth, Marla, Kurt, Brad, and Eric—even Beth's friends, Imani and Priyanka. Kylie must have told them to call him Dan. He saw his fifth-grade teacher and a lot of his old classmates. And there, sitting with her dad, was his new friend Hannah. The disagreeable girl had decided to come after all. He waved frantically. "Let's do this," he shouted, just before receiving the Go signal.

Danny became a creature from Greek mythology. He was carried by the wind, not helpless but working with the wind. He was flying, swift, a galloping horse—in charge of this amazing machine, his body. In no time at all, he was in the last lap. Was he behind? Ahead? He couldn't tell, and it didn't matter. Running was all that did. Then it was over, and he stopped, although he was sure he could go on forever.

Then, he became aware of the watchers, on their feet and cheering. "Kennedy! Kennedy!" the chant continued. Someone handed him a towel and a bottle of water. Yes, he was thirsty and sweaty and tired. Exhausted. He sat on the bench and looked around. Where were his team members? There they were in the distance coming to the goal. He was first, but what was his time? He crossed his fingers. Please, let it be at least a ten!

A few team members slapped him on the back or demanded a high five. He could see Porter, dragging himself to the end, but he wasn't last. Each team sat impatiently while the coach announced the five top players from each grade, the ones who would go to Forest Meadows, the site of the final meet of the season—the big Conference in early November. Danny was certain he'd make it, but what was his time? He was no longer in competition with others—just himself.

Speaking too loudly into a microphone, the head coach made the announcement. "Representing the first sixth-grade class at Castle Bluff Middle School will be: Sarah Barkley, 11 minutes, Kendra Yu, 10 minutes, Joe Pappas, 10 minutes, Stephen Boulder, 9 minutes, and Dan Kennedy, 7 minutes!" The crowd and team members went wild, including Danny. He ran the 3K in only 7 minutes? He'd never run that fast before!

But the coach had more to say. "A few more items. The newspaper is here to take photos of the members of all of the teams, including the champs. Obviously, all of you are really champs, and I wish each one of you could participate at the Conference. But think how long that race would be?" The crowd laughed good-naturedly. "Parents, we appreciate your efforts in encouraging and driving your children, especially in light of our scheduling problems. One last thing before you leave. With his time today of 7 minutes for a 3K race, Dan Kennedy from the sixth-grade class broke an all-time record for Castle Bluff Middle School."

"For all grades?" someone in the crowd yelled out.

"Yes! The other coaches and I are very excited and proud."

SCENE 7 – COME AT ONCE!

SO MANY PEOPLE WERE SURROUNDING Danny. He was a hero. He wouldn't care if Hannah said anything to him or not. "Let's go, Dad," she said. "I'll congratulate Danny tomorrow."

"Sorry, honey, I've got to rush to pick up Martin. I'm going to be late, but he'll wait at the restaurant next to where the orchestra is rehearsing today."

"But—"

"You go with the Kennedys," Dad said. "Look, Mr. Kennedy is coming now. I'll see you back home. We might be late again." He gave her a quick peck on the cheek and raced to his car.

"Again?" Hannah struggled to hold back tears, but Danny's father definitely noticed. "I'm starting to feel like an orphan," she said quietly.

Dan Kennedy put his hand on her shoulder. "You must feel very much alone sometimes," he said softly. "Come next door whenever you wish. They'll work it out. It takes time."

"I don't understand why Uncle Martin can't take the train—at least occasionally."

"Your father thinks it's too dangerous. He's afraid Martin might be attacked. There are so many hateful people in the world."

Hannah stared at him. "You know?"

"I suspected that in your family there are two fathers—that Martin isn't really your uncle."

Hannah shrugged. "Actually, he is. But he isn't Dad's brother; he's my mom's."

Mr. Kennedy whistled. "Oh, my, that must have been difficult."

"Awful." Hannah looked into his eyes and saw nothing but sympathy and kindness. He wasn't judging. "Thanks. I guess I understand better why they're always late. I thought they just didn't want to be with me."

"Always helps when we know why people do something. Now, let's go see Danny, and then we're all going out to dinner to celebrate."

"Me, too?" Hannah smiled her thank you. "It will be nice not to have macaroni and cheese again."

Danny wanted to go home—to stretch out on his bed with the lights out and go over and over one of the best moments of his life. Not just the winning and learning he was the best runner at a school that hadn't even opened yet. No, it was the running, the flying, the complete exhilaration and joy. He couldn't wait until practice tomorrow or the final meet coming in just a few weeks. Sure, he was signed up for soccer and that would be great, but it couldn't be like running. Soccer would be working with a team, not flying solo. Maybe he'd take up flying someday—learning to fly a real plane would be awesome!

But his family wanted to celebrate him, and that was awfully nice of them. He was definitely hungry. Starved, in fact. And it was fun to see Hannah look at him like he was a real hero.

Smithy's wasn't elegant, of course, but it was affordable and offered the juiciest hamburgers around. When Smithy saw how many families had come for the occasion, he opened up the back room, where Porter's family joined them—all of them, even Beth and Porter's younger sister, Kelly, and the baby, Zoe.

Before the hamburgers came, Kylie suggested toasts. "To my brother, Dan," she said. "I'm proud to be his sister."

"Hear, hear!" Beth shouted.

Then Porter raised his glass of 7Up. "To my best friend. The greatest sixth-grade runner in town—maybe even the whole world!"

Danny suddenly felt very grown up. "I have a few toasts, too," he said, raising his bottle of root beer. "Thank you, Mom and Dad, for making it possible for me to do sports and not minding too much when my grades aren't terrific. To Kylie, my friend as well as my sister. To my new friend, Hannah. I miss Roe, but I'm glad you moved next door. Most of all, I'm proud of my best friend, Porter, who is always a good sport."

Everyone applauded; some felt teary. They were grateful when the hamburgers arrived. Mr. Kennedy and Mr. Walters split the bill, leaving a generous tip.

Home, Danny thought. Home at last. He was happy, his stomach was satisfied, and he was more tired than he had ever been. Quickly, he put on his pajamas and brushed his teeth. He should shower, but he just couldn't. He'd do it first thing in the morning. He was too tired to even review the day. He turned out the light, only to turn it back on. A light was going on and off next door.

He looked out the window. Yes, Hannah was sending him the agreed-upon signal for SSC—the emergency one, meaning *come at once!*

"Now what? This better not be some game you're playing." He replaced his pajama bottoms with jeans. "Stay, Bingo, and be quiet." Bingo opened one eye and closed it again. You're not the only one who's had a busy day, he seemed to say.

Creeping in bare feet down the back way, careful that Mom and Dad wouldn't hear him in the living room where, thankfully, the TV was on, Danny went out the mudroom door.

Hannah opened her door immediately and pulled him inside. "What's wrong? You look scared to death."

"Almost," Hannah said, her voice shaking. "Someone broke in."

Danny looked around the kitchen. "How can you tell? It looks okay to me."

"You see those dishes on the drain board?"

"So?"

"So, when I left this morning, they were in the fridge, and there was food on them. The leftover mac and cheese I was going to have for dinner, for one thing. Also missing—salad, about half a cake, and maybe a quart of milk. And they washed the dishes."

There must be a reasonable explanation. Danny supposed Hannah could be trying to get attention—she was lonely, alone so much—but he didn't think so. His gut told him something was terribly wrong and that they needed help. "Could your Uncle Martin have come home and then left again?"

Hannah shook her head. "No, he left before we did this morning and planned to be in rehearsal all day—until Dad picked him up tonight. Late because Dad wanted to go see you at the meet."

Danny didn't think she was implying it was his fault, although he might have thought that if she'd said it differently. She was just telling it like it was.

He'd try to be a Super Sleuth. "Any windows open or doors unlocked?"

Hannah could play her role, too. "No sign of forced entry. Doors and windows all locked. Another thing, I'm almost certain someone was in my room."

"Anything taken?"

She shook her head. "Not from my room, anyway. Just a feeling I had that a few things weren't where I left them. I'm not sure, but I think a whole bottle of aspirin is missing from the upstairs bathroom. I know I saw it when I brushed my teeth this morning."

"It's got to be the prowler," Danny said. "Maybe someone hungry and sick. Homeless. But how did he get into the house? Do you have a spare key under a mat or somewhere?"

"I don't know. It's possible, I guess."

Danny started toward the back door. "I'm sure no one will come back tonight. But lock everything, and then go to your room. Your dad will probably be back soon. If you get scared, flash your lights. If you think there's anyone in the house that shouldn't be, call my house or the police."

"What should we do next?"

"Think. And let's talk to Porter tomorrow. Since it's Friday, he's staying over tomorrow night. We can have an urgent meeting."

"Thanks, Danny. Oh, one more thing. About a gun and a knife, I-uh-sorta made that part up."

Danny smiled. "I sorta figured that."

"But there really is someone."

"I believe you. Goodnight, Hannah."

Beth heard a noise. "Kylie," she whispered. "Are you awake?" No answer from the other twin bed. Beth was having a long-overdue sleepover at Kylie's. No school tomorrow at the high school because of an institute day, and Beth had most of her work done for the week. A little tweaking tomorrow morning, and she'd send the completed assignments to her teachers.

There. She heard it again. Someone was walking down the hall toward the back steps to the kitchen. Beth didn't think Aunt Jane and Uncle Dan had gone to bed yet. That left only—Danny. What was he up to? A late-night snack or maybe Bingo had made an urgent request to go out? She probably should make sure. Danny's head was so inflated by his success, he might have told himself he needed to run. Grabbing her cellphone, in case she needed its flashlight app, Beth tiptoed down the hall. Halfway down the stairs, she heard the mudroom door open, then close stealthily. Whatever he was up to, Danny wanted to keep it private.

"We'll see about that," Beth whispered. Danny was like her second brother, so she felt right in interfering. Keeping all lights off, she pulled out a stool in the mudroom, and sat, prepared to wait for—I'll give him ten minutes, she decided, checking the phone for time. If he's not back by then, I'll tell Aunt Jane and Uncle Dan.

Ten minutes was a long time when you're sitting in the dark, waiting, especially if you don't know if you are making the right decision. But Danny was a good kid, and she'd give him the benefit of the doubt.

The long heart-to-heart with Kylie had enabled them to catch up on everything. And in case they hadn't, Kylie had talked her into staying another night. "Porter will be here, too, starting tomorrow night," Kylie had said. "The four of us can play your Castle Bluff Monopoly game."

"If Mom and Dad approve, you're on," Beth said. "I've got Drama Club Saturday morning. Maybe you'd like to come, too." She was sure now that her friend would support her and not try to take over. She told Kylie the positives and negatives of Drama Club so far. "Kurt has agreed to give an improv demonstration the following Saturday. I still need to talk to Mr. Markey about a Halloween party. I keep putting it off."

"How about I go to the castle with you tomorrow afternoon?" Kylie suggested. "It would be good to see Mr. Markey again—"

"And the newly-transformed Leland," Beth added, giggling. "Thanks, Kylie."

"You okay about Kurt?"

"Yes, I understand now."

"I told Brad, but he didn't seem to care."

How Beth wanted to reveal what Kurt had confided! It was hard to be asked to keep something a secret, when it meant you'd be disloyal to another friend.

"Maybe instead of asking Brad what's wrong, you could tell him how you feel. Tell him how hurt you are, and how much you've missed him. Ask him if you've done anything wrong."

Kylie had sighed. "I'll think about it. You're probably right. It's a good suggestion. Thanks."

Beth stood and stretched. She couldn't sit in the dark another minute. "Okay, Danny, time's up." She checked her phone once more, just as the back door opened. "Danny, it's me, Beth. Don't freak out!"

Danny had been all set to scream, but Beth's words entered his brain in time. He tried to pretend it was no big deal. "Oh, hi, Beth. What's up?"

"About to ask you the same thing—sneaking out of the house! I was going to tell your parents when you opened the door. I know it has nothing to do with Bingo, so that's one excuse off the table. I'm still going to the living room unless you tell me why I shouldn't."

"Uh, okay. But can we go back upstairs so we don't have to talk in the dark?"

Beth followed Danny to the spare room, where he closed the drapes and turned on a small lamp. It didn't give much light, but it was better than Beth's cellphone app.

"Kylie isn't with you," Danny said.

"Obviously. She's sound asleep. Out with it! And stick to the truth." She'd known Danny all his life and could see right through him. She wasn't as angry as she sounded. Mainly, she was relieved he was all right. Now that he was back, she realized how scared she'd been. Scared for his safety, and scared that she was making a huge mistake. She still might be.

"I went to see Hannah," Danny said. "Her father and uncle aren't home yet, and she was spooked."

"She's alone a lot, according to Porter. Why tonight, especially?"

Danny shrugged.

"Wait a minute," Beth persisted. "The phone didn't ring here, and you don't have a cellphone. How did you know?"

One secret was about to be revealed. "Her bedroom is right across from mine. We have a lights code—one for emergencies—and she used it tonight."

Well, that was a Danny-thing to do, Beth thought. The bedroom right across from Danny's was Mateo's old room, not Roe's. She was a little surprised by that.

"Go on," she said. "What was the emergency?"

Danny gave up. Beth wasn't going to stop. In a way he was glad. It was becoming too serious for even the SSC to handle. He blurted out the whole story. "But if we're going to tell Mom and Dad, could we wait until tomorrow night? It doesn't seem right not to talk it over with Hannah and Porter first. And maybe Kylie, too."

Beth nodded. Both Uncle Dan and Aunt Jane would be leaving for work very early the next morning—Dan to Milwaukee and Jane to a house-viewing several towns away. That was one of the reasons Beth had stayed over, to help Kylie make sure Danny got off to school okay. Hannah's dad would drive, if he came home, that is.

"It's a deal, Danny, except for one thing. Hannah is not going to stay alone next door. She's frightened and nervous, and I don't blame her. Are you sure the man isn't still there? Did you look in every room, even the basement?"

Danny shook his head, mouth open. "I didn't think of that."

Beth handed him her cellphone. "You know the number?" Danny nodded. "Then tell her she has to spend the night here. She can have this room. She should pack just what she needs and write a note to her father so he won't be worried."

Danny called. "I got caught," he said. "Porter's sister, Beth, found out. She says you have to stay here tonight." He gave Hannah all of Beth's instructions. "She'll meet you at our back door."

He returned the phone. "She didn't try to argue. She'll be right over. Are you sure you don't want me to go down?"

"You have school tomorrow. I don't. Try to get some sleep now. We'll find out what's going on, I promise."

Danny nodded. "Thanks, Beth," he said.

SCENE 8 – THE MOST IMPORTANT INGREDIENT

IN SPITE OF THE TROUBLESOME night, Danny managed to awaken before Kylie or Beth. First thing, he looked out the window. Hannah's father's car was parked in the driveway. He came home. One less worry. Danny peeked into the spare room. "Hannah," he called softly. "Hannah, wake up."

"Wha—? Oh, it's you, Danny. I almost forgot."

"Your Dad's car is in the driveway, so they came home all right."

"Oh, good."

"Maybe you should have breakfast there. Then we won't have to tell my sister what you're doing here." Danny was certain Beth would tell her everything, but at least he wouldn't be part of the discussion. If Mom and Dad were there, it would be a super huge discussion.

"Okay. Close the door, so I can get dressed."

Danny obeyed, but he could hear her say on the other side, "Thanks, Danny."

Beth didn't tell Kylie what had happened until they were on their way to Markey Castle. Kylie had slept late while Beth completed and turned in her school assignments. She loved her essay on friendship and emailed a copy to Roe, as well as to her teacher. She also printed a few copies on the Kennedy's printer that made its home in the kitchen. She wanted Kylie to read it—maybe even Kurt. Beth thought she'd captured exactly how she felt—longing for new discoveries and friends, but also yearning for the way it used to be. She was pulled, wanting to grow but also to remain the same. Her best friends probably felt the same way.

She and Kylie fixed a grand French toast and bacon brunch, and then were off. "I really hope Mr. Markey approves of a Halloween party at the castle," Beth said.

Kylie laughed. "He won't be your problem. He'll be excited. Leland and Mrs. Hunt will be the ones to grind it into reality. Just as well. Drama Club would be in big trouble if the party got out of hand."

"Speaking of out of hand—" That was Beth's segue into last night's adventure.

Kylie stopped short. "What got into those kids? Why didn't they tell Mom and Dad immediately?"

"You mean like you told Roe's dad immediately about the Crofts family last summer at Shimmer Lake?"

"Well, we were just waiting for the right time."

"So are Danny and Hannah. They're planning on telling Hannah's father, but they want their club to meet first."

Kylie hooted. "Their club? How infantile can you get?"

Beth nodded. "Well, certainly not mature, like a certain group of friends wanting to solve the mystery at Camp Shimmer Lake, deciding that a play was more important than reporting people who were trying to kill you."

"Okay, you got me. I guess we needed to do a lot of growing up, too. I used to be the one giving you advice, but now—what happened, Beth?"

"No idea." Then she giggled. "Danny, Porter, and Hannah even have a name for their club. The SSC. Danny wouldn't tell me what that stands for."

"Secret Service something? It does sound silly."

"Yeah, but Danny and Porter are only in sixth grade. I would have thought it was cool then, too. But honestly, Kylie, I think the club might be Danny's way of helping Hannah to fit in. She's really unhappy, and I think it's more than just being new. She doesn't even try to be friendly. I'm not sure Danny totally believes her creepy prowler story."

"Danny was really pleased she showed up at his meet, though. He seems to like her, and my parents think her father is great—"

"Oh look, Kylie," Beth interrupted. "Doesn't the castle look beautiful? This time last year we were in our last rehearsals for *Mouse*, and I was getting mighty sick of it. Remember?"

"I miss it so much," Kylie admitted. "Not the weather exactly. It was getting really cold."

Both of them gazed at the beautiful castle, now surrounded by colorful and crumbling leaves. They would keep the memories of this place, where new friendships were formed and old ones became stronger or were broken. Beth and Kylie walked up the wide staircase, and Kylie knocked, just as she had over a year ago.

Leland opened the door. "Welcome, stranger," he said to Kylie. Beth grinned at Kylie's expression. Grandly, Leland led them in and introduced Kylie to his wife, Janet.

"I hope you're here for a long chat," Janet said, leading them into the now-comfortable parlor.

Mr. Markey stood on tiptoes to hug Kylie. Beth knew she had always been his favorite. And why not? It was because of Kylie that his life had changed for the better.

It all pretty much went as Beth expected. Mr. Markey was thrilled and began to plan his costume. Leland and Janet gave their approval, with reservations. They were worried about numbers and safety.

"We don't want to spoil your fun," Janet said, "but this doesn't seem very well thought out. When exactly will it be, who will you invite, and what will you do at the party?"

"I'm mainly concerned about security," Leland said. "I think it's too risky having the back door unlocked, the one you use for club meetings. Older people you don't even know could go up the stairs, and then wander around the castle without our knowing." Even though he didn't use the words, Beth could tell he was thinking about alcohol, drugs, and sex. Leland had come a long way in accepting their group, but that didn't apply to teens he didn't know.

"Maybe Janet and someone like Gee could be in the ballroom kitchen," Kylie suggested. "They'd notice anyone coming in from the back."

"People in the kitchen would be good," Beth said, "but I agree with Leland. The back door should stay locked. Everyone should use the main entrance."

"Okay," Kylie continued, "and maybe Leland and Mr. Markey could greet them at the front door—"

"In costume," Mr. Markey interrupted.

Kylie smiled. "In costume. Drama Club could have a member stationed at the top of each landing, making sure people keep going and don't go down any halls."

Beth shook her head. "That would be boring—unless—oh, I know. We'd have a cut-off time on the invitation. At that time, the front door would lock, and no more guests admitted. Once the party starts, Drama Club members could take turns watching the ballroom doors, so no one goes down to the other floors."

"And Janet and Gee would make sure no one went down the back stairs in the kitchen," Kylie added. It was starting to come together.

Janet nodded. "That could work. I've got another idea. Halloween is on a Saturday, but does your party have to go until late at night? Why not make it start late afternoon—say around five? It would still be atmospheric. You could have refreshments and play theater games. End your party at eight and trick-or-treat your way home."

Parent permission slips, Beth thought, since Drama Club was sponsored by the middle school. "I think that's a really good idea. We have Drama Club here tomorrow morning. Janet, would you be able to come? Early so we can run it by Mrs. Hunt. Then club members can help figure out the rest."

All of them nodded. It was a good plan. Probably not as wild and glorious as first perceived—but doable, safe, and fun.

Refreshments were always a part of castle visits. Soon, in spite of brunch, they were enjoying slices of Janet's pound cake and glasses of cider.

"Any parts for you yet at high school, Kylie?" Mr. Markey's eyes twinkled.

Kylie snorted. "Not even an extra. But we started late, although not as late as middle school. I went to one Drama Club meeting, but— well, you know—probably back to small parts. Auditions for *You Can't Take It with You* are next week. I'll try out, but I don't expect much."

Janet made a face. "That old pot-boiler? We did that when I was in high school. No, don't get me wrong. It's a great play; just done too often, perhaps. Do you have a script?"

Kylie shook her head. "I don't know anything about it, except it's a famous comedy."

"Before you go," Janet continued, "I'll take a look at the bookcase in Anna's room. I'm certain she has a copy you may borrow."

Right. Miss Armstrong was Janet's niece, now living at the castle. Beth caught Kylie's look of uncertainty. She'd never told Beth why she'd turned against her former theater teacher.

Soon, armed with a whole pound cake and a script, the girls left the castle, determined to get home before the boys and Hannah arrived.

Again, Hannah's attention hadn't been fully on her schoolwork. Getting good grades came easily and kept teachers from getting on her case. She liked them not paying attention to her—taking it for granted that she'd do well. Mom probably wouldn't have minded if she flunked out, as long as it didn't involve her. Once she'd found out about Dad and Uncle Martin, she divorced Dad and, it seemed, her daughter. Hannah shrugged. "Who cares?" she whispered. She'd rather live with Dad and Uncle Martin. They always said they were proud of her grades but didn't make a big fuss. Other things were just as important as school.

Today, whenever she could get away with it, Hannah wrote lists. Why it would be good to tell both dads and maybe the Kennedys about the strange man, and why it wouldn't. She also made a list of what she needed to know, such as was there a key to their house hidden somewhere, and had Dad changed the locks when they first moved in? If they hadn't changed the locks, could there be a key someone hadn't turned back in? The Kennedys might know, not that she suspected them of anything. If Dad had hidden a key—where? And could the prowler have taken it? Under reasons to tell, she listed that she was scared for herself—and for Dad and Uncle Martin, in case someone was gearing up for a hate crime. It could happen, even here.

Reasons for not telling were simple: she didn't want to worry Dad and Uncle Martin, and she didn't want to ruin the secret club. Would they continue to have SSC if adults were in on the mystery? She pretended not to want friends, but that was just her being prickly, trying to keep from being hurt again. She thought about telling Danny that she'd just made the whole thing up—that she'd actually eaten all the food and that she'd never seen or heard a prowler. She'd say she'd been mistaken about the missing bottle of aspirin. No, that would only prove to the boys she was crazy, something they probably thought already. She thought about how scared she'd been, all alone last night, and how grateful she was when Beth insisted she sleep at Danny's house. She guessed she'd wait and see what the others thought about telling. Beth and Kylie were older. They might be able to see things more clearly.

In the halls, Danny lived the life of a star. *Way to go, Dan! Hurray for the champ! Can't wait for the big event, Dan!* It was great! But the story was different in the classroom. D on his science test. "Try harder," the teacher wrote. An incomplete on an English paper, a failure on a math quiz, and finally, a note from his counselor, asking to see him at the end of the day.

At least coach said no practice on Friday afternoon, Danny thought at 3:15, the end of a wonderful horrible day. His counselor, Mrs. Arnold, greeted him with a smile. "Sit down, Danny." He sat next to her, not across from her desk. "Don't look so worried. You aren't the only one in this situation." He waited, knowing the *situation* but not wanting to state it himself. "First, congratulations, on your stunning victory yesterday. Your whole school is proud of you."

Danny relaxed. This might not end up so bad.

"Now, let's see what we might do to keep you from being disqualified from the final conference. That would be a big hit on the school's pride and not do much for yours, either."

"What?" Danny stood quickly, but sat again slowly as Mrs. Arnold waited.

She nodded. "Right. If you continue doing as poorly in your schoolwork as you are now, you won't be allowed to compete. Those are the rules that you and your parents agreed upon when you signed up for your vigorous sports schedule. Sports are important, Danny, but not as important as why you're here—to learn to the best of your ability, in order to be ready for the next step, seventh grade. It is your teachers' responsibility and mine, but mainly yours, to make sure that happens."

He and Mrs. Arnold went through each of his classes and discussed ways he might improve. He admitted he hadn't even tried to do well. "But I will," he said. "You wait and see."

"I'm sure you mean to, but suppose we meet every few days to check on how you're doing? The conference isn't until the Thursday after Halloween. I will need to make my final decision a few days before. See me after school next Wednesday. I won't keep you long; I know you have practice. Danny, I know how confusing this year has been—sixth grade for the first time in middle school and not in the correct building. Believe me, you are not the only one in your predicament, although possibly the one with the most to lose."

Danny left the building to the glad cries of *Hurray for Dan! He's our Man!* But he didn't feel like an important Dan the Man anymore. As he walked to Mom's car, where Porter and Hannah were waiting for a ride home, he was Danny, a scared and humbled little boy.

The SSC met after a supper prepared by Danny's father because his mom was visiting a sick friend. Hannah was invited but decided to eat at her house, even though her dad had left already to pick up Uncle Martin, in hopes of getting home early for a change. Non-club members, Beth and Kylie, joined members on the back patio because—well, they insisted.

Hannah and Danny summed up everything. They knew more than Porter, although he added a few pieces of information. Beth could tell that the three of them were reluctant to divulge anything. She understood and, obviously, so did Kylie.

Kylie smiled at them. "Look, Beth and I get it. More than a few times last year we wanted to shut parents and teachers out. We wanted to solve things ourselves—our gang and no one else. Well, we did do a lot—most things—but there were some things so serious we needed help. A prowler that broke into your house, Hannah, is dangerous. You don't want anyone to get hurt. Don't worry, though. The three of you will still have your club."

Beth nodded. "We must find out who this man is and if he means harm. Maybe it's someone who needs our help."

"We considered that, too," Porter said. "We should tell Hannah's dad."

Hannah scoffed. "If we ever see him. He was supposed to come home early; didn't happen. If we must tell an adult, how about Mr. Kennedy? He was pretty nice to me."

"Your father is nice, too," Danny said. "Just very busy."

"All the time." Hannah sighed.

"Okay, Dad it is," Kylie said. "I'll go get him."

Porter said he needed to use the bathroom, and Beth said she should call home—leaving Danny and Hannah staring uneasily at each other.

"Why don't you want to tell your father and uncle, Hannah?"

Hannah turned red. "I'm afraid they won't believe me."

"Because?"

"Because I don't always tell the truth," she said softly.

Danny nodded. "I know. Sometimes I wasn't sure whether to believe you."

"But you did, finally?"

He grinned. "When you took out the gun and knife parts. I finally decided you were the girl who cried wolf. I saw how scared you were last night. If that was fake, you belong in Drama Club. Besides, I heard you talking about how you would have had leftover mac and cheese if you hadn't had dinner with us. That was while we were in the restaurant. If that was a lie, it was a totally stupid one."

"I'll try not to lie anymore, Danny. Sometimes it's just more interesting than my real life."

Changing the subject, Danny told her about his up-and-down day.

"I'll help you catch up, Danny. I really will."

Danny smiled, realizing suddenly that he now had two best friends and that perhaps the most important ingredient in friendship was honesty.

SCENE 9 – A DRAMATIC SUCCESS

BETH, KYLIE, AND HANNAH TROD cautiously on the crunchy ground to the castle. An overnight hard frost had announced that autumn days soon would end. They planned to meet Porter and Danny there. Yes, both Danny and Hannah were going to Drama Club in return for Beth's help. "You owe me," Beth insisted, after Uncle Dan, hearing the whole story, said he'd take care of things with Hannah's father. Thanks to Beth and Kylie smoothing things over, none of the adults would be angry.

"It might have helped if you'd told us earlier," Mr. Kennedy said, "but I think I understand why you didn't. Until last night, you really couldn't be certain something was wrong. It's easy to imagine a stranger lurking around, but missing food and medicine is different." He didn't know if the locks next door had been changed but would check with his wife. She had been the agent who'd sold the house and might have an answer. He'd also talk with Hannah's dad to see if something could be worked out so that she wasn't alone so often. He ruffled Hannah's hair. "That house! Always something! First Roe and now you — both fine girls."

Hannah had had a snack with the boys — microwaved popcorn in the kitchen — until she'd heard her dad and uncle pull into the driveway. They confided to each other that they did not want to go to Drama Club, although privately Hannah thought it might be cool to see the castle, and Porter wanted to support his sister. Danny felt blackmailed. Oh, well, he would run from eight to ten on the blocks near the castle. Beth didn't say he had to go more than once. And Kylie said she'd help him with schoolwork in the afternoon.

Hannah laughed at the grotesque troll doorknob when Kylie insisted that she do the honors. Gleefully, Hannah grabbed the troll's nose.

"And who do we have here?" Mr. Markey answered the door, unusual for him. "A new friend, I see."

Instantly, Hannah fell in love with the old man, her very image of the perfect grandfather. Thinking of her own grandfathers, though, she decided Mr. Markey might be old enough to be a great-grandfather. Whatever, Hannah didn't have either now, seeing that both sides of her family had given up on Dad, Uncle Martin, and even her. She shook Mr. Markey's hand. "I'm Hannah," she said. "You have a beautiful home, Mr. Markey."

"That I love sharing with young people like you. Please come inside. The weather is becoming quite nippy."

Beth could tell that Mr. Markey longed for a visit but knew they had to go upstairs. "We'll come back once the meeting is over," she said.

Mr. Markey smiled. "Come for sandwiches. Leland will be back from shopping by then. Anna and Robbie have gone to the city—you keep missing them. Janet is upstairs already. I'm the greeter today." He seemed pleased by the unaccustomed role.

They started up the stairs. "I think I'm in love," Hannah said.

Kylie laughed. "That's how I felt," she said, "from the very first time we met him."

"I'd forgotten that Mr. Markey always wants a visit," Beth said. "I'll need to add that to my schedule."

"I remember those days," Kylie said. "But it looks like the visits are going to be a lot more comfortable than they used to be—both because of the furniture and the new Leland."

Beth nodded. "Because of the prowler, we're running late, but I don't suppose we're the only ones."

She was wrong, for as soon as they opened the ballroom door, she was greeted by a mighty cheer. "What—?" Everyone from last week seemed to be there, plus Porter and Danny, although they were the only middle school boys. And seated unobtrusively, at least for him, in a corner, was Kurt, who grinned and waved at her.

Imani walked over and dragged Beth into the room. "Enter, Madame President," she said.

Mrs. Hunt smiled. "It seems that in your absence you were unanimously elected. Serves you right for being late."

Priyanka shook her head. "Mrs. Hunt is joking. We figured that since you were doing the most work—there probably wouldn't be a Drama Club without you—you should be president this year. That is, if you'll accept."

Wow! Would she! They'd never had a Drama Club president before. Because Mrs. Hunt was so new, officers did make sense. "Thank you!" she said. "I'd love to."

"That doesn't mean you have to keep on doing all the work, though," Priyanka nodded.

"I can't. As soon as school officially opens, I'll have Art Club, too." Beth vowed that she would not become so overwhelmed with activities that she let her schoolwork slide, as Kylie had done last year.

"Perhaps we can elect additional officers at another time," Mrs. Hunt suggested. "Suppose you start the meeting now, Beth. We have a lot to do this morning."

Right. First, Beth introduced their guests. Mrs. Janet Duncan, who said they should call her Janet, would take Mrs. Hunt's place when she couldn't come. "And I'll provide cookies often," she said to applause.

"And this is Kylie Kennedy and Kurt Brockway. Both were in Drama Club last year and starred in the first play. Kylie directed a winter play here at the castle. Would you like to say a few words, Kylie and Kurt? Just a few, Kurt." Those who knew Kurt laughed.

Kylie stood. "Well, I just want to say I'm sure you'll have a wonderful year and that I'll try to help if you need me. I'll be auditioning for the play at CBHS next week, so it would be nice if you'd send me mental Break-a-leg wishes."

She would not try to take over, Beth thought. Kylie understood it had to be their club now. And what a good idea Kylie had just given her—they could have a meeting sometime to explain the traditions and superstitions of theater, such as Break-a-leg. She couldn't wait to see their expressions when she told them why actors were called Hams. What fun!

Then Kurt bounced up to talk about next week's meeting. "Foolishly," he said, grinning, "Beth invited me back to lead you in improvisations and theater games. We'll have a blast, so be sure to come. Please encourage your friends, too. It would be nice to have more boys, but don't worry if you don't get them at first. More are sure to come once Cross Country is over and you're all back in your real school. And there are plenty of great scenes and plays for girls, so it won't be a problem for you. If the boys aren't interested, that's their loss."

Beth had never thought of it that way. Could be that Kurt was growing up, too. She and Kylie looked at each other and smiled.

"I'll see you next week," Kurt said, "but I gotta go. Let me be the first to tell you that I have to rush over to Crofts for Read-Through."

"What?" Beth, Kylie, Imani, and Priyanka shouted at the same time.

"Yep. Found out late last night. Crofts is doing a senior-written adaptation of *A Girl of the Limberlost*. I don't know anything about it."

Suddenly a normally quiet, sullen girl shouted, "That's one of my favorite books! I love it!"

Beth stared. Hannah? She hardly recognized the excited girl.

"What part did you get?" Hannah insisted.

"Billy," Kurt said. "As I said, I don't know anything about it. Auditions were just improv and monologues from other shows."

"Oh, you'll be perfect," Hannah breathed. "Elnora is the main character, but Billy is the most important boy — I think — at least in the first part of the book."

The old Kurt reappeared. "A lead?" he shrieked. "I got a lead? At Crofts? Thanks — ?"

"Hannah," she said, the shy voice returning.

"Hannah! I'll tell you about it next week. I'm outa here!" Kurt practically flew down the stairs.

"Well, that was amusing," Mrs. Hunt said, "and pure Kurt. You're in for a good time next week."

The meeting was going too quickly, Beth thought. They hadn't even talked about the Halloween party. "I need to have a short conference with Mrs. Hunt and Janet," she said. "Priyanka and Imani, will you explain about our scenes and monologues show? A lot of you picked your parts last week, but not everyone. Remember, if possible, your scene partner should be someone from another grade."

The girls agreed, and Beth and the two women exited into the kitchen.

Danny watched the proceedings. Drama Club might work out fine for Hannah, he thought, noticing how pleased she seemed when an eighth grader named Gabrielle approached her with a scene. Soon he saw their two heads together, reading lines. He wondered what the scene was. Porter looked shocked when Imani pulled him away to another corner and pleaded with him to do a scene with her. Danny thought Porter might resist until he looked over the scene, and then seemed as excited as Imani. Porter and Imani doing a scene together—strange, but interesting. Danny decided he'd like to see that, but be in a scene? No way! His face must have shown his disinterest, for not a soul approached him. Three things mattered to him: taking care of Bingo, running, and pulling up his grades. Other than that, everything else was an afterthought. Probably even the SSC. With Dad and Mr. Rendina taking over, they'd lost their mystery, and it was unlikely a new one was on the horizon. Oh, they'd keep the club, mainly because they loved its name—SSC, so cool! The initials needed to stand for something else, though. No more Super Sleuths. Secret Spies? No, wrong era for that. Supreme Scandals? Sounded like a bad rock group. How about Super Shitheads? Danny laughed out loud, causing a few students to gaze at him in wonder. That was it! Perfect! No one would ever guess, especially Mom and Grandma, who really mustn't find out. He couldn't wait to tell Porter and Hannah!

By the time Beth, Mrs. Hunt, and Janet returned from the kitchen, practically every student had signed a form telling what scene or monologue they would do. A few were undecided but said they'd email Priyanka and let her know. They planned to find something they liked at the library.

"Everyone promised to get together whenever possible to rehearse," Priyanka told Beth. "I think we can be ready by the Saturday before Thanksgiving weekend. That's the plan, anyway."

"Sounds good," Beth said, grateful that Pri had taken charge. "I think Mr. Markey will let us put on our show here, even though we should be back in school by then. That way we can use the kitchen and serve refreshments. Janet, let's ask Mr. Markey and Leland after the meeting."

Janet smiled smugly, as if she knew who would have the deciding vote.

"We need a name for the show," Imani said.

"The Speakeasy!" Hannah blurted out, only to blush when everyone stared at her. "You know, like in Al Capone times. They had secret places where illegal alcohol was served. I read a book about it. A speakeasy would be a play on words."

"And we could serve root beer and pretzels," Porter offered. "It's perfect, Hannah! I've read about it, too. Admission could be a secret password."

Soon all agreed. Drama Club would open the very first speakeasy in the history of Castle Bluff Middle School!

Finally, Janet and Beth explained the rules for the Halloween party — pretty much what had been determined earlier. Each Drama Club member could invite one other person, with the stipulation that they attended CBMT now or were former Drama Club members. "No one from a different school," Beth warned. Imani said she would type up the rules and send them out, and also distribute invitations the following Saturday.

At a little after noon, Beth dismissed the meeting. A great success, everyone agreed.

Back home, Hannah, alone again and wearing her warmest jacket, climbed into her tree fort. Her homework was done, so she could read and dream. Instead, she decided to memorize her lines for the scene she was doing with Gabrielle. It was about this girl who found out she had diabetes and wouldn't be allowed to eat much sugar. Hannah would play that girl. Gabrielle played the best friend, who was trying to make her feel better by offering strange alternatives to sugar. Finally, they indulged in a last ice cream cone. The scene was funny and sad at the same time. She was going to like Drama Club, at least while it met at the castle. The kids didn't act like she was weird. They thought she was clever and had good ideas. Lots of them said that calling the show Speakeasy was brilliant. She looked forward to seeing that boy Kurt again, too. And Mr. Markey said she should come and visit anytime she wanted.

Hannah didn't mind being alone for a while. Dad and Uncle Martin promised to take her out for dinner and a movie. They hadn't done that in a long time. She thought Mr. Kennedy had talked with them. That was probably why they were going to a restaurant—a different place to mull things over.

It was getting dark—too cold for tree forts. The weather had been nice during the day lately, but as soon as the sun went down—Boom! Freezing! It was like summer turned instantly to winter. She was starting down the tree, with her books and papers on her back, when she saw him. The prowler, all in black—black pants and black hoodie. He was in the Kennedys' garden, about to detach a pumpkin from its vine. There were only a few, and Danny expected to carve them for Halloween. What would a vagrant do with a pumpkin? Eat it raw? Hardly! This was vandalism—completely nasty. No longer scared, Hannah was furious!

"Hey!" she yelled. "Leave it alone! Get out of there!"

The man turned and stared at her. She finally got a good look at him. He was younger than she'd expected. More like an old boy than a man, and way too skinny. Not bad looking—just not healthy—and definitely frightened. Just as Hannah was about to shout out an offer of help, he bolted over the back fence and fled into the night.

Inside, Hannah called Danny. Too late for anyone to do anything now, but she could describe the man. Why was she always the only one to see him?

SCENE 10 – A NOTHING-TO-DO DAY

DANNY DIDN'T SEE HANNAH UNTIL after church the next day. She showed him exactly where she had seen the man in the garden. "You stopped him just in time," Danny said. The medium-sized pumpkin had been severed from its vine.

"I wonder why he wanted it?" Hannah said. "Can you eat it?"

"I guess. But I don't think it would taste good raw, and it would be hard to chew."

"He might be desperate," Hannah said quietly.

Just in case, he and Hannah picked all five of the pumpkins and placed them as decorations on the Kennedys' front steps. "Maybe we'll carve them tonight," Danny said, "and hope they last until Halloween."

Danny was all caught up with his schoolwork but wanted Kylie to look it over one more time. "It has to be perfect because the grades will be lowered on the ones that are late."

"Are your subjects really hard? Mine are easy in comparison with my old school."

Danny shrugged. "Not hard. I just don't want to do the work. It's boring."

Hannah laughed. "Well, if you're going to be the big sports hero of CBMT, I guess you'll have to pretend to like it."

"That's what Kylie said."

"Where is she? Couldn't she check your stuff now, so we could tell her about the pumpkins and figure out what to do next?"

Danny shook his head. "She's meeting her boyfriend someplace." At Hannah's look of disgust, he said quickly, "No, I'm glad. Brad is great, but I think something's wrong. I can tell Kylie's worried."

"Usually, I think it's okay not to have a brother or sister," Hannah said, "but you and Kylie and Beth and Porter seem to be good friends. Maybe you're lucky."

"Most of the time," Danny agreed.

A walk to the park made sense, they decided. They would take Bingo along. Maybe they'd see the stranger. He had to be hiding out somewhere. Something needed to pep up this nothing day, Danny thought.

Beth was getting a head start on the week's schoolwork. Fortunately, it was brainless, for her head was full of Drama Club plans, Hannah's mysterious visitor, and Kylie's problems. "Call Brad," she had urged. "Call and ask if you can meet somewhere. Not Smithy's—too crowded. Maybe down at the bluffs. The lake should be gorgeous today."

Kylie called back, all excited, to say she had followed Beth's advice. "I'm heading to the bluffs now. Thanks, Beth."

"Let me know what happens." Beth hoped Brad would tell Kylie about his parents. It felt wrong knowing about Brad when his own girlfriend didn't. And she hoped Kurt liked his part in the play. Funny, Hannah knowing about some book Beth had never heard of. She was definitely a weird kid, but maybe a good kind of weird.

No, she couldn't concentrate on school. Maybe Porter would like to do something. Watch a show or bake cookies, seeing that they were stuck here with Zoe while Mom and Dad were out with Kelly. But when she asked him—"Beth, would you watch her yourself, this time? I'll owe you. Danny called and wants me to meet him at the park. Please?"

Beth nodded. "Okay, but yes, you'll owe me. I guess I'll work on Drama Club plans." Nothing else to do. Yesterday was crazy, but she preferred it to today.

"Thanks, Beth. I think it's great that you're president!"

Beth guessed she thought it was, too, although she wasn't quite sure if she'd be any good. Priyanka and Imani had taken over the Speakeasy plans. Beth grinned, remembering Hannah's suggestion. She doubted anyone else would have thought of it. Imani was going to make invitations for the Halloween party and send out the rules to everyone by email. Janet would take charge of refreshments.

She could think about her Halloween costume, but that had nothing to do with being president. Games at the party were important, but she didn't think she was the right person to come up with them. Gabrielle was clever. Beth sent her a quick text, to which Gabrielle answered immediately. "I'd love to, but I might not be at the party because my grandfather is really sick. I'll come up with some games, though, and give them to you."

"Thank you, Gabby. Sorry about your grandfather. Hope he's OK!" Maybe being a good president was about delegating, getting everyone involved in some way.

So the Halloween party was settled, other than finding someone to lead the games Gabby found and thinking of a guest to invite. Probably Kurt. And she had been so busy talking with Mrs. Hunt and Janet about the Halloween party she'd never chosen a scene or monologue. She didn't think she wanted to participate, as an actor, anyway. I could be an announcer, she thought. She'd write a short emcee script, tying the scenes and monologues together. "I can't do it until I know what the scenes are," she said, sending a quick email to Priyanka and Imani, asking for the list. "I'll figure out the order and write an emcee script," she wrote. Then added, "I'm really happy you're doing so much."

"I wish Mom and Dad would come home," she whispered. But she didn't want Zoe for company. She'd rather be bored than listen to Zoe howl the way she always did when she first woke up. And then there'd be a gross diaper to change. Beth would read, she decided.

Back to thinking about school. In English, they were expected to read a book of their choosing and write a synopsis. She looked at the bookshelves in her room, in Porter's, and in Dad's study. Nothing appealed. But she had book credits on her Kindle. What was the name of the book that Hannah mentioned? The one Kurt's play was adapted from? Fortunately, she had scribbled down a few minutes after the meeting. Here it was—*A Girl of the Limberlost.* She looked it up. She wouldn't even need credits; Kindle had it for free! And after the first chapter, Beth had an idea for Drama Club. Theater trips! The club would go see *You Can't Take It with You* at CBHS—fingers crossed for Kylie— and *Limberlost* at Crofts. A great idea, and a perfect excuse to call Kurt!

She punched his number but was rewarded only with his silly not-at-home message. "I would really like this day to be over," she said, returning to Kindle.

Danny and Porter were also in a complaining mood. But not Hannah. How could anyone think this day was boring? Friends playing with a sweet dog on a beautiful day at a super park, with colorful trees and mysterious paths that might lead anywhere, and always in the distance, the sound of waves crashing against the bluff. Hannah wished she could make the boys understand what this meant to her. But they took good friends for granted and were seldom alone for long. They had sisters who were friends and normal moms and dads. They even had grandparents who loved them, no matter what their parents might do. Hannah loved Dad and Uncle Martin more than anyone, of course, but it would be nice if things were more normal—if they didn't have to hide who they were. "I have two fathers, and it's okay," she wanted to yell. But she couldn't—because of all the people who would tell her it wasn't okay. She wanted to tell Danny and Porter. Maybe they'd understand—after all, Mr. Kennedy did. No, she wouldn't take a chance. "I wish I had a dog," she said instead.

The boys stopped crabbing about how bored they were. "Well, why not?" Porter asked. "I can't because my mom is allergic. But why can't you?"

"Well, we've always rented and moved a lot, and—"

"But now you don't," Danny said, suddenly excited and interested in the conversation. "You have a house with a big backyard, and your dads have great jobs. You definitely need a dog, and Porter and I will help you find one."

Hannah gasped, and her mouth stayed open. What did he say? *Your dads?* Afraid that she had misheard, she tried not to react further. Instead—"You will? Help me find a dog? That would be terrific! I'll need permission, of course."

"Piece of cake," Porter said. "You can say you need a watchdog—protection from the evil stranger." He grinned. Hannah thought Porter might believe she was lying about the stranger, but she didn't care. He was her friend, anyway. And Danny definitely was—her very best friend.

SCENE 11 – THAT'S ALWAYS THE QUESTION

"Now what?" Danny muttered, opening a note the study hall teacher had just given him. Here he was, making good use of his study hall, doing all of his Monday morning assignments, determined that his counselor would be pleased with him on Wednesday, only to be sabotaged by his English teacher asking to see him immediately. Kylie warned him about this. Said it had happened to her last year when they kept scheduling Student Council meetings during her study hall. Didn't the teachers want them to succeed? Well, hopefully, Miss Grant wouldn't keep him long and knew that he hadn't done anything awful.

Danny was greeted, though, by a wide smile. "Danny," Miss Grant said. "Thank you for coming so quickly. I won't keep you. I just wanted to ask your permission."

"Permission?" Danny's whole face was a question.

Miss Grant laughed, holding up Danny's composition about his first Cross Country meet. "This is fine work, Danny. I felt as if I were running along with you. You made me feel absolutely joyous, and I don't even like to run."

Danny noticed the big fat A on top and grinned. "Thanks. I'm glad you like it, but you wanted permission?"

"I'd like to submit this to our school literary magazine. The deadline was last week. Mrs. Hunt is the sponsor, but I'm sure she and the student editors will accept it—especially since you will represent your class in the final meet. Would you allow me?"

"Wow, Miss Grant! I'd love that!" He'd keep it as a surprise for his family. "Could I tell my counselor? I'm meeting with her on Wednesday. She hasn't been too happy about my grades."

"Definitely." Miss Grant laughed. "And Danny, you'll do just fine as long as you complete your assignments and remember to turn them in."

Danny returned to study hall, resolving to become a good student—something he'd never cared about before. He'd remember to thank Hannah for her suggestion. "Write what you care about," she'd said. She was right.

Hannah was good and mad at Dad and Uncle Martin. Okay, they had finally kept their promise on Monday, instead of Sunday, and had taken her out to dinner. No movie, though. Dad had even taken a half-day from school and gone into the city early to fetch Uncle Martin. But it was Tuesday night now, and again she was alone, with no idea where they were. She hadn't seen much of Danny because of his Cross Country practices and homework. She was glad he was doing better, but she was lonely.

At dinner last night, Uncle Martin started the conversation. "Hannah, I wouldn't blame you if you resented me. I've really screwed up your life."

Hannah shrugged. That was a bit extreme; she loved Uncle Martin. She was just sick of being alone. The only ones she resented were Mom and the other family members who'd turned against her—as if she'd done anything wrong. "I don't resent you or Dad, Uncle Martin. I'm just mad that you didn't keep your promise about taking me out to dinner and a movie when you said you would. You were going to make it so I wouldn't be alone so much. But I am, practically every single night. Sometimes I'm scared." She told them the latest—about seeing the stranger in the Kennedy's garden.

"Maybe we should call the police," Dad said. "We haven't wanted to draw any attention to ourselves, but—"

"That's okay," Hannah said. "I don't think they could do anything." That's your job, she wanted to add, but retreated into silence instead. At least steak and fries beat frozen microwaved whatever. She also wanted to tell them about Danny and Porter saying they'd find her a dog. But she'd wait. The boys probably had forgotten about it. Besides, she'd feel even worse if Dad and Uncle Martin said no.

"Well, let's tell you about some plans we've made that might help," Dad said. "We've made an appointment to have all the locks in the house changed. We should have done that when we first moved in, but we were so busy we didn't even think about it."

"We didn't leave a spare key outside," Uncle Martin said, "but we found out the Kennedys did. Mrs. Kennedy forgot. When she looked, the key to our house was gone."

"So that's how the prowler got inside," Hannah said. Wait until she told the SSC. But it was still a big mystery. "How did he know it was there?"

The men shook their heads. No idea. "You'll be safer with the new locks," Dad said, "but that doesn't solve your loneliness. Your Uncle Martin and I have been checking our finances, and we're pretty sure we'll be able to afford a secondhand car soon."

"Then I'll be able to drive myself back and forth, and your father will go home with you every day."

Hannah smiled briefly before frowning again. She knew where Uncle Martin worked. "You'll have to leave the car in a parking garage. Will you be safe?"

"That's always the question, isn't it?" Uncle Martin said ruefully. "I've talked to some of the other musicians in the same situation.

We've agreed to look out for each other. They'll accompany me to my car."

"Mr. Kennedy said you should pop over any time you like," Dad said. "He thinks you're a good influence on Danny."

"Me?" A good influence? Crazy! Should she chance it? Oh, why not? "Danny and Porter said they could help me find a dog. I've always wanted one, and I'd feel a whole lot safer."

Dad and Uncle Martin exchanged glances and nodded. "We've got the space for one," Uncle Martin said. "As long as you agree to take care of it, I think it's a fine idea."

A dog of her own! Maybe he and Bingo would play together. And she'd never be lonely again! But meanwhile it was Tuesday night, and she was alone.

Beth couldn't wait for Saturday. She'd spent hours on the phone, talking with Imani and Priyanka—Imani had asked her and Pri for an overnight Saturday, and Mom had said yes. She also caught up with Kylie, who finally knew the truth about Brad. Beth didn't tell her she already did. That was part of keeping Kurt's confidence.

"It didn't have anything to do with me," Kylie said. "He was working up the courage to tell me because he was afraid I'd be upset. I was, of course, but pretended I wasn't. He doesn't want to leave Castle Bluff. It might not happen, but he doesn't think he should sign up for anything and run the risk of letting people down."

"That sounds like Brad," Beth said. "How is he taking his mom and dad splitting?"

"He's sad, but he said he's not surprised because they fight all the time. He's mainly worried about his little brothers and sisters. They're bewildered. Why would parents who are not getting along have six children?"

"I guess it seemed like a good idea at the time," Beth said, causing a slight chuckle from her friend. Then she shut up. She knew, of course, what Kurt had told her, but she hadn't known how bad it was.

"Beth, I asked him if he'd like to come to your Drama Club this Saturday to see Kurt show off, and he said yes. I know I should have checked with you first. I hope it's okay."

"The more the merrier," Beth said. "I'm glad he's coming."

"I'm just glad we're talking again. I told him we'd stay in touch, no matter what."

Well, Beth hadn't spent much time talking on the phone with Kurt because he was so busy. He was beyond thrilled with his part in the play. "It's totally cool, Beth. I play a troubled kid—a brat, at first. I wish you could help with the set and lights. You'd be a whiz at depicting the swamp in Indiana. If they tried to make it look real, it would only look amateurish, so they're just giving an impression."

"Yes, it would need to be stylized," Beth said. "I'm reading the book now, and it's wonderful. I'm glad Hannah mentioned it."

"Yeah, that Hannah. She's going to be a big help in Drama Club."

"About Drama Club, Kurt, I was wondering if the club could come see your performance and the one at the high school, too. We could take theater fieldtrips. What do you think?"

"It's a great idea, but the tickets at Crofts are pretty expensive. I'll ask the director. It might help that Miss Armstrong and Imani's dad are teachers there."

"Thanks." Then, hoping that Kurt hadn't forgotten in his excitement, "Are you still coming Saturday? I've been telling everyone. You don't have a rehearsal?"

Kurt chuckled. "Don't worry, kid. I've got your back. I listed it as one of my conflicts. I've been excused, and the director thinks it's a terrific idea. He's the same director Roe had for *Anne Frank*—great guy!"

Beth marked her calendar. This Saturday, improv, the following would be Halloween, and one more meeting after that. Then they'd be back at Castle Bluff Middle School, if they were lucky. She would be sorry to leave the castle, but doing school online was getting old. It was past time to be with friends, to meet new kids, and be taught by real teachers.

SCENE 12 – HAVING A BLAST

DANNY DIDN'T EVEN KNOW HANNAH could laugh — at least not like that. Sometimes she'd laugh at Bingo, but this was different. She was laughing so hard at Kurt's pantomimes that tears were rolling down her face and she was clutching her stomach. "Ouch," she said, but kept on laughing.

Well, Kurt was funny, Danny thought. It was just that he'd seen him plenty of times — pretending to be Frankenstein's monster, a cat playing with a ball of yarn, and a small child who has dropped his sucker. When Kurt was done, he gave a sweeping bow, basking in the wild applause.

Then Kurt turned serious, which sort of surprised Danny. He'd only seen Kurt's serious side once, last summer at Camp Shimmer Lake, when so many dangerous things were happening. Danny preferred him when he was just joking around.

"I love doing pantomime and making you laugh," Kurt said, "but you should know that it's a serious art form. Probably the most amazing mime ever was the French actor, Marcel Marceau. His famous character was Bip the Clown. You can watch him perform on YouTube. Maybe when you're back at CBMS, Beth could request equipment so you can watch together at a Drama Club meeting. Then you'll discover that I'm a beginner." Kurt laughed, which made people like him even more.

Danny guessed he understood. He was plenty serious about sports, even though they were fun. Maybe he'd look up that clown on YouTube, if he could remember his name.

Kurt continued. "Now, before I ask for volunteers — don't worry, Danny and others, you don't have to try unless you want to — I'd like to give you a few basic rules. They sound simple, but you'll find out they're anything but. First, don't talk! And, ladies, that includes giggling. I'm looking at you, Hannah." Of course, that caused all the girls in the room to giggle and the few boys to look superior. "Next, remember that you're playing a scene and that it must be clear. We must know almost immediately who you are and your location. For me, the cat was the easiest and the little boy the hardest. Another rule is that everything you do, especially your facial expressions, must be exaggerated. The audience won't understand if you're trying to be subtle." After noticing some confused faces, Kurt said, "In this case, that means difficult to understand; you do not want that! Be sure that all your motions are precise — carefully done. Your gestures must be elaborate. Pantomime is not a guessing game. You want the audience to know. There are some great theater guessing games, but mime isn't one of them. You must keep your scenes entertaining, or the audience will throw ripe tomatoes at you or worse, go home. And the last rule is the same as the first: Don't talk!"

Danny wasn't sure he liked being singled out, but then he noticed Hannah. She was smiling like crazy. Kurt had remembered her name. Suddenly, Danny understood. Kurt wouldn't have mentioned them if he wasn't sure they could take it — that they'd be good sports. He could relax and just enjoy watching.

A few volunteers tried their own pantomimes and learned quickly how difficult it was to perform every task, using only motions and expressions. Hannah would have been okay as a little girl who tried to jump rope but kept missing, if she hadn't broken down in laughter each time. But everyone was so good-natured about it she didn't seem to mind. Porter was really good pretending to be a boy climbing up a hill and then falling down again, but his audience didn't quite get it. "I needed a Jill to come tumbling after," he said. "It's hard pretending that another person is with you." Porter is the coolest friend on the planet, Danny thought, especially because he doesn't know it.

Beth thought the best mime was by an eighth-grade boy named Joe. She had never met him before and wondered if he was new to the school. Tough, she thought, to be brand new and also stuck having your classes online. She'd be sure to talk to him before the meeting was over. Joe pretended to drink from a fountain. It looked so real Beth thought she almost saw water. Joe received a huge applause and praise from Kurt.

"I think you might not be a beginner," Kurt said. Joe admitted that he had just moved to Castle Bluff and had done theater at his old school and with a private company. Kurt nodded. Beth thought he might be examining new material for Crofts.

Beth looked at her watch. Almost an hour had gone by, and only an hour remained. They still had so much to do. She'd ask Kurt if he could come back again sometime. Maybe he could help with games at the Halloween party. He was about to start another activity when a youngish elderly lady came into the room, carrying a tray of something that smelled incredible.

"Gee!" shouted everyone who knew her.

"Heard my grandson was here, showing off, as usual," she said. "Thought the occasion called for homemade donuts." Everyone, whether they knew Gee or not, cheered.

At first, Beth was irritated, but it didn't last long. I just learned something, she told herself. When it comes to being president of Drama Club, I need to be flexible. Probably we'll never have time to do everything I plan. She remembered her grandpa's expression. *I'm going to have to roll with the punches.* And Gee's donuts were the most delicious things in Castle Bluff.

She managed to grab Kurt for just a few seconds. "It's going great, Kurt, but we won't get much more done today. I was wondering if you could lead our games at the Halloween party next Saturday. Gabby has been working on them, but she could use some help."

Kurt looked sheepish. "I can't, Beth. I'd love to another time. It's just—"

"Oh, right. I forgot. Another time would be great." Crofts' dance was on Halloween.

"I'm really sorry."

"Forget it. The kids are having a blast today. You've really helped the club. It's getting late, but maybe we'll have time for one more thing."

"Did I spend too much time on pantomime?"

Beth shook her head. "No, it was perfect. Things always take more time than we think they will." Then she called out to the group. "We have time for one more activity—I think. Kurt has promised to come back sometime. Before you go today, be sure to take an invitation for next week's Halloween party and a list of rules, if you didn't get them by email. Imani and Priyanka will pass them out. Raise your hands, Imani and Pri!"

Then Kurt asked everyone who wished to be in a scene to divide into groups of three or four. He pulled some index cards from his pocket. "I'll give each group a scene to play. If you just want to watch, please sit on the stage." Danny, wearing a stubborn expression, went to the stage. No surprise, Beth thought, although she might tell him in private sometime that good sportsmanship was important outside of sports. He did look sheepish when Kurt gave him a disapproving look.

But Beth was surprised and pleased when Joe asked her to be his partner. "I think it's only us, though," he said.

"That's okay. Be warned, though, I'm not nearly as good as you. Your mime was great. I could see the water."

"I have had a lot of experience," Joe said, adding that his last name was MacCracken. "It took forever to learn that water trick. I probably was showing off, but I did want to be noticed. I really need this club. I haven't met anyone in town yet."

"You'll meet a lot of kids once we're back in school," Beth said. "But Drama Club won't be like this—just one more after-school activity in a classroom, lasting only 45 minutes. We won't have time to do much."

"Couldn't you stay here? Two hours on Saturday morning?"

Beth stared at him. "I hadn't thought of that. Maybe. I could ask Mr. Markey. He really likes having us here. But I don't know how many new kids we'll get if we don't meet after school."

Kurt interrupted, handing them a scene. "I don't know if it will work for two people," he said. "I guess I could join you."

But Joe waived Kurt away. "Shall we just skip it today and keep on talking?" he asked Beth.

Beth nodded happily. She wanted to talk to Joe, and she couldn't help enjoying Kurt's reaction. Kurt was jealous! She led Joe to a corner. One of the greatest things about the ballroom was all the space. They could not spread out like this in a classroom.

"I wonder if we could have two meetings," she said. "Once a week at school where we plan things and do simple activities, and then again on Saturday here at the castle for kids who are more serious. Mrs. Hunt, our advisor, probably would just want to be at school. But Janet—she's a lady that lives at the castle—or Gee would come on Saturdays. I'm sure of it."

"Or maybe we could meet here every other Saturday. I think it's a great plan, Beth."

Then Beth found herself telling Joe about the Halloween party and her disappointment that Kurt couldn't come and lead them in more theater games. "Gabrielle is finding some, but we'll need more. If there's not lots to do, things might get out of control."

Joe thought a bit and then cleared his throat. "Beth, you don't know me, but—well—I was in a performing arts troupe back in Minneapolis, and we did lots of theater games and taught them to people, even teenagers and adults. If you think you could trust me, I'd love to lead the games. We could talk about it during the week."

"Oh, would you? That would be such a relief! Thank you, Joe!"

Suddenly, both of them were aware of laughter and applause. "We'd better watch," Beth said. After all, she was supposed to be the president. But she was doing a good job, she decided. Yes, she was making a lot of decisions, but other officers hadn't been elected yet, and Mrs. Hunt didn't seem interested in doing more than observing and learning. She was completely different from Miss Armstrong, who decided everything and didn't want officers. Beth wasn't taking over; she was delegating. Imani and Priyanka were taking charge of planning the Speakeasy and some parts of the Halloween party, and Joe would lead the party games. They were using members' ideas, including Hannah suggesting the name for their scenes and monologue show. The Speakeasy could very well become a Drama Club tradition.

Hannah was in the last scene of the day, which didn't give her group more time to practice because they had to watch the other scenes. But it did give them more thinking time. Her scene, with Porter, Imani, and a seventh grader named Seth, was to give reasons for why they were late for an event. They decided the event was Imani's birthday party. It would have been better if they had more people, but it was still okay. Porter went on and on about his mom's car having a flat tire. After it was fixed, he got a ticket for speeding, and then forgot

Imani's present and had to go home again. After each excuse, Imani rolled her eyes and made sarcastic comments. Then Hannah gave her excuse. "A scary burglar was robbing our pumpkin patch," she said. "It was terrible! He was cutting them from the vines, and they were howling in pain. I tried to call the police, but our very old-fashioned telephone wires were cut. Finally, I chased him away and then ran as fast as I could to get here. I'm sorry that I forgot the present."

Imani and Porter made faces and gave her a hard time until Seth came up from behind with a pretend gun—his hand and a pointed finger. He growled. "Hand over all presents, or I'll shoot first, and then squash you with a pumpkin." Only a few knew that Hannah's excuse—preventing a notorious thief from robbing a pumpkin patch—was based on fact. She could hear Danny laughing the loudest.

Seth's acting left something to be desired, Hannah thought, but it was all in good fun. In fact, the whole morning had been enjoyable. She hadn't felt sour or shy even once. "Thank you," she whispered to Beth before leaving. "I had a great time!" She wondered if she'd enjoy Drama Club as much when they were back in school.

SCENE 13 – GOOD THINGS COMING

"OKAY, WHO IS HE? WHAT'S going on?" Imani demanded.
She and Beth were ready for confidences in Imani's lovely bedroom, where Beth would spend the night. Her first overnight with Imani in ages!

"I can't imagine who you're talking about," Beth said airily.

"Come on, Beth. I'd tell you!"

"Well, okay, his name is Joe MacCracken, and I think he's going to be a big deal in Drama Club this year."

"That's a start," Imani said. "But it doesn't explain why your face matches your hair, and it doesn't explain why Kurt was glowering all over."

Beth giggled. "That was fun. He didn't have any reason to be jealous, but I loved it. Joe moved here from Minneapolis, where I guess he was a theater bigwig in his middle school."

"An eighth grader?"

"Yep. I don't think Kurt would have noticed if Joe wasn't the tallest boy to come along since Brad Michaels. The timing was great, too." Beth explained about Crofts' Halloween dance.

"Phew! Kurt asked Kylie instead of you? I'll bet you were furious."

"Well, more like hurt. Then I sort of understood after Kurt explained. He was afraid of being teased if he took an eighth grader. He called himself a coward."

"He was right, of course, about being teased, that is. Aniya says they're as stuck up as ever over there, even after that awful senior class graduated." Imani's sister was a dance student at Crofts, and their father, one of the art teachers. "It's good he didn't ask you, Beth. Then you'd have had to back out or not go to the Halloween party."

"I know, but I'm sorry that Kylie and Kurt can't come. I wanted Kurt to lead our games again. He's so good. Then Joe offered to do it." Beth sighed without realizing it, but Imani did.

"Watch out, Kurt. Here comes Joe! And watch out, Beth. Don't jump into another crush so soon." Imani was alluding to the crush Beth had had on her Social Studies teacher—a crush that could have been a disaster.

"That was different," Beth said.

"True, but be careful anyway. About Joe—are you sure he'll come through? I mean, you don't even know him."

"I thought of that. Maybe as a backup, we should make a list of possible games, just in case. You know, a Plan B to bring out if he lets us down. I don't think he will, but—"

"Not a problem," Imani said, grabbing a notebook and pencil. "A lot of the games could be about costumes. You know, guessing what the costumes are, prizes for the best and worst. Pri and I will buy some cheap prizes."

"And maybe we can divide into groups for skits."

"And whatever costumes they wore would have to be part of the skit. Good idea!"

"Joe says he'll call during the week to talk about ideas. If he does, I'll give him Gabrielle's phone number, in case she had time to find some."

"Gorgeous, unreliable Gabby? Don't count on her."

"I think she might have changed," Beth said.

The evening evolved into pillow fights and giggles. The girls forgot they were teenagers—thirteen, practically grown up. Aniya had given them permission to go through her old dance costumes and select anything they wanted for the party. Beth chose a Robin Hood outfit while Imani became Maid Marian—the chubbiest Maid Marian ever, she declared.

"If I sit down or breathe, this zipper is going to pop. But you're going to be stunning, especially with your figure and red hair." Imani styled Beth's hair in a low ponytail, and then applied makeup that covered her freckles. "There," Imani said, stepping back to check her masterpiece. "Beth, you are really pretty, practically gorgeous. And you're consistently nice—something no one would say about Gabby."

Beth checked the mirror and smiled. "I guess I make a prettier boy than a girl."

"You can keep the makeup. I'll show you how to apply it so no one knows you're wearing it."

"Not even my mother?"

"Especially not your mother."

Giggles and skirmishes resumed until Aniya knocked on the wall. Aniya, now seventeen, wanted her beauty sleep and thought her sister and friend were far too childish. Still giggling, Beth and Imani got ready for bed and resumed quiet chatter throughout the night.

I don't mind being alone today, Hannah thought, once more perched in her tree fort. Danny and his family were off to church and would then go to his grandparents' house for Sunday dinner. She almost asked if she could take care of Bingo while they were away but didn't have the nerve. Danny was protective of his little dog, and Hannah couldn't blame him. But she'd remind him that he'd offered to help her find one of her own.

Yes, being alone was okay today when things were about to go her way. Hannah laughed at her instant rhyme. Uncle Martin would soon have a car, so Dad could be home every night. They had gone to the city for a concert, but at least they had asked if she wanted to go along. It sounded boring—some modern composer she'd never heard of—but it was nice to be asked.

"I'll go for a walk," she decided, "and if I meet anyone I know, I'll be friendly and say hi." She stood precariously. "They like me here!" she yelled, not caring if anyone heard. "I have friends! I am happy! It's going to be okay!" She'd zip into the house first and get some money, so she could buy lunch in town. Maybe at Smithy's, if there was a place to sit. Or maybe she'd go into the Food Mart and buy a sandwich to eat at the park. This was her town now!

Drama Club really made the difference, even more so than Danny and Porter. She laughed and had fun, and the others liked her ideas. Maybe kids at school would like her, too—if she gave them a chance.

While walking along the sidewalk toward town, she tried to figure out a Halloween costume. She hadn't participated in Halloween for several years, not since Mom and Dad were together. She had been a clown back then. She no longer had the costume, but it wouldn't have fit anyway. Besides, a clown was a little kid thing to be, even though a lot of people thought they were scary.

"Hey, Hannah!" Two girls approached. One was Beth, but she didn't remember the other girl's name; just that it was kind of weird. She recognized her, of course, because she'd been in Hannah's skit.

"Oh, hi," Hannah slowed down.

"Where are you off to?" Beth asked.

"Oh, just walking, but I thought I'd get lunch somewhere. Maybe Smithy's, if it isn't crowded."

Beth looked at her watch. "Church crowd should be out of there by now. Mind if Imani and I join you?"

Imani—that was her name! Hannah restrained herself from shouting, "that would be great!" No, too eager, too needy. Instead, "I'd like that."

"Shall we stop off at your house first to drop off your bag?" Imani asked Beth.

"And be stuck babysitting the rest of the afternoon?" Beth laughed, looping her free arm through Hannah's. "Let's not go anywhere near my house."

I'm just another Castle Bluff girl, going to Smithy's with friends, Hannah told herself.

Fortunately, Smithy's was almost empty. Hannah ordered a cheeseburger, fries, and a Coke. All she'd had for breakfast was a bowl of Fruit Loops covered with what was left of the milk. Beth and Imani had eaten but ordered chocolate shakes, to keep Hannah company and because Smithy's shakes were yummy.

"Have you figured out your Halloween costume yet?" Imani asked.

Hannah shook her head. "No ideas." And no way to get one if I had, she added silently.

Perhaps Beth guessed her thoughts. Kylie had told her that Hannah often fended for herself. "Imani's got lots of costumes in her attic. You could help, couldn't you, Imani?"

"No problem. Could you go back with me to my house, Hannah?"

Hannah grinned. "No problem. Thanks."

"Wish I could join you," Beth said, polishing off her shake, "but I promised to help Porter with a science project."

"Hannah and I will be fine," Imani said. "I've got some ideas already."

Hannah felt a little shy once Beth left, but Imani was nice.

Imani concentrated on finishing her shake. Perhaps she, too, was wondering what to say. Finally—"You and Porter are pretty good friends, aren't you?"

Hannah nodded. "I guess. Mainly because he and Danny are such good friends."

"I'm glad you and Porter joined Drama Club. Any chance Danny will do it, too?"

Hannah shook her head, grinning. "No chance," she said.

"Well, finish up, and we'll go see about that costume. Beth will be the cutest Robin Hood you ever saw. And me—well, actually, I was planning to be Maid Marian, but I think you'd be better than me. You're much slimmer, and your long, white-blond hair is perfect. We've got plenty of medieval gowns. I'm too heavy for Marian, but I will make a terrific Friar Tuck. For some reason, we have a monk's costume." She laughed. "Mom thinks I should give up Smithy's shakes, but I don't think so—Hannah, what's the matter?"

Hannah sat suspended, holding up her burger, staring at the kitchen door. "Oh, nothing. I was just thinking about being Maid Marian."

But something was the matter, or at least strange, for coming out of Smithy's kitchen was the stranger Hannah had last seen trying to steal a pumpkin from the Kennedys' garden. He stared at her, then gave a slight smile and wave before returning to the kitchen.

Should she say something? No, Hannah didn't know if Beth had told Imani what was going on. Maybe she wouldn't say anything to anyone. After all, it had been a friendly smile, even if he seemed startled to see her. If he was getting his act together, working for Smithy, she did not want to wreck it for him. Everyone deserved a new beginning.

"I'm ready," she said to Imani. "Let's go look at those costumes. It's really nice of you."

Sunday dinners at his grandparents were often a drag, but Danny was enjoying it today. So many good things had happened lately, and so many more were coming. And he was all caught up with his homework. The only thing he needed to think about was his Halloween costume. He'd call Porter to see if he had ideas.

"That Cross Country Conference of yours is getting mighty close, isn't it, Danny?" Grandpa pretended the date wasn't clearly marked on the kitchen calendar. He winked at Grandma.

"Yep. The Thursday after Halloween, right after school. You're coming, aren't you, Grandpa?"

"Well, let's see . . . " Grandpa put a hand into his pocket. "Let me check my appointment calendar."

"Oh, stop teasing him, Dad," Mom said. "The whole family will be there, Danny."

"Even if it's too cold or snowing," Grandma promised.

"Even Kylie?" Danny wasn't sure his sister could make it—a high school student on a Thursday afternoon.

"I put it down as a conflict," Kylie said, "and they're sure to honor it."

"A conflict? What? You made the play?" Danny shouted. He knew acting was almost as important to his sister as running was to him.

"Why didn't you tell us, dear?" Mom asked.

"The cast list was sent out late last night," Kylie said. "Everything was so hectic this morning that I thought it would be more fun to tell you here."

"It's a fine old play," Dad said. "*You Can't Take It with You.*"

"Old is right," Grandma said. "We did that when I was in high school."

"Did you get a named part or an extra?" Danny had been around Kylie and her theater friends long enough to speak the language.

"A good part, actually, and different from anything I've ever done. I'm Essie, a ditz, who thinks she's a ballerina but is terrible. I'm going to ask Imani's sister for help."

"Anyone else we know in the cast?" Mom asked.

"Yeah, Miss Armstrong's kids did okay. Eric plays a tax inspector, a really funny part. Marla made it, too. She's Gay Wellington. She wanted the part of the countess, but I think the director wanted a large person for the role. It went to a junior, who is huge. Marla is happy with her part, even though it's small, because she gets to be drunk and pass out."

Grandma made a noise of disgust.

"Now, Grandma, Marla has changed."

"Hmmm . . . we'll see." Grandma muttered something about leopards and spots, but the others ignored her. Grandma didn't always make a lot of sense, at least to her grandchildren. "And did anyone let Miss Armstrong know how great her kids did? She'll be hurt if no one contacts her. Did you, Kylie?"

Kylie shook her head. Danny thought his sister looked troubled whenever her former theater director was mentioned. He tried to help. "Well, she left CBMT and went to Crofts. That wasn't very loyal."

Mom chimed in. "CBMT might not have wanted her back, after leaving so abruptly. Did you ever find out what happened, Kylie?"

Kylie didn't answer. She just shook her head again.

"What about Brad?" Dad interrupted, perhaps hoping to change the subject to something that wouldn't upset his daughter. "I would think he'd get a very good part."

"He wasn't able to audition," Kylie said. "Later," she mouthed to Dad, who gave her a puzzled nod, realizing his change of topics had not been successful.

As was often the case, Grandpa came to the rescue. "I must say this family is full of good news. But anything else must wait until after dinner and maybe a game of Parchesi. I don't know about you, but I'm hungry. And something smells mighty good, Edna."

Danny smiled to himself as they sat at the table. He would wait until the literary magazine came out before he told them about his article. In fact, he'd try to get extra copies, so each of them could have one. He didn't suppose he could afford to send the whole magazine to Roe in Spain, but he could rip out his article and send that. Schoolwork was back on track, and his counselor was pleased. She wanted to see him once a week until the meet was over, but it all looked good. And so did Grandma's roast beef dinner.

SCENE 14 — HALLOWEEN HAPPENINGS

OCTOBER 31, HALLOWEEN — COOL BUT DRY. Perfect anywhere, but especially at a gingerbread castle high on a bluff overlooking Lake Michigan. All day, Leland and a hired crew had worked, stringing white lights on trees and castle eaves, causing the yellow, orange and red leaves, aided by an almost-full moon, to shimmer mysteriously. The moon seemed to provide a spooky path up the front steps to the gargoyle doorknocker. All guests would be thrilled, especially those who had never been in the castle before. Leland and Mr. Markey had rented costumes — the creepiest monsters available.

Inside, a team of decorators, led by Priyanka, Mrs. Hunt, and Janet had hung black and orange streamers and branches of colorful leaves around the ballroom walls. On the stage, plastic skeletons from Mr. Markey's storeroom, surrounded by cornhusks and bright grinning pumpkins, prepared to leer down at soon-to-appear guests. Enticing odors of homemade donuts and brownies from the kitchen wafted into the ballroom. No one, even those who had consumed an early supper, would be able to resist. Gee, the baker, and Janet, her helper, would soon don their costumes, characters from Beauty and the Beast. Priyanka would become a gorgeous Indian princess, right out of Aladdin, while Mrs. Hunt turned into a totally authentic Mary Poppins, a role that suited her personality.

Arriving first was president of the Drama Club, Robin Hood, in awe of how splendid the ballroom looked. "Even better than our *Mouse* cast party," she whispered. "I wish all of the kids from last year could come." Yes, she would be showing off a bit, but so what?

Following Robin closely behind was the breathtaking Lady Marian, in a medieval gown of black, wine, and deep blue. Not the dress Imani had planned to wear, but one just right for Hannah's slim figure. She wore her long hair down with white blond tendrils, created by stylist Imani Jones, also known as rollicking Friar Tuck. Merry men, Little John and Will Scarlet—Porter and Danny by day— brought up the rear. Possibly the bow and candy arrows, created by Hannah's dad, had convinced them to join the merry band.

But wait! Who could that be? Even Robin wasn't sure. Breathing evil, up to no good, entered the Sheriff of Nottingham. A sword at his side, the sheriff marched up to Robin, and gave her an evil look before taking off his mask and grinning. "Joe MacCracken, at your service, ready to complete the cast."

Beth smiled. "Thank you, Joe!" How in the world had he found out their costumes? Never mind Imani's warning, Beth was on the verge of another crush.

Soon, Beth welcomed everyone—quite a large group as it turned out, and she hoped there wouldn't be any problems. No sign of Gabrielle; she hadn't even returned Beth's text. Oh, well, her loss!

At the agreed-upon time, Leland put a sign on the front door, announcing that the party had begun and, as the invitation had stated, there would be no latecomers. Then he and an elderly ogre got into the new elevator and joined the party. The back door was locked, and Mrs. Gee Potts and Chef Janet Bouche would keep an eye on things in the kitchen, with Monster Leland occasionally wandering in to give his wife a smooch.

Beth then introduced the Master of Ceremonies, Joe, also known as the Sheriff of Nottingham. "The Sheriff is here to arrest me but also to make sure you have a great time."

First, Joe divided them into groups for skits, in which they had to incorporate their characters. "Alas, Robin Hood and her Merry People will be separated," he said. Beth was pleased he was using her skit idea. Groups were formed by counting from one to five. Those who didn't want to participate sat in audience chairs. They would serve as judges. Participants had ten minutes to figure out their skits.

Peter Pan, Mickey Mouse, a ghost, Cinderella, and Maid Marian were in Group Three. Group Four consisted of Harry Potter, Snow White, Tarzan, Friar Tuck, and a creepy clown right out of a Stephen King thriller. Beth decided not to participate. Acting was something she no longer enjoyed. Designing sets and posters, writing, and coming up with ideas were her thing. Maybe directing someday. She thought she might be good at that.

When the skits were done, judges huddled together to pick the winner. Danny was chosen to make the announcement. "They were all great," he said, "and it was hard to choose. We finally went with the group that was careful to include everyone. No single person took over." Danny had learned the importance of that from Kylie and Roe.

"The winner is — drumroll please — Group Three!"

Winners and losers cheered good-naturedly, especially Hannah, who was overjoyed. The skit, in which each of them reacted to the scary ghost, had been her idea. Every person was equally important, and the skit was something they could put together quickly. She was pleased with her prize of a full-sized Snickers bar, but that wasn't what mattered. Beth thought Hannah looked as if a light had gone on inside her. With a start, she realized that Hannah wasn't merely pretty; she was beautiful. The best thing was that Hannah didn't know it.

Then Joe had them try the classic mirror game. "Everyone needs a partner. If it doesn't work out evenly, Beth or I will fill in." Everyone scrambled to find a partner. Porter grabbed Danny and wouldn't take no for an answer. Beth noticed Hannah smiling when another seventh-grade girl claimed her. She was happy it all worked out evenly. Beth knew the mirror game well but preferred to watch.

Joe continued. "One of you is the leader; the other the mirror. Decide fast. Now face each other. Okay, your mirror will not be full length today. Move only from the waist up. Leaders, you'll make simple gestures or movements. Mirror, you must duplicate your leader's movements exactly. Leaders, you're not trying to trick your mirror; you must cooperate with each other. Remember what it's like if you look into a mirror. If you lift your arm, what do you see?" A few people nodded; they got it. "It will help if you maintain eye contact. If you talk or giggle, you're doomed." Everyone laughed. "You'll be concentrating so hard, you won't be able to see the other couples. Robin Hood and I will judge, and then the winners will demonstrate."

There was a lot of talking and giggling at first, but finally the groups settled down and took the exercise seriously. It was both fun and difficult at the same time. Beth and Joe wandered around watching, with Joe occasionally giving advice. Then he and Beth had a conference.

"Okay, time's up," Joe said. "Time to announce the winner. The team that managed a reflection that was smooth and continuous, with no lagging, was Porter and Danny. They did it so well we couldn't tell who was the leader and who was the mirror."

"Hey, we won!" Danny yelled.

After their demonstration, Porter admitted that he had been the leader and Danny the mirror. Both were pleased with the full-sized Butterfinger prizes and ate them immediately. The smells from the kitchen were driving everyone crazy.

They should have saved their candy, though, for in came Gee and Janet with a huge platter of donuts and paper cups of cider. Eating and just talking with friends were important parts of any party, Beth reflected, raising her cup of cider to Mr. Markey, who winked at her and raised his.

Beth took the opportunity to ask him about Drama Club still meeting at the castle once school opened. She explained the reasoning.

Mr. Markey smiled. "I'll need to talk it over with Leland and Janet," he said, "but I can't see any reason why it wouldn't work. If your Mrs. Hunt doesn't want to continue coming on Saturdays, I'm sure either Janet or Gee would love to help. I could also be a substitute. I used to act, myself, a million years ago."

It was getting late. The party would end at seven, so that it wouldn't be too late for trick-or-treating. Joe took charge again. "For our last game at this terrific party, we'll play To Question is the Answer."

Beth had never heard of it. Joe must know it from his old school—or he made it up. She thought he was creative enough to have done so.

"I'll call out a question, and whoever I choose must answer. No, I don't know your names, but I've got them on cards that I'll shuffle right now." He made such a big deal out of shuffling that everyone laughed. "Okay, I'm ready. Now your answer must be spontaneous, and it won't hurt if it's ridiculous." Joe smiled. "Anything goes, so don't be shy." He looked at a card.

"Porter Walters, why don't you like spinach?"

Porter stood and cleared his throat. "I don't like spinach because it's green and slimy. I hate green." He pointed mischievously at his green costume. "Besides, Popeye told me he'd beat me up if I took any of his spinach."

Everyone cheered. Porter had done just fine. It was always hard to be first. Beth was proud of him.

Joe glanced at the next card. "Kamirah—hmmm, different—Williams. Kamirah Williams."

That was the girl who had been Hannah's mirror. Beth would make a point of talking to her later.

"Kamirah, why are you afraid of chickens?"

Kamirah stood, shaking with nerves, but seemingly determined to try. Beth smiled encouragingly. Her nervousness suited the question, though. "Afraid? I am absolutely terrified! They look at me with their beady eyes, and I can tell they're determined to peck mine out. They'll kill me someday, I tell you. They're bound to get back at me for eating their Great Uncle Henry last Sunday!"

Everyone howled, especially Hannah. Beth vowed to ask Joe to come up with more crazy questions. They'd play it again at a Drama Club meeting.

Then Mrs. Hunt joined Beth and Joe onstage and held up her hand. "Cars are starting to line up outside," she said, "and it's past seven. This has been a wonderful party, and I'm sure we're all sorry it's over. Beth, would you like to say anything?"

"Yes," Beth said loudly. "First, thank you all for coming. If you think you like us and that Drama Club might be the right group for you, please give us another chance by coming to the castle next Saturday. We meet from ten until twelve. You can help us plan our activities for the rest of the semester. Now, special thanks to our hosts, Mr. Markey, Leland, and Janet. This party wouldn't have been possible without their kindness. Thanks also to one of our best friends, Gee, who has done so much for us and makes the best donuts ever. We're always grateful to our sponsor, Mrs. Hunt, who puts up with us and even seems to like us. And lastly, a huge round of applause for the Sheriff of Nottingham and terrific emcee, Joe MacCracken!"

Joe received his huge round of applause. If he had ever been worried about his welcome in the new town, he no longer was. Mrs. Hunt came forward and raised her hand. "And let's hear it for our president, Beth Walters, who never minds sharing the spotlight and makes everyone feel important."

Beth then received her share of applause, causing her face to match her hair.

"One last prize," Joe announced, taking charge again. "The first and only prize for costumes and being great sports goes to the terrifying monsters. Misters Harold MacLain Markey and Leland Duncan!"

The men beamed, and Beth nodded in approval. They were great sports—especially Leland. What a difference happiness made!

The ballroom, of course, was a mess. Joe said he wished he could help, but he'd promised to take his little brother trick-or-treating. Beth was surprised little brother hadn't gone out earlier with his parents, but she assured Joe it wasn't a problem. "We've got it covered," she said.

And boy had they! With Zoe in a stroller, Mom and Dad had escorted Kelly and her friends trick-or-treating while it was still daylight. Porter would follow Drama Club members, filling their sacks with candy as they made their way home, and then spend the night at Danny's. Mrs. Kennedy would scrutinize every morsel before they were allowed one bite. As far as what was consumed en route, what she didn't know wouldn't hurt her.

And Beth? Well, it was too thrilling! She, Imani, and Priyanka were the cleanup committee, with a bonus for their efforts. Early that morning, they'd brought their sleeping bags and personal gear for an overnight in the castle! They were too old for trick-or-treating, they'd decided, but the perfect age to pretend to be scared to death by the castle ghosts. Mrs. Hunt left with the others, but Gee and Janet helped set the ballroom to rights, and then they all joined Mr. Markey and Leland downstairs for a late-night pizza. Beth didn't think she'd be very comfortable in a sleeping bag on a hardwood floor, but so what? It was doubtful they'd do much sleeping anyway.

Hannah walked with Kamirah—"call me Kammy"— while Danny and Porter walked just ahead, although they stopped often to punch each other and wrestle. They were definitely in a boy mood, Hannah thought. Probably too much candy.

"I wish we'd had more time for that question game. Yours was great, Kammy."

"Thanks. I was so scared."

"But it fit, so no one noticed," Hannah assured her.

"You're in my math class."

Hannah nodded. "Yes, but that's the only one. We might not have met if you hadn't come to the party."

"I almost didn't. I was afraid I wouldn't fit in because, well, I don't think there are many Black kids in Castle Bluff, like there were at my old school. I'm not sure what it will be like when CBMT opens up."

"I don't know either," Hannah said. "Oh, I don't mean about you. I'm talking about me. I don't usually fit in anywhere."

"You? But you're white and really pretty."

Hannah laughed. "Well, the pretty is kinda new, thanks to Imani. But there are all kinds of prejudices."

Kammy shrugged. "I guess. Well, Drama Club seems okay. If I go again, will you be there?"

"Definitely," Hannah said.

They were approaching her house, but the lights were off. Hannah was hoping Dad and Uncle Martin would be home. She didn't feel like being alone after such a wonderful time. And it was Halloween and scary, and she didn't think they'd bought any candy for trick-or-treaters.

"Looks like your parents aren't home yet," Danny said. "I think you'd better come to my house until they are."

Parents, he'd said. Hannah liked that. "Okay," she said, relieved. She didn't think the prowler meant any harm, now that he was working at Smithy's, but still . . .

"This way Aunt Jane can look through your candy, too," Porter joked. "But beware, she'll steal the Reese's."

Hannah wouldn't mind, not if it meant being part of the Kennedy family, for even a little while. "What about you, Kammy? Can you call someone to pick you up?"

"Nah, no phone, but I don't mind going on alone."

Danny shook his head. "Bad idea. Some weird guy has been prowling around the neighborhood. We'll walk you home. No more trick-or-treating, though. Most of the front porch lights have been turned off. Imani is sleeping over at the castle. You're her sister, right?"

Stopping cold, Kammy glared at him. "Why? Because I'm Black?"

"Whoa!" Danny said. "I didn't mean anything. I just know that Imani has a sister, and I thought you were her."

"Because I'm Black."

"Well, yeah, I guess. I'm sorry."

Hannah wanted to tell her to just chill but was afraid that would make matters worse. She didn't know Kammy, and besides, she sort of understood her reaction.

Porter, as usual, smoothed things over. "An honest mistake," he said. "Imani is one of my sister Beth's best friends. She's also one of the most popular girls in town. Imani has an older sister, Aniya, who is a dancer at Crofts. Danny didn't mean to offend you. Now, lead us to your house, or come inside the Kennedys' to phone your parents. You are not walking home alone."

Hannah grinned. Every now and then she realized that Porter was the most mature of the three of them.

"To my house then. As I said, we don't have a phone yet."

They would pretend it had never happened, but Hannah could tell Kammy had not made a good impression on the boys. Later, when she saw where Kammy lived, Hannah understood even more why her new friend was so prickly. The circumstances of Kammy's family couldn't be more opposite to those of Imani's. Kammy lived on the small western corner of Castle Bluff, between two major highways, where the poorest people lived. No way should she have walked there alone.

"See you Monday," Hannah said.

Without answering, Kammy dashed inside a townhouse.

"Wow," Danny said, as they headed back east. "I never met anyone who lived there before. I'm not even allowed to cross the highway."

Porter nodded. "Me neither. I feel sorry for her. Not because she's poor exactly, but because she was so embarrassed. I hope she'll stay with Drama Club."

"I'll try to talk to her on Monday," Hannah resolved.

"And I'll tell Beth what happened," Porter said. "Maybe she and Imani can help."

"I didn't mean to put my foot in it," Danny said glumly.

"I know," Hannah said. Danny had no way of understanding how Kammy felt. She did. Money wasn't a huge problem for her family, although they had to be careful, but she certainly was no stranger to prejudice.

"Come on," Porter said. "Let's make a run for it!" And they dashed across the highway — safe again in their own part of town.

Back at Hannah's, the lights were on. "Oh, Dad and Uncle Martin are home." She reached into her bag and pulled out three packages of Reese's Peanut Butter Cups. "Here, Danny, give these to your mom from me and tell her Happy Halloween!" The evening, mostly wonderful, was over. She wished Danny hadn't mentioned Imani, but how was he to know?

No more Drama Club for me, Danny decided. He had had a good enough time at the party, but the drama afterwards dampened it for him. Theater people were too emotional. Sports people weren't like that. They were determined, of course, but practical. They wouldn't get down on a guy just because he made an honest mistake. They would never think someone was trying to hurt a buddy's feelings. No, he'd leave the skits and plays to Porter and Hannah. His big meet was in five days. After winning, he would be a good sport to all the boys who didn't. Starting tomorrow until next Thursday, he would concentrate on running, schoolwork, and taking care of Bingo.

"Hey, Mom, we're home," he cried out. "Come steal our candy!"

SCENE 15 – A TRAGIC PROPHECY

ETH AWOKE, SORE ALL OVER. How she wished she could take a shower. Guess she'd have to wait until she got home. At least the Walters had no plans for the day. What time was it? She checked her phone. Noon! Time to rise but not shine. A text from Gabrielle, saying she hoped that the party was a success and that Joe had been able to use some of the games she'd sent him. That was odd, Beth thought. Joe hadn't said a thing. But they'd better get moving.

"Imani, Pri, wake up!"

Even louder demands and considerable shaking were required before that finally happened. Both girls stretched and groaned.

"I take it all back," Imani said. "We didn't talk all night. I had a great sleep. It's early now, and I got all of my chores done before the party."

"Sure you did." Beth showed her the time.

"Mom will kill me," Imani said.

Priyanka rose slowly, not saying anything but looking troubled, maybe fearful.

"Pri? Is anything wrong?"

"Yes, Beth, but I don't know what."

"Oh, no," Imani groaned. "Not again."

"What? What's going on?"

"Priyanka's long-dead great-grandma," Imani said, "making herself known in her usual spooky way."

"Well, I don't know about that," Priyanka said, but her voice shook. "She was a Hindi seer and often predicted the future."

"And is that what you're doing?" Beth asked. "Predicting the future? Are you a seer, too?" Not that Beth knew what that meant.

"I don't think so, but I have a strong feeling something terrible is about to happen."

Imani laughed. "Something terrible will happen if we don't get out of here. If I don't clean my closet, I can say goodbye to sleepovers for a long, long time."

At least they'd packed everything the night before. "You're probably right," Beth said, picking up her phone and calling for a ride. "Let's wait for Dad outside." Mr. Walters would take them home.

Still looking worried, Priyanka followed.

"Something troubling you?" Uncle Martin asked Hannah at breakfast. "I thought you'd be pleased at having us home for the day."

"Oh, I am." Hannah gave him a hug. "It's definitely unusual, though, and I'll believe it when it happens. All day? Really?"

Dad grinned. "Well, I do have papers to grade this afternoon, and no doubt Martin needs to practice, but I thought we might go to a movie later. Maybe that new place that opened up on the west side of town."

The west side of town. Hannah looked worried again.

"What's wrong?" Uncle Martin asked gently.

Tentatively, Hannah told them about Kamirah and what had happened on their way home. "Up until then, we were having the best time."

"Danny and Porter insisting on escorting her home was the right thing to do," Dad said.

"I know that. But Danny isn't a racist, Dad. He really thought Imani and Kammy were sisters."

"Would he have made that assumption if either of the two girls were white?"

Hannah shook her head. "No, but—"

"But there are very few African American families in Castle Bluff, and Danny knows Imani has a sister. It was unfortunate but understandable."

Hannah nodded. "Danny was really embarrassed. I sort of understood how she felt, though."

Uncle Martin sighed. "Because you've been the victim of prejudice, too—both unintended and deliberate. You might be just the person Kammy needs for a friend."

"I liked her until she turned on Danny that way. Danny is my best friend." Then Hannah told Dad and Uncle Martin where Kammy lived. "Danny and Porter aren't allowed there. I don't think they'll tell their parents."

Dad frowned. "I'm familiar with the West Village Flats. I don't want you going there, either—at least not without an adult. That area is dangerous."

"Okay. Anyway, I don't think I'll be invited to Kammy's. She seemed embarrassed."

"After you know Kammy a little better and I'm home more, you might try to invite her here," Dad said.

The three of them cleared the table and washed dishes together—like a normal family, for once.

Hannah made sure all of her school stuff was ready for the next day, before heading outside to her tree fort with a blanket and an Agatha Christie book. Uncle Martin had a whole shelf of them. She decided to give one a try. She thought Danny had gone out running after church. Maybe they could play with Bingo later in the afternoon.

"Brrr," she said. When summer came again, she would ask Uncle Martin to help her turn the fort into a tree house with walls. She wouldn't be able to read here much longer.

Perry, a fellow team member, kept time while Danny ran around the track at Community. Too bad the final meet wouldn't be held here. He was used to this track and liked it. On Thursday, he'd climb onto the school bus with the other CBMS winners and travel a few towns over to Forest Glen Consolidated. Dad and Mom planned two carloads, filled with friends and family. Danny was certain it would be the most exciting day of his life, so far. He had never felt stronger. He would win. He just knew it!

He came to the end where Perry slapped him on the back. "Seven minutes again," Perry cried. "Super! Now my turn."

Danny sat on a bleacher and held the timer. Perry was a good, consistent runner. He'd probably never set a record, but he was a valuable team member and a good sport. Danny would miss Cross Country once it ended, but soccer started the week after. A short season this year because of the lateness of school opening. Auditions were Friday, the very day after the meet. He chuckled to himself. Auditions! He'd meant tryouts, of course. He'd grown accustomed to Kylie's theater talk. He was pretty sure he'd make the team, but if not, hockey was right around the corner, and he had all that new equipment from Uncle Carl. He hadn't seen him in ages. Maybe he'd come down for Christmas. Danny wished Roe would come, too, but that wasn't likely. All the way from Spain! She'd sent him a good-luck email.

Perry did his last lap and jogged over to him. "Eleven minutes," Danny said. "Good job!"

Danny jogged home. He would practice after school with the team for the next three days, and that would be it. He was ready. He felt pretty grownup. Mom and Dad had allowed him to stay home alone today. They'd gone to Grandma's while Kylie went to see a friend. She didn't get home from the dance until after midnight and was excused from church this morning. Not Danny, but that was all right. He'd grab some lunch and then maybe see if Hannah wanted to do anything. He did not want to talk about the Halloween party and that walk home. Heck, he hadn't meant anything. At least he'd been friendly with the new girl. Walking her home had been his suggestion. But the party had been cool, and he was glad he went. Drama Club was over for him, of course. Nothing would interfere with sports. That was what was important!

After a quick ham sandwich, Danny checked Hannah's backyard, where he thought he might find her. Yep, reading a book, propped high up on the board she called her tree fort. "Hey, Hannah," he called. "Want to toss around a Frisbee for Bingo?"

"Sure," she hollered down. "Just one more page and I'll be done with the chapter."

"I'll get Bingo," Danny shouted. Throwing the Frisbee would keep them from talking—at least about anything too serious. He didn't realize that the incident with Kammy was the last thing Hannah wanted to discuss.

Danny let the Frisbee fly into his backyard. With an excited bark, Bingo went after it.

"Any luck finding me a dog, Danny?"

"Not yet. Porter and I haven't had time. Did you ask your dad and uncle?"

"Yeah, they said yes."

"I'll ask around as soon as the meet's over," Danny promised.

"Thanks. How did your practice go?"

"Great. Perry timed me. Seven minutes again."

"You're sure to win," Hannah said. "I'll try to get a ride."

"Your dad can't come?"

"Probably not. It will be different once we have a second car, and Uncle Martin can drive himself." Hannah hesitated. "It's hard to carry a cello on a bus and train." She giggled. "It's almost as big as I am, and besides—"

"He's gay and might be attacked."

Hannah's mouth dropped. "You know? I wasn't sure."

"I guessed. Then I talked it over with Dad."

"You don't mind?"

Danny shook his head. "Heck, no, your dad and uncle are super. Mom and Dad like them, too."

"You won't tell?"

"Of course not. I'm not exactly dumb."

Without thinking, Danny and Hannah had wandered onto the Kennedy's driveway, forgetting about Bingo, who had not forgotten about them. Eagerly, he presented them with the Frisbee, pleading that the game continue.

"Okay, Bingo." Hannah let it fly. Too hard, and she hadn't considered the direction. She let it go, and it sailed away, right into the street as a white pickup truck approached.

A mere truck wouldn't stop Bingo. He was determined to get that Frisbee.

"Bingo, stop!" Danny yelled, in pursuit. "Heel, boy!"

Heel—when the prize was a Frisbee?

"No, Bingo!" Danny raced after him, failing to see that Bingo had managed to get beyond the truck.

"Come back, Danny," someone yelled. "Now!"

Danny looked back, just as the truck struck his side, throwing him practically to the sidewalk. Then, as if nothing had happened, it kept on going.

Hannah rushed over. "Danny," she sobbed. "Are you okay?" Bingo, unharmed, returned with the Frisbee. He seemed to realize that the game was over.

"Hannah," the stranger said. "Go call for an ambulance. I'll stay here until you return. Take Bingo with you." It was their prowler— the young man she'd seen at Smithy's.

"Who are you?"

"Go, Hannah. Then come right back."

Danny looked up. "Mateo," he managed to say before losing consciousness.

"Hannah! Now!"

Hannah ran into the house, and alerted 911. Then she yelled upstairs for Dad and Uncle Martin. As soon as he saw her, the stranger took off running. In the distance, she heard the ambulance.

SCENE 16 – ANSWERS AND QUESTIONS

HANNAH'S DAD DROVE TO THE hospital, so there'd be an adult there for Danny. "Try to find Danny's parents," he ordered before leaving.

"Any ideas?" Uncle Martin asked.

"They usually go to Danny's grandparents after church," Hannah said, wishing Danny had gone, too. "I'll call Porter. His family might know where they live." Thanks to the SSC, Hannah had Porter's phone number.

The Walters were able to contact the Kennedys immediately, but no one seemed to know where Kylie was. Beth offered to call around until she found her. Hannah would take care of Bingo.

Beth's mom insisted on picking up the Kennedys and going to the hospital, too. "They shouldn't drive, and Jane will need me," she said. She and Danny's mom had been best friends since they were children. "You keep calling, Beth. Dad will pick up Kylie and drive her to the hospital as soon as you find her. Porter, I'll let you know something as soon as I do." Porter was sitting at the dining room table, crying his heart out.

His dad tried to comfort him. "I'm sure he'll be okay." Meaningless words. "As soon as Beth finds out where Kylie is, we'll go to the hospital. You, too." Porter nodded. Yes, that would help. He needed to be there. Then Mr. Walters called a neighbor to come watch Kelly and Zoe.

Beth grabbed her cellphone. All of their mutual friends' numbers were on her contact list. Briefly, she thought of Priyanka's great-grandmother, the Hindi seer. "Something terrible did happen," she whispered. "Pri was right."

First, she called Kurt. After all, he and Kylie had gone to the dance together.

"Beth! How was the Halloween party?"

"Fine, but I can't talk now. It's an emergency. Do you know where Kylie is?"

"Sorry, my parents dropped her home about midnight. An emergency?"

"Danny was hit by a truck. He's in the hospital. That's all I know, but I've got to find Kylie."

"Danny? Oh, no! Could she be at her grandparents? She usually goes there for Sunday dinner."

"Not today. Look, Kurt, I've got to keep calling. You try, too. I'll let you know later what's happening."

This was going to be hard. All their friends liked Danny. Beth teared up at the thought of Danny's surprise birthday party almost a year ago. No time now, she scolded herself. Keep calling.

Next call was to Brad. "No, Beth, I haven't seen Kylie for a few days, and I'm at work now." Brad had kept his job as handyman at the castle. "Anything wrong?" Beth explained quickly, once again.

She doubted Eric would know, but maybe Marla. After that, she had no ideas. She didn't know what new friends Kylie might have made in high school.

"Marla, is Kylie there? Oh, thank goodness. Listen, Danny was in an accident. He's at the hospital. No, I don't have any details. My dad will drive to your house to get her. Try to keep her from worrying." What a stupid thing to say, Beth thought.

By the time they got to the hospital, the waiting room was full of frightened family members and all their friends. If more people arrived, there wouldn't be enough places to sit, Beth thought. After rushing into her parents' arms, Kylie sat next to Brad, firmly holding his hand. Surprisingly, Kurt held Beth's. Then they waited, no one sure what to say.

Hannah sat, miserable, between Dad and Uncle Martin. This is my fault, she thought. I shouldn't have thrown the Frisbee, especially not so hard and not in the driveway. Danny was the best friend she'd had. How could he ever forgive her, even if he was okay? She had seen his leg, twisted under him, and the one on top, cut and bleeding. He would live, but there was no way he would run in any race in only four days—maybe not even for the rest of the year. Sports— what mattered most to him. She turned to Dad and sobbed quietly into his jacket.

The doctor entered, and everyone stood. He smiled. "I believe this must be the Danny Kennedy fan club. Which of you are his parents?"

Mr. and Mrs. Kennedy rushed over, and the doctor led them into the hall to talk privately. Kylie tried to go, too, but her grandfather stopped her. "We'll find out soon," he said. "You stay here."

When they returned, Danny's mother was crying and his father had turned white. "They're taking him into surgery," he said. "Both legs are in pretty bad shape, but they'll try to save them. He also has a mild concussion. Other than that, he's checked out okay. The surgery will take awhile. You might want to go home, and we'll call you once we know anything more."

Eric and Marla gave Kylie a hug and said they'd be praying. Kurt asked Eric for a ride and told Beth he'd call her later. "I'm staying," Brad said. It appeared everyone else was, too, at least for a while.

Beth's parents offered to bring back coffee and sodas from the cafeteria—better than what's offered in the machines, they said.

All was quiet until—"This is my fault," Hannah sobbed loudly. "You should all hate me, and I won't blame you!"

"I doubt if you're to blame for anything," Mr. Kennedy said. "But come sit next to me and tell me what happened."

The Walters returned with the beverages and quietly passed them out. It was obvious something had happened.

Hannah's sobs turned into hiccups, but she was determined to speak. "We were playing with Bingo in the backyard, taking turns throwing the Frisbee, and by mistake we ended up in the driveway. Then it was my turn, but I threw too hard, and it went into the street, and Bingo went after it. A truck came along, too fast, I think, and could have hit Bingo. So Danny went after him. The truck would have run over Danny, if that weird man hadn't yelled for him to go back, so I guess he saved his life. But Danny didn't, but at least he stopped. At least the truck didn't run over him, but it did hit him."

"The truck didn't stop?" Beth mother asked, shocked.

Hannah shook her head.

"What happened next," Mr. Kennedy urged.

"The man knew Danny's name and mine, and Danny knew him, too. Then the man told me to go call 911 and to come back. I did, and I yelled upstairs for Dad. Oh, the man told me to grab Bingo, too. He knew Bingo's name. When I went back out, I heard the sirens, and then he took off."

"Hannah," Mr. Kennedy put his arm around her, "this is not your fault. You might not have been thinking when you threw the Frisbee, but Danny wasn't, either, when he ran into the street. Bingo was just being Bingo; a dog wouldn't know better. If there's any blame here, it's the truck driver, going too fast in a residential area and not stopping. The police will sort that out. You'll probably need to give them a description at some point. Did you see the driver?"

"Uh-huh, and the other person in the truck. But if I hadn't thrown—" The sobs returned.

Kylie joined them. "Hannah, stop. Don't blame yourself. But this is important. You said Danny knew the stranger—I assume that's the man who's been prowling around our houses and that you think broke into yours. Did Danny say anything?"

"Yes, right before he passed out. He said, 'Mateo.'"

"Impossible!" a few people said.

"Mateo Santos? But he's dead!"

Mr. Kennedy shook his head. "Maybe—maybe not. You said he saved Danny?"

Hannah nodded. "He wasn't scary at all. He was nice, and he tried to help. I don't know why he didn't stay."

"We must find him, and I must notify Carlos," Mr. Kennedy said.

"I think I know where he is," Hannah said. "I saw him working at Smithy's, but I didn't know who he was." She still didn't but knew better than to ask then. It helped a little that people didn't blame her.

Danny ran around the field. Ran? He flew around the field. Faster and faster and faster—faster than he had ever flown before. The crowds were cheering him on, although it sounded more like crying. That was strange. Bingo was barking triumphantly. He had run his race, too, and a golden Frisbee was his prize. A banner proclaiming, *Dan Wins!* was on top of a dirty white truck, and his coach yelled into a large speaker, "four minutes, the all-time best score for anyone, anywhere! A new world record!"

"He's regaining consciousness," a strange voice said. "Too soon. Nurse, give him another injection."

"My boy, my boy," someone was crying. It was Mom. Sure, she was proud of him, but she shouldn't cry. That was just embarrassing.

Why was he lying down? How silly! He should be dancing for joy. He'd get up now. But his legs—they wouldn't cooperate. He couldn't feel them. Then he couldn't feel anything.

ENTR'ACTE

Beth looked around Kylie's hideaway, also known as the Kennedy basement. One could almost imagine that the last year had never happened. Almost. Certainly the weather was different. Almost Christmas, and still no snow. Her old friends had gathered again to celebrate Danny's birthday. Almost like last year. Almost. Danny had been happy back then. Today, they would be lucky to see even a glimmer of a smile. Porter, always faithful, was with Danny in his improvised bedroom, now downstairs in the room that had been his father's study. And the side steps, leading to the driveway, had become a ramp for wheelchair access.

But they were all back together, including Roe. She had returned from Spain, not just because of Danny, but also her brother. They were anxious to hear the full story of Mateo, but all seemed hesitant to ask.

"Okay," Roe said finally. "I hear you, even if you're not saying anything. It's a long story, and I don't know everything. Mateo's forgotten a lot. I hardly know where to begin."

"Maybe at the bridge?" Kylie suggested.

"Well, you know, obviously, that Mateo didn't die. We assumed he did because his body was never found, even though the other boys were. Mateo isn't sure what happened next. He was washed ashore somewhere, unconscious. Some people picked him up and took him to a facility, maybe a hospital, where he was detoxed. He said it didn't work, though. Somehow he left, and then got into bad company and more drugs. He was beaten when he couldn't pay. He doesn't know where he was but remembers he was left under a bridge to die. He thinks the police picked him up and threw him into jail. During all that time, he wasn't quite sure who he was or where he belonged."

"Amnesia?" Beth wondered.

"Sort of. The drugs really scrambled his brains. He might never be totally okay."

"Three whole years, Roe," Brad said, sounding suspicious.

"Yes. Well, in time he got help. A policeman found a place willing to try. He was there for a long time and finally remembered who he was. He was in Nevada then. He worked a few jobs until he had enough money to come home."

"But when he got to Castle Bluff, his family was gone," Kurt said.

"Right." Kylie picked up the story. "I guess he wanted to approach Mom and Dad a couple of times but didn't have the courage. He remembered where we hid our key, and when he looked, he found his family's back door key as well. Mom put it there when she was trying to sell the house but completely forgot about it; it was easier for her than constantly removing the lockbox. He went inside because he was hungry and getting bad headaches, but mainly because he was trying to find an address or anything, really, to tell him where his family was. Nothing. He was pretty desperate when he finally asked Smithy for help."

"And Smithy gave him a job and let him stay in a back room of the store," Roe said.

"Has he changed?" Eric asked.

"Oh, yes. I don't know him at all. He doesn't seem like my brother. Dad is going to help him. He is Dad's adopted son."

"And your mom?" Beth asked.

"We went up there. She didn't know him or me, but she seemed pleased to have visitors. She hardly eats anything. She's just skin and bones." Roe sighed. "Mateo blames himself completely for Mom's condition. He's pretty upset. Dad says that part of her collapse might have been brought on by thinking Mateo was dead, but that she probably would be sick anyway. I don't know if I agree, but I didn't say anything."

"Drugs, Roe," Eric said. "They took over. It wasn't Mateo's fault."

"Maybe." Beth could tell Roe wasn't convinced.

Then they put one sad topic away and brought out another: Danny. Gathering their gifts, they went upstairs, praying they could bring some cheer to a hurting, very depressed friend.

ACT TWO

If you cried a little less, the audience would cry more.

— Edith Evans

SCENE 1 — CARRYING ON

"OKAY, BOOTS, JUST ONCE MORE, and then it's time for your nap." Danny threw the catnip mouse to the playful kitten, who had learned quickly that for the game to continue she needed to hop back onto Danny's lap. Boots, all black with white boots, was Danny's favorite of the many presents celebrating his twelfth birthday. At first, another pet seemed disloyal to Bingo, but Hannah, when she gave him the tiny creature, assured him it was not.

"You and Bingo will always love each other best, and someday you'll be able to run around with him again. But I will not throw Frisbees in the driveway—at least not toward the street."

Danny hadn't answered. He'd grown tired of saying it was not her fault—of trying to make her feel better. Really, it was everyone's fault or no one's. It was an accident, and he was the one who must suffer, at least physically. He saw pain in many eyes, especially his parents', but it wasn't his job to make them feel better. Besides, he didn't want to.

"Time for rest now, Boots." Danny put the mouse into his robe pocket and patted an invitation for the kitten to sleep under the tartan rug covering his legs—Boots's favorite place to sleep.

Everything belonging to Boots was in this room or in the adjoining bathroom. While Danny had been in the hospital, Dad hired a man to open the wall enough so that his wheelchair cruised through easily. Boots's litter box was there, as well as a walker and a special chair attached onto the toilet. There was also an alarm bell for Danny to call his family, in case he needed help. He'd had to use it twice, which he found mortifying. Those with working legs had to use the upstairs bathroom or go to the basement. The first floor one belonged strictly to Danny and Boots. His world had become very small. Fortunately, the doorway of the converted bedroom was wide enough for Danny to join the family for meals. Mom insisted that he come, even when he didn't want to.

As soon as Hannah exercised Bingo, she would bring him into Danny's room, where he would curl up in his dog bed. Sometimes, Boots cuddled next to him. The dog and cat had initially reacted as expected but quickly decided they'd prefer being comrades. Danny wondered if they knew he needed them to get along.

His other birthday presents were fine. So many cards — one from each member of the Cross Country team, wishing him well and making wild prophecies for next year, or even spring track. Everyone tried to stay positive — everyone but Danny. His team had lost the meet, of course — the heart had gone out of it. The school literary magazine, with his essay inside, stayed on a shelf, unread.

Kylie's friends had even tried to duplicate last year's surprise party — to date the best one Danny ever had. They'd meant well, but Danny wished they hadn't bothered. Happy memories made him sadder.

The only present that made him think positively about the future was from Kurt — Speedo swimming trunks. "Not yet, of course," Kurt had said, "and you'll want to talk to your doctor, but swimming is a terrific sport, and with the new pool at CBMS, there's bound to be a swim team someday. It could be fun and help your legs, too."

Danny reached over and took the trunks from the box. He shrugged. Swimming. Someday that might interest him. Not much did right now.

And it was winter break again, and soon it would be Christmas. No snow yet. He wished it would. Then there'd be something to see out the window, other than dead grass and leafless trees.

The grand opening of Castle Bluff Middle School had been delayed again but was supposed to take place after the holidays. He would not be part of the excitement. All of his assignments would be done right here in this wheelchair.

A knock at the door and a face peeked inside — "May I come in?"

"Sure, Roe." Roe coming home was one of the few good things to happen lately, although she was planning to return to Spain to celebrate Christmas with her grandparents.

Roe pulled a chair over next to him. "How's the little bundle of fur?"

Danny lifted the rug so she could see the sleeping kitten. Roe knew not to ask him how he was, the way everyone else did. "Wiped out," he said. "That mouse you gave her does the trick every time."

"She's adorable," Roe said. "Such a good idea of Hannah's. I like her, Danny. And I like that she's living in my old house."

"Yeah, she's cool. I wish you were staying, Roe, but upstairs in the bedroom next to Kylie's — not next door."

Roe didn't point out that that room was now Mr. Kennedy's study, perhaps for a long time to come. "I'll be back at the end of the school year. Not sure where, exactly, but at least here in the same country. We'll see each other more often."

"I don't see why you can't stay for Christmas. Wouldn't your relatives understand?"

Roe sighed. "They would, Danny. It's — complicated."

Danny made a face. "That's what people always say when they don't want to explain."

"Well, I'll try, but it's hard. It's about Mateo."

"I think he's great. He probably saved my life when he called me back." And my legs would have been saved, too, if I'd obeyed immediately, Danny thought.

"Yes, it's good he was there. I don't know him anymore, and maybe I didn't back then, either. He and Dad have a lot to work out. Mateo is legally dead, so Dad has to bring him back to life, legally, that is. I had to talk to the police this morning—tell them what happened three years ago."

"Why?"

"In case they wanted to charge him with something. I mean, drugs were involved, and two people died."

"But Mateo pushed you out of the car! He saved your life!"

"That's what I told the police."

Roe's voice sounded funny, Danny thought. Almost as if she were lying. No, that couldn't be. Roe never lied.

⚷

Beth, Hannah, and Porter were on their way to the castle that cold December morning. Beth, too, wished it would snow. It was cold enough, so why didn't it? True, snow would make it harder to walk, but it would be more exciting. Well, maybe her idea for Drama Club would pep things up a bit. She couldn't blame Porter and Hannah for being down in the dumps. For their sakes she wished Danny would at least try to be cheerful and work harder at his physical therapy sessions. Not his fault, but it made things really difficult for those who cared.

Mr. Markey, Leland, and Janet had been pleased Drama Club wanted to continue using the ballroom, even when school opened again. "We're used to your being here," Leland said, "and it does Mr. Markey a world of good." Everyone had been worried about Mr. Markey's recent bout of bronchitis. They had just managed to keep him out of the hospital.

The recent Speakeasy that they managed to squeeze in right after Thanksgiving had been a great success, and even the sixth-grade members thought it should become an annual event. Porter wanted to bow out because of Danny, but he couldn't leave Imani without a partner. Actually, Porter's unhappiness made the scene about two kids looking for their fathers' names on the Vietnam Wall even more powerful.

Hannah, too, was devastated about Danny and might have given up her part if Beth hadn't said, "Your quitting won't help Danny." And *you do not want Gabrielle for an enemy,* she added mentally. Beth had learned that from Roe's experience last year, although Gabby seemed to have changed.

Roe. It had been so good to have her with them again. In fact, having everyone back together for a reunion and an attempted reenactment of Danny's famous birthday party had shown Beth a truth. Even though she was too young and even though she sometimes pushed him away, Kurt was still the one for her. Beth thought he knew that, too, because he told her that the very next time Crofts had a dance, she would be his date. "And if anyone laughs, so what?" he said. Beth had already decided to ask him to CBMS's Valentine's Day dance.

The three of them were too quiet, Beth thought, all of them in their separate worlds, mostly involving Danny. "How are things going with Bingo, Hannah?"

"Good. It's more fun with Danny, of course, but I like it when Porter comes to help."

"Danny really loves that kitten," Porter said. "Boots might have been the only present he cared about."

Beth knew Porter was disappointed by Danny's reaction to the video games, so she changed the subject quickly. "I wouldn't mind having a kitten, myself, if Mom weren't allergic to all wildlife except humans."

"And some of them," Porter said, grinning.

"What's next for Drama Club?" Hannah wondered. "I think you know. How about a hint?"

Beth laughed. "Just you wait. Actually, Marla gave me the idea. She's coming to the meeting to explain it. All I'll say is that I'd like you to be my partner, Hannah."

Hannah nodded. "It's kind of strange to agree to something without knowing what it is, but I guess I can trust you."

"You can, Hannah. I promise."

They made their way to the back of the castle where Beth, to her great pride, had been entrusted with a key. Marla was waiting there with a smaller number of Drama Club kids than usual, but it was winter break.

Beth unlocked the door and let everyone go first. The old-timers knew where all the lights were, and it was possible Gee or Janet was already there. First she wanted to talk with Marla. Joe lingered behind, looking anxious.

"I need to talk with Marla, Joe. See you upstairs." Shrugging, Joe followed the others. He was becoming really annoying, Beth thought. When they first met, she thought she liked him. Not acknowledging Gabby's contributions at the Halloween party hadn't been a red flag, exactly, but it had been a pink one. Since then, he seemed to be trying to push her aside as president. He wanted to emcee the Speakeasy, and when she said no, he suggested being a co-emcee. Maybe he would have been a better president, but she had been elected unanimously, and it was her job. She turned to Marla.

"I'm glad you could come, Marla!"

Marla gave her a hug. "And I'm glad you called and reminded me how much I've missed the castle."

They had both been at Danny's flop of a surprise party but hadn't had a chance to talk privately. Besides, it had seemed to Beth that Marla had been more interested in Eric than in her, and maybe was a little jealous since Roe was back in town. That could have been true, but it didn't mean the two of them weren't still friends.

"I've missed you," Beth said, "but I guess I thought you were too busy."

"Well, there's school and the play, but mainly it's been hard at home. Mom can't seem to move on from the divorce, and Marta has fallen way behind in school. I've been trying to help without letting myself get down. I'll do better at keeping in touch, Beth. I promise."

Beth smiled. "We'd better get upstairs before Joe declares himself president." At Marla's questioning look — "Tell you later."

Indeed, Joe was attempting to take charge, with Gee trying valiantly to wait for Beth. "Ah, here she is now." Gee threw a look that said, *Don't be late again!*

"Sorry," Beth said. "I was just touching base with our guest. Everyone, this is Marla Gray. She was in *Cinderella, Cinderella* here at the castle last year. You might also have seen her over the summer in *Play On!* Right now, she's in *You Can't Take It with You* at CBHS."

Those who knew Marla applauded heartily. A few others exchanged glances. They'd heard their parents discussing the scandal connected with Marla's family.

Marla smiled, ignoring anything negative, just as Eric had suggested she do.

Marla gave Gee a hug and then addressed the group. "It's great to be back at the castle and to see old friends and, I hope, make new ones. Beth says you plan on coming to see the show at CBHS in January. Kylie Kennedy is in it, too. It's going really well, and I think you'll love it. And I've got good news for you — not even Beth knows. I talked with our director, and he's invited you to come to opening night, free of charge. It won't cost you a dime. Trust me, it's unusual for our director to do this."

This was indeed fine news, and Beth led the group in the applause. "I'll get the details from you, Marla, and email everyone. A lot of people aren't here today." But Beth could tell that, other than those who were away on vacation, the most serious members of Drama Club had come. "Now Marla, tell everyone your idea."

"This is something they did at a boarding school I attended for a short while. I wasn't a part of it, but I thought it sounded fun. I know that CBMS will finally open soon but that you won't be able to use the stage for a regular play until maybe April. You'll have a spring show rather than a fall one. Only classrooms for meetings, of course, but it's terrific you can continue to use the ballroom on Saturdays. What could work for you might be a one-act playwriting contest. Maybe you could write in teams of two, with an end of winter break deadline." Marla laughed at the looks of dismay. "No, that isn't much time, but think about it. Not everyone will want to do it, and you'll be too busy when school starts. I was thinking maybe Mrs. Hunt and some of the other English teachers could be the judges and pick two or three winners. Even a play that needs only a few suggestions could still win."

"Would we put on the plays?" Joe yelled out, sounding skeptical.

"Well, yes," Marla said. "Some of you could direct and others could act. Some artistic types, such as Beth, might like to come up with a simple set that would work for all the plays."

Beth could almost see light bulbs turning on in their heads. She bet that Joe would want to direct. Priyanka and Imani exchanged glances—definitely a formidable writing team. Beth felt her own inner light bulb begin to glow.

"Would we put the shows on here?" Hannah wondered.

Marla nodded. "And another thing to think about, depending on the scripts you get and if any are suitable for children, you might take a show on the road—libraries and kids' birthday parties, things like that. Moms might even pay if Drama Club took charge of a birthday party." Excited smiles were on everyone's faces and the necessary chatter followed.

"Thanks, Marla," Beth said. "I don't think we'll need to vote." She grinned as Gee brought in a platter of large chocolate chip cookies. "While we enjoy Gee's treats, let's decide how we might participate. Some of us might choose a writing team. That's what I'm going to do. I've already asked Hannah to be my partner, although she didn't know for what. And we've still got lots of scenes that weren't picked for Speakeasy. How about anyone wanting to direct, pick out a scene and then find actors willing to work with you? At an early meeting in January—probably the first one, so get together over break—you can present your scenes, and the rest of us can vote for the best people to direct the winning scripts. I'm sure we'll find something for everyone to do."

Hannah noticed Kamirah watching her with displeasure. Had Kammy wanted to be her writing partner? Honestly? They were still friendly but had barely spoken since Halloween night. She'd invited Kammy over a few times but had always been turned down. Kammy had never invited her. Not that Dad or Uncle Martin would have allowed her to go. She smiled at Kammy. "Sorry," she mouthed. But how would that have worked? A writing team that couldn't meet?

Relieved, Hannah noticed Joe quickly grab a scene for several players and beckon Kammy and a few other sixth- and seventh-grade girls. Joe must know exactly what scene it was and who he wanted in his cast. If they'd rehearse at the castle, that might work for Kammy. Joe was certainly popular. He might have been chosen president if he hadn't been new this year. It was better this way, Hannah thought. Beth wasn't interested in being important. She just wanted Drama Club to be enjoyable for everyone.

Other than worrying about Danny, life was improving for Hannah. Dad and Uncle Martin had bought a used car in such good condition it was practically new. Now Uncle Martin and his cello traveled safely back and forth to the city, and Dad came home once his classes were over at Community. Underground parking garages in the city were dangerous, of course, but Martin's musician friends parked close together and escorted each other to their cars. Between Dad and Danny and Bingo, Hannah would not be lonely again. And once Danny cheered up and tried harder to get better, everything would be perfect.

A cookie in hand, Beth beckoned Hannah to join her. "You okay with being my writing partner, Hannah?"

"Yeah, I guess. Just surprised. Why did you pick me? You don't know anything about the way I write."

"Well, no, but I do know you've got a great imagination, and I've heard you get good grades."

"I do okay, but is that the only reason?"

Beth shook her head. "That's two reasons, but also because you live next door to Danny."

"Danny? He won't be interested. He's not interested in anything lately."

"Except Boots. She's got to be the best present of all times, Hannah."

Hannah smiled. "So what does my house and Danny have to do with anything?"

"You and I can write while Porter visits Danny. Then we can have Porter and Danny read boy parts while you, Kylie, and I do the girls'. Because of Zoe and Kelly, my house is a zoo these days, but your house is just right, and Aunt Jane is used to me coming in and out of theirs. It's a way to help Danny. We've got to!"

They made a date to meet the following afternoon. "This afternoon and tonight, let's brainstorm ideas," Beth said. Then she raised her voice. "Time to clean up, everyone. Be sure to take whatever materials you need with you. Two more meetings here before and after Christmas—and then we'll be back at CBMS. Finally!"

As if on cue, Leland came into the room. It was unusual for him to make an appearance. "I just overheard what Beth said. I hate to put a damper on your plans."

The students looked at each other. Damper?

Leland chuckled. "Sorry. What I meant to say is that I hate to ruin your plans. I'm afraid you won't be able to meet back here until the Saturday after New Years. We've decided—that is, Mr. Markey,

Janet, and I plan to lock up the castle for the holidays and join Miss Armstrong and Robbie in New York. Robbie is going to see a specialist about a new treatment, and we're going to see some plays and museums. Janet plans on spending all of my money." He laughed while the others waited. "We think it would be safer if no one comes inside during that time."

Beth cleared her throat. "We understand, Leland, and hope Robbie gets some good news. We'll be okay. Practically everyone here signed up for an activity, and I'll send emails to all members. I'll also send contact information to the directors, so that they can email or phone their casts — I think only one member doesn't have an email address. If you're writing, directing, or acting, you should plan on getting together at each other's homes over break."

Leland wished them happy holidays and went downstairs.

Actually, this would work out better for Beth. Dad had just broken the news that for Christmas this year, the whole family would go to Colorado and visit Grandma and Grandpa Walters in their new home. Beth had planned to ask Janet to take charge of Drama Club meetings. She shrugged. This might mean fewer scene participants, but it was not her problem.

While Beth again reminded the group not to leave anything behind, Hannah wandered over to the window — the non-bluff side of the castle. Could it be? Finally! Oh, how beautiful! "Come look!"

Everyone rushed to the window. "Snow," they said in unison, as if it were a prayer. "Snow!" Nothing was as exciting as the first snow of winter.

"I wonder if we'll be able to go sledding today," Porter said.

Joe shook his head. "Probably not, but if this continues, I'll be looking for a steep hill tomorrow."

"I am so glad we moved out of the city," Hannah said.

But Kammy, standing next to her, muttered, "Snow. Disgusting, cold, wet snow! This ruins everything!"

What was wrong with her now? "Kammy?"

To Hannah's amazement, Kamirah's eyes filled with tears. She even seemed frightened. "Can't talk now. Gotta go. It's a long walk home."

It was too long, and her jacket had already seen too many winters—a limp puffer, once white with black dots. Hannah wondered if some of those dots were holes. She could call Dad from the kitchen and ask for a ride. He would be willing to drive Kammy home. But, no, she didn't want to. Yeah, she was being selfish, but she couldn't wait for her first walk home in the snow!

SCENE 2 – A FEW STRANGE THINGS

As SOON AS SHE WAS certain everyone was out, Beth locked the door. She and Marla were going to the Grays' house, first to pick up Marta, and then to Beth's to get Kelly. They planned on taking the little girls to the matinee performance of a Disney movie they had been clamoring to see. It sounded amusing enough, and Beth and Marla were looking for acceptable reasons to stay out of their houses, where certain chores awaited.

"We'll need to rush if we're going to be on time," Beth said.

"Maybe we should just meet at the theater," Marla suggested.

Beth shook her head. "No, we'll walk fast."

"Oh, no! Beth, wait!"

"Now what?" Kamirah ran up to her. "What is it, Kammy?"

"I am so sorry. I was on my way home when I remembered I left my script inside. Please may I go back upstairs and get it? I don't have an email address yet; we don't have a computer. It'll just take a second."

"Well, okay. I'll unlock the door and then set it, so all you have to do is slam the door and make sure it locks. Okay?"

"Okay. Thank you!"

Kammy disappeared inside.

"Come on, let's hurry," Marla said. "Kammy can walk with Hannah and Porter."

Marla and Beth jogged quickly away while Porter and Hannah stood outside the castle, deep in conversation.

No one noticed that Kammy did not make sure the door was locked. In fact, she inserted a small thin piece of wood in the hinge to make absolutely certain it wouldn't.

"Gotta run!" she shouted to Hannah and Porter. "Merry Christmas!"

"You, too!" they yelled, and continued to talk all the way home.

"We've got to find ways to cheer up Danny," Hannah insisted. "That's why Beth wants to write a play with me—so she can somehow rope Danny into helping us."

"But the problem is he's not interested in plays. He might do it to help you and Beth, but—"

"Well, at least it's something for him to do. But I know what you mean, Porter."

"We can still do jigsaw puzzles and play video and board games, of course—"

"And maybe have Bingo and Boots in the living room, if it's okay with Mr. and Mrs. Kennedy."

"Uncle Dan and Aunt Jane would allow them on the roof if it helped Danny laugh again. This is a good lesson for us, Hannah—especially me. It's important to have lots of interests. All Danny wants is sports, and—don't tell anyone—I overheard Aunt Jane tell my mom that the doctor says Danny may never walk again unless he tries harder. He complains all through his physical therapy and then doesn't do the exercises at home."

"I'm sure they hurt, but—"

"I hate to admit it, Hannah, but we could use a reason for that club of ours to meet again—a reason for SSC to continue. But it has to be a real mystery, like Mateo. Not something we just dream up."

Porter was right, Hannah thought. But how were they going to find a real mystery—at least one to discuss, if not solve?

From his bedroom window, Danny gazed at the falling snow. He didn't notice when tears fell, too. So cold, so beautiful—how he wished he could run outside and make snowballs and throw them for Bingo to catch. He'd have to tell Hannah to do it, so he could look out and watch.

He bent over and pressed his nose against the glass. Now his nose was cold, and it felt good. But his face was wet. Crying again? Honestly! He had to stop feeling sorry for himself, or at least cry in the dark when his family was asleep. Everyone was trying so hard to please him. Mom, who had been trying to diet for years, resembled a scrawny, sad sack. Sorrow was no way to lose weight. And he was sick of Dad pretending to be jovial.

Danny wondered if they knew what the doctor had told him. "Danny, whether or not you walk again is up to you. There will be no more operations and no medicine will do the job. It's going to take painful therapy. I guess we'll find out if you have the courage to handle it." That's when Danny asked him about swimming. "That could help," the doctor had said, "but forget about some winning team at the Y. Maybe someday, if you start small. After the holidays, let's try the warm whirlpool at the hospital, and then work up to the pool. It's for therapy, though, not for anything fancy."

The doctor had been really strict, almost mean, and Danny didn't like it. But it actually might have helped him. In not so many words, the doctor had implied that Danny should be thinking of others. Already, Danny had said to Mom and Dad, "Everything you've done so I could be downstairs and have my own bathroom must have cost a ton of money. And the doctor bills must be awful. It's okay if I don't get much for Christmas."

Dad had smiled and patted his shoulder. "Thanks for understanding, son. Yes, we're planning to cut back this year." So maybe, Danny thought, he was entering a positive stage, for once.

Danny continued to watch the snow, accumulating nicely now, with a snoring dog and a contented kitten nearby. He had almost nodded off himself when Kylie burst into the room. "Shhh," he whispered, pointing to the dog and cat.

Kylie grabbed a box off a shelf and whispered back. "You're leaving this room now." Then, without giving him a chance to object, she wheeled him into the hall and closed the door.

"What?" he demanded.

"This," she said, putting the box across his lap. "This game, given to you by Mateo Santos for your birthday. Purchased with money he earned at Smithy's. Pretty generous of him, I'd say, under the circumstances. I'll bet you haven't even looked at it."

"I have. It's Monopoly. Big deal!"

"Actually, it's the new Anti-Monopoly Game, and it was a big deal—for him, at least. Saving your life and caring about your birthday—not exactly the Mateo I remember."

Kylie was right, of course, and he looked sheepish. "So what do you suggest?"

"Other than writing a thank you note as soon as we have an address, I suggest we play the game, so you'll have something to write about."

Danny agreed, mainly because arguing with Kylie was something he didn't enjoy, mainly because she always won. Besides, it wasn't a bad idea. To get even, though, he would not let her win at Monopoly—Anti-Monopoly, that is.

The two were ready to come to blows when Dad entered the dining room. "The sounds of your fighting are music to my ears," Dad said. "You'll have to continue the war after dinner. Kylie, I've put up a card table in the living room. Help me pick up the board. Danny, put everything else carefully into the lid."

Kylie stood. "Don't cheat," she told Danny.

Danny thought it was almost like old times as they sat around the table. Mom suggested a movie they might watch together once they'd ended the game. Then she turned to Dad. "You seem kind of quiet, Dan. Anything new on your mind?" Other than him, Danny realized she meant.

"Yeah, something I heard on the radio. You know that townhouse complex west of here?"

"West Village Flats? Not a very safe part of town."

"That's the one. Looks as if there was a stabbing earlier today. An elderly man was severely injured. So far, no suspects."

Mom gasped. "In Castle Bluff? Hard to believe, but I've always told Kylie and Danny not to go over there."

Danny looked down at his steak, hoping his appetite would return. The West Village Flats—where Kammy lived. He would not tell Mom and Dad he had been there Halloween night. If only he had a cellphone and could call Hannah and Porter. Or if he had his old bedroom upstairs, he could use the lights signal. Even if he could do it downstairs, Hannah wouldn't see. Maybe one of them would come soon. Then he could let them know they needed an emergency SSC meeting. Of course they couldn't solve an attempted murder, but they could talk about it and figure out how to find out more about the strange girl, Kamirah Williams.

SCENE 3 – RETURN OF THE SSC

BETH AND MARLA DID MAKE it in time to take their sisters to the movies. Beth had hoped they'd have a chance to talk alone without two silly girls listening in. No chance, but as soon as they left the theater, Beth had an idea.

"Just a second, Marla. I want to make a phone call." Thankfully, Beth was able to reach Mom. "Hi, Mom. I was wondering if Marta and Marla might come back to our house for a sleepover. The girls are having a great time, and Marla and I haven't had good visit in ages. I haven't said anything to Marla, and she'd have to ask her mom. We'd play with Zoe, too," she added, hoping that would sweeten the deal, as Gramps would say. Mom thought it was a fine idea, but of course they'd have to get Mrs. Gray's permission.

"Before you say anything to the little girls."

Quickly, Beth pulled Marla aside. "I'm sure it's okay, but I'll call," Marla said, removing her cell from a pocket and punching a contact number. The answer was short and definite. "No problem. Mom is delighted to get rid of us."

"And I think my mom wants a break from Kelly and Zoe," Beth added, hoping Marla would feel less bitter about her mother. They didn't get along very well.

"We'll stop off at my house and pick up our overnight stuff," Marla said.

Then they told the little girls, who were overjoyed. Soon, Beth reflected, she'd have to stop treating Kelly as if she were an annoying child. Kelly was almost ten, and it wouldn't be long before she was old enough for middle school. Thank goodness I'll be in high school then, Beth thought. Porter was different. He was a friend — one who'd always given her plenty of space.

Finally, baby Zoe, cuter than usual for Marla's benefit, was asleep for the night, and Kelly and Marta were in Kelly's room, happily giggling and sharing their own confidences.

"Alone at last," Beth breathed, flopping on her bed. It was full-sized, so they'd have no problem sharing it. "You're lucky having only one sibling."

"And you're lucky having such a happy family."

Beth nodded, ashamed. "I know. I really shouldn't complain."

"I'll trade you Marta for Porter."

"No way!" Beth threw a pillow at her, mainly to put a halt to a discussion that was becoming serious. Talks like that were meant for the dark times of a sleepover, when the only thing remaining was sleep.

A rambunctious pillow fight ensued, which even nine-year-olds would declare childish, ending with the ringing of a cellphone.

"Yours or mine?"

"Yours, I think."

Beth grabbed it while Marla tidied the disaster of a bed. "It's Kurt," she said. Marla grinned. "Hey Kurt, what's up? No, Marla is spending the night. We just had a pillow fight. I know, I know — definitely juvenile. Sure, that would be fun. I'm free early in the week. Not on Christmas, of course. A gift for me? You didn't have to. Well, as a matter of fact —" Beth tried to ignore the faces Marla was making — "Tuesday at Smithy's would be good. Three is fine. No, we're not having Drama Club until after vacation. Mr. Markey and everyone are going away, and Leland thinks it would be better if no one was in the castle while they're gone. It's okay. I'll be in Colorado anyway. We figured out what we were doing at the meeting this morning. A light? Well, Leland didn't say when they were leaving. I'm sure it's okay. He didn't ask me to keep an eye on things. What? You're kidding! In Castle Bluff? Is he dead? Oh, Kurt, I've got another call—from Joe. I'd better take it. I'll see you Tuesday at three. Bye."

"Phew!"

"I'm sorry, Marla. I'll keep it short."

"Okay, but I am going to want details."

"Joe, what's up? No, sorry, I haven't had a chance. I had to take my little sister to the movies this afternoon, and now I have an overnight guest. Who?" Was he nosy, or what? It was Beth's turn to make a face at Marla. "My friend Marla. You met her this morning. Why would you think I meant Hannah? Never mind. I chose Hannah because it's a family thing. I'm not sure what you're implying. She lives with her father and uncle. Look, I'll send out the contact list tomorrow. I doubt if anyone else even thought about it. Yes, I promise. Then you can call again if you have any questions. Gotta go now, Joe. Bye." Firmly, Beth pressed the end key.

"Wow! You didn't just turn off your phone; you turned off him, too."

"I didn't exactly mean to. He's a great addition to Drama Club. An eighth-grade boy, who is really interested."

"And really cute."

"Yeah, that, too. And tall. He'll be great for the spring show, whatever play is chosen."

"He couldn't keep his eyes off you during the meeting. I got the idea that he was hoping the two of you might be a team and was disappointed you picked Hannah."

"I noticed. But working with Hannah makes sense. Porter and I want to spend a lot of time with Danny, and Hannah is right next door. We think it might help Danny to get involved in what we're doing. And, well, it is a family thing and none of Joe's business."

Marla shook her head. "I don't think I've ever known anyone who's changed as much as you. You're not the same person I first met last year."

"Look who's talking!"

"Okay, okay, I guess I asked for that."

"Just a little. Anyway, as far as Joe goes, I'm picking up some vibes that bother me. Haven't made up my mind yet."

"Maybe because he picked all younger girls for his scene? Like you're thinking of Mr. Carroll?"

Beth shook her head. "That isn't it. I know the scene. It's terrific — all girls and the younger the better. He might also have thought they'd be more likely to follow his directions. It's nothing I can pin down, exactly. Just a feeling. But there's also Kurt."

"Kurt. Now that was a fascinating conversation. Especially the ending."

"I almost forgot. He said that a man has been stabbed over at the West Village Flats."

"Murdered?"

"Kurt wasn't sure. At least attempted murder. 'A late-breaking story,' was how he put it."

"Sounds like Kurt. Anything else."

"Not much. We were talking about getting together Tuesday at Smithy's. Then Joe interrupted."

"And you were sure to let Kurt know. Trying to make Kurt jealous, are we?"

Beth smiled. "Maybe a little. But you should talk. Like you weren't trying to make Roe squirm at Kylie's party."

"Guilty as charged. Just wanted to see if I could. Didn't work, of course; Roe doesn't play games like that. I always had the feeling she gave me Eric as a going-away present, even though she was the one going away."

Beth had had that feeling, too. "So what is it with you and Eric?"

"I like him, even though he treats me like he's my stern uncle, and I'm a naughty child. He is easy to talk to. But everyone says that about him."

Beth nodded. "That's Kurt, too—easy to talk to—but not everyone agrees."

"My turn. What else about Kurt? You broke up with him last June. Are you back together now?"

Beth shrugged. "I think we're headed in that direction. I broke up with him because, well, he was going to Crofts, and I would only be in eighth. I felt so young and unimportant, and he is so popular. Well, you know . . ."

"I think so, although it's possible you've evened things up. Does Kurt like Crofts?"

"Not really, but he does want to be a professional actor someday, and he thinks he'll have a better chance if he graduates from Crofts and skips college. He's determined to stick it out, especially if they continue to give him a full scholarship. He got a lead in their first play, which is unusual for a freshman."

"Lights out, girls," Beth's mom called. Hoping for more overnights soon, Beth obeyed.

Before falling asleep, though, Marla confessed that one of the problems at home was that her mother desperately needed to find a job. Her father was out of jail but had heavy fines and about a million community service hours to fill. "A lot anyway. He doesn't have money to give us—even if he wanted to."

Silence. Beth wondered if Marla had fallen asleep, but Marla continued, maybe choosing her words carefully.

"Eventually, he'll have to pay child support, but then he could demand visitation. Mom will not let that happen, but right now, she doesn't know what to do about Marta because she doesn't want her to be home alone. But East Elementary gets out way earlier than the high school. She can't afford to pay anyone to watch her. My play is almost over, so I guess there won't be more theater for me this year."

It was Beth's turn for silence, for thinking. She wished getting along with Marla's mom was easier. Still, Mom might agree. "Marla, let me talk with Mom. Marta and Kelly get along great, and they were really good with Zoe—mainly because of Marta being here. Maybe Mom will agree to letting Marta come home with Kelly. That way, either your mother or you could pick her up once you were done with whatever."

"Oh, gosh, Beth—if only."

"I'll ask first thing tomorrow," Beth said.

The next afternoon, Hannah was the one with the guest. That hardly ever happened. But Dad and Uncle Martin were both home, watching a football game in the family room. Once they were both armed with beer and popcorn, Hannah claimed the kitchen. She decided to stick with popcorn, since the smell was intoxicating, making it hard to want anything else. Hannah microwaved a few bags and brought cold Cokes out of the fridge. Then with laptop, paper, and pencils at hand, she was all set for Beth. Together, they would create a winning script. All they needed was one decent idea, and Hannah thought she had one.

Beth was running late. Hannah had seen Porter arrive next door shortly before Mr. and Mrs. Kennedy and Kylie left for church. The Walters were more flexible about church attendance. Hannah wasn't sure she'd ever had a religion. If she had, church had never been a part of it. Porter would keep Danny company while his family was away. And then, she thought, the grandparents were coming for dinner. It might be nice to have grandparents who cared about you, Hannah thought, not for the first time.

A knock at the back door. Oh, good! Hannah opened the door. "Hi!"

Beth brushed the snow from her jacket. "Sorry I'm late. I had to talk to Mom before Marla and her sister went home. They stayed overnight, and we were up so late we slept in. You know what that's like." Actually, I don't, Hannah thought. "Then," Beth continued, "just as I was leaving the house, I remembered that I promised to send out the Drama Club contact list, and I didn't want us to be interrupted by my phone exploding every two minutes. And yes, please. I'd love some popcorn. It doesn't matter that I had some at the movies yesterday. Nothing smells so good — except maybe bacon."

Soon the girls had their heads together at the kitchen table. This was what most girls had all the time, Hannah thought, vowing never to take it for granted. A home, a friend visiting, and loving parents in the other room. She grinned as she heard Dad yell, "Oh, no! You idiot!"

"Football," she said. "Uncle Martin hates it, but he puts up with it for Dad's sake."

Beth grinned. "My dad, too. I think Porter is relieved to get away from it. Maybe Danny will invite him to stay for dinner, so he can avoid it."

"Unless Danny wants to watch, too."

Beth shook her head. "Not if the grandparents have their way. And believe me, they will. The TV will be turned off during Sunday dinner. That's a major part of the Kennedy's religion. Now, any thoughts?"

Actually, Hannah had been thinking of little else since the meeting yesterday morning. "Yes, I do."

"Phew!" Beth said. "I haven't had time at all." Then, as if waiting for the cue, her phone rang. "Darn. Joe again." She muted the phone. "Let him leave a message. We've got work to do. No more interruptions."

"Ump? Are you out of your stupid mind?" Hannah's dad again, although he used a different word for stupid.

Both girls burst out laughing. "Okay, here's what I was thinking," Hannah said. "Do you know the musical, *Into the Woods?*"

Beth confessed that she'd heard of it, but that was all.

"Dad took me to see it in New York," Hannah said. "Uncle Martin was playing in the pit."

"Pit?"

"In the orchestra. Well, it's about all these well-known fairy and folk tale characters who get lost in the woods, and whose stories start interacting with each other's. The first act is light and funny, but the second act is pretty dark. I thought we could do something similar to the first act. Throw some characters from different stories together, and maybe have someone like a sarcastic fairy mess everything up. I was thinking we could keep it simple but clever and easy to do. You know, easy to transport—just any stage would do, or no stage at all."

"I love it," Beth said, "and the idea of performing at birthday parties. My little sister is having a birthday soon, and I'll bet Mom would pay plenty if we took it off her hands."

"Maybe," Hannah said. "I don't really like the payment idea, unless we need the money. I think it would be cool if Drama Club could just do something for Castle Bluff."

Beth nodded. "What my church calls Community Outreach. We could ask for contributions to a charity in town. You're right, Hannah."

Next, they decided to work separately and come up with a list of up to eight possible characters. Then they'd go over them together and pick the best ones.

"And here I thought I'd be leading our little team," Beth said. "Boy, was I wrong, and boy, am I glad!"

Hannah chewed on the end of her pencil and thought—and wrote.

Beth, still not getting down to work, listened to her phone message. "Hannah, Joe says there's no email address for Kammy.

Well, I knew about that; I thought he did, too. But he says there's no phone number, either. Do you have it?"

Hannah opened the contacts on her laptop. "Yeah, I've called a few times; they finally got a phone."

"I'll send it to him in a text," Beth said. "Then I'll turn off my phone for at least an hour."

Danny and Porter were playing video games in Danny's bedroom when Dad opened the door. "Dinnertime. Grandma and Grandpa just arrived. Care to join us, Porter?"

"Thanks for asking, Uncle Dan. I'd love to." Danny had already assured Porter this would happen. They were both hoping Hannah could come later for an SSC meeting.

"Oh, one more thing," Dad said. "Let's not get Grandma angry by discussing the stabbing. I've got more news that I thought you two would like to hear."

Danny and Porter shared glances. Had Dad somehow guessed that the club was meeting to talk about that very thing? Of course not!

"It seems that the man didn't die, although he might still. He's in bad shape at the hospital. I asked my friend, Sergeant Lodge, about him."

"Do the police know who did it?" Porter wondered.

Dad shook his head. "Not yet, although the manager of the flats, if he can be believed—not a nice fellow—says that the man doesn't live alone. Another man, maybe a friend, lives there, too. But he seems to have disappeared, so he's a suspect at the moment. The police checked the apartment and found possessions that might belong to a young teen, but the manager says the old man's granddaughter visits sometimes. Well, come along to dinner before we get into trouble."

"Okay, but Dad, how did the cops find out?"

"Some kid called 911—from a payphone." Dad shrugged. "Didn't know we still had any in Castle Bluff."

The boys looked at each other and mouthed, "Smithy's." Smithy had the only payphone left in Castle Bluff. And he kept it outside—just in case some kid was in trouble, he always said. Wow! A real mystery for their club! And then they mouthed something else. "Kammy!"

"I can't stay long," Hannah said. "Dad and Uncle Martin want the three of us 'to bond,' now that the football game is over. I think what they have in mind is a thrilling board game." She giggled. "That's their idea of bonding. I'm not complaining. It's good to have them home more often. Why did you want me to come?"

"SSC," Danny said solemnly.

"What? You mean you've found a mystery?" She stared at Porter. After all, it was only a thought—an idea to keep Danny amused.

"Oh, yeah," Porter said.

The boys got Hannah up to date on what Mr. Kennedy had told them about the attempted murder.

"Oh, my God, a young teenage girl! Are you guys thinking what I'm thinking?"

"Of course," Danny said, "but we didn't tell Dad about walking Kammy home. We're not stupid."

"How come your dad knows so much?" Hannah didn't mention that she'd told her parents about Halloween night.

Danny explained about his father's friendship with the policeman. "They go way, way back—maybe even to St. Joseph days. They meet for drinks—too often, according to Mom. In fact, the reason we weren't talking about it at dinner was because of Mom, not Grandma. Grandma loves a good murder mystery, but Mom thinks Sergeant Lodge tells Dad too much."

"Interesting," Hannah said, "but how can this be our mystery?"

Porter explained. "We won't be able to solve an attempted murder, but we can find out more about Kammy."

"And just maybe," Danny added, "we will discover a killer. Wouldn't that be something?"

Hannah and Porter stared at each other. Maybe reviving the club had succeeded too well. Danny was enthused all right, but even attempted murder could be dangerous. Hannah crossed her fingers that they hadn't made a gigantic mistake.

BETH HAD THOUGHT SHE'D SLEEP forever, but that old Monday morning body clock kicked in, and she was wide awake, dressed, and joining her mother at breakfast by eight.

Mom grinned, giving Zoe another spoonful of cereal, ignoring her when she spit it back. She just wiped it off and kept on spooning. "Poor Beth — wants to be a slug, but the flesh isn't willing. Porter doesn't seem to have your problem. I don't think we'll see him before noon."

"How about Kelly?"

"She'll be up soon. Her friend Carrie is coming, so you're officially off childcare duty today."

"Phew!" But Beth was only kidding. Mom had always been reasonable. A great mom, in every way, Beth thought, scrambling herself an egg. That, toast, and orange juice would do her fine. Marla was hoping they'd get together, but Beth decided she needed to get serious about Christmas presents — what to buy and what to make. "That was really nice of you, Mom — agreeing to let Marta come here after school."

Before answering, Mom cleaned Zoe and set her down on the kitchen floor. "It's not a problem; in fact, I think it will help. Lately,

Kelly has been nagging constantly to go here or there or wanting to ask someone over. Neither you nor your brother were like that."

"Porter is practically a saint, Mom, and he's also a boy. Think of Kelly as your middle child."

Mom sighed. "Maybe you're right. Grab her, will you, Beth?"

"Come back here, you silly goose." Beth tackled and tickled Zoe just as she was about to have a second breakfast of dust bunnies. Zoe giggled as Beth plunked her into the bouncy chair and gave her a favorite toy giraffe. Content, Zoe began chewing the giraffe's ear.

Mom continued the conversation. "Marta is a sweet girl, and that family has been through too much. I'll help as much as their mother allows me. Mrs. Gray isn't easy to know."

"Neither was Marla," Beth admitted, "but we're really good friends now."

"She's certainly changed," Mom said, perhaps a little wary.

Beth laughed. "I told her that last night—after she accused me of changing. What does Gramps always say? Something about a pot and a kettle? I'm starting to get it."

Beth's cell phone rang. "Oh, sorry, Mom. It's about Drama Club, and I should take it. I'll keep it short and then do the dishes."

"It's okay, dear. You run along. I'll do them. Zoe seems happy."

"Hi, Joe," Beth said, ignoring her mother's shrewd look. "What's up?"

Beth listened, chiming in occasionally with an "I see," or "I understand." Finally, "look, Joe, I've got an idea, but it involves going to Imani's house. Would you be able to? No, I don't mean you should go alone. Of course I know where she lives. She's one of my best friends. You can? Okay. I'll call Imani and ask her. I'll call you right back." Beth sighed. "Yes, Joe, I promise. Just hold on."

"I'm hearing your suspicious voice," Mom said. "Everything okay? Joe's that new boy in Drama Club, right? The one you think is going to be terrific?" Terrific had been Beth's word.

"Yeah, he's fine. He's just sort of demanding. I'm not sure about him now. I've got to call Imani, Mom."

"Imani?" Quickly, Beth made her request. "Okay, thanks." Then she called again. "Joe? Imani says we can. Where do you live? Uh-huh. Then let's meet at Smithy's in, say, fifteen minutes. That's the midway point. Then we can go to Imani's from there. Okay, bye."

"So where does he live?" Mom asked.

"On Adelphia," Beth said softly. It had been great talking with Mom, but she was becoming too inquisitive.

"So close by. He could have met you here. Does he know your address?"

Beth shook her head. "I don't know why I didn't tell him," she said.

"You're learning to obey your instincts," Mom said. "Good for you!"

On the way to Smithy's, Beth went over her gift list. Almost everything was homemade, although she still needed to buy some supplies. Maybe more wrapping paper. She wanted Kurt's present to look especially nice, and she would give it to him tomorrow. She shivered in anticipation, although it was plenty cold. Not snowing now, but more predicted tonight. Kelly and her friends might be able to go sledding tomorrow. Maybe Porter, too, unless he decided to visit Danny instead. Poor Danny! And maybe poor Porter, if it meant giving up sledding and ice skating in order to support his friend.

The present for Kurt was Beth's favorite, and it had taken the longest to complete. After doing a lot of practicing with oils, following Imani's dad's suggestions, Beth had finally risked it — an oil painting of Kurt as Puck in A *Midsummer Night's Dream*. Kurt, in his costume and at his most Puckish, stepped out from the magical tree that had been the dream tree Beth had created for Roe at Camp Shimmer Lake. She painted the forest background that all the plays had used. High in the tree that glittered with every fruit imaginable was Brad the lion, Witch Kylie, Eric as one of Shakespeare's men, and Roe, herself, with a wide smile, playing her favorite role. Mr. Jones had framed the painting, at a fraction of what it would have cost Beth elsewhere.

"Beth, this is something my students at Crofts would be proud of." Her private lessons were working out great. She would be sad to say goodbye to the painting, but she had sketches, as well as photos for her portfolio.

Danny's painting was a watercolor of Bingo playing in the snow. Beth had sketched that last winter, shortly after Bingo had become a member of the Kennedy family. Kylie already had a painting of the castle, so Beth made her a beaded friendship bracelet. An invitation for a train trip to downtown Chicago for lunch and to check out the after-Christmas sales was an additional present that Dad had agreed to finance. Imani, Priyanka, and Marla would also receive friendship bracelets.

At the last minute, Beth decided she wanted to give Hannah something. This was one of the reasons Beth wanted to stay home today. It was too late to start a painting, but Beth thought she could do a sketch of Hannah in her backyard tree fort, looking down—just as Beth first saw her. She wouldn't give Hannah a sour expression, but a happy one would look phony. Instead, she would try for interested but questioning—a typical Hannah expression. At the Dollar Store, Beth would purchase an inexpensive frame.

Mom and Dad would receive sketches also: Mom, kind of a Madonna and child portrait of Mom and Zoe; Dad's showed him playing catch with Kelly and Porter. She had already found simple frames for those. Kelly and Porter's gifts took money, although Porter might have liked a sketch. Beth just didn't have any ideas. Porter would get an illustrated book of Tolkien's Ring Trilogy. He'd read it a thousand times at least, but this copy was so beautiful she was certain he'd cherish it. For Kelly, a new outfit for her American Girl doll — one that cost more than an outfit for her.

After today, there would be one broke Beth — allowance all gone as well as babysitting savings. Good thing Kurt was treating tomorrow.

And finally, there she was in front of Smithy's, and there was Joe, looking as if he'd been waiting for hours. Bad impression, Joe, she thought. After all, I'm doing you the favor. In fact, that's what she would say, if he dared to complain.

"Oh, good, let's get going," seemed to be as far as Joe was going to push it. "Fill me in on how you think Imani can help. She's the other black one, right?"

"I might not have put it that way, but okay," Beth said. "I know the scene you're doing, and it would be best if an African American girl played the part. If Kammy doesn't come through or Imani won't do it, you'll either have to settle for another race or find a different scene. First, tell me what happened with Kammy."

"Well, as I said, she never answered."

"Maybe she just wasn't home. I know Hannah has called her before." Beth didn't reveal that the calls were never satisfactory.

"I thought that, too, so I kept on trying. Then, an operator stepped in and said the phone had been disconnected. I tried again later, and it didn't ring — just blank, dead."

"Okay, so we ask Imani," Beth said. "She a wonderful actor and would be perfect in the part. The thing is, you can't take it away from Kamirah. You don't know she isn't with some relative for Christmas and learning her lines right this minute. I'll admit it's weird, but you can ask Imani to be backup, an understudy, just in case. Imani is a quick study, but she'll have to agree to learn the part with no guarantee that she'll perform it."

Joe smiled. "Sounds like a great plan. So we're heading east. I don't know that area of Castle Bluff. The poor section of town, right?"

"What makes you say that?"

"Oh, you know . . ."

"Right." Homes east of here, the North Shore, next to Lake Michigan and near the castle, must be the poor section for African Americans. Buddy, you've really got it coming, but I'm not saying a word. "One thing, Joe. Remember that Imani is already on a writing team. You will be asking her to do you a favor. She doesn't owe you anything." And neither do I, Beth added silently.

Beth led him up a long, curving driveway, surrounded on both sides by sweet-smelling pines, ending at one of the most stately homes in Castle Bluff. She lifted her arm. "Behold, the poor section of town."

Joe's mouth dropped. "She lives here?"

Beth grinned, making a stab at being friendly again.

Imani opened the front door. "Come inside and warm up."

⚷

"She's really nice," Joe said, as they left after a very short time. Imani was busy, too. "And wow, that house! Those paintings could be in a museum!"

"Imani's father is the artist. He's the head of the art department at Crofts and also displays at a studio downtown. His paintings go for thousands. Her mother is a scientist at Abbott Labs."

"Well, I hope Kamirah doesn't come back. Maybe I'll just give Imani the part, anyway."

"Oh no you won't. Imani made the terms clear. It's Kammy's part, and Imani is an understudy only."

"Maybe I can make her change her mind." He wiggled his eyebrows and attempted a sexy voice that just sounded silly. He really did think he was the greatest, Beth thought.

"As I said before, no, you won't. I won't let you, and neither will Mrs. Hunt. You got lucky, Joe. Accept it and move on. I've got some shopping to do, so I'll say goodbye and Merry Christmas."

"I thought we could go back to Smithy's for a shake or something. Please?"

"Sorry, not today, but thanks." Beth walked away quickly. She couldn't help feeling disappointed. She was hoping he might become a friend, if not a boyfriend. Now, she didn't think she even liked him. Then she remembered that Marla had changed—a lot—and she might have had more to change than Joe. Maybe once he got used to the way people were in Castle Bluff, he'd stop playing his macho male act—unless he was just a bigot and not acting. Beth wasn't certain he could change that. He'd implied stuff about Hannah's family and assumed Imani was poor because of her race. Beth's vibes were definitely tingling, and she'd remain on guard.

Hannah, too, was thinking about Christmas shopping. Too crowded to go into the city, but Dad would take her to Libertyville as soon as she finished walking Bingo and taking him back to the Kennedys' mudroom. She made short work of that, much to Bingo's displeasure. "Danny will be home soon," she said, "and then you can be with him and Boots." Bingo gave a short yap. He had quickly learned the name of his new friend, Boots. Hannah gave him a treat. "See you later, Bingo. Be good." Danny would return from physical therapy, probably in a terrible mood. She'd see him later, too—much later!

"Okay, Dad, I'm ready," she called out. This was going to be so much fun. Uncle Martin was in the city, preparing for the concert on Christmas night at Orchestra Hall, and Dad had promised her a new dress for the occasion. They hoped to find that in Libertyville. Many of the shops there were just as grand as those in Chicago. They would be crowded, too, but not as bad and not so far away.

"Any ideas?" Dad asked, once they were on their way.

"Not really." Hannah paused, figuring how to approach it. "You see, Dad, I don't have any money."

Dad laughed. "Hannah, no twelve-year-old could have worked any harder than you have since we came to Castle Bluff. You fix your own breakfasts and lunches, and often dinner for the three of us. You do laundry, take care of your room, and get top grades in school. And you comfort your friend and take care of his dog, putting off having one of your own. Don't worry about money. You've earned it and more. Now, who is on your shopping list?"

"Well, you and Uncle Martin, of course, so I'll need to have some time alone—with money. It's too late to mail something to Mother, but I don't think she expects anything." Hannah didn't add that she didn't think her mother would send anything, either, or even ask to see her. She guessed that hurt a little, but not as much as it should. She could tell Dad was on the same train of thought and not enjoying it. Time to say more—quickly. "I need to buy something for Danny, Bingo, and Boots, and Porter and Beth. I guess it would be polite to get something for Kylie, too, and maybe Imani because she helped me with the Halloween costume. I think that's it." There was Kammy, but she didn't think she'd see her, and Mr. Markey, but he was out of town. "Maybe I should wrap up a few boxes of candy, just in case. Doesn't have to cost a lot."

"A very good idea. I have you and Martin, of course, so I, too, will need time alone—with money. Then I thought a large basket of fruit might be nice for the Kennedys—you know, the kind that includes candy and little Christmas trinkets."

Hannah could visualize it. "Perfect!"

Libertyville should be called Christmas Town, Hannah decided, especially since it was snowing. She and Dad stuck to the historic section, with its fine shops and beautiful homes—some with large white pillars, almost like mansions.

"We'll eat first," Dad said. "No sense shopping on an empty stomach."

"And we'll be more sensible when we go into a candy store." Hannah giggled.

"Let's give this a try," Dad said. "Casa Bonita? Okay with you?"

Hannah smiled. Everything was okay today.

It was crowded, but Hannah didn't mind waiting, especially since she and Dad were in such splendid festive moods. And, for once, Dad had nothing else demanding his attention. He ordered two large tacos, fajitas, and a seafood platter for them to share. "And ginger ale on the rocks for two," Dad said, grinning at the waiter.

While eating, Dad turned momentarily serious. "Not to make a big issue of it, but you could order a bouquet of flowers or a plant for your mother. It would be delivered to her before Christmas."

Hannah thought, and then shook her head. "Let's wait first and see what she does. I don't even know if she's home." She didn't say, I'm not even sure where her home is now.

"Okay. We'll wait and see, but the offer stands. Now, let's see if we can waddle out of here."

Hannah giggled. "I am immune to candy."

Next, Dad suggested a first separation and handed her a great wad of money. Fortunately, she'd brought a small purse, even though there wasn't much inside. He also plunked his watch inside the purse. "I can check the time on my phone. Let's meet back at that bench in the pavilion at, say, two. If we need more time or you need more money, we'll talk about it then."

Surely she had enough money to last the rest of her life, Hannah thought. It would be fun if they could keep on shopping together, especially for a dress, but there needed to be secrets and surprises.

As if Dad knew what she was thinking, he added, "and then we'll look for a sophisticated, elegant dress for you, and then load up on candy so you'll be too fat to wear it."

Hannah laughed out loud. Everyone in the world was always saying she was too skinny. Then Dad took off. Hannah pretended not to notice, but Dad's first stop was a jewelry store. For her? Probably not. Oh, she guessed it! Dad was going to buy a wedding ring for Uncle Martin. Even though they were married, they didn't wear rings. Hannah thought they'd never felt comfortable enough before. Her eyes welled up with unexpected tears. Uncle Martin was going to be so happy! She could hardly wait!

Better start spending money, she thought. She was proud that Dad felt she'd earned it.

Hours later, they drove home, content, each with a small bag of candy and two extra ones for Danny and Uncle Martin. Hanging from a hook in the back seat was the most beautiful dress Hannah had ever owned. "A rich cabernet," was how the salesperson described the chiffon and lace, swirly, full-skirt creation. Hannah thought the color was like the dark wine Uncle Martin sometimes had at dinner as a special treat. It was sleeveless, which worried Dad until he insisted on buying a silvery-gray long winter dress coat. Hannah had never owned a dress coat before. She wondered how often she'd wear it, but she was thrilled.

"Shoes?" she said, reluctantly. She didn't want Dad to spend one cent more, but she could hardly wear gym shoes.

"Of course," Dad said, and they found silver flats, decorated with rhinestones, and sheer stockings. "Makeup?" he wondered.

"I'll ask Kylie for help. Dad, you spent a lot of money."

"I did," he said, "and it felt great!"

Danny spent the day brooding. Winter break, no school, no friends, and nothing to do. Physical therapy had been difficult and painful—so was getting into and out of the car two times. Sid, his therapist, usually pleasant, was not today. He'd even accused Danny of not trying and let him know he was not the only one with problems. He knew that; Sid didn't need to be so grumpy. How would he feel if he couldn't build a snow fort or play hockey? Well, actually, Danny didn't know anything about what Sid might enjoy doing. Maybe he'd ask next time. Maybe . . .

He wished Hannah and Porter would come. It wasn't as if he could do anything to solve the mystery without them. Failing that, he wished that someone—anyone—was home. Dad was at work, still commuting most days to Milwaukee, Mom had a house showing, and Kylie had a date with Brad. That was okay. Danny liked Brad and knew there had been some problems. He liked all of Kylie's friends; they had been good to him—especially Kurt and Roe. That gave him an idea and a possible way to stop feeling sorry for himself while he waited for Hannah and Porter.

With a camera he hadn't used in ages, he would take photos and make Christmas/thank you cards. The hard part was being downstairs when all the art supplies were either in the basement or upstairs in Dad's office. Danny could take the photos, but he'd need help with everything else. Why hadn't his family asked him how he was going to get presents? Wait, he told himself. Why didn't you ask?

Okay, who could help? Beth had lots of cardstock. That might be a good first step. Carefully, he wheeled himself out into the living room and called the Walters. "Aunt Sue, is Beth home?" No surprise; Porter wasn't there, either. "Maybe you can help." Danny explained the problem and exactly what was needed.

"A fine idea, Danny. I'll gather some cardstock and a few fine-line markers—Beth will never notice—and have Porter take them to you as soon as he gets home. I'll package them up, so he won't know. Try to take all of your photos now and give Porter the camera card in a large envelope. I'll print them right away and get them to you. Will that work?"

"Yes! Thank you, Aunt Sue!"

But what pictures could he take? It wasn't as if he could get around much. Briefly, he thought about crawling up the stairs but gave it up as a really bad idea. Coming to the rescue, though, was Bingo. He gave a loud yawn, causing Boots to jump straight up, prepared to fight. Seeing her frenemy settle back to sleep, Boots curled up next to him.

"You two are my subjects," Danny said, laughing. "I'll keep on taking pictures of you until Porter comes. Sleeping pictures come first, but then you'll simply have to get up and perform again."

SCENE 5 – HOLIDAYS AND HAPPENINGS

"NO WAY," HANNAH SAID. "NOT before Christmas."

"Not a good idea, Danny." Porter shook his head. "I have no intention of getting into trouble—especially not before Christmas. Why ruin the holidays?"

Danny turned grumpy again, after finally being in an almost-decent mood. "Then I don't understand how we're going to learn anything more about Kammy and if she has anything to do with the murder."

"Attempted murder," Hannah corrected. "The old man isn't dead. And thinking Kammy has anything to do with it is just plain crazy."

"Maybe not," Porter said. "Beth was trying to get in touch with her because of a Drama Club scene."

Hannah nodded. "Beth got the phone number from me."

"But the phone has been disconnected," Porter said. "Whether or not that's connected with the, uh, mystery—"

"Okay, maybe you can't go, Porter, but Hannah could. Her parents never said she couldn't go there. Besides, Kammy is her friend. I would think she'd want to know if Kammy is all right."

"Hello," Hannah waved at him. "I'm right here. Don't talk about me like I wasn't. That part of the village is dangerous—even when it isn't dark out. I am not going, especially alone." When Danny started to object, she added, "Look, I know you don't understand, but I think this is going to be the best Christmas of my whole life, and I have a new dress, and I don't want anything to spoil it."

To his credit, Danny didn't say this was going to be his worst Christmas. "I get it," he said. "I can't keep asking Dad for information, though. He's going to start getting suspicious."

"Tell you what," Porter said. "How about Hannah and I go there after Christmas and sometime before New Year's? If we went around noon on a weekday, we'd be safe enough."

Hannah nodded. Maybe something would come up that would make going not necessary. She did not want the boys to know she'd told Dad and Uncle Martin about walking Kammy home Halloween night. Maybe if they kept putting it off, Danny would forget about it. Oh, yeah? Fat chance!

"Gosh, Beth, gosh!"

Beth smiled happily. She didn't think she had ever seen Kurt speechless before. "I think that means you like it."

"Like it? I love it—more than anything! I can't believe you painted this. And in oils! I didn't know you could oil paint."

"I've been taking lessons from Imani's father. He says our lessons can continue even when Art Club starts again."

"I'll bet he's better than any middle school art teacher. Heck, I'll bet you're better than any middle school art teacher. There's Brad and Kylie and Roe and Eric—all my best friends from last summer— except you, Beth."

"Well, you'll just have to pretend I'm the tree."

Kurt nodded. "That makes sense. Without you, we wouldn't have had the tree. At least, not like this one. Beth, thank you. I will treasure it always!"

Their date at Smithy's had been completely successful, Beth thought, touching the rose-gold, heart-shaped necklace around her neck. She had taken a peek at the certificate that had come with it. *Ten-karat gold with diamond accents*! "This is the most gorgeous thing I own. Kurt, you must have been saving up for this, like forever."

"Pretty much," he agreed.

"Mom said I can get a new dress for the Valentine's Day dance. And I'll make sure it's perfect for the most beautiful necklace in the world!"

By the time shakes were consumed and gifts properly admired, over and over, it was definite that Beth and Kurt were girlfriend and boyfriend again. "No matter what grade we're in or what school we attend," Kurt said. "It's an added Christmas bonus!"

Christmas morning was the best, Hannah thought, especially calling and thanking everyone, once all the presents were opened. Most of Hannah's gifts from Dad and Uncle Martin were small and inexpensive—she hadn't expected much because of her new outfit. Then she opened another small package. "Dad! Uncle Martin! Thank you!" At last, a cellphone of her own!

She had to call the Kennedys, of course—on her cellphone. "Just a minute, Hannah," Kylie said. "Danny will call you right back. And thank you for the book. I know I'll love it." All of Hannah's presents were books. Kylie's was a biography of Judy Garland.

"Thank you for the jeweled headband, Kylie. I'm going to wear it to the concert later."

Soon Hannah received a phone call from a number she didn't recognize. "Merry Christmas, Hannah!" It was Danny on *his* cellphone! "Porter got one, too. He called me from Colorado. This will really help SSC! I'll see you tomorrow!"

Danny forgot to thank her for the book of true spy adventures and didn't give her a chance to thank him for the super photograph of her playing snowball catch with Bingo. But it was okay. As Danny said, they'd see each other tomorrow.

One of the best parts of the morning was seeing Dad and Uncle Martin exchange rings. Uncle Martin had surprised Dad, too.

Hannah admired herself in the full-length mirror in the upstairs hall. "Why, I'm pretty," she said, amazed. It hadn't been Halloween magic. Then she tried on an unaccustomed smile. "Maybe too much." She switched to a slight smile — more natural, more her. Then she swirled, and her skirt swirled with her. "Cabernet," she whispered. "Cabernet." An elegant sound for an elegant Hannah. She wore the headband Kylie had given her like a crown, rather than a regular headband. It matched her silver, sparkly shoes. She'd applied makeup just as Kylie suggested — minimal, understated. You couldn't tell she was wearing any. She just looked like a better Hannah.

"Look at our princess," Uncle Martin declared. "Picture time!"

"Take one on my phone, too. Then I can send it to Danny."

"Aha!" Dad joked.

Hannah insisted on taking pictures of Dad and Uncle Martin, too. She had never seen them looking so handsome at the same time. She was used to Uncle Martin being all dressed up for concerts, but not Dad. In one photo, the two men held up their left hands, showing off their rings. Hannah didn't think the three of them had ever been so happy. They belonged together. They were a real family!

Uncle Martin needed to be at Orchestra Hall an hour before the concert, to tune up and everything, and because of the snow. Hannah looked down at her feet. "Snow," she said. "My shoes! They'll be ruined!"

"I thought of that, and your dad gave me your shoe size. Two more presents — just from me. Not wrapped, though." Uncle Martin presented Hannah with a box and a bag. In the box she found a pair of gray boots with fur tops. They would keep her warm and dry but were soft and would fold easily. The other present was a carrying bag. "You can put your shoes in it and change at Orchestra Hall."

They sat in box seats that would cost most people a fortune, but Hannah and Dad had complementary tickets. Hannah had learned to call them comps. As first cellist, Uncle Martin could be seen easily. It wasn't a long concert—just the right length for a Christmas evening—a medley of famous Christmas carols and unfamiliar ones. Hannah decided her favorite was Leroy Anderson's "Sleigh Ride." It wasn't really a Christmas carol—more of a rollicking, jolly tune that fit the season. Dad's favorite was "Carol of the Bells." Of course they had to wait again for Uncle Martin when the concert was over, but that was okay. The lobby was a beautiful, comfortable place.

"I'm proud of Uncle Martin, aren't you?"

"Oh, yes," Dad said.

Hannah wished she had a small purse to match her outfit. That way she could have brought her cellphone along, even though Dad had said he didn't want her to become too attached to it. "And no social media groups before high school. I will check, Hannah." She could have taken photos of the lobby, though. Oh, well, now that Dad said she would have a regular allowance, maybe she'd save up for a purse—if she didn't go back to normal old Hannah and buy a book instead.

"All set?" Uncle Martin, carrying his cello, smiled at them. "Did you like the concert?"

"It was amazing," Hannah said, before remembering to change back into the new boots.

The plan was to get a bite to eat on their way home. Uncle Martin knew of a wonderful pancake house in Wilmette. They headed for the parking garage, talking happily about their favorite songs, when Hannah became aware of a rough-looking group of men behind them. They were making weird sounds and saying things Hannah couldn't quite hear, as they came closer and closer. Her friend Beth would have talked about bad vibes. Then Hannah noticed Uncle Martin about to take Dad's hand. Quickly, she stepped between them. "Look, Dad," she shouted, "there's the restaurant where Mom said we should meet. I can't wait to see Aunt Clare again, Uncle Bob." Dad and Martin glanced back, just as Hannah grabbed both of their hands and pulled them inside the restaurant.

"That was quick thinking," Dad said.

"Every time you think it's all right to feel safe . . ." Uncle Martin was shaking.

"Do you have a reservation?" the receptionist asked. "If not, it's not a problem."

"Only for our wallets," Dad whispered, as a man in a suit fancier than Uncle Martin's led them to a table.

"It will be fine," Uncle Martin said, seemingly recovered. "The pancake house isn't cheap either. Hannah, thank you. I am so proud of you."

"Do you think they . . .?"

"Yes," Dad said. "Now let's put it behind us, and see if there's anything inexpensive on the menu. Then I think we'll call for a cab to take us the rest of the way to the parking garage."

Finally, Hannah understood why a second car was necessary.

SCENE 6 – So Much to Do – So Little Time!

"THE TIME BETWEEN CHRISTMAS AND New Year's Day is the shortest and longest time of the year," Hannah said two days after Christmas. "It goes by in a flash, and it also drags—maybe because there's not much to look forward to. Soon, I'll want school to start again."

"I used to feel that way," Danny complained. "Now everything drags. I can't wait for Porter to come home. Then you and he can go investigate the West Village Flats."

"Well, I want the Walters to come home, too, but not for your reason. I am not looking forward to that. But Beth and I need to work on our script. I think I've written most of it— unless she's been doing stuff I don't know about."

"When is the deadline?"

"Right when we get back to school—which is okay, because we won't have time after that. While the judges are picking the winners, we'll see the scenes and choose who gets to direct. Then the directors will get their scripts and hold auditions and rehearse."

"How much time will you have for all that?" Danny asked.

"Including performances? Probably late February or early March."

"Phew! Writing the one-acts seemed like a good idea, but now it sounds really complicated."

Hannah nodded. "Now it sounds really impossible."

A knock interrupted them. A Dad knock, Danny thought. Besides, Dad was the only one thoughtful enough to knock. "Enter," Danny bellowed.

Dad opened the door, laughing. "For a moment, I thought Leland had taken up residence."

Hannah laughed, too. "Just Danny giving a butler imitation. Maybe there'll be a butler part in the spring play."

"A butler in a wheelchair." Danny sneered. "Wouldn't that be a hit?" Silence. "Sorry, didn't mean to sound so grumpy."

"Well, I think a butler in a wheelchair could be a huge hit, especially if the butler did it. I wanted to congratulate Hannah. Your dad told me what you did on Christmas night. I doubt if an adult would be that quick witted."

"What?"

Hannah blushed. "I haven't told anyone about it."

"Well, I'll leave you to it. Don't let her go modest on you, Danny. She was very brave. I'll see you later, but let's leave the door open, so Mom doesn't get concerned."

"Hannah and me? No way! Honestly, Dad? I'm twelve and in a wheelchair. What does she think will happen?"

"Defies the imagination," Dad said, "but leave the door open."

"Mothers," Hannah said, as soon as Mr. Kennedy left. "Makes me almost glad I don't have one — well, hardly."

"You didn't hear from her on Christmas?"

Hannah shrugged, as if she couldn't care less. "A package came yesterday from Germany, where I guess she is now. It's a doll — a Christmas doll. She's given me a doll every year of my life. It's beautiful, but—"

"You'd rather have a baseball mitt."

"I'd rather have a phone call."

"So, what happened Christmas night? Why did Dad say you were brave?"

Briefly, Hannah told him about the gang of thugs, although she dearly wanted to forget about it.

"Do you really think they would have hurt your dad and uncle?"

Hannah nodded. "And maybe me, too."

"Wow! I don't know if brave is the right word. You think fast, and you have terrific instincts. Between you and Porter and what little I can do, I think we will solve the mystery!"

Hannah sighed. She was afraid it would come back to that.

Beth unpacked and found places for her Christmas presents. They had had a wonderful time with her Grandma and Grandpa Walters at their new home in Colorado. It was a snowy wonderland—much more so than Castle Bluff, which seemed kind of boring in comparison. She was sorry that Grandma and Grandpa had moved so far away, but it was much more fun visiting them in Manitou Springs than in Waukegan. Not many days of vacation left now, and so many things to do. She wanted to have overnights with her friends, and she wanted to see Kurt loads of times, and—

"Beth," Porter yelled. "You've got like forty million phone messages from Hannah, wondering when we'd be back."

"The answering machine won't hold that many," she yelled back. She wondered why Hannah hadn't called her cellphone. Beth looked. Oh, she had. Beth just hadn't checked her calls or texts in days. Her friends knew where she was and wouldn't have bothered, other than Kurt, who had called Christmas day. Beth wondered what Hannah wanted so urgently.

"Oh, my God! The playwriting contest!" Scripts were due—she checked the calendar—in only a week! "And it was my suggestion, even though Marla presented it. Marla wouldn't have even attended

Drama Club if I hadn't asked her." And she'd stuck Hannah with the whole task!

Beth raced downstairs and explained the problem to her mother. "Mom, if Hannah says it's okay, can I go over there? I know we just got back, but—"

"Go ahead," Mom said. "I hope you haven't bitten off more than you can chew, as Gramps would say." Beth grabbed the kitchen phone.

"Hello?"

Hannah sounded cold, or was Beth just feeling guilty?

"Hi, Hannah, it's Beth. We just got back into town, and I saw your messages."

"And your cell?"

"Honestly, Hannah, I hardly used it the whole time we were in Colorado. I'm so sorry. Mom says I can go over to your house now, if you're not busy. I still have your Christmas present."

"That would be okay. I've got your present, too."

Porter decided to go along. He'd visit with Danny while Beth saw Hannah. "Meet me there when you're through at Hannah's," Porter said. "Danny and I still need to exchange presents. That's the problem with going away for Christmas. When you come home, it's over for everyone else, but you haven't finished."

Beth nodded. "We should have taken care of presents before we left, but somehow we ran out of time." Except for Kurt's present, she thought. That had been top priority.

"Do you want me to take your present to Danny?"

"No, thanks," Beth said. "I want to see his reaction."

"I don't blame you. All I'm giving him is another dumb video game."

Both Beth and Hannah were thrilled with their gifts. "Dad will try to claim this," Hannah said, examining the sketch of her peering down from her tree fort. She laughed. "I'll bet this is exactly how I looked back then. 'Go on, prove that you really want to be my friend.' That was definitely my attitude."

Beth smiled. "That's sort of how I felt when I first went to middle school—like I was a loser and would never fit in." Kurt and Kylie had changed all that for her, she thought. "Soon you'll have lots of friends. And even if you don't know many kids in seventh grade now, Drama Club will change that."

Hannah handed Beth a wrapped package. "This is for you."

Thank goodness I had something for her, Beth thought. "Oh, Hannah, a book about painting with oils. Thank you!"

"Look at the author," Hannah said, acting as if it were no big deal.

"Troy Rendina," Beth read. "That's your last name, Hannah."

"Uh-huh, my dad wrote it. I thought you'd like it."

"I sure do. I'd forgotten he taught art at Community."

Then Beth looked over the printed copy of Hannah's script and made a few suggestions. For the most part, she couldn't improve upon it. "Hannah, this is your work, and only your name should be on it—not mine. It wasn't even my idea."

Hannah squirmed. "Whatever you think is best, Beth. I don't mind."

"I'll have plenty to do just being president," Beth said, "but I feel guilty at letting you down. Tell you what. I'm a better typist than you. I'll fix the typos and clean things up a bit, and then type the final for you to turn in. You're the playwright, and I am your editor. Okay?"

"Super," Hannah said.

Beth's phone gave its jingle. "Porter, what's up? Yes, I think we're done here." She turned to Hannah. "Porter wants me to go next door now. I'll type the script tomorrow and send it to you. You can check to see if it works."

Hannah nodded. "I'll go with you. I've got something for Porter, too. He was the hardest."

Oh, dear, Beth thought. Did Porter have anything for Hannah? Nothing she could do about it. "We'll be right over, Porter."

Good thing Beth was there, Hannah thought. Without her, Danny would insist on calling the SSC to order and scheduling a time for her and Porter to visit the West Village Flats. Hannah didn't want to and was certain Porter didn't, either, but Danny would nag them unmercifully, as soon as he could get them together — alone!

"Awesome wheelchair, Danny," Beth said. "Is it a Christmas present?"

Hannah stared. She hadn't even noticed.

"Yes. It's from Uncle Carl, Roe, and Mateo. Dad took back the rental. Watch this — it's motorized." Danny gave a demonstration. "I plan to enter wheelchair races." Then, at their odd looks, he added, "Joking!"

They laughed, just because it was great to see Danny in such a good mood.

"It's going to really help you get around," Porter said. "Will you be able to go back to school?"

Danny shrugged. "Not right away, because of all the physical therapy. But I'm swimming now — not just hanging out in the hydrotherapy pool."

"Maybe you will be on the swim team someday," Hannah said.

"Is Kylie home?" Beth interrupted. Danny nodded. "I need to see her, so let's open presents now."

Hannah wished she'd waited. "I've already given mine to you and Danny."

Danny wheeled over to his bedside table and held up his book about famous spies. "Thanks, Hannah."

"And I love my —"

"Shhh," Danny commanded.

Hannah nodded. "Got it." Danny probably made similar cards for everyone. It wasn't like he could go shopping.

Soon, the giftwrap was flying. Danny was both pleased and saddened by his gift from Beth. He gazed at the painting of him in the backyard playing with Bingo. "Next summer," he vowed. "This will be me again next summer."

Hannah and Porter were surprised by their gifts to each other. Porter gave Hannah a pair of binoculars. "That's so you can spy on everyone from your tree fort, once the snow and ice go away. They weren't expensive but should do the job."

"Maybe you can use them even sooner," Danny said. Hannah and Porter glared at him, but Beth didn't seem to notice.

"Thank you, Hannah." Porter shook his head. "I don't know what else to say." His gift was a small book about friendship. Each page had a beautiful photo and a quotation from a famous person.

"I gave everyone books," Hannah said, "even my parents. I wasn't sure about you until I saw this. It's because you are the best person I know at making friends."

The others nodded and looked at Porter—until he blushed. It was true. Porter made and kept friends. He supported them in their activities, whether or not he was interested. And he never said anything mean about anyone.

"This is my favorite," Hannah said. She took the book and turned to a page of two people sitting on a bench, looking out at a lake. She read, "Friends are those rare people who ask how we are and then wait to hear the answer."

"That's you, Porter," Danny said. "You won't even let us get away with saying 'fine,' unless it's the truth."

Beth laughed. "This is getting way too sentimental, especially since you're talking about my brother. I'm going to find Kylie. See you spies later."

As soon as Beth shut the door, the SSC looked at each other in dismay. "I didn't say anything," Porter said. The others shook their heads. They hadn't either.

"Never mind," Danny said. "She doesn't know what we're doing."

"We?" Hannah asked warily.

"Well, you two, with me checking in with you by text. You haven't heard anything more about Kammy, have you?"

Hannah shook her head.

"And I haven't heard anything about the attempted murder. I don't even know how the man in the hospital is doing. So, you're going to take a trip to the West Village Flats tomorrow?"

"All right," Porter said, and Hannah nodded. Danny was not going to give up. "After lunch, we'll meet here. My mom will just think I've gone to see you."

SCENE 7 – THE WHITE TRUCK AGAIN

HANNAH MET PORTER OUTSIDE THE Kennedys' house. "It's awfully cold," Hannah said. "I've been trying to think of ways to get out of going, but—" She shrugged.

"Me, too," Porter admitted. "But we're dressed warmly, and it's not supposed to snow anymore today. We might as well get it over with. If we don't go today, Danny will insist that we go tomorrow. Shall we go inside and see him first?"

"For more orders? No thanks. I saw him before. We're supposed to text him when we arrive. And he'll probably text us often. Too often! He said he's Command Central."

Porter sighed. "He just wants to be a part of things. I'm not sure what we're supposed to be looking for, but I am sure my parents don't want me anywhere near the West Village Flats."

"It was dark on Halloween," Hannah said, "so I couldn't see much—just a bunch of run-down townhouses. A rotten location."

"Between two busy highways that I've been told often enough not to cross. You'd think they'd know I'm old enough to look both ways. Parents!"

Hannah's experiences had been different, so she didn't say anything. No need, for she heard a ping on Porter's phone.

He laughed. "Text one." He returned the text quickly and showed Hannah. "No news. 2 blks from U."

"He's definitely going to be a pain in the you know what." Hannah shook her head. "You know, I don't even remember crossing a highway when we walked Kammy home that night."

"Not much traffic. I was pretty scared, though."

"You didn't let on." And that summed up Porter fairly well, Hannah thought. You could never tell what he was thinking.

"Just a couple more blocks before we cross the highway," Porter said. "We'll text Danny on the other side. At least we don't have to cross the busiest one."

"Why did they build a housing development in such an awful location?" Hannah wondered.

"Why do you think? It's low-rent housing, and the town council finally approved when they learned our fine village residents would be protected from the low-class riffraff." Hannah had never heard Porter sound bitter before. "My church fought for a decent location, but no one would listen."

"And are the people riffraff? Whatever that means."

"I guess it means no good. Many who live there do get into trouble, especially with drugs and alcohol. Lots of fights. I don't believe anyone is no good, though. Maybe they'd do better if people didn't expect them to be scum."

"How do the children get to school?"

"I think there's a bus to the elementary school on the west side. The middle and high school kids have to walk across the highway, unless their parents can drive them."

"No wonder Kammy was unhappy to see the snow," Hannah said.

They walked the next block without talking, each with their own thoughts. Hannah was mainly worried about Kammy, whom she could no longer reach by any means. Porter broke the silence.

"I was thinking about the book you gave me, Hannah. I really like it, but it also bothered me."

"Bothered you? I'm sorry."

"No, I'm explaining it wrong. It's just that you had a hard time figuring out what to give me. Everyone does. Mom asks what I want for Christmas or birthdays, and I never know what to tell her. Beth always has a list—clothing, CDs, art supplies—Kelly wants every doll in the Libertyville toyshop. Even Zoe has hobbies—balloons and bubbles and Mr. Giraffe. Danny's list, before the accident, was as long as his useless legs. I feel like a boring nothing sometimes."

"You like to read and were in Cross Country. Now you're in Drama Club." Hannah didn't like to hear Porter so down on himself.

He shrugged. "That's to support my sister. And the only reason I did Cross Country was because of Danny, until I finally had the nerve to quit. I don't even enjoy video games that much. I just go along with whatever my friends are doing and don't do anything that's just for me."

Hannah hardly knew what to say. This was the longest conversation she'd ever had with Porter. He'd always been sort of an appendage of Danny's, rather than a person in his own right. "I don't think you need to worry, Porter," she said carefully. "Maybe you're lucky that you're not all wrapped up in things yet. In the meantime, you're an awfully good friend."

"Thanks, Hannah. Well, here we are." Then, after looking both ways, they held hands like little children and dashed across the busy four-lane highway.

"It was around here that Kammy left us," Hannah said, "but I don't know which townhouse is hers."

"I don't want to knock on any doors," Porter said, "not even in daylight. But we can walk around and if we see anybody outside, ask."

"Okay. Preferably a woman."

Finally, they came upon three small children building a snowman. A woman was supervising them. Hannah thought the children looked well fed and were dressed for the weather. They certainly were having a good time. She approached the woman.

"Hi," she said, hoping she didn't sound nervous. "We're trying to find a friend. Her name is Kamirah Williams, but we call her Kammy. She lives in one of these town houses."

"She's sort of disappeared," Porter added. "We're worried about her."

"Well, I don't know. . ." the woman started.

"Yes you do, Mama," said one of the little girls, who looked about eight. "Kammy played Hide and Seek with us. She had the best hiding places. She lived with that man who got hurt."

"Stabbed!" a boy who might have been the girl's twin said with relish. He picked up a stick and stabbed the snowman, causing the smallest child, bundled so thoroughly Hannah couldn't tell if it was a boy or a girl, to cry.

"Now, now," the mother said. "Alec, settle down and repair the snowman. Nora, there's no need to cry. Kamirah lived with her grandfather in unit 26, but I haven't seen her since the old man was attacked. Perhaps she was taken to the Home."

"We did play Hide and Seek," Alec said. "Alice is right. Kammy knew the best hiding places."

The best places was right, Hannah thought. It was obvious, though, that the woman would not allow the conversation to continue. Perhaps fearing more questions, she hustled her children inside — to Unit 22.

"Thank you," Hannah called out, as she and Porter walked away.

"Well, I guess we know a little more now," Porter said. "I had a hunch Kammy was connected somehow with the man who was stabbed."

"Her grandfather. That's horrible! The woman mentioned a home. What home?"

"The Winter Markey Home for Children. It's for orphans and children whose families can't take care of them. It's pretty nice, actually. They even have their own school."

"I know Mr. Markey, but Winter?"

Porter smiled. "Yes, it's strange, but that was the name of Mr. Markey's great-grandmother."

"It's kind of pretty. I once knew a girl named Summer, so I guess Winter isn't too weird. Do you think Kammy could be there?"

"It's possible, I guess. I don't know if the people in charge would tell us, though."

"We could try," Hannah said.

"Okay, but not today."

A familiar ping on Hannah's phone this time. "Back ASAP," she texted, and then she showed Porter.

"Yeah, we've been here long enough. The traffic is going to get much worse soon."

At that, a white truck pulled into a lot near them. Hannah gasped, and turned on her phone's camera.

"What's wrong?"

"Shhh." Hannah pulled Porter away and had him block her. "I don't want to be noticed." Quickly she took several photos of a man and woman, as they got out of the truck and went into one of the units. Then, as the door closed and she couldn't see them in any of the windows, she approached the truck and began photographing it, especially the license number. "Okay," she said. "Let's get out of here."

They crossed the highway, just beginning rush-hour traffic. On the other side, back in familiar territory, Porter stopped. "Okay, Hannah, what was that about?"

"Can't you guess? That was the truck that hit Danny!"

SCENE 8 – A TEAM SPORT

"DONE!" BETH ANNOUNCED. BABY ZOE looked up from the bouncy seat, and then returned to her serious play with a set of plastic keys. Kelly and her friend Marta ignored her; dressing their dolls was far more important. Beth was fortunate that babysitting had been simple, for once, and that Mom would be home soon.

She removed two copies of the script from the printer. *Bob's Woodland Adventure* probably would be a winner. Hannah had done a fine job, but Beth had made enough corrections and revisions to include her name without feeling guilty. The playwrights were Hannah Rendina and Beth Walters. What seemed like a grand idea for Drama Club now looked uncertain. It might have been different if Mr. Markey and the rest hadn't gone away for the holidays, and the directors and actors were able to rehearse their scenes at the castle—but maybe not. All of them, including Mrs. Hunt, had forgotten how little gets done over the holidays. "Who knows?" Beth shrugged.

"Who knows what?" Kelly asked.

"Who knows if Drama Club will have enough time to do everything? That's a nice outfit Daisy is wearing, Kelly." Daisy had been Beth's favorite doll only a few years back.

"She's going to Abigail's birthday party," Marta said. Beth thought Marla's sister seemed much happier now that she was spending so much time with Kelly. At home, the little girl had been soaking in her mother's tension.

"What's Marla doing today?"

"She's on a date with Eric. Maybe he'll kiss her." The little girls giggled.

"Well, I can see that everyone is happy here!" Beth's mom had returned. She scooped Zoe from her bouncy seat and gave a sniff. "One diaper change, and then time for a nap."

"No," Zoe said. "No, no, no!" But she grinned. She was just showing off, proud of that all-powerful word.

"Yes, yes, yes!" said her mother. "The girls will be fine, Beth. You go ahead and do whatever you'd like."

Beth held up a folder. "I finished the script, so I need Hannah to check it over. Then I'll go see Danny, too."

"I think Porter is there," Mom said. "Just be home for dinner and bring back all clothing. We're running out of mittens and scarves, and I refuse to buy more."

Mom was being so understanding lately, Beth thought, as she started the cold walk toward Hannah's house. She shivered. Thank goodness she'd worn her warmest clothing, even gloves, which she loathed because she was always losing them. She wouldn't be surprised if Mom sent a reminder text closer to dinnertime. Beth wasn't on babysitting duty nearly as much now that Marta was coming to the house. Marta thought Zoe was cute. Kelly, who was eager to please Marta, went along with including Zoe. Just having her younger siblings get older would help the whole family, Beth thought.

Wondering whether Hannah might not be home, Beth rang the doorbell. It would be easier to talk with her alone before they went next door. Hannah's house was quiet—almost solemn. Movement and noise were a constant at the Kennedys'—dog, cat, different music from multiple locations, blending together in a startling din. It was fun, of course, especially now that Danny had a more positive attitude and could be somewhat independent in his motorized wheelchair.

She rang again. No answer. She was about to leave when the front door opened. "Sorry, I was upstairs and didn't hear the bell at first. You're Beth, right? The artist?"

Beth blushed. "Well, maybe someday. You're Hannah's dad. I recognize you from the photo on the back of the book Hannah gave me. I love it. The book, I mean, not the photo. I mean—"

Mr. Rendina smiled. "I know what you mean. And I am crazy about the sketch you did of Hannah. I would like to talk to you about your art."

Did he mean now? With or without Hannah? She felt prickles up her spine—the warning sensation she had had ever since the incident with that awful teacher last year.

"That would be nice sometime," she said. "Is Hannah home?"

Hannah's father shook his head. "No, I think she's with Danny and your brother. Someday soon, you, Hannah, and I can take a look at your drawings. I'd like to see what else you've done."

He understood. He didn't mean now. The disturbing prickles went away. "Thanks, Mr. Rendina. I'll go check next door. We need to go over our script for the contest."

Danny was working a jigsaw puzzle at the card table in the living room. Boots was asleep on his lap, Bingo snoozed at his feet. Bingo looked up as Beth entered the room, perhaps hoping for a walk.

"Sorry, Bingo," Beth said. "I'm not Hannah, and I almost froze my toes off out there."

Danny put his puzzle piece down. "I thought you'd be Hannah and Porter."

"They're not here? That's weird. Where do you think they are?"

"They got tired of hanging around with me. They went for a walk."

Oh, dear, Danny was feeling sorry for himself again. That wouldn't do.

"I'm sure they'll be back soon. I'm surprised I didn't see them." Beth held up the copies of the script.

"It's finished? Is it good?" A spark of interest from Danny.

"I think so. I need to hear it read aloud. Look, while we're waiting, would you read with me? You can take the boy parts."

Danny shrugged. "Might as well, I guess. I don't have anything else to do."

Even though Beth had thought she was just killing time, reading with Danny proved to be enormously helpful. She spotted some things that needed changing, including some typos that somehow she'd missed. More important, she learned something about Danny.

Snow White: *My stepmother hates me so much, just because I'm younger and prettier than she is. She sent me out here with her huntsman so he could kill me, but he wouldn't. He loves me too much. So, he left me here, but I'm going to die anyway. I don't know what to do.* (Bursts into hysterical sobs.)

Bob: *Hey, it's okay. You're not going to die. I know a place you can live, if you're willing to work for your keep. Just over that hill is a house with seven men. They are looking for a housekeeper and will protect you.*

Snow White: (shocked) *Live with seven men! What kind of girl do you think I am?* (Pause) *But I do need a safe place to stay.* (Exits, muttering)

Bob: *Everyone is so cranky today.* (Enter Red) *Where are you going?*

Red: *I'm going to Granny's, and I'm going to take the shortcut today.*

Bob: *That's not a good idea. I just came from there and saw a very hungry wolf. Take the other path.*

Danny was a natural but probably didn't know it. Beth thought he was especially good as the villain, Roger. Of course villains were easier to play than straight parts—they were so overdone. Beth played Rebecca.

Roger: Hey, Becky! I've done it! I closed the land deal just outside of town. Now I can buy the boat and club membership and the new sports car and those golf clubs I've been wanting.

Rebecca: Roger, the dryer quit working again today. You said that if the land deal worked out, you would buy me a new one.

Roger: But if I do that, I can't buy my new golf clubs, can I? I'll look really low-class on the club course with old ones, won't I?

Rebecca: Well…

Roger: Just call the repairman again. Have him fix it, and take the money out of your household budget.

Rebecca: Well…

Roger: What's for dinner?

Rebecca: Fried calves liver.

Roger: What? I hate that stuff.

Rebecca: Well, I'm sorry. I'm trying to stay within my meager household budget, and that was what was in the clearance meat bin this week.

Roger: Meager? I generously give you ten dollars a week to buy groceries, pay the bills, and put gas in your car. A lot of women would think that is more than plenty. I'm surprised you don't give the leftover money back to me.

Rebecca: (explodes) I don't have any left over! I rob Peter to pay Paul every week as it is!

Roger: (furious) Stealing from a strange man to pay a guy named Paul? Unbelievable! And I'm not eating that liver! I'm going out. You eat the liver. (Storms out)

Rebecca*: That no good, lying, selfish . . .* (Walks off, muttering angrily)

They read a few more pages, and then—"Oh, I get it!" Danny yelled, causing Boots to jump off his lap, hissing in dismay. "It's like that famous Christmas movie Dad made me watch. Bob finds out what it would be like if he'd never been born."

"Right," Beth said. *"It's A Wonderful Life, A Christmas Carol,* and a few fairy tales, all bunched together."

"I like it, Beth. I think you and Hannah will win."

How much should Beth tell him? Should she say that he was a good actor? No, she'd scare him off. "It really helped to hear the lines, Danny. Thanks."

"It was fun," Danny admitted. "Not like reading a play in a dumb old English class. Not as good as sports, of course."

"Theater is a team sport, Danny," Beth said softly. She might have said more if her brother and Hannah hadn't charged into the room. "Wow, you look frozen!"

"We are," Porter said, teeth chattering.

Both he and Hannah were staring at Danny. It was obvious the three wanted to talk in private. Beth was in the way. Something was going on. Maybe she could pull it out of Porter later. "How about I go into the kitchen and fix us some hot chocolate? Aunt Jane always has instant mix handy."

"Great idea," Porter said. "Thanks."

Beth tried to stall, but stirring chocolate mix into hot water was not time consuming. She placed four filled cups onto a tray, added a small plate of cookies, and returned to the living room. There, she almost laughed out loud. Uncle Dan had joined the group, having no idea how unwelcome he was. The expressions on the SSC members' faces were priceless. How could Uncle Dan not see how frustrated they were? Meanwhile, it was getting late, and she and her brother needed to go home soon. Yep—her phone pinged.

"OK," she responded. "Drink up, Porter. You're about to be plunged back into the deep freeze. Mom wants us home for supper."

Porter gulped down the hot drink. "I'll call you later, Danny." Then he gave Hannah a meaningful look that meant, well, something. Beth thought it looked like a warning.

"Maybe we can get together tomorrow, Hannah," Beth said. "Danny and I read over the script. I need to make a few changes, but I'll email you the revision tonight. I'd like you to read it again before we send it in."

"Sorry I wasn't here before," Hannah said. And Beth thought she sounded sorry—really, really sorry. Whatever had happened on their unlikely walk together, neither Hannah nor Porter was pleased.

SCENE 9 – REAL SCHOOL AT LAST

HANNAH REACHED OVER AND TURNED off the alarm. Right. No more sleeping late. Today meant back to school, and not in just a few rooms at Community, but in the newly renovated Castle Bluff Middle School. Hannah was nervous. Ridiculous, she told herself. Sure, there would be new kids to meet, but she had friends in Castle Bluff now. True, they were either in sixth or eighth grade, but that was a good start. Other kids probably had jittery stomachs, too. Groaning, she got out of bed and looked out the window. Blowing snow.

"Hannah, get cracking, kid, if you want a ride with me."

"Okay, Dad."

She dressed more carefully than she would on a normal school day, but today felt more like the first day of school, only in winter. She wore a Black Watch plaid skirt, a black pullover sweater, and black tights and her new boots. To add a little color, she added a chunky gold chain necklace. She wanted to wear her hair down, the way she did for the Christmas concert, but the wind was fierce today. Instead, she swooped her hair back into a low ponytail and pulled down a knit cap, almost covering her eyes. No time for more than a strawberry Pop-Tart and a glass of milk. She'd buy her lunch at school. "I'm ready, Dad," she said.

He was just coming inside. "The car is all warmed up." Then he took a good look at her. "My, don't you look nice! A special occasion?"

Hannah nodded. "The first day of real school. Finally!"

"Then let's do it! You are not the same girl, peeking down from her tree fort, just a few months ago."

"I don't even know that girl now," Hannah said, determined not to go back to unfriendly ways, no matter what.

Over the last few days, she and Porter, separately, had managed to tell Danny about their adventure at the West Village Flats. Both agreed not to tell him about the white truck. Hannah was certain it was the vehicle that had struck Danny, but neither she nor Porter knew what to do with the information. It wasn't really the driver's fault, at least not the hitting part. The criminal part was leaving the scene without helping. If Hannah and Mateo hadn't been there, Danny would have been alone, terribly injured—maybe dead. But how would Danny react if he learned they'd seen the truck? Maybe too risky. Hannah had the photos of the driver, the truck, and the license plate number. To do more, they'd have to admit to prowling around the Flats, a place where they were forbidden to go.

In the end, they'd stuck to Kammy's story—or lack of story. They knew the old man who had been stabbed was her grandfather. What they didn't know was her present whereabouts or how her grandfather was doing.

"Maybe I'll see Kammy today," she said.

Dad looked startled, deeply engrossed in his own thoughts. "I hope you will," he said, "and you'll meet other seventh graders as well." He pulled up to the drop-off point. "Well, here we are. You have a very good day. Try to get a ride home, but if you can't, call me."

"I'll probably take the bus, if I can figure out how it works. Oh, there's Beth. I'll walk with her." She had dreaded going in alone. "Bye, Dad."

Beth and Porter walked to school. Their home was too close for bus service. "Go ahead, I don't mind," Beth said, when Porter spotted some sixth-grade boys he knew walking ahead. "Not cool to be seen with your sister."

Porter grinned. "It's very cool," he said, "but maybe not today. Thanks," and he raced away.

Beth didn't mind some thinking time alone. Classes hadn't even started, but she felt heavy weights on her shoulders. She needed to contact Mrs. Hunt about when to resume Drama Club—at school and in the castle. The deadline for scripts had passed. Beth wondered how many had been turned in. Short scenes that were supposed to be rehearsed over break—but probably weren't—must be performed before directors for the One-Acts could be chosen. Beth knew that Imani would act in Joe's sketch; Kammy had never contacted anyone and, thus, lost her part. Beth hoped Kammy wouldn't be disappointed, but she didn't blame Joe for dropping her.

Then, arrangements were needed for the trips to Crofts and the high school to see Kurt's and Kylie's shows. Both of them had been so busy rehearsing over the holidays that Beth had hardly seen them. Kurt's play was next week, and Kylie's the week after. "If I had been smart, I would have taken care of permission slips and everything before we left on vacation." No, she was being too hard on herself. "I've got to make it clear that I can't do it all myself," she resolved. Then she sighed. "I never realized how much Miss Armstrong used to do for us." Mrs. Hunt was a fine English and social studies teacher, but she didn't seem the right fit for Drama Club. And could she really direct a main-stage spring play?

"Beth," someone yelled. "Can I walk in with you?"

It was Hannah. She probably felt like the new girl, all over again. "Sure," Beth yelled back, waiting for Hannah to catch up.

Danny was in no mood for physical therapy. It had been hard watching Kylie dash out to catch the bus — even harder to see Hannah get into her father's car. Hannah, Porter, and all of Danny's friends would be at the grand reopening of Castle Bluff Middle School, but not Danny. Instead, he was propped up between two parallel bars, trying to swing his legs as if he were walking. It was hard, really hard. He wished Sid, his therapist, would let him try on his own. But Sid insisted on standing behind him. "We can't take a chance you'll reinjure yourself."

"But it would be my chance," he wanted to say. It would be his risk to take. But no, he didn't mean that. In this case, taking chances was stupid, if he wanted to walk again and have his old life back. At least, no therapist had to move his legs for him now. He was making progress.

"Okay, a short rest before we try the next exercise. You are improving, Danny, even though—"

"I'm in a crappy mood?" Danny grinned, pleased to use a word that would be forbidden at home. He shouldn't take it out on Sid. "Sorry. I'm just kind of down because the middle school finally opened, and all my friends are there. Mom went over to get work for me."

"Well, you have been studying at home since the accident, haven't you?"

"Yes, but it's different now."

"Then let's get you in good enough shape so you can go, too."

In a wheelchair, Danny thought. Relying on the school elevator. Everyone would look at him and gossip about how he would have been the fastest runner in the whole school, if—he stopped. If he hadn't gone after his dog chasing a Frisbee.

Next came massage therapy, followed by the heated whirlpool tub. The massage therapy hurt, but that was a good sign. At least he had feelings in his legs. Now if he could only get them to work better. The whirlpool was the best part.

Danny was drying off, getting ready to go home, when he overheard his mother talking to the physiotherapist in charge, Dr. Anthony. "Yes, he's making some progress," the doctor said, "but he should be further along. I'm starting to wonder if part of the problem is psychological. The reports I'm getting indicate depression. Of course, I've seen this in many patients. It might be just a stage."

"Do you think he should see someone?"

Danny shook his head. I don't want that, he thought. Of course I'm down. I am missing all winter sports and don't know if I'll ever play anything again. But I'm dealing with it. He'd better convince the grownups. He needed to pretend — to act.

He scooted himself into his wheelchair, even though it was difficult, and greeted his mother with a huge smile. "Hi, Mom. I did great today, but I'm starving! Let's get some lunch." Beth had thought he was a pretty good actor the other day. Well, he'd be a great actor now — minus a script.

After lunch, which he made sure he did justice to, Danny wheeled himself into the improvised study area in the living room and examined his workload. His English teacher wanted him to read a novel of his own choosing that had at least 200 words. "Write a short summary of each chapter," she'd written, "just to show that you've understood what you've read. Then I'll send you some questions and possible essays. I hope you are able to return to school very soon."

What book should he read? Hannah had lent him a stack of her favorites. He selected one — probably a girls' book — *A Girl of the Limberlost*. That was the play Kurt was in at Crofts. Maybe he'd go see that play. That would show mom that his attitude was fine — that he didn't need to "see someone." He opened the book. Now what part was Kurt playing again?

Hours later, it seemed, he closed the book, just as Mom called him for dinner. "I'm almost done reading the whole book," he said. "I don't think I've ever done that before, except for little kid books."

"You must have enjoyed it," Kylie said.

"Yes and no. The first part was better than the last. I won't have any trouble writing the chapter summaries. I took notes."

"What did you like best about it?" Dad asked.

"The setting—it's cool—and the character, Billy. He's really funny, and I think it's the right part for Kurt without him being typecast."

"That's what Beth says," Kylie said. "It's a wonder that Kurt got any part at all, but a lead as a freshman is amazing."

"So, Danny," Dad said, "you and your wheeled chariot are going to venture out—someplace besides the doctor's office and physical therapy?"

Danny nodded. "I want to see that play. I think I'd want to, even if Kurt weren't in it. Maybe I'll read other books by that author someday. And I'd like to see what's left of the Limberlost. It's in Indiana—that's not far. But not in a wheelchair. I will need to walk once I get there."

Mom, Dad, and Kylie looked at each other. This was the first time Danny had mentioned wanting to walk again for any reason except sports or playing with Bingo. And Kylie couldn't help grinning at Danny's remark about being typecast. At least he'd picked up some knowledge of theater.

"I must say," Mom added, "it's been a pleasure to have such a literary conversation at the dinner table."

Kylie stood. "I'll get dessert," she said. "I made it."

"Uh-oh," said Danny, but he didn't mean it. Dinner and the conversation had been a pleasant change. No one had seemed worried or angry about anything.

SCENE 10 – WINNERS AND LOSERS

A T THE BEGINNING OF EIGHTH period, Beth finally got the note she'd been waiting for. A request from Mrs. Hunt, asking to see her as soon as school was over. All day — at lunch, in class, passing in the halls — people had been asking when Drama Club would meet. "I think on Wednesday," she'd said. "I'll let you know for sure."

Drama Club hadn't seemed this complicated last year, even when Miss Armstrong disappeared. Because I wasn't so involved, Beth thought. Maybe Kylie wouldn't agree.

In the cafeteria, Beth had tried to figure out who had turned in scripts for the contest and what scenes were ready or almost ready. Imani and Priyanka admitted they'd given up on writing a script. "We didn't have time or ideas," Imani said. "Pri was away practically all vacation, and Joe had tons of rehearsals — all at my house."

"No Kammy?"

Imani shook her head. "Joe tried calling, but no service. I guess the phone was disconnected. It wasn't Joe's fault, Beth."

"No one's fault but Kammy's," Beth said. "Maybe not even hers. I haven't seen her today, have you?" Neither Imani nor Priyanka had, but it wasn't likely they would. The way the school was redesigned, they hadn't seen many seventh graders.

Drama Club wasn't the main subject at lunch, though. It was the Valentine's Day dance. Giggling, Imani admitted that she was hoping Joe would ask her. "He's nice, Beth. I think he was just trying too hard before. Maybe because he's new."

Priyanka hoped someone would ask her. "If not, maybe I'll go alone."

"Most people won't have dates," Beth predicted. "I asked Kurt ages ago, but I need to find a dress. Mom said I could have a new one."

"Let's go shopping together," Priyanka said. "Just us three. I'll ask Mom if she can take us to Libertyville."

"Or maybe downtown," Imani said. "That would be special."

"Art Club on Thursday, Beth. You going? I know you're awfully busy with Drama Club."

"I'll be there." Drama Club was taking too much space in her brain. She would talk to Mrs. Hunt about it. She didn't mind being president, but she shouldn't have to do all the planning.

⚷

"Beth, sit down." Mrs. Hunt patted the chair next to her desk. "We have a lot to talk about."

"Everyone wants to know if we're having a meeting Wednesday." Beth didn't bother with introductory small talk.

"That won't be a problem." Mrs. Hunt sighed. "But what comes after is."

To Beth's dismay, Mrs. Hunt said she wouldn't be able to continue with Drama Club. "You know I already sponsor the literary magazine. Now the administration insists I coach the girls' volleyball team. Well, I don't have to spell out what that means."

Beth nodded. No need for Mrs. Hunt to explain. This was not her fault. Sports at CBMS would always rank before theater or any of the arts. "Did you mention Drama Club to them?"

"Yes, and the spring play. They just said we needed to find someone else. I've asked around, but all the teachers are too busy. Everyone feels overburdened and behind this year. Don't get me wrong, but I'm kind of relieved. Not so much about Drama Club—you've done practically everything—but about the spring play. I'm really not qualified to direct it."

"There needs to be one," Beth said. "The music department had their musical in the fall. They kept it simple, so we could have our show in the spring. Cancelling would not be fair to anyone. Well, I'll think about it. Let's talk about what we'll do on Wednesday. Do you have the winners of the playwriting contest?"

"Yes. There weren't many entries, but we have two winners."

"I was hoping for three," Beth said.

"I know, but only two are good enough to be performed without a great deal of work. We'll have a first and second place, and the others honorable mention, so no one who tried will feel hurt. Do you want to know the names of the winners?"

Beth shook her head. "No, that's okay. I'll wait. You can make the announcement. I asked around at lunchtime, but only Joe's group rehearsed its scene. His group can perform Wednesday, unless they'd rather wait and do it at the castle." Beth shrugged. There was no sense in sharing the problems with Mrs. Hunt. She wasn't going to be around anyway. Beth expected that *Bob's Woodland Adventure* was one of the winners. Probably the only winners, though, would be the playwrights' scripts. The big losers would be Drama Club, itself, and its members.

"Other than announcing the plays and maybe watching Joe's scene, what else do you have planned for the meeting?"

"Figuring out our trip to the dress rehearsal at Crofts," Beth said. "It's next week on Thursday after school. Not enough time to arrange us going together. I think I'll just do a handout of the information and give a time to meet in Crofts' lobby. That way we don't have to bother with permission slips. Parents will take and pick up. I'll call Kurt tonight and get an approximate playing time."

"That makes sense. Anything else?"

"Yes!" Too loud—she must remain calm. "We need more officers. There's just me, and I can't do it all. Art Club is starting Thursday, and that's important to me. I never thought I would have to do so much."

Mrs. Hunt nodded. She didn't say anything, but Beth knew the teacher realized that she had let the group down. It wasn't exactly Mrs. Hunt's fault. She was like Beth—taking on too much, trying to help. Just trying to be nice.

⚷

Hannah dropped off her books and headed for Danny's house. He'd texted her three times during the day, and she needed to tell him not to do that anymore. She could get into trouble. Big trouble. Fortunately, after the first text, she'd left the phone in her locker. She hadn't learned how to turn it off. She'd ask Dad tonight.

It had been a confusing day but not as bad as she'd feared. The school was big, her locker was too far away from most of her classes, and she got lost a few times. But so did other kids. All of the sixth and seventh graders were in the same boat. Even some of the eighth graders had trouble figuring out the new addition. "The stairs are in the wrong places," Beth had complained when Hannah passed her in the hall.

"Finally!" was Danny's welcome. "What kept you?"

"Other than school and then going around to get your work, only to find out your Mom picked it up, so I missed my bus and had to call Dad, but he had a meeting, so I had to wait for the late bus— nothing. Hello to you, too." Maybe that wasn't very friendly, but Hannah was growing tired of Danny's constant demands.

Silence, then, "Sorry. I should have said I'm really glad to see you. I guess I got used to seeing you and Porter every day."

He had been impatient, but so had Hannah. "I'm sorry, too," she said. "Let's start again. How are you?"

"Okay." He patted the novel on his bed—*A Girl of the Limberlost*. "I finished it."

"That was fast. What did you think?"

"The first part was cool when her mom was so mean, but I didn't like the rest."

Hannah nodded. "Well, I liked the whole thing, but I agree about the beginning. It's so much better. Once the mom is nice, everything gets kind of preachy. Should I take the book home?"

Danny shook his head. "I still need it for school. I'm wondering how they can make a play of it. Really hard to stage." Danny knew he was showing off a bit.

"Guess we'll find out next week. Are you going?"

"Yes, especially since it's a dress rehearsal, and Kurt is my friend. I wouldn't go to a regular performance, though."

Hannah bit her tongue. She wanted to ask him a question, but the timing still seemed wrong. Maybe she and Porter could do it together. She was determined to invite Danny to the February dance. If they could make it a threesome—Porter, Danny, and her—would he agree? She thought of her lovely Christmas dress that might not fit next year and sighed. She would call Porter that very night.

Outside, she heard a car pull into the driveway next door. "I can't stay much longer," she said. "Dad's home. Let me see your schoolwork."

"I can figure it out," Danny said. "Tell me about our mystery. Did you see Kammy?"

Hannah shook her head. "Absent, and she is in some of my classes. Maybe she'll be back tomorrow."

"I don't think so."

Hannah didn't either.

Beth texted Kurt—"Can u talk?"

"Going on stage. Will call soon."

Beth was relieved she'd texted rather than called. Crofts was gearing up for tech and dress rehearsals. The performance was a little over a week away. She tackled her homework, even though she needed to type the theater trip information. She finished the last algebra problem just as the phone rang. "Kurt, hi. How are rehearsals going?"

"Horrible, but don't tell anyone."

Beth grinned. She remembered what *Hell Week* was like. Last year, Miss Armstrong preferred that they call it *Tech Week*, so they compromised and called it *Heck Week*. "I won't tell; I promise. I decided that Drama Club members should go separately to your dress rehearsal. They'll get information on Wednesday. That way I don't have to worry about permission slips and things like that. They'll find their own rides there and back. It would help if I had a playing time."

"Good question." Kurt let out a dramatic sigh. On purpose, Beth knew. "Figure two hours, including a fifteen-minute intermission. Don't stay after, though. The director will give us notes, and that takes an eternity."

Beth thought he sounded exhausted but didn't mention it. Instead, she told Kurt about everything going on in Drama Club. "So, after Wednesday, we won't have a sponsor or a director for the spring play. And we've got the one-acts and—I really don't know what to do."

Quiet for a moment, then—"Beth, I've got a wild thought. I heard a rumor today that Miss Armstrong isn't coming back—that she quit. Crofts hasn't been fair to her. She's being treated as if she never put together a prompt book. I guess that's the way they treat new teachers here."

"Wow! And she wanted to teach there so much!"

"Yeah, but she's still living at the castle. Why don't you call her and ask for help? You have her cellphone number, right? Oops, my cue. Gotta go!"

Miss Armstrong. Having her back would be wonderful. But was it possible? Nervously, Beth checked her contact list and made the call. Miss Armstrong answered immediately and listened to Beth's stammered request.

"Beth, you've given me a lot to think about. Perhaps we can help each other. Could you meet me at the castle after school tomorrow? Upstairs in the ballroom kitchen, so we can talk alone?"

"I'll be there," Beth promised. She crossed her fingers. "Please make it happen," she whispered.

After dinner, Danny sat at his table in the living room. Mom was nearby in case he needed help. Dad was better at math but had a late meeting in Milwaukee and was staying overnight. English assignment done—chapters summarized, questions about the book answered, and he'd come up with a vocabulary list. "Mom, will you proofread this before I turn it in?" He handed Mom his laptop before turning to math, the assignment in a book, rather than on the computer.

He missed Porter, and he missed Hannah staying longer. In some ways, it was worse than before vacation. Back then, he just felt rotten physically. Now, he was feeling better but was antsy and lonely. He couldn't believe he was so excited about seeing Kurt's play next week. And he missed real school. Maybe—just maybe—if the Drama Club kids didn't treat him differently because of the wheelchair, he would consider attending a few classes that didn't require the elevator. He put on a happy smile. Just keep on fooling Mom, he told himself. It was weird, but pretending to be happy actually did seem to make him happier.

SCENE 11 – A GHOST AT THE CASTLE

A NOTE FROM MOM MADE it possible for Beth to take a school bus that stopped close to the castle. It was too far to walk now that it got dark so early. Dad would come and get her, Mom promised. Beth used the key to open the back door for the first time since the last club meeting. She kicked away a piece of wood that looked something like an old splintered door wedge.

Miss Armstrong was waiting for her at the kitchen table, with a notebook and a pile of scripts next to her. "Good to see you, Beth. Help yourself to some hot chocolate and banana bread." She gestured toward the stove.

Beth felt huge weights drop from her shoulders as she poured a steaming cup of chocolate, grabbed a slice of banana bread, and sat across from Miss Armstrong. CBMS's former director looked as if she'd never left—like she was in charge again. "You're back, aren't you, Miss Armstrong?"

Miss Armstrong smiled. "I have been very busy today." Miss Armstrong summed it up. She had talked with Mrs. Hunt and the school vice principal. Mrs. Hunt would be in charge of Drama Club the next day, but Miss Armstrong would also attend. "Then I'll run the following meetings and direct the spring play," she said. "That pleases me very much."

A part of Beth—the tired part—wanted to let Miss Armstrong have her own way, but most of her was troubled. She, Beth, was president. Was that to be discounted? Beth wasn't used to standing up to authority, and she needed to. But she told herself to proceed carefully.

"Miss Armstrong, when I saw you here with the piles of scripts, you wouldn't believe how relieved I felt. It was like my mom's reaction when she finally gets Zoe to sleep at night. But then she says, 'as happy as I am when she goes to sleep, I'd go out of my mind if she didn't wake up again.'"

"I'm not sure what you're getting at, Beth. Just say what you mean."

Maybe it wasn't a good enough parallel. "It's just that—I don't want to brag, but if it weren't for me there wouldn't be a Drama Club this year. I do need help, but—"

"But you don't want me to take over," Miss Armstrong finished. Beth couldn't tell how Miss Armstrong felt about that.

"I don't want to hurt your feelings, and we do need you—a lot— but mainly as advisor and sponsor of the club and director of the play. Without you, there won't be one. Last year, our main play was great, but Drama Club hardly existed; it was all about the play. Then you were gone, and Kylie directed *Cinderella, Cinderella*. In the spring, Drama Club just did improv and theater games. The kids suggested what to do, and teachers and subs kind of took turns just being there as chaperones. We didn't even have officers last year."

"True. I never saw the need for them. But what has the club done this year under your leadership?"

Uh-oh—was Miss Armstrong being sarcastic? She sounded kind of snarky. Quickly, Beth told her about the Halloween party, games led by Kurt, the Speakeasy show, and the one-act playwriting contest. "We couldn't use the school, so everyone came here Saturday mornings. Next week we're going to Crofts to see the dress rehearsal, and the following we'll see the performance at the high school."

Miss Armstrong nodded. "Mrs. Hunt told me about the field trips and the play-writing contest. She indicated you were in over your head."

"A little." Beth shrugged "But my dad says that's an important part of learning—finding our limitations. We were doing okay, but the holidays and not being able to rehearse at the castle during that time set us back. The trips will work out, though, and probably the playwriting project, too. Maybe we won't do as much as we'd hoped, but enough so it still will be worthwhile. Mrs. Hunt says there are two winners in the playwriting contest. She would have told me who they are, but I'd rather find out tomorrow."

"How do you see my role, Beth? Just someone who hangs around and watches?"

"No." Beth shook her head slowly. "It's been too time-consuming for me. I just wanted to keep the club going; I never wanted it to take over my life. I think we should elect more officers, and then I'd like you, me, and the rest of the officers to plan meetings together. Then advise us when we're going off track and make suggestions, too. We could really use your feedback on scenes. But let the officers run the meetings. Won't you have enough to do—choosing a play, and then casting and directing it?"

Miss Armstrong laughed, apparently feeling better. "Well, you're right about a lot of things. I was so busy with the fall play last year I let the club fall to the side, and then I left when possibly I shouldn't have." She shook her head. "Beth, I would rather you not repeat this, but I'm no longer at Crofts because I wasn't valued. I decided that because Robbie and I are living here, rent-free, I could afford to tackle some personal dreams. I'd like to write and submit some of my own plays. I've started to write an adaptation of this." She showed Beth the title. "I believe it's something we could do."

"Warning, Miss Armstrong, we don't have many boys."

She laughed. "Let that be my problem. I'll keep the cast small, and I think I might be able to work out something with the English teachers. Something involving extra credit, perhaps."

"I love the book, of course, and—oh, Miss Armstrong—I have the most amazing thought!" Leaning close to Miss Armstrong, although there was no one else around to hear, Beth whispered her idea.

"Wouldn't that be wonderful? Well, we'll just have to see, won't we? Suppose you write out a simple agenda for tomorrow's meeting?" She handed Beth a piece of notebook paper and a pen.

But Beth pulled out her own paper. She had already written one, so all Miss Armstrong did was suggest a different order for a few things. Then she said she'd prefer that the scene Joe directed be performed on Saturday at the castle. "I think Joe would like that better, too," Beth said. She and the teacher were starting to work together.

"It's getting late. I'd better text Dad to come get me."

"Beth, see if you can stay for supper. I'd like to tell you about something going on here. I'll drive you home."

Dad called right back. "Supper is okay, but ask Miss Armstrong to drop you off at the Kennedys. Porter is helping Danny with math and will eat there. I'll come and get you when you're ready."

Later in the car, Beth tried to listen to Miss Armstrong and think at the same time. "Obviously, there isn't a ghost at the castle," Miss Armstrong said, "but there must be an explanation for the missing food from the first-floor kitchen."

Beth agreed. "And neighbors reporting various lights going on and off while you were away." They'd made a big joke of it at the dinner table, where Beth had her best meal since the Christmas feast at Grandma's. The cooking team of Janet and Leland could easily put Smithy out of business.

"It's about time this castle had a haunt," Mr. Markey said, laughing. "All these years without so much as a chain rattling." He seemed pleased by this new development—the way he was about most things. Anything different was an adventure. But Beth thought Leland and Janet were worried.

Leland pulled her aside while Miss Armstrong went for her coat. "I don't want to alarm Mr. Markey," he'd said, "but money is missing from my desk, as well as a spare key to the back door—like the one you have. Our neighbor thought she saw that door ajar a few times— or at least not closed completely—when we first went away."

"Ghosts don't need keys, money, or food," Beth said. "There's got to be a reason, Leland, but I'm not sure how I can help."

Leland patted her shoulder. "Just be aware," he said. "Keep your eyes and ears open. I would prefer not calling the police, but I will if anything else happens."

As soon as her supper was over, Hannah, too, went to Danny's house. He'd texted earlier, asking her over to talk about the mystery. There wasn't much to talk about, since neither she nor Porter wanted to mention the truck. But she wanted to find out if Danny had learned anything more from his dad about Kammy's grandfather. "She wasn't in school again today," Hannah said.

Porter shrugged. "Maybe she's moved away since her grandfather can't take care of her."

"Then someone better let the office know," Hannah said crossly. "Our homeroom teacher marked her absent again, and he looked annoyed."

"The school probably thinks her family is still on vacation and didn't bother to let them know," Danny said.

"We don't even know if she has a family." Porter shook his head. "Has your dad said anything else, Danny? Like maybe her grandfather's last name? I wonder if it's the same as Kammy's. I don't remember it."

"Williams," said Hannah. "Kamirah Williams. I was thinking I should go to the office and ask about her. But I'm new and, well, I don't even know where the office is."

"I've got it!" Porter blurted out. "Maybe we could ask—"

"Hi, guys!"

"Speak of the devil."

"Excuse me?"

Porter grinned at his sister. "Sorry, I meant *almost* speaking of the devil. I was about to suggest that you do something when you made your grand entrance."

"Right," Danny said. "Beth could do it."

"First, Beth needs to know what she might do. Suppose you tell me, Hannah. You, at least, may be reasonably sane."

Yes, the boys were right, Hannah thought. Beth was a friend and discreet. "Well, we know a few things you don't," she started.

"I imagine you do, considering you have a secret club. Out with it."

"Okay, but we're not saying how we know. We found out that the old man who was stabbed at the West Village Flats is Kammy's grandfather."

"What?"

"I know, it's awful, and we don't know what's happened to her. You haven't been able to contact her, and she hasn't come back to school."

"She probably moved," Beth said, as Porter had before. "Poor kid. She seemed to like Drama Club. But what can I do about it?"

"If she's moved, the office doesn't know about it. She's being marked absent. You're president of Drama Club, Beth, and tomorrow is our meeting. If she doesn't come, could you go to the office on Thursday and check? Porter and I aren't even sure where the office is. You could say that you tried to reach Kammy over break and that the phone has been disconnected."

Porter nodded. "You could even say that some of the members are worried about her. That's true."

"It certainly is. And now that you've told me about her grandfather, I am, too. Yes, I'll go, or maybe I'll ask Mrs. Hunt."

"An adult," Hannah said. "Yes, that would be better, unless Mrs. Hunt blows you off."

Beth shook her head. "She won't. She listens. I can guarantee that."

The door opened. "Sounds kind of serious in here, but I'll need to remove the Walters delegation. How are you doing, Danny? Haven't seen you in a while. That must be the fancy new wheelchair."

"I'm good, Uncle John. I'm planning to enter the electric wheelchair Olympics."

Beth and Porter's dad laughed. "That I'll be sure not to miss."

"I think Beth wanted to say more," Danny said. "She knows something."

Hannah shrugged. "Maybe she's just tired. She probably still has homework."

"Maybe, but there was more. I know her pretty well."

"I don't think we told her too much, do you, Danny?"

"No, just right, I think. But Beth is smart. She's figured out our club solves mysteries."

"Or tries to." Hannah giggled. Then a pinging noise made her look down at her phone. "Dad wants me to come home—now! He used an exclamation point, so I guess he means it. I'll see you tomorrow, Danny."

"Right after Drama Club. I want to know what happens."

"I'll try."

As soon as she was gone, Danny stared down at his useless legs. "This is nuts!" His friends must think he was a nuisance, relying on them for everything and nagging them to do something that could get them into trouble. Aunt Sue and Uncle John had made it clear to Porter he was not to go to the west side, and he was fairly sure Hannah's dad and uncle wouldn't want her there, either, if they knew what it was like. Probably the only reason they'd gone was because they felt sorry for him. "Stupid legs," he said. He could stand up, with assistance from his physical therapist. Maybe he could do it here, too—on his own. First, he made sure the wheelchair brake was on. Then, slowly, he gripped its arms and stood. It was hard, but maybe if he did it a few times each day and—

"Danny, what are you doing?"

He almost fell and would have if Kylie hadn't grabbed his arms and eased him back down.

"I was doing fine, Kylie."

"You almost fell."

"Only because you startled me. Why is Dad the only one who knocks?"

"Okay, I will. But knocking might have startled you, too. You did stand, though. Didn't you want anyone to see you?"

Danny shook his head.

"I think I understand. How about you just do it when I'm the room? I won't tell anyone. And you can make a sign for the door."

"Mom will ignore it, but thanks, Kylie. I'd like that."

"Not until after rehearsals, of course. Now I thought I'd take Bingo out one last time before bed."

All the little dog needed was to hear the word "out," and, leash in mouth, he was at Kylie's side.

Soon, Danny decided, he wouldn't need anyone's help for anything. He'd walk his own dog, find his own adventures, and run. Yes, most of all, he would run. Meanwhile, he'd wait for Dad to come and help him into his pajamas.

SCENE 12 – The Key to Everything

AS BETH PASSED OUT THE notices about the theater trip to Crofts, she caught Hannah's eye. "No," Hannah mouthed, shaking her head. That meant Kammy had not returned to school and clearly was not in Drama Club. The room they'd been assigned didn't have enough chairs for all members, never mind enough space for theater games and skits. Not only would Beth have to ask Mrs. Hunt to check in the office about Kammy, she would also need to request a larger room. This was not going to work. Thank goodness, they could meet at the castle. She looked at Joe, and he rolled his eyes.

Then Mrs. Hunt introduced Miss Armstrong, letting the club know the change in plans. "I have enjoyed my time with you," she said, "but am unable to continue because of other duties. And you are fortunate that Miss Armstrong is back at the helm. She has more experience than all of us put together."

Miss Armstrong smiled and addressed the group. "I know many of you eighth graders and am looking forward to getting acquainted with all of you. Under Beth's guidance, you've certainly accomplished a great deal. I will ask Mrs. Hunt to do one more thing for us. Please ask the administration to please, please, please find us a larger space!"

Everyone applauded and cheered. Miss Armstrong continued, "I hope you'll all come to the castle on Saturday. I understand that we will be treated to a scene, directed by Joe, someone I don't know. Raise your hand, Joe."

Joe stood, smiling and waving, in presidential mode, Beth thought. She stood, too, just as a reminder that she was president. "Joe's group was the only one that managed to rehearse over break," she said. "They deserve a lot of credit. We will be planning other events this Saturday, so please be sure to come, where we have room, and the refreshments are always yummy!" That brought the usual applause. "Now, before we rush out to catch the activity bus, Mrs. Hunt has a special announcement."

"While only one scene was prepared, several people managed to enter the One-Act contest. In fact, we have two winners and two honorable mentions."

Although Beth hadn't had time to care before, suddenly she was nervous. Would she and Hannah win? She knew Mrs. Hunt was just being kind by having honorable mentions.

"The first-place winning script is a one-person endeavor," Mrs. Hunt announced. "The play, a satire called *Nevermore, Uncle Edgar*, was written by sixth-grader, Lee Lester." While all applauded, the sixth graders were loudest. Beth exchanged glances with Hannah, who smiled and shrugged.

"How did you ever think to write this, Lee?" Miss Armstrong asked.

Lee blushed. "My dad still insists on reading to the whole family. We all protest, but we really like it. Dad is a big Edgar Allen Poe fan. After he read "The Raven" and a few short stories, I got the idea of making Poe a crazy guy who had a niece. I think it worked."

"It did indeed," said Mrs. Hunt. "It might be wise for everyone to read the poem before seeing it performed. Now then, second place and also a show that will be performed is *Bob's Woodland Adventure* by seventh- and eighth-graders, Hannah Rendina and Beth Walters. The two plays are unique and will appeal to different audiences."

Beth smiled but barely listened to the applause. It was good that new people, such as Lee and Hannah, had won. It was also good that as president, she hadn't come in first. Later, when she got home, she realized that she hadn't even heard who'd won honorable mention. Drama Club needed a secretary to take minutes.

She stood to end the meeting and thank Mrs. Hunt once again, adding, "We're so happy to have Miss Armstrong back with us and hope to see all of you at the castle this Saturday morning at ten."

Beth managed to stop Mrs. Hunt on her way out. "I'm sure Kammy is fine, Beth, but I will check. It's good of you to care."

To Beth's surprise, Porter was waiting to walk home with her. "Nice but unexpected," she said. "What's up?"

"Thought you might know more than Hannah and could save me some sanity when Danny starts calling."

Beth smiled. "I imagine it's getting old. His friends and family must want him to walk again almost as much as he does. Kylie said she caught him trying to stand on his own. She promised to help him, but she's got a lot of rehearsals now."

"So what do you know? Hannah told me Kammy still isn't in school. Did you have a chance to talk to Mrs. Hunt?"

"Yeah, that's why I was late getting out. She'll talk to the vice principal today or tomorrow."

They just turned onto their street when Beth's phone rang. "It's Mrs. Hunt," she whispered to Porter. "Yes? Of course I'll let you know if I hear anything. Yes, her friends are, too. Thanks for getting back to me. Goodbye." Beth walked in silence.

"Well? What did she say?"

Beth shook her head. "The office doesn't know anything, other than she's been absent. No one in her family has contacted the school. They can't reach her, either; phone disconnected, just like Joe and Hannah said."

"Did you tell Mrs. Hunt about Kammy's grandfather?"

"Not yet," Beth said. "I think you and your mysterious club know more than you're saying, Porter."

"Maybe, but so do you, Beth."

"Yeah, I guess I do, but . . ."

"But?"

"But I need a little more thinking time. We'll put it all together soon. I think Drama Club on Saturday is going to be important. See if you can get yourself invited for an overnight with Danny on Friday. I'll do the same with Kylie. We'll pool our knowledge, and then decide what to do. Tell Hannah not to go anywhere."

Porter nodded. "And let's make sure Mom and Dad don't have plans that require babysitters."

Dad had a late meeting at Community, and Uncle Martin wouldn't get back from the city until at least seven, so Hannah was able to dash over to Danny's without worrying about being reminded of homework or chores. The only chore absolutely necessary was a quick walk with Bingo. "Why can't you be like other dogs and hate the cold and snow?" she complained.

Bingo gave her a look as if to say, "What do you know about other dogs?"

"You're right, Bingo, but just you wait until spring. If no one wants to help me, I'll find a dog myself. This time next year, I'll be an authority on dogs." Hannah could have sworn Bingo shrugged before making one last run through the backyard, returning with a sorrowful-looking bone. "Okay, you can bring it inside, but it stays in the mudroom, understand?"

"Where's Bingo?" Danny growled at her.

"Hello to you, too," Hannah said. "He found an old bone he must have buried in the fall. He wouldn't be parted from it, so they're both in the mudroom."

"Thank you for walking him," Danny muttered. "I guess I should say that more often."

Hannah nodded. "Yes, you should." She sat next to him at the card table in the living room, where he had made a start on a jigsaw puzzle of a mountain scene. She stared at his bleak face. "What's wrong?"

"Adults all day long." Danny sighed. "And having to pretend to be cheerful so they don't decide I'm depressed and need a psychologist."

Hannah, who had needed a few, thought that a psychologist wouldn't hurt Danny one bit. "Well, I guess I'll go home then. I don't want you to pretend for me, and I'm not in the mood for downers."

"Hannah, wait!" But she was gone.

She wasn't out of hearing, though. She'd separate Bingo from his bone and let him back into the house, where he'd go straight to Danny. Maybe Bingo would cheer him up, but it was not her turn.

⚷

"Hey, fella." Danny leaned over and gave Bingo a scratch. "So Hannah didn't go straight home; she let you inside first. But she didn't tell me anything, even though she must have known I'd been waiting to hear. She didn't have to be so mean. She didn't even ask me how my day went." Bingo gave him a quizzical look. "Okay, so I didn't ask her, either." He'd give her a chance to cool off before texting her. But first, he'd call Porter.

"Hi, Danny, I was about to call you. Guess Hannah told you that Kammy still isn't back."

"Uh, no," Danny said. "I don't know anything. Did Beth talk to Mrs. Hunt?"

"Yes. The school is concerned, too. Beth wants us to get together at your house Friday night."

"Us?"

"Yeah, you, me, Beth, and Hannah. Beth hopes she and I can stay overnight. She's going to call Kylie, but would you ask your parents?"

"Sure, but why?"

"Beth says we need to share everything we know, even if we think we might get into trouble. She thinks we're holding something back, and she said that she is, too."

I knew it, Danny thought. "Porter, I think we might solve the mysteries after all." He waited for Porter to disagree or make fun of him. He wasn't prepared for Porter's reaction.

"I think so, too," Porter said quietly. "And I think Kammy is the key — to everything."

"Maybe not everything," Danny whispered, after they said goodbye. He reminded himself again. But how many reminders did he need? Friendship was the key — to everything. He looked at the cellphone, still in his hand. "Hannah, I'm really sorry," he texted. "Please forgive me."

SCENE 13 – MORE LIKE A GAME

HAD SCHOOL EVER DRAGGED ON so slowly? Hannah glared at the classroom clock that Thursday afternoon. She'd texted Danny at lunchtime. "It's okay. Can't see U today because of Smithy's and homework. Ask Kylie to walk Bingo. Till tomorrow nite. Can't wait."

Well, it was true about wanting tomorrow night to come, but she was nervous. They were going to tell each other everything? That meant she would have to show the photos of the white truck. She wondered what Beth and Kylie would think they should do about it, but mostly she hoped Danny wouldn't go ballistic because they hadn't told him before. She was telling the truth about homework, and she'd promised Uncle Martin she'd clean her room. As for Smithy's, a bunch of seventh-grade girls asked her to go, and she decided to say yes. Dad promised to pick her up there. "You need some girlfriends," he said.

But it was also true she was being mean. She hadn't responded to Danny's apology last night. He hurt her feelings when he took her for granted. She was tired of apologies, although she owed him one, too. How would she feel if she were stuck in a wheelchair while her friends were out doing things? But Danny should at least pretend he cared about other people. He was safe, in his nice house with plenty to eat and people and pets who loved him. Whereas Kammy . . . Where are you, Kammy?

The bell rang at last, and her science class joined the hordes filling the halls. Hannah waved at Beth, clutching her sketchbook, on the way to Art Club. "Over here, Hannah!" yelled a girl named Avery, who seemed in charge of gathering the group going to Smithy's. Smile, Hannah, she told herself. Be friendly. She waved and joined Avery.

Danny knew he was being punished. Hannah had returned briefly to that grim girl he'd met last August, and it was his own darned fault. It would be okay, but he'd better give her some space. He couldn't even count on Porter to relieve his boredom. Porter had texted after school that he had to go right home and babysit Zoe. His parents were going out tomorrow night, but he'd talked them into hiring a babysitter so he and Beth could have their overnight. "Can't push it," Porter wrote.

In other words, Danny concluded, other people have lives, too — even his good friends. If the accident had never happened, wouldn't he be busy with winter sports and guilty of ignoring them? Something to think about. He stroked Boots, cuddled up in his lap, causing her to jump down in alarm. "Sorry, Boots. Were you having a nightmare?" Cats definitely dream. At least, his cat did. That had to be what all the whisker twitching and chattering were about. "I'll bet you were about to catch a bird, Boots, and I ruined it." He patted his lap. "Do you want to come back up?" But Boots did not. It was time to box Bingo's ears and tackle his tail. Bingo, who had been sleeping at Danny's feet, yawned, and then looked up expectantly. "Surely it's time for a walk," he seemed to say.

"Look what waking one sleeping kitten did," Danny said. "Bingo, sometimes I wish you were a different kind of dog. I wish I could roll to the mudroom, open the door, and have you dash out to do your business and come right back. It's only five above out there, but you would think it was a balmy spring day and keep on going. You and I must be patient until Mom or Kylie comes home. And neither of us is very good at patience."

Sighing, but filled with positive resolve, Danny did his sitting exercises and then returned to schoolwork.

Study halls at the end of the day on Friday didn't make sense, if you didn't have weekend homework. Wouldn't it be nice if they'd just let Beth go home early? Well, no, maybe not. Mom would be certain to have chores waiting. As it was, she wasn't thrilled about hiring a babysitter tonight because of losing her built-in ones. What Mom didn't know was that Beth had talked Marla into doing it and that Marla would refuse payment. Marla wasn't interested until Beth explained a little about the urgency of the meeting, promising she'd give Marla the whole story sometime soon. "Okay, but you'll owe me!" Then Marla grinned and said Beth would owe her another overnight as soon as the high school play was over. Definitely something to look forward to, Beth thought, especially if all the SSC drama was over, too.

She'd used this time to make lists. First Art Club. That was relaxing, for a change. She'd been nominated president but had turned it down because of Drama Club. Actually, she might have preferred it, but Drama Club happened first. The club's sponsor, Mr. Henderson, asked them to bring their sketchpads next week. If they didn't have one, they were available at the school store. They were also to make suggestions for a theme for the club's spring exhibit. Beth wrote down her idea—Seasonal Sketches of Castle Bluff. It was okay. Maybe someone would come up with something better.

Next, a Drama Club agenda for Saturday. Easy. She emailed it to Miss Armstrong for approval. Then she thought of the last list, the trickiest one of all. What did she want to tell and find out during the sleepover tonight? She wanted to know exactly how Porter and Hannah knew the old man in the West Village Flats was Kamirah Williams's grandfather and anything else the secretive club was keeping from her and Kylie. Then she wanted to let them know about her dinner at the castle and Leland's worries about a ghost—one that stole food, money, and the back door key.

"The back door," she whispered, suddenly recalling the piece of wood she'd kicked away. At the time, she'd thought it looked like an old-fashioned door wedge, the kind in her elementary school when she was in second grade. Unbidden and to her horror, she also remembered what had happened after the last meeting at the castle, the one before the holidays. She and Marla had been in a hurry to pick up their two sisters and go to the movies, but Kammy wanted to go back into the castle because she'd forgotten her scene, and Beth said, "I'll unlock the door and then set it, so all you have to do is slam the door and make sure it locks." And that night, Kurt told her he'd seen a light in the castle. She'd thought that meant they hadn't left yet or that Leland had a light on a timer. That could have been the case. She had winter break on her mind and wasn't concerned. But now, putting it all together, maybe she was taking a giant leap forward—but she didn't think so.

Finally, the bell! Time to meet Porter at his locker. Mom had dropped off their belongings with Aunt Jane that morning, and given them a note of permission to take the bus stopping the closest to the Kennedys' house. Beth crossed her fingers. It was going to be some night!

⚷

Danny, of course, wanted to start the proceedings immediately. He held in his frustrations admirably, Beth thought, while he waited for his mother and father to leave for a dinner party in Milwaukee. Aunt Jane and Uncle Dan were pleased that Danny's friends would be keeping him company and that Hannah's father next door had promised to keep an eye on things. "Hang in there, Danny," she whispered. "We still have to wait for Kylie to get home. How about we talk after dinner? For now, just have fun, okay?"

"Okay." Danny smiled at her. When was the last time he'd had a good time? He relaxed when he was playing, in a limited way, with Bingo and Boots, but even the SSC meetings were depressing because he couldn't really participate. Then he remembered his resolve to care about his friends. Beth left him to take her overnight bag up to Kylie's room. Porter had gone to Danny's old room upstairs. But Hannah was there now, right in front of him—just returning from walking Bingo—and looking around uncertainly. Other than a couple of texts, they hadn't communicated since their big blowup the other day. "Hey, Hannah," he said.

"Hi, Danny." She sat at the card table next to him. And then— "Wow, Mrs. Kennedy! You look gorgeous!"

"You sure do, Mom, and way to go, Dad!" Their entrance served to break the ice. "You look almost like your wedding pictures."

"Almost is right," Mom said. She kissed him on the forehead.

"No wild parties now," Dad said, "and don't wait up for us."

"Don't worry, Mr. Kennedy. My dad and Uncle Martin are on high alert. Have a good time."

As soon as they left, Danny shook his head. "I am not used to my parents looking so, well, romantic."

"I am about mine," Hannah said. "That's because it's all kind of new to Dad and Uncle Martin. For the longest time, they wouldn't even hug or hold hands in front of me." She told Danny about the exchange of rings on Christmas morning. "They finally decided they lived in a place where it was safe."

"That is so cool," Danny said. "Uh, did you have a good time at Smithy's?"

Hannah shrugged. "It was okay. One girl was nice enough, a sixth grader named Laurel. The rest wanted to talk about boys and knock down other girls—especially Laurel's sister, Avery. Regular cats. No offense, Boots," she said to the little black kitten kneading the blanket on Danny's lap.

"I never had the chance to be part of the Smithy's after-school crowd," he said. Then, perhaps fearing that Hannah might think he was feeling sorry for himself — "Maybe I won't want to when the time comes."

"We'll be our own crowd, once you walk again," Hannah said. "You, me, Porter, Laurel, and maybe Kammy."

"Yeah, Kammy. That would be nice," Danny said.

Beth and Porter interrupted them, and soon Kylie arrived. "Home from rehearsal at last," she sighed.

"How's it going?" Danny asked, ignoring Kylie's startled look. For how long had he given the impression of not caring about anyone but himself?

"How is it going — a question that should never be asked less than two weeks before a show," Kylie answered.

Beth grinned. "That bad, huh? Kurt screams when I ask. But his show is in exactly a week."

"Sorry," Danny said. "I forgot how loaded that question is."

"I don't understand," Hannah said.

"You will!" all replied in unison.

"On that, I shall order the pizza," Kylie announced. "We can have whatever we want. Dad called this morning and gave his credit card number."

"Great!" Danny said. "I, for one, am starving!"

Kylie wrote down the complicated order, then made the call. "Gotta go upstairs. Beth, open the door if the pizza comes before I'm back down. Dad took care of the tip already. Hannah, I wish there was room for you to stay overnight."

"Not a problem. I'll stay late and be wide awake for Drama Club tomorrow."

"Don't remind me." Beth groaned.

All of a sudden, Danny felt left out again. His friends were going to Drama Club in the morning, and his sister would have Saturday tech at the high school. Could he go to Drama Club, too? There was a ramp next to the front steps of the castle and a new elevator inside that went all the way up to the ballroom. That part was easy enough. But Dad or Mom would have to drive him and the wheelchair, and they wouldn't be getting home until late tonight. Should he text them? No, that wouldn't be fair. He'd think about it, and then if he decided he wanted to go, he'd leave a note.

Every slice of pizza had been consumed, and Hannah had taken Bingo out for another jaunt around the yard. Finally, the group moved into the living room—an odd place for a party—if it was one—but the basement was out of the question for Danny. Everyone looked expectantly at Beth.

"Okay," she said. "I guess because I called for this gathering, it makes sense for me to—"

"Be the referee," Porter interrupted, causing laughter all around.

Beth continued. "I hope it won't come to that. First, I'd like everyone to agree not to get angry or upset by anything that is said. Except for Kylie, we're all keeping things back. I know I am."

"I just don't want to get into trouble," Porter said.

"And I don't want Danny mad at me," Hannah added. Danny stared at her. She shrugged.

"The thing to remember," Beth said, "is that we're here to figure out what happened to Kamirah Williams—why she disappeared and where she is now. I have a good idea about the where and when, but maybe we should talk about the why. Who wants to start?"

"I will," Danny said. "I don't think I know much, but I kind of started it."

Then he told Beth and his sister about walking Kammy home after the Halloween party. "It was dark, and she didn't have anyone to come get her."

"We didn't know where she lived, at first," Porter said.

"The West Village Flats," Danny said.

"What?" Kylie and Beth shouted.

"Referee yourself, Beth," Hannah said. "I told Dad, and he said it was the right thing to do, but he didn't want me to go back again without an adult."

Beth nodded. "Our parents would flip, but it was the right thing."

"Maybe," Kylie said, "but it might have been better to get her a ride, but if you didn't know where she lived just then . . . Go on, Danny."

"I think it was after my accident—I don't remember exactly; I'm a little messed up on time—Dad told us about the man being stabbed at the West Village Flats. And, uh, I thought maybe our club could solve the mystery." Kylie made a rude noise.

Beth shrugged. "Actually, Kylie, I think they're pretty close to doing just that. Right around that time is when Kammy disappeared. She was supposed to be in a scene that was rehearsing over winter break, but she said she didn't have an email address, and the phone number she gave us didn't work."

"Disconnected," Hannah said, "and it worked fine when I called her before break. She was never allowed to do anything with me, though. Then we did something that might get us into trouble—at least Porter and I did."

"My fault," Danny said loudly, causing a sharp bark and a startled hiss. "I guess Bingo and Boots blame me, too."

"Not really your fault, although you nagged us plenty. Hannah and I didn't have to go along with it."

"It was our choice," Hannah admitted. "Danny was only Command Central."

"And a super pain-in-the-rear texter," Porter added

The three SSC members grinned at the memory. "After Christmas, Porter and I returned to the West Village Flats." Hannah held up her hand, cautioning the older girls to keep still. "We went around noon this time—not safe, exactly, but not as dangerous as nighttime."

"And there was hardly any traffic," Porter added.

"We wanted to see if we could find Kammy. Well, we didn't, but we learned plenty—from a mom playing outside with her little kids. The kids were nice."

"Kammy had sort of been their babysitter. Hannah and I didn't think we'd find out anything about the man who had been stabbed, although Danny was hoping we would."

"And they did," Danny said. "The old man is Kammy's grandfather."

"So that's how you found out," Beth said.

Hannah nodded. "We learned Kammy's address and something that doesn't have anything to do with her, but that doesn't matter now."

Beth stood and stretched. "I need to send a text, and I think we should take bathroom breaks. I don't know about you, but I had way too much soda."

"One if by land, two if by sea," Porter yelled incongruously, racing upstairs. Danny wheeled quickly into his bedroom and to the adjoining bathroom. Sighing, Kylie made her way to the basement, beckoning Hannah to follow.

Beth sent a joint text to Miss Armstrong and Leland. "Please ask everyone at the castle to come to Drama Club tomorrow. We need you! Gee, too, if she's there." Then she sent a private text to Leland. "We're close to figuring out your ghost. We need everyone in the ballroom, away from the rest of the castle."

Soon there were two responses. "Will do," Miss Armstrong wrote. And then Leland sent a "thumbs up." Leland using an emoji? Hysterical!

"Okay, Beth, your turn," Danny said, as soon as they came back together. "We've told everything we know."

"Okay, here goes. I've made one colossal mistake." Quickly, she explained how she'd been remiss at making sure the back door to the castle was locked. "Marla and I were late getting to the movies, but I should have waited and checked." Then she told them about much later finding the wooden wedge and learning that neighbors reported seeing the door ajar and lights—at a time the castle residents were away.

"Interesting but not conclusive," Porter said.

Hannah nodded. "Makes you wonder, though."

"I'll now head closer to conclusive, to use your fancy word, little brother, and then you can tell me what you think."

All leaned toward Beth. She sounded formal and mysterious—unlike herself. A twinkle in her eye indicated she was acting that way deliberately. "Then I found out on Tuesday that the castle is haunted; it has its very own ghost!"

"What?"

"No such thing!"

"You're kidding!"

"Are they scared?"

Beth laughed. "One at a time. No, I'm not kidding. As for being scared, Mr. Markey is delighted. He said it's about time they had a haunt. Janet and Miss Armstrong are nervous, and Leland is concerned. He told me that food and money are missing, as well as a spare key to the back door." Beth paused, enjoying their shocked faces. "Now, mystery clubbers, what is your conclusion?"

"Kammy!" Hannah, Porter, and Danny shouted.

"Exactly," Beth said. "And tomorrow, we're going to find her. I sent Miss Armstrong and Leland texts, asking that everyone staying at the castle come to the Drama Club meeting tomorrow morning. Then, when everyone is eating refreshments, Hannah, Porter, and I will go on a ghost hunt!"

Danny definitely wanted to go to Drama Club now. It might not be a good idea to text his parents, but he was going to anyway. He took his phone out of his pocket. Hey, they'd beat him to it! He was concentrating so hard he hadn't heard the ping.

"We're fine," he wrote back. "Lots of fun. Do you think I could go to Drama Club tomorrow? There's a ramp into the castle and an elevator inside. Mr. Markey is going to attend the meeting. Would you be able to give me a ride?"

Dad answered with a happy face. Even though he'd be plenty tired. Dad was always excited when Danny wanted to do anything positive—Mom, too. He hoped they would understand when they learned why he was so anxious to go.

Then Hannah also received a text. "Dad wants me home, even though Uncle Martin is coming over to wait until Mr. and Mrs. Kennedy get home."

"Time to break things up, anyway," Beth said. "We all have to get up early tomorrow, except—"

"Except no one," Danny said. "Dad just said I could go to Drama Club. So I'm going to be a ghost buster, too!"

Porter walked Hannah to the mudroom. "I'll go out with Bingo," he called to the rest of the group. But he whispered to Hannah, "I want to talk to you. Did you decide not to tell about seeing the white truck?"

"Yeah, the most important thing was Kammy. I decided nothing should distract from her. The truck is important, too, but in a different way. That's more of a police matter. I'll explain what happened to Mr. Kennedy and show him the photos. He'll know what to do."

"Good idea. I wonder what will happen tomorrow. That ghost hunting plan sounds more like a game than anything. What if we don't find her?"

"No idea," Hannah said. "But what if we do? She doesn't have a home to go back to. What then?"

Porter shook his head. "See ya, Hannah."

"See ya, Porter." Shivering from the cold and a sudden revelation, Hannah rushed to her back door. Danny was still her best friend, of course, but for some reason she felt closer to Porter.

SCENE 14 – A GHOST REVEALED

"RISE AND SHINE, SON."

Danny made a groaning noise. Really, he was having the best dream. Oh, well, he forgot what it was about. "Okay, Dad."

"Your choice. Sleep or go to the castle. Doesn't bother me."

"Oh, right. Thanks, Dad. I think I can dress myself. I'll give you a shout if I have trouble."

"Sounds good. Everyone slept late but Kylie. I dropped her off at the high school at eight. Your mom will pick her up. You can text me when you're ready to come home. Beth and Porter are just stirring now, and the lights are on next door. You get ready and feed the pets, and I'll fix breakfast."

Danny eased himself into the wheelchair.

Dad started out, then turned back. "I don't know if it's a good time, but you did seem interested. We heard it on the radio coming back last night. The man who was stabbed at the West Village Flats didn't make it."

"Oh, no! That poor man!"

Dad seemed surprised. "Well, yes. I expected you to say that it's now murder."

"Yes." But instead of acting excited, Danny looked sad. Unless there were relatives somewhere they didn't know about, Kammy was homeless.

Dad gave him a penetrating glance, and then left for the kitchen.

"I wonder," Danny whispered to Boots. "Do you think Kammy knows who stabbed her grandfather? Is that why she disappeared—because she's scared?"

Boots stared at him, and then blinked. "That's exactly what I was thinking," she seemed to say.

"And someone called 911 from a payphone, Boots. I'll bet it was Kammy, calling on the only payphone left in town, the one outside of Smithy's."

Dressed and in the kitchen, Danny managed to whisper to Porter, "Dad just told me Kammy's grandfather died. Tell Beth."

And then Beth would pass it on to Hannah. We're playing a grown-up version of telephone, Danny thought. Except this isn't a game.

Beth called Drama Club to order. First on the agenda was to distribute trip information to anyone who hadn't received it or who had lost it. She decided to make the visit to the high school the same deal—parents providing transportation. It was too hard to arrange carpools until she had more help. "We'll be seeing the actual performance at the high school," she said, "but we won't be charged admission. Please let me know during the week if you're coming, so I'll know how many comp tickets to get from Kylie."

Next, she brought up the topic of officers. "We won't have a Wednesday meeting this week because of the trip to Crofts on Thursday. But elections will be the following Wednesday. Please be thinking about who to nominate—I think a vice president and a combined secretary/treasurer should do it—and if you'd be willing to serve if you're nominated. I'll now turn the meeting over to Joe and his group of actors."

"Five minutes tops to set up," he said.

Only five minutes? Pretty amazing, considering that they'd had no rehearsal time at the castle. From the kitchen, she could smell the incredible odor of deep-fried donuts, Gee's specialty. Surely if Kammy were hiding somewhere close by, she would not be able to resist. Gee insisted that after the program, everyone should file into the kitchen for mugs of hot chocolate. Janet and Leland would bring platters of donuts into the ballroom.

"Okay, Gee," Beth had said loudly, "but leave a few extras." (For Kammy, who might be listening.) She led Gee into the ballroom, away from the kitchen door. "Then please stay in the ballroom with the others. No one should go back into the kitchen until Hannah or Porter say it's okay. No seconds on hot chocolate or needing the sink or anything." As president, Beth decided she'd also stay in the ballroom. Her absence might be noticed. Hannah and Porter, who knew Kammy, would be the ghostbusters.

"I'll bring in plenty of paper towels," Gee promised.

The five minutes were almost up. Mr. Markey was chatting with Priyanka, and Danny looked pleased, sitting next to Robbie. Beth wondered if Robbie's seeing-eye dog was downstairs somewhere and if it was a problem for Kammy—if she's here, Beth thought. Don't get so sure of yourself.

"Showtime!" Joe announced grandly. "Everyone take your seats, please!"

Beth thought the actors did a good job with their scene about a group of young girls excluding another because of the color of her skin, especially since all of them, except for Imani, were brand new to theater. Something about the scene bothered her, though, but she wasn't sure what. Not the content because it was well written—the characters in the scene (if not the director) did learn a lesson—but something else. She and the entire audience clapped while Joe gave his cast a standing ovation. Tacky, Beth thought. But what did Miss Armstrong think? "Would you give us your critique, Miss Armstrong?" she asked politely.

Miss Armstrong stood, smiling. "I'd love to," she said. "First, let me commend all of you for your effort. Joe, you did an especially fine job of making good use of space. Actors, your projection was excellent, and I felt that you understood your characters.

"Imani, you had the most difficult role, and we were with you until the very end—when, I'm afraid, you lost us. Audience, I'd like to ask you about Imani's display of emotion. How did you feel about it?"

That was the right question, Beth thought. Miss Armstrong had spotted the problem, even though she wasn't sure why it was one. She watched the Drama Club members looking around, each perhaps hoping someone else would go first. Hannah raised her hand slowly. Miss Armstrong, not knowing her name, nodded.

"When Imani let loose crying, I noticed that the audience was uncomfortable. We were squirming, maybe embarrassed. Imani was really good, though." Hannah's voice faltered.

"Yes, she was. Anyone else?"

Porter raised his hand. "Porter?" Beth wondered how Miss Armstrong knew his name.

"I don't know about anyone else, but I felt manipulated—like Imani was instructing me how to feel. So I stopped empathizing with her."

Beth grinned. She was always both amused and proud when Porter displayed his super vocabulary. He wasn't showing off—he was just Porter.

"Exactly, Porter," Miss Armstrong said. "There's a famous theater quotation I'd like you to know. No need to write it down or memorize it; just remember its meaning: *If you cried a little less, the audience would cry more.*" Miss Armstrong repeated the quotation, and then looked around at the students trying to grasp it.

"Oh, I get it!" To Beth's surprise, it was Danny waving his hand to get attention. "We would have felt sorrier for Imani if she tried not to cry. We would have thought she was really brave if she tried to hold back her tears. It's like if you feel too sorry for yourself, maybe other people won't. But they'll admire you if you have courage—even if you feel terrible."

Beth watched Hannah and Porter nodding to each other. They saw their friend not only understanding the quotation, but also applying it to himself.

"Very good, Danny," Miss Armstrong said. Then she asked Imani to run that part of the scene again, following Danny's suggestion. Everyone saw the difference; it was so much better.

"You did fine, Joe," Miss Armstrong said, noticing he looked glum. "Directors with years and years of experience make that error. And sometimes, actors suddenly overact during a performance, even if directed not to. 'My character took over,' the actor might say. No, sorry, characters aren't allowed to take over. Actors, even more than directors, control their characters. Always remember that."

And that is exactly why we need Miss Armstrong, Beth thought.

"One last thing before we break for refreshments," Miss Armstrong said. "Joe, you'll definitely be a director for a one-act. I'd like to request, though, that casting, rehearsing, and performing wait until after the spring play we'll try to present before spring break." Then, seeing Joe start to object, she continued. "I will announce and cast the show in the next few weeks, but I won't allow anyone working on another play to be involved in the main stage spring show." That was enough to keep anyone from objecting, including Joe.

Gee charged in from the kitchen at that point and said she couldn't keep the hot chocolate hot much longer, and Beth adjourned the meeting.

Finally, everyone had their paper mugs of hot chocolate and returned to the ballroom to tackle Gee's donuts. It worked out perfectly, Hannah thought, for she and Porter lingered behind and planned what to do. Porter whispered that he would use the steep back stairs from the kitchen, start on the first floor of the castle and work his way up, searching as many rooms as possible. He would send her a quick text if he found Kammy.

"I'll hide here behind the soda crates. I don't think she'll be able to resist the smell of those donuts." Hannah pointed to a small platter on the table. "I'm having trouble, myself, keeping my mitts off of them."

After promising Porter she'd text if she found Kammy first and after watching the last Drama Club member return to the ballroom, Porter and Hannah took their stations, Porter to search and Hannah to wait.

It didn't take Hannah long to wish she were also a searcher. Crouching down in a corner was not comfortable. And there were weird flip-flops going on in her stomach. Nervousness, yes, but mainly it was those darned donuts. She stood and stretched. Maybe just one, she thought. As she approached the table, she heard an odd noise. Kind of a whimpering sound, a little like Bingo when he wanted to go outside but also wanted to be polite. The sound came from behind the door—the one Drama Club used to go down to the back door and outside.

Carefully, Hannah opened it and there, crying into her fist with eyes almost swollen shut, was the castle's miserable, cold, dirty little ghost. "Hi, Kammy," Hannah said softly. Startled, Kammy stood and was about to bolt down the stairs and outside, but Hannah grabbed her arm. She shook her head. "No, Kammy, it's too cold out there. I'm here to help you. Let's go eat the donuts and hot chocolate Gee left for us."

Kammy nodded but looked scared to death, Hannah thought. "I didn't mean any harm," Kammy said. "I just didn't know what else to do."

"We know that, and you didn't do anything wrong. Sit down and I'll fix you some hot chocolate. You're freezing. But please leave two donuts—one for me and Porter."

"Porter?" Kammy's speech was garbled as she hungrily devoured a donut.

"He's searching the castle for you while everyone else is in the ballroom."

"They'll come in here."

"No, they won't. But just to be sure—" Hannah shoved a chair against the door. "Now let me text Porter that I've found you." Quickly she texted, "Come back. Keep cool." She hoped Porter understood that meant don't overreact.

"Oh . . ."

"It's okay, Kammy. You're safe now. We've been so worried about you."

"How did you know I was here?"

"I didn't, but we started to figure it out when Leland told Beth that the castle was haunted."

"By me? That is so funny!" She laughed briefly but without humor. "Did I scare them?"

"Mr. Markey was delighted that the castle finally had a ghost. But I think the rest were more worried than scared. They noticed things were missing."

"I'm sorry—"

"It's okay, Kammy. They'll understand, I promise."

Porter opened the door. "Hey, Kammy, good to see you again. Oh, thank you! You saved me a few donuts. I could smell them all the way downstairs."

"I was just explaining to Kammy about people thinking she was a ghost."

"I don't understand why you've been looking for me. Why do you care?"

Porter took a gulp of chocolate, now more tepid than hot. "Because you're our friend, of course. Friends care. After Christmas, when we couldn't reach you by phone, Hannah and I looked for you at the West Village Flats."

"We talked to a woman and her little kids and found out that the man who was hurt was your grandfather," Hannah said. "The kids liked you a lot."

Porter seemed hesitant, and then determined. "Call it a hunch," he said, "or just spending too much time around Danny and his mysteries, but Hannah, show Kammy the photos you took."

"But they don't have anything to do with—"

"Maybe, but show her."

Hannah opened her iPhone and scrolled to a photo of the white truck.

Kammy trembled violently, making the whimpering sounds she'd made before. "Please don't let them find me," she said. "They'll hurt me. I need to hide again." She tried to stand, but her legs gave out. Instead, she buried her head in her arms, a temporary hiding place.

"I think we've talked enough," Porter said. "No one is going to hurt you, Kammy, but we need some help. It's starting to snow big time, and the cars are coming to pick up kids. They'll have to come through here to go downstairs for their rides. You won't want to be here. We can ask Gee or Janet or Leland to help. Which one?"

"Janet—and Leland," Kammy said.

Hannah was surprised Kammy selected Leland, too, but she was glad. Janet and Leland basically ran the castle. Hannah stood—the decision made. "Kammy, let's go downstairs to the parlor. Porter, wait until we're gone before removing the chair. Then get Janet and Leland."

"Aye, aye," Porter said, "but Hannah, my Dad is coming for Beth and me now. I won't be able to stay. You're going home with Danny, right?"

"Right. Ask Danny to go downstairs in the elevator but maybe wait in the entryway. He shouldn't come into the parlor. He can let his dad know that he'll text when we're ready."

"Understood. I'll see you soon, Kammy. I'm glad we found you."

❧

Danny was growing more and more anxious. Practically everyone knew their rides had arrived and that the earlier snowflakes were turning into a major blizzard. A few kids had started to wonder about church tomorrow and even school on Monday. They were getting serious texts from their parents, but Gee fiercely guarded the kitchen door. No one would proceed to the back steps until she gave the okay. Finally, Porter opened the kitchen door and Gee signaled them through, as if she were a newly appointed, proud member of the fifth-grade safety patrol.

First, Porter sought out Leland and Janet, whispering a little about what had occurred. The couple hurried out of the ballroom. One minute—Porter held up his finger to Beth. Then he turned to Danny and whispered. "We found her. She's in the parlor with Hannah; Leland and Janet are going down now. Text your dad and tell him you'll let him know when to come. Go down in the elevator with Mr. Markey and Robbie. Tell them and Miss Armstrong not to go into the parlor. I'll let Gee know that she can go home."

Beth grabbed his arm. "Come on, Porter, before Dad has a cow. He and Mom are going out later. Tell me what happened once we get home."

"Right," Porter said. "Just have to tell Gee something. Danny, I'll call you later."

Danny followed orders, deciding there was nothing to do but remain patient. At least Kammy had been found.

Robbie and Miss Armstrong decided to stay in the kitchen and help Gee clean up while Mr. Markey and Danny waited in a small room opposite the parlor. Danny gave Mr. Markey an update.

"So she's been haunting the place since your winter break began. Why, that's over three weeks! The poor child! I enjoyed having a ghost in residence, but it might be better to help a little girl in trouble."

"We found out this morning that Kammy's grandfather died. I don't know if Hannah told her. It might be better not to say anything yet, Mr. Markey."

"Mum's the word," Mr. Markey said.

Soon, Hannah came out of the parlor. "You can text your dad now, Danny. Mr. Markey, they want you to join them."

"What about Kammy?" Danny asked.

"She's staying here for now. She needs a bath, good meals, and a comfortable bed." Hannah teared up. Then, as if to stop further emotion, she hugged Mr. Markey. "We'll see you soon," she said.

"You had a hard time, didn't you, Hannah?"

She nodded. "I'm exhausted. I'll go over to your house later, Danny, and tell you everything. One thing will please you, though. It looks like we will solve the murder mystery. Kammy knows who did it, but she's not talking yet. She's too scared."

"Does she know her grandfather died?"

Hannah shook her head. "We were afraid to upset her even more."

Danny felt his phone vibrate. "Oh, Dad is here now. I'll bet he's been waiting all along. The snow is pretty bad."

⚷

Mr. Kennedy lifted Danny and carried him inside. Not their usual order of doing things, but with the snow piling up, it was better to take his time removing the folded wheelchair. He couldn't take a chance of falling on the slippery snow. "I'll see you later," Hannah called. But she waited until Danny's father returned for the wheelchair.

"Mr. Kennedy, I need to touch base with Dad and Uncle Martin. Then I'm coming back to take out Bingo and talk to Danny. But I really need to talk with you privately."

"Of course, Hannah. Sounds serious." Hannah nodded. "Well, sneak upstairs and knock on my office door—our old spare room. Better do it before you see Danny."

"Thanks, Mr. Kennedy."

Hannah would show him the photos of the white truck and tell him everything. It didn't matter now if they got into trouble. It looked as if the people who had hit Danny and kept on going were the same people who killed Kammy's grandfather. Mr. Kennedy, the police, and perhaps Kammy would determine what happened next.

SCENE 15 – THE WAY FORWARD

BETH LOOKED OUT HER BEDROOM window and practically purred. Mother Nature was in charge and had taken away the necessity of doing almost everything. The snow was blowing so hard that she, Dad, and Porter wouldn't be expected to shovel. She might have to take a turn watching Zoe, but even that sounded relaxing. A no-rush, leisurely breakfast was the first order of business.

"Good morning, dear," Mom said. She and Dad were sharing the Sunday papers while sipping large mugs of coffee. Zoe was in her highchair, gumming Arrowroot biscuits and playing with Mom's car keys. Warmth and contentment were in that kitchen. "Pancakes on the stove. Help yourself."

"Porter not up?"

Dad peered over the entertainment section. "Unlikely, and Kelly is engaged in whatever her latest hobby might be."

"Designing clothes for paper dolls," Beth said. "I used to love doing that." In fact, if she remained in this ethereal mood, she might give Kelly a hand. No sense in mentioning it and committing herself too soon. She helped herself to pancakes, bacon, and juice and joined her parents at the table. "Oh, I love this kind of day!"

"Might be a different story tomorrow," Dad said, "but enjoy it while you can."

"School tomorrow?"

Mom shrugged. "I doubt it. Do you have homework?"

"Nope. I think I'll do some sketching. It's been awhile since I started anything new. And let me know if you want me to watch Zoe."

A day that didn't require much thinking was just what the doctor ordered. She might call Leland and find out how Kammy was doing, but maybe not. Kammy had been found, and now it was up to adults to figure things out. Porter filled her in yesterday on what he knew, but she didn't need to know anything else today. "Let it snow," she whispered.

⚷

"We're snowed in!" Hannah said. "I don't think I can even get to Danny's house."

"I wouldn't chance it," Uncle Martin said. "Our side door is completely blocked with snow. Your friend Bingo will have to make do with newspapers in the mudroom."

"So, what are your plans on this friendless day?" Dad asked.

When was the last time the word "friendless" applied to her? Not for a long, long time. "I might go back to bed and read—a whole book!"

Uncle Martin smiled. "That would be a treat. And you might do it again tomorrow. Community has already called off classes, and I'm sure CBMS will follow soon."

Hannah wondered how Kammy was doing, but she had no way of contacting her. Mr. Kennedy probably couldn't do anything until at least Tuesday, unless he called his policeman friend ahead of time.

Talking with him had been so easy. He didn't act shocked or surprised, although he must have been, and he didn't scold at all. "It looks as if that club of yours—the SSC—has done it again."

Hannah had gasped. "You know about it?"

Danny's dad grinned. "I've heard it mentioned. Can't say I know what the letters stand for."

"I'm not sure I know anymore; we change it so often." Hannah decided not to mention the Super Shits.

She wondered if the club still existed. "Now, what book shall I read today?" she asked herself.

Danny was not pleased by weather that would keep his friends from coming to see him, but he couldn't complain because of all the excitement yesterday. He had a few aches and pains that he'd sensibly keep to himself. Maybe Hannah or Porter would call later. Hannah had already texted her apologies to Bingo.

"No PT for you tomorrow," Mom said at the breakfast table. "Good news, I imagine."

Danny shook his head. "Not really. I'm making progress. In fact, I think I'd like to try school again soon, if Sid thinks I'm ready. Mainly right now, I'm feeling sorry for Kurt and Kylie. Especially Kurt. His opening night is Friday, and they won't be able to start final rehearsals tomorrow."

Mom and Dad looked approvingly at him, and it felt good. He thought about Miss Armstrong's quotation. It was time to stop crying—time to end the self-pity. Even though he was in a wheelchair, he could control it, and his arms were stronger than they'd ever been. Danny would show his friends and family that at last, this stage of his life was over.

ACT THREE

In the first act you get your hero up a tree.
The second act, you throw rocks at him.
For the third act, you let him down.

—George Abbott

SCENE 1 – MEMBERS OF THE AUDIENCE

BETH SAT, LOST IN MEMORY. Only a year ago she was there, seated next to Kurt, hearing his guarantee that she'd be watching him on that stage—in only a year. While he wasn't as happy as he'd expected, he did keep the promise. Soon the curtain would rise on his first Crofts play. He had been right, and she, thinking that he would no longer be her boyfriend, wrong. She fingered the heart necklace he'd given her for Christmas, possibly her favorite possession.

The necklace reminded her of the Valentine's Day dance, coming in a few weeks. She still needed to find a dress. Priyanka had mentioned a shopping trip. Beth would bring it up again after the show. If Pri couldn't do it, Beth would ask Mom.

Everyone from Drama Club had shown up, except for Miss Armstrong. She should be here, Beth thought, if only to support the club and Kurt, her former student. Miss Armstrong was good at avoiding things that made her uncomfortable; she'd done that before. Gee was their excited chaperone today. She'd probably attend all of the performances. If there were a proud Grandma award, Gee would win it, hands down.

Beth had hoped Kammy could come, but Uncle Dan said it might be awhile before they would see her. In fact, Beth, Hannah, Porter, and Danny weren't even allowed to tell anyone Kammy was at the castle. Uncle Dan said Kammy must stay hidden for the time being.

The warning bell rang, lights dimmed. "Break-a-leg, Kurt," Beth whispered. He had been so worried about losing both Monday and Tuesday rehearsals to snow that Beth assured him she'd go to a real performance Saturday night. Mom and Kelly were going, too. She thought that Kylie and the old gang would come to the Sunday matinee.

Hannah sat between Porter and her new friend, Laurel, whom she'd met at Smithy's and talked into joining Drama Club. Laurel was in sixth grade. Her older sister, Avery, was in seventh. Fortunately, Laurel was completely different—not an awful gossip, like Avery. Porter already knew Laurel from his fifth-grade class last year. "She's nice," Porter had told her, "and a really good singer." Then Porter shook his head. "Her sister, though, is the worst bully I've ever seen. We practically had a celebration when she left East Elementary." Hannah was not surprised and vowed to avoid Avery.

If Kammy returned to middle school, Hannah would finally have a seventh-grade friend. Right now, that was one big if. Danny's dad had talked with her and Danny on Tuesday, the second snow day in a row. They were not to tell anyone about Kammy staying at the castle. Danny said his dad had even called Gee and warned her. "Kammy knows who killed her grandfather. She is a material witness in a murder case. She must be protected, just in case she's in danger." Thinking of Kammy's reaction to the photos of the white truck, Hannah knew Kammy was certain she was in danger.

Hannah wished she were sitting next to Danny, so they could whisper about the show. From the cast list in the program, she could tell that the play would cover only the first part of the book—the time Elnora's mother was cruel. That would please Danny, who didn't like the romantic second part. The curtain opened and the audience, mainly Drama Club members, gasped, and then applauded. The Limberlost set was absolutely gorgeous!

No one was paying any attention to Danny or his wheelchair. He'd ask Sid at PT tomorrow about returning to school, at least on a limited basis. Maybe a few half days a week. He'd even use the elevator if he had to.

He'd continue with Drama Club, too, although maybe just the meetings at the castle. For the first time since the accident, he felt almost lucky. That's what talking with Robbie had done for him. She'd confided that she wished her aunt and sister would accept that she was blind. "I'm dealing with it," she said, "but they can't seem to. They don't even listen to doctors anymore but keep trying to find ones who'll say something different." But Danny's doctors told him he would walk again—if he put in the work.

And he was certainly luckier than Kammy. SSC had started just as something to do. He'd wanted them to solve a mystery but never expected the mystery to be so, well, awful. Imagine seeing your grandfather stabbed, and then be afraid the killers would come after you! Dad's friend, Sergeant Lodge, had come for lunch yesterday. He told them that officers would interview Kammy on Friday. They hoped Kammy would tell them whom she'd seen. At least they'd identified the owner of the truck, although they couldn't be positive it was the one that had hit Danny. He understood why Hannah and Porter hadn't told him. Yes, he would have gone slightly crazy. Hard to admit, but they'd done the right thing.

The curtain opened. At first, Danny frowned at the audience's applause. He remembered what he'd learned from Kylie. If the audience claps for a set, it's a bad set, but he wasn't sure he agreed. The Crofts' tech crew had done an amazing job of portraying Indiana's large swamp, the Limberlost. They deserved a lot of credit.

"Break-a-leg, Kurt," Danny whispered, "just not the way I did."

"I think the acting is excellent," Porter said during intermission, "especially the girl who plays Elnora's mother."

Beth nodded. "Cress Morgan—I know her."

"Yeah," Danny said. "She was in Roe's play at camp last summer. She's good, but Kurt is the best."

Beth smiled. "Of course." While perhaps not best, Kurt was perfectly cast as Billy, a funny but pathetic little boy. "I wonder, though, how many understand the show. We might not if—"

"I agree," Joe chimed in. "The acting is okay, I guess, but the play doesn't make sense."

Why did he have to stick his nose into everything? Beth wondered. Kids wanted to like Joe but gave up when they got to know him—even a little. She saw Hannah bristle. Hannah no longer pretended.

"What Beth was about to say, before you interrupted, is that we understand the play because we took the trouble to read the book."

Joe laughed. "As if I had time to read chick lit."

Porter entered the fray. "It happens to be a classic. I suppose you think *Harry Potter* is macho lit—something girls shouldn't read because the main character is a boy."

Let Hannah and Porter argue with him, Beth decided, drifting away from the group. But it didn't work; Joe followed her.

"So, is Kurt still your boyfriend?"

"He is."

"Even though he took someone else to the Crofts dance?"

"I'll be at the next one. I had the Drama Club Halloween party."

"Is he your date for the Valentine's Day dance?"

"He is. Look, Joe, why all the questions?"

"I hoped you'd broken up and that I could ask you. How about it?"

Beth shook her head. "As I said, I'm going with my boyfriend, Kurt. Dates aren't necessary for middle school dances, but if you really want one, why don't you ask Imani?"

Joe made a noise. "You're kidding, right?"

"Why not? You got to know each other when you worked on the scene, right?"

"That was different. Other people were with us. It wasn't like anyone would think she was my girlfriend."

"You didn't mind using her house for all your rehearsals."

"It's a great house, but I think you must be teasing me. What would my dad say if I went to the dance with someone —"

"Black? Got it. Oh, good, there's the bell for the second act." I am so done with you, Joe, Beth thought.

Walking behind Joe was someone about to cheer Beth up immensely. "I may not like the play, Gee," Joe said, "but your grandson is a good actor. I wonder if I should come to Crofts next year."

"Yes, Joe, I really think you should," Gee said. "You'd fit in splendidly."

Beth turned back and grinned. She was rewarded by Gee's delighted wink. Joe had no idea that Gee had just insulted him.

SCENE 2 – STILL WATCHING

SITTING NEXT TO GRANDMA AND Grandpa, waiting for the curtain to open, Danny was glad he'd been allowed to attend the dress rehearsal of *You Can't Take It with You*. Going to a real performance with his friends in Drama Club might have been more fun, but the crowds would have been too much for him, as well as his grandparents. Other kids' grandparents, including some in wheelchairs, were there, too.

The snow that had been predicted changed its mind, but Kylie had been a nervous wreck until it did. "We can't afford to lose a dress rehearsal," she'd whined. And then she told Danny not to tell anyone about the play. "I want them to be surprised."

"I'll just tell them everyone was good but that you sucked." She stuck out her tongue. Then the two of them laughed because fooling around felt so normal. "Good thing Mom isn't around," Danny had said.

Again, Danny was sending out Break-a-leg wishes. But *I'm done with shows for a while*, he decided. The next play he'd see would be CBMS's spring show, at least two months away. He'd probably find out about it Saturday morning at the castle. Hannah said that the Drama Club meeting at school yesterday had been kind of boring. "They just talked about the show at Crofts, going to the high school play, and electing officers to help Beth." Talking about *The Girl of the Limberlost* would have been interesting, Danny thought, but that was it.

"Sid told me I can go back to school three mornings a week," he whispered to Grandma. "Just to my classes on the first floor when it's not snowy or icy."

Grandma gave him a hug. "I'm proud of you," she said. That's what was so great about grandparents, Danny thought. They're always proud of you, even if you don't deserve it. But that got him thinking about Kammy and her grandfather. Did she have other relatives? Who would take care of her now? It would be weird going back to the castle without knowing if she were there. If Dad knew anything more, he wasn't talking.

Time to stop thinking. The director walked out on the apron to welcome the visitors. "And because it's starting to snow again, if you have family members in the cast, they may leave with you directly after the rehearsal. I will email their notes, though, in truth, they are so wonderful I doubt there will be many." Everyone laughed and applauded as the director left the stage.

Yes, Danny thought, as the lights dimmed and the curtain opened. Kylie was right to come here. It was a happier place than Crofts.

Mom checked the thermometer again. "A little lower—one-hundred and one—but you're still not going anywhere."

"I know." Beth raised herself slightly and sipped her peppermint tea. A combination flu/bronchitis bug had taken over her life a whole week ago, the day after the Drama Club trip to Crofts. Thank goodness she'd been able to see Kurt perform at least once. She hoped she didn't get anyone else sick.

"It's still morning, of course," Mom said, "so your temperature might rise again this afternoon. You want anything else to eat?"

"No, thanks. Jello was fine. I don't want to start coughing again."

"I'll let you rest then," Mom said.

Dr. Patel, Priyanka's dad, had sent over a prescription. If possible, he did not want her going to the office. "A good place to pass on germs or get new ones," he said. And she was feeling somewhat better. Her big hope was that she would make it to *You Can't Take It with You.* Not tonight with Drama Club or tomorrow night, but maybe, if she were very lucky, the Sunday matinee with Kurt and the rest of her friends.

She turned on the radio to her favorite station. Her eyes hurt to read and daytime TV was boring. Porter had brought home her schoolwork, but she couldn't possibly—not yet. Porter was her lifeline, though, to what was happening. Mom and Dad allowed him into her room, figuring that he'd already been exposed. He'd given her an update on Wednesday's Drama Club meeting and would tell her all about the Saturday one at the castle.

"I nominated Joe for vice president," Porter had told her. "Hannah would have killed me if I hadn't told her I was following your orders. Why, Beth? The jerk has a big enough head as it is. And he'll try to take over—you know he will."

It was a little hard to explain, but Beth gave it a try. "Well, his ego has taken a few hits lately. As for taking over, Miss Armstrong is more than his match." It was also true that Beth's ego was stronger than it used to be, but she didn't mention that. "Joe really cares about the club—maybe more than I do—and he'll work hard to make it a success. I'd rather concentrate on art and doing technical stuff for the spring play."

Beth knew Joe could be a mistake, but she was willing to chance it. She was hoping he would turn out to be like Marla—someone who could benefit from positive people—or maybe like their sometimes-friend, Jaimie. Everyone seemed to have lost touch with the troubled girl since her family followed her to Florida.

"Well, at least Priyanka will be great as secretary/treasurer," she whispered. She swallowed a couple of Tylenol tablets with the rest of her tea. "Maybe I'll go back to sleep for a while."

"So how was the show?" Uncle Martin asked at breakfast Saturday morning. Hannah and her family fended for themselves during the week, but weekends were breakfast celebrations. Waffles and sausages were Uncle Martin's specialty.

"It was good," Hannah said. "Better, I think, than the play at Crofts."

Dad nodded. "Not surprising. One student-written, and the other an award-winning comedy. Not fair to compare them. How was Kylie?"

"Hysterical. She's really talented. She was accepted to Crofts, you know. She just decided she'd be better off at the high school."

"And how is our artist feeling?"

"Beth? Still sick. She hopes she can go to the Sunday matinee, but—" Hannah shrugged. She took her empty dishes to the sink and gave them a good rinsing before adding them to the dishwasher. "I'd better get ready for Drama Club." Mr. Kennedy was driving her and Danny to the castle.

Hannah wondered how Joe would act when he took charge of the meeting. She thought Beth had made a mistake asking that he be nominated for vice president. He had certainly tried to act the big shot at the high school the night before, even cautioning Drama Club members to behave themselves when they hadn't been doing anything other people weren't. Talking to each other before the curtain opened, for heaven's sake! Big deal! A couple of times she saw Miss Armstrong watching him, maybe amused but also considering when and where to strike. She was no pushover, Hannah decided.

"I don't know if it will be any fun without Beth," Danny said, after he and Hannah were in the car, before his dad had lifted in the wheelchair.

Hannah shrugged, although she had been thinking the same thing. "Joe will probably lead the discussion of *You Can't Take It with You*. That might go okay if he doesn't start acting like a know-it-all. Miss Armstrong will announce the spring play and talk about auditions. That will be very interesting."

"Not to me," Danny said. "But at least I'm out of the house." He looked sheepish. "Not feeling sorry for myself—mainly for Beth. I'm hoping Gee made donuts. They're beyond interesting."

As Hannah predicted, Joe opened the meeting wanting to compare the Crofts and CBHS shows. "Come on, everyone," he said, when no one responded. There was something about his manner that was, well, off-putting. Hannah had read that expression recently, and it seemed to fit Joe. She raised her hand. Joe nodded toward her as if he didn't recall her name. "Yes?"

"I enjoyed both shows," she said, "and the acting was really good." When Joe started to interrupt, she cut him off. "I'm not finished. I don't think it's fair to compare the plays. One was student-written and the other a prize-winning comedy by master playwrights." Thanks, Dad, I owe you.

Porter quickly raised his hand. "I agree with Hannah. I thought the Kaufman and Hart show—" That's right, Porter, show off, Hannah thought—"was awfully slow starting, but when it picked up, terrific."

Miss Armstrong smiled. "Many critics have made that comment about the play, Porter."

A few more students made comments, especially about the actors they liked, and then Danny raised his hand. "Danny," Joe said, almost dully.

"What helped me most was knowing both stories. *Limberlost*, because I read the book, and the other from helping my sister learn her lines. The student at Crofts did a good job of picking the best parts of the book. I liked the high school show best because it was funny and because, well, Kylie was in it."

"You got to go to the dress rehearsal, right? How come? Because of your sister?"

Hannah and others stared at Joe. Did he not know how unpleasant he sounded? Fortunately, Danny could handle him.

"She's only a freshman, so she doesn't have much say," Danny said. "As for me, I was a very important member of the electric wheelchair brigade."

Everyone howled, and then applauded. Hannah and Porter gave Danny a thumbs-up. Also laughing, Miss Armstrong said, "On that note, I say we break for refreshments. Then, before we go home, I'll announce the spring play."

Hannah had just managed to grab a cookie when someone tapped her shoulder—Janet, placing a finger to her lips, beckoned Hannah to follow. Making sure no one was watching, Janet led her down the kitchen stairs.

"Just a few minutes, dear," Janet said, "and don't tell anyone."

More cookies and juice were waiting for Hannah in the downstairs kitchen, as was—"Kammy!"

Kammy, friendlier than she'd ever been, gave Hannah a hug. "I am so happy to see you, Hannah!"

"Oh, me, too! I didn't know what was happening and—Oh, Kammy, you look terrific!"

"Better than the last time you saw me, anyway. You can't stay, but I talked Janet and Leland into a few minutes. I can't tell you much."

"That's okay, as long as I know you're here—and safe."

"I wish I could go back upstairs with you. Maybe someday."

Janet interrupted. "Time to return, Hannah. I'm sure you'll come again soon."

"Uh—okay. Uh—I'm sorry about your grandfather, Kammy."

"Thank you. And thanks for finding me."

Grabbing another cookie, Hannah rushed back upstairs. She heard Miss Armstrong give the name of the play and audition information, but it didn't register until later. All she could think about was her good friend Kammy.

Porter knocked softly on Beth's door and waited.

"Come in," Beth croaked, just loud enough for him to hear.

"Are you feeling any better?" he whispered.

She shook her head. "Not really, but why are you whispering?"

He grinned. "I have no idea. Just seemed kind of solemn in here."

"That's a good word for how I'm feeling—solemn. My fever has broken, but Mom won't let me go to the matinee tomorrow."

"I don't blame her. You sound awful!"

Beth reached for her hot lemonade. "Yeah, I know. Mom checked with Dr. Patel. I can't even go to school again Monday. I might be able to do some homework tomorrow, though."

"And maybe look at this." Porter handed over a large manila envelope. "From Miss Armstrong."

Beth peered inside. "Oooh, *The Secret Garden*! The script! And there's a note inside." She read quickly. "She wants me to be her technical director and to start working on a set design as soon as I feel well enough. Ha! This is almost enough to cure me!"

"Miss Armstrong wrote it, right?"

"She adapted it from the famous book—like the student at Crofts did with *Limberlost*."

"Hmm, maybe I should read it then. Reading a book sure made a difference at Drama Club today." Porter grinned. "Joe was no match for Danny, Hannah, and me."

Beth sighed. "Poor old Joe. Was he totally obnoxious?"

"Almost. Miss Armstrong didn't do a thing. She let us handle it."

Beth laid her head back on the pillow. Just this little chat with Porter was becoming too much. "I think I need a short nap. Maybe we'll talk later."

"One more thing. Miss Armstrong talked to me in private. She wants me to audition. I don't know why, do you?"

"Mrs. Hunt gave her a link to our Speakeasy. Miss Armstrong thinks you're good. Look through the top shelf of my bookcase, Porter, and happy reading. Close the door when you leave, please."

SCENE 3 – A LONELY AFTERNOON

DANNY WAS LONELY AND ALONE again, although it had been a pretty good day. He would have liked to talk about the Drama Club meeting with Hannah or Porter — especially Hannah, since he'd noticed her following Janet and figured it had something to do with Kammy. But Hannah had texted that she was going out with her father and uncle. Just "Out," without mentioning where or why. Porter wasn't going to the mysterious "Out," but his parents were and wanted him to stay home and keep an eye on Beth, in case she needed anything. Hannah said she'd check in tomorrow.

"What's with everyone today?" he said loudly, causing a sharp bark from Bingo. Kylie, coming up from the basement with a large box of party supplies, took a detour into the living room.

"Oof!" She set the box down on his card table. "Mom and Dad are out. Not sure where, and I have costume/makeup call for five."

Danny grinned. "At least your plan is specific. Everyone else seems to be heading to the unknown place called 'Out.'"

Kylie sat next to him. "I'll bet you're longing to join them there."

"I am. Going out and it not being a major production — without Mom complaining about the wheelchair being heavy and hard to fold, without worrying if I'll slip on the ice getting out of the van or if there'll be ramps. I never knew that going out without thinking about it was true freedom. 'Where are you going, Danny? Out, Mom! Well, just be home for dinner.' What a wonderful world that was!"

"Never thought of it that way. You're right. So what will you do this afternoon?"

Danny shrugged. "Jigsaw puzzle, watch a movie, I don't know. No one can come see me. Dad and Mom going to the show tonight?"

"Tomorrow. How did you like it, Danny? You didn't say."

"Only because I haven't seen you. I liked it a lot—you best, because you were really funny."

"I'm having a good time. I'll be sorry when it's over."

"Too bad about Beth."

"Yeah, but we've got a surprise. Because she's a friend of the techies and helped them last summer, the director is allowing the lights crew to film the show tonight—just for her."

"Cool. Maybe Mr. Markey can see it, too."

"Well, as long as they don't tell anyone. It's illegal to tape. Should I let Bingo out for a few minutes?"

"Thanks! That would make both of us happy. What are you doing with the old party stuff?"

"Mom says I can have it for our cast party after strike tomorrow. We're going to decorate the gym with anything we've got handy. Should be fun."

"Sounds like a blast! Break-a-leg again, Kylie!"

"I intend to. Come on, Bingo!"

"Oh, one more thing . . ." But Kylie was gone. He shrugged. She probably didn't have it anyway. He reached for his Kindle, although he preferred real books. Miss Armstrong said she'd adapted her play, *The Secret Garden*, from a book. Well, he loved secrets, of course, and everybody liked gardens. Maybe he'd buy it, if it didn't cost too much. He checked. Free? Good deal!

Beth awoke again in a dark room. She should be slept-out by now. That's about all she'd done for how long? Did she feel better? Maybe. Not well enough to go to the show tomorrow. She'd lost that battle with Mom. She knew she wasn't well enough, although she would have liked it to be her decision. She switched on the light above her bed. Almost eight. Should she ring her waiter for supper? She started to giggle but stopped when it came out a croak. Porter would not want to be called a waiter, but he might think it funny if she called him her babysitter.

That would depend on what kind of mood he was in, which would depend on if he were really babysitting Kelly and Zoe. She was hungry. Might as well give it a try. No bell, unfortunately. A text would do.

He came almost at once. "So, you finally woke up. Feeling better?"

"Maybe. I'm not sure yet."

"Hungry?"

She nodded

"Well, me, too. Also lonely. You and I are the only ones home. Kelly went with Marta and her mom to the show, and Zoe is with Mom and Dad—playing bridge at someone's house. Mom left a phone number. Shall we have supper in here?"

"No, I need to get out of bed for a while."

"Good idea. Best to keep the chili off your blankets. But get up slowly."

"Hannah, we heard from your mom," Dad said, as soon as they placed their order for hot dogs and fries at a favorite diner outside of town, one that looked as if it belonged in the 1950s—juke boxes, checkered tablecloths, the works.

"Oh?" Hannah asked warily.

"She wants to know if you'd like to live with her for a while."

Silence.

"Is it really my choice?"

Dad nodded. "She said she isn't certain whether you'd be at her house or her new boyfriend's, but she thinks you'll like him. She wants me to text her back tonight."

"What?" Hannah felt her rage building.

"Steady, dear," Uncle Martin said. "We have to handle this carefully."

Hannah knew he was right, of course. If Mother became angry, she would threaten them with lawyers and court and could easily win. "Okay, I get it. Please tell her that I love her but that I'm really happy here. I am doing great in school and have made a lot of friends." Hannah crossed her fingers. "And say that I'm going to be in a play and that I'd like her to come see it."

Uncle Martin nodded. "In other words, don't mention your dad or me. That might work. And we could say that you'd like to visit this summer."

"Right," Hannah said. "By that time, she will have ditched this boyfriend and moved somewhere else. I don't even know where she lives now."

"We don't know either," Dad said. "Wait a minute! You made the play?"

"Not yet, but I will. I'm determined. Auditions are next week!"

The hot dogs were a welcome arrival. They needed a break from thinking about Hannah's mother, Dad's ex-wife, and Martin's sister—painful memories for all concerned. Hannah supposed she could text or call, but she was afraid to. Mom always caused confusion and made Hannah's brain tie up in knots. It was not her fault that Dad and Uncle Martin loved each other, and it was not her fault that she loved them better than she did Mom. And it was not Hannah's fault that she was happier in Castle Bluff than she'd ever been anywhere!

QUIETLY BUT COMFORTABLY, BETH AND Kurt sauntered to the Walters' home, where Kurt had been invited for supper that Friday night. Then they planned to go to the movies, their first date in ages. Finally, Beth felt well enough to be doing normal things, although both Mom and Dr. Patel had warned her not to overdo.

"Are you sorry you turned Miss Armstrong down?" Kurt broke the silence.

"Nope." Beth grinned. "If I were her assistant director/stage manager, I would have no life, especially since I agreed to be tech director. I'd have to go to every single rehearsal and would probably have to give up Art Club. But—"

"But—you'd like to be a fly on a certain castle wall right now."

"In a way. As long as you could be another fly next to me."

Kurt laughed. "An artful answer, Miss Walters. So, who's the suck—I mean, AD/SM."

"Gabrielle."

"Our Gabrielle? You mean she isn't holding out for a lead?"

Beth looked troubled. "I don't know everything that's going on, but Gabby says there are problems at home. She worked something out with Miss Armstrong so she could do this and maybe have a small part. Priyanka agreed to substitute at rehearsals when Gabby can't come."

Kurt whistled. "Problems at home—the theme of the year. I know more about Brad, if you promise not to tell." Kylie and Brad planned to join them at the movies. Not only a date—a double date!

"I promise. I won't tell anyone. Does Brad know if he's leaving Castle Bluff? Kylie hasn't said anything."

"It might be good news. No one is leaving—for now—at least this year. Brad's siblings are not doing so hot—trouble in school, crying, wetting the bed, that kind of stuff. His parents finally woke up and decided to try again, with a family counselor and therapy for everyone."

"Oh, I hope!"

"So do I, although Brad isn't sure it's a good idea. He wants to stay but if his parents can't start treating each other with respect, he wishes they'd just split, so everyone could start adjusting."

"Makes me feel guilty that I complain about my parents," Beth said, mainly thinking about her mother.

"Yeah. We're so darned lucky."

"Okay, okay, jeez, all right already!" Danny gave up. "I'll do anything if you guys will stop nagging!"

"Yes!" Hannah gave Porter a high-five.

Porter grinned. "Hannah wants to be the only one to show up at the dance with two dates."

"Even if they are a year younger," Danny added.

Hannah smirked. "Actually, I just want to wear my Christmas dress again."

Actually, you really, really like Porter but know that he won't ask you or go if I'm not there, too. Of course, Danny did not say that out loud. He'd been around Kylie and her friends long enough to know there's a big difference between an almost 7th grader and an almost 8th grader. A bigger difference than you would think with only a year apart. Time to change the subject. They'd talk another time about one of those dates being in a wheelchair.

"So, you both auditioned today, right? How did it go?"

Simultaneously, Hannah and Porter crossed their fingers.

"Okay, I think," Porter said. "There aren't really any small parts, unless Miss Armstrong writes in woodland animals and has me playing a skunk."

Hannah shook her head. "Not gonna happen. She kept going back and forth between Dickon and Ben Weatherstaff. Then she dropped Ben and stuck with Porter reading Dickon."

"All right! That's like the male lead." When they stared at him, Danny grinned. "Okay, so I read the book. What about you, Hannah?"

"I'm afraid to jinx anything, but I think I have a shot at Mary Lennox."

"You gave the best reading for her," Porter said, "and I can't see you in any other role."

"Maybe we'll both be skunks."

"When will the cast list be posted?"

"It won't be," Hannah and Porter said together.

"Miss Armstrong will send out an email as soon as she decides," Hannah said.

Hannah had just fallen asleep when her cellphone woke her. "What? What time is it?" She reached over and checked the ID. Porter— calling her? That hardly ever happened. "Porter, is everything okay?"

"Everything is great, Hannah! Check your email and call me back!"

What time was it? 11:30? Really late, and Porter never sounded excited. Hannah turned on her bedside lamp. Thanks to the new phone, she could check her email without going downstairs to the computer. And there it was—the Cast List, posted just a few minutes before. Porter must have waited up, just in case.

Cast List

Narrator/Ayah	...	*Priyanka Patel*
Martha	...	*Laurel Mullen*
Doctor Craven	...	*Timothy Howard*
Mrs. Medlock	...	*Imani Jones*
Mary Lennox	...	*Hannah Rendina*
Ben Weatherstaff	...	*Seth Edwards*
Dickon	...	*Porter Walters*
Colin Craven	...	*TBD*
The Robin	...	*Kamirah Williams*
Mr. Craven	...	*Joe MacCracken*
Susan Sowerberry	...	*Gabrielle Soleigh*

Be sure to contact Miss Armstrong this weekend if you do not accept your part. Read-through will be held Tuesday at the castle, after school until 5:30. Be sure to arrange your ride.

Hannah began to cry. "This is silly," she scolded herself. "I can't call back Porter if I'm crying. Stupid to cry when I'm happy!" She grabbed a tissue. Mary Lennox! She was Mary, the lead in *The Secret Garden*, maybe her all-time favorite book. And Porter, the coolest, smartest boy in the world, was Dickon. Why, they'd have lots of rehearsals together. True, Porter wasn't at all like Dickon in real life, but he looked the part, with his spiky red hair and outdoorsy complexion, not at all like his pale sister. He looked like he should be climbing a tree instead of reading a book about it. But Porter could act, and obviously Miss Armstrong recognized that.

Her phone interrupted her thoughts. Porter again. "Why didn't you call back? I couldn't wait any longer."

"Sorry. I was about to." Darn, her voice sounded weepy.

"Crying, huh? I was a bit sniffly myself. I guess we're not going to be skunks after all."

"I can't believe it!"

"Believe it! It's going to work out perfectly. Doing anything tomorrow?"

"Not really."

"Good. I'm going to call for an emergency SSC meeting at Danny's house."

"SSC? Porter, why?"

"Think about it. There is one main part that hasn't been cast. Who do we know who could play that role?"

"Oh, my God! And if—"

"Exactly! Beth isn't home from the movies yet, but I'm going to wait up for her."

"I'll bet she can help."

"Oh, I just heard the door open. Gotta go, Hannah. Talk to you tomorrow. And congratulations!"

"You, too—" But Porter was gone. Had she ever heard Porter so enthused? It looked as if he finally cared about something.

Hannah wished Dad and Uncle Martin were awake, but they had crashed early. She wondered briefly if Mother would come to see the play. Probably not, but at least she hadn't lied about being in one. The rest of the cast looked great. She'd play some scenes with her new friend, Laurel. Kammy hadn't auditioned, but she was the Robin. What kind of part was that? Of course there was a robin in the book, but it didn't talk or anything. She'd find out soon. In the meantime, she would wait—and try to sleep.

I T WAS MIDNIGHT WHEN Beth opened the door to her bedroom. Mom and Dad hadn't waited up for her, which was a first. The movie had been so-so, but going to Smithy's afterwards had been great fun. And the walk home with Kurt, ending with a first kiss, sublime. She closed the door before turning on a light. If possible, she'd prefer that Mom and Dad not know how late it was. A note on her bed. Not from Mom, thank goodness. "Beth, come see me when you get home, no matter what time. P." Porter? Weird. Something was wrong.

His door was closed, but a light shone underneath. Beth tapped lightly before opening the door. "Porter, are you okay?" Porter was sitting at his desk with an oversized grin on his face. "I guess you are. What's going on?" she stage-whispered.

"Close the door." He pointed to his computer screen. "Come look."

"The cast list? So soon?" She glanced quickly. "Porter, you're Dickon? Oh, my God!" Beth pulled her phone from her jeans pocket and checked her emails. Yes, Miss Armstrong had sent the list to her, too. She hadn't bothered to look at her phone all evening. She sat on Porter's bed and studied the list more closely. "This is a great cast. Perfect, in fact. You and Hannah are the leads."

Porter nodded. "I can't believe how excited I am."

Beth studied his face. How many times had she ever seen Porter like this? She couldn't even count once before now. This really mattered to him, and he was surprised, too.

"You might notice," Porter said, "that one major role hasn't been cast. I'm wondering if you can guess what I'm thinking."

Beth smiled. "Of course. When I first learned Miss Armstrong was considering *The Secret Garden*, I thought of Danny. He could play Colin Craven, the boy in the wheelchair. But will he?"

"Hannah and I are meeting at her house tomorrow morning to discuss strategy. Then we're calling an emergency SSC meeting for, hopefully, tomorrow afternoon. Will you come, too?"

"Definitely, if Mom doesn't need me. But I think we'd better tell her what we have in mind. She'll be pleased about Dickon, and she knows Danny needs to get involved in something. That's according to Aunt Jane, Danny's doctor, and his physical therapist."

Porter nodded. "Sid. But don't tell Mom about SSC."

Beth laughed. "I wouldn't know where to begin. But what about Kylie?"

"Probably not yet. Danny can be stubborn if he thinks people are ganging up."

"I hear you. It should work out. Marla and Eric joined us at the movies, and Kylie went home with Marla for an overnight. I was invited, but Mom wanted me home because of being sick. Most likely, Kylie will be at Marla's for most of the day." Beth looked at Porter's alarm clock. Almost one. "We'd better get some sleep or else we'll be good for nothing tomorrow."

"You mean today," Porter said.

The plan fell into place quickly. "Okay," Hannah said, taking the role of spokesperson because they were at her house, "we know what we're doing. Porter and I will go first. Our strategy will be to explain why being Colin will help Danny. When we need you to come, Beth, I'll text you."

"And what am I supposed to be doing in the meantime?"

"Stay here. No one is home. Have a Coke. Look at a magazine. I don't think we'll be long. I'll text Danny now."

Porter nodded. "Just say we're coming over for an emergency SSC meeting—in his room."

Danny texted back. "OK. Door unlocked."

Leaving Beth, Hannah and Porter rushed across the driveway, through the mudroom, and into Danny's bedroom.

"Hey," Danny said. "Don't you think we should solve the mystery we've got before we tackle new ones?"

Hannah pulled a chair next to the wheelchair, and Porter sat on the bed. "What unsolved mystery do we have?" Porter asked.

"Oh, you know. Like who killed Kammy's grandfather and drove away after knocking me down? Probably the same person."

"Not our mystery anymore," Hannah said. "Maybe we'll find out someday. For now, it belongs to Kammy and the cops."

"Kammy and the cops." Danny laughed. "Good one, especially if you spell cops with a K. But how come the meeting?"

Porter handed Danny a folded paper. "First, this bit of good news. The cast list."

"Hmmm, I'd forgotten about auditions. Got the skunk parts, did you?"

Hannah grinned. "Just read it, will you?"

"Right. Oh, wow! Mary and Dickon! You did it! The leads are a sixth grader and a seventh! Congratulations!"

Porter beamed. "Thanks!"

Danny looked back at the list. "Kammy is the robin? I don't understand."

"We don't either," Hannah said. "She never auditioned, but of course she and Miss Armstrong both live in the castle. They see each other all the time."

"A talking robin? I don't think I like that."

Hannah and Porter nodded. It didn't appeal to them, either.

"Okay," Hannah said. "Now for the SSC part. If you'll agree, it will stand for Secret Surprise Club."

"Huh?"

"Look at the list again," Porter instructed. "What part is still to be determined?"

"Oh no, you don't. Just forget that. I will not play Colin, the sickly kid in a wheelchair! I'm through with plays. Sid and I figure that if I work hard, I might make it back into sports next year."

"And we want that for you, Danny," Hannah said. "Don't you see how playing Colin might help make that come true? What happens at the end of the book?"

"I don't want to talk about it."

"Then just think about it," Porter said. "Mary, Dickon, and Ben help Colin walk again, and then he surprises his father. What if—"

Hannah interrupted. "Oh, I heard Dad's car pull in. Think it over, Danny. I've got to tell Dad and Uncle Martin about the play. They weren't home when I got up this morning."

"Wait, Hannah. We forgot someone."

"Oops! I'll send her over. See you later!" Hannah rushed out.

Danny knew exactly what his friends had in mind. Yes, it would be the best surprise ever if he walked at the end of the performance, with Mom and Dad not knowing it would happen. They'd have to know he was in the play, of course. "But what if it didn't work, Porter? What if I couldn't walk again in time?"

"Beth will be here soon. Let's ask her what she thinks. Besides, you haven't auditioned. It's really up to Miss Armstrong."

"And me," Danny said. "I haven't decided anything."

They heard a tap at the door. "You forgot me," Beth said.

Danny shook his head. "Not my fault. I suppose you're here to nag me into being Colin."

"Of course, but something else came up. Got to tell you fast in case Hannah comes back. It's about Valentine's Day."

"Hannah already talked Danny and me into going to the dance, Beth."

"I know. It's something else. I looked at their kitchen calendar, and, well, the 14th is not just Valentine's Day, it's Hannah's birthday! Did you know that, Danny?"

From Danny's lap came a loud yawn. Danny laughed. "No, but I guess Boots does." Bingo, who had been sound asleep in his bed, raised an ear. "Maybe Bingo knows, too. I guess that makes sense. They do talk things over."

"Maybe that's why the dance and wearing the dress mean so much to her," Porter said. "Because it's her birthday, too."

"Thought you'd like to have time to figure out presents," Beth said.

Danny and Porter looked at each other, both remembering at the same time. "We promised to find her a dog," Danny said.

Porter agreed. "Nothing else will do."

"Might not be easy finding one this time of year," Beth cautioned. Bingo gave an in-his-sleep yip. "But of course you're right, Bingo. It is possible."

"I'll ask Dad to help," Danny said. "I'm really glad you saw that calendar, Beth."

"Now back to Colin. What do you think, Danny?"

"It would be a terrific surprise, but what if it didn't work? What if I couldn't walk in time?"

Beth nodded. "I have a few ideas about that. The high school tech department has agreed to lend us a scrim. I thought we'd use it to make the garden scene a big reveal. With the right lighting, a scrim can be transparent; it's a really cool effect. But it can be used in other ways. Depending on what Miss Armstrong thinks of the idea, Colin walking at the end could be in silhouette. Another person about your height could sit in the wheelchair and stand up and walk."

"That could work," Porter said, "and here's another idea. What if we did it that way for the first performance, and then if Danny can walk, skip the silhouette in the second. He'd walk in the last scene, and come out for curtain call. That way, we'd have all bases covered."

"Says the big baseball fan." Danny laughed. "Yeah, that would be awesome. Okay, I'm willing to audition. What's next, Beth?"

"Next, I'll call Miss Armstrong. Right this minute."

SCENE 6 – VALENTINE HEARTS AND PUPPY DOGS

"A GRAY DRESS? YOU'RE KIDDING!"

"Just try it, Beth," Imani urged. "You know that Pryanka has a perfect eye for fashion. Besides, it's not really gray—more like pearl."

Beth had lost count of the number of party dresses she'd tried on. She was also losing count of the number of times her mother had texted to find out if she was ready. Mom and Pri's mother were having high tea in the elegant Walnut Room upstairs. Coming downtown to shop was a special treat for all of them.

"I thought I wanted something floral, like this one." Beth touched the green chiffon with pink roses she thought would look nice with the heart Kurt had given her for Christmas. She'd worn the necklace just to make sure.

"The dress and necklace do look nice together, but—" Priyanka hesitated.

"But not on you," Imani concluded. "Not enough on top, dear. Maybe in a few years."

"Or maybe never." Beth sighed.

"But you could wear it in a larger size, Imani. Go find one," Pri said. Then once more, Pri handed her choice to Beth. "Come on, give it a chance."

Beth shrugged. She felt the soft knit. Sure it was gray, but not a boring gray. The neckline was higher than the others she'd tried on. She wondered if the chain on her necklace was long enough. The dress was longer, which would please her mother. Face it, she told herself, Mom would not approve of any of the other dresses and would not be willing to pay for them. "Okay, here goes nothing. Zip me up, Pri."

It felt beautiful, and the chain was the right length. Now to check the mirror. Yes, it was beautiful and, amazingly, she was beautiful wearing it. It fell to just above her knees. The flared A-line skirt was stretchy and full. Mom would like the round neckline and hidden back zipper. The dress wasn't sexy—just very feminine.

"It's perfect," Beth said. "You're a genius, Priyanka. Please text your mom and say we're ready." She checked the price tag. Expensive, but she wouldn't need to buy anything else. The new black flats she'd worn on Christmas would do fine, and she wouldn't need to do a single thing to her hair. She was pretty sure she could borrow one of Kylie's wraps if Mom didn't have anything. "I'll leave it on so Mom can see," she said.

Imani held the green and pink, floral creation tightly. "I'm glad my mom isn't here to vote. I love this and am going to pay for it right now. Meet you at the register."

Priyanka offered to wait for the two mothers outside the dressing room. "Do you think your mom will like it?"

"She has to." Beth crossed her fingers.

And then Mom was there with tears in her eyes. "Mom?"

"It's the most beautiful dress I've ever seen, on the most beautiful girl—inside and out."

"It's kind of expensive."

"I don't care. This is your dress."

Danny was in his room, learning Colin's lines. It was going well, he thought, and Miss Armstrong was pleased. Mom and Dad were happy he was participating, especially since Miss Armstrong agreed that most of his rehearsals would take place at the castle, where it was easier to transport the wheelchair and where using the elevator was not difficult. They had no idea of the super surprise Danny had in store for them. Each day, he was becoming more and more certain it would happen. Like Colin, Danny would walk again. They were even keeping it a surprise from cast members, other than Hannah, Porter, and Seth, sworn to secrecy. Beth insisted that Joe, playing Colin's father, should not know. She did not trust him to keep quiet. "Besides," she said, "think how powerful his performance will be if he doesn't suspect. He'll end up thanking us."

Well, Danny didn't know about that, but he agreed that the fewer people who knew, the better. Sid and Kylie were in on the surprise because he needed their help with exercising. Sid had attended a rehearsal at the castle, in order to see the old-fashioned wooden wheelchair in Mr. Markey's storeroom and to figure out how Danny might use it safely. "A play is not more important than your recovery," Sid said.

Danny agreed. It must all lead to him back on the field, running next fall.

A tap on his door meant Dad. "Come in, Dad." No one else bothered to knock.

"Busy?"

"Just working on lines. Grandma okay?"

"A bad cold—we didn't stay long. I've got some news. I may have found the birthday puppy." Dad handed Danny a photo.

Danny stared at a creature too adorable to be real—curly tan coat, soft floppy ears, and the most charming grin. "Is he alive or a toy?"

          Marilyn Ludwig

"That was my first reaction. *She* is very much alive—and very much in need of a home."

"Is she a poodle? No, that isn't right."

"A cross between a poodle and a lab retriever—an Australian Mini-Labradoodle. Nice breed. I contacted our vet, who happened to know another vet in Wisconsin, trying to find a new home for her."

"She's a puppy, Dad. She couldn't have had a home for long. Why does she need a new one? Is something wrong with her?"

Dad shook his head. "No, but it's a sad story, far worse than Bingo's. She belonged to a little girl who had cancer. Well, the child died, and the parents didn't feel up to taking care of a puppy. The vet has been searching for a family."

"Hannah will flip. I say, yes!"

Dad nodded. "And Troy and Martin approve. I thought if we drove to Milwaukee the afternoon of Valentine's Day, you could present her to Hannah that evening. That way, Betsy wouldn't need to meet Bingo and Boots quite yet."

"Betsy?"

"That's what the little girl named her. Certainly Hannah could change the name."

Danny burst out laughing. "Bingo, Boots, and Betsy! Hannah will love it! It will be the best surprise ever." Well, almost the best, he amended silently. "I can't wait! Please tell the vet in Milwaukee that we'll take her."

"One more thing. I've talked it over with your mother. Betsy has been spayed and has received all her shots. A lot of money has been invested in her, but she'll actually cost us only a fraction of what she's worth."

"Oh, no!" Money? Why hadn't Dad told him that in the first place?

"Your mother agrees that it's right to do this."

"Mom said okay?"

"We talked about all that Hannah has done for you since the accident—taking care of Bingo, giving you Boots, helping you with your schoolwork, and—"

"And never letting me give up." Hannah and Porter—no one had ever had such good friends!

Worriedly, Hannah looked out the window. The only car next door belonged to Danny's mom. He and his dad weren't home yet, and it was almost six. Danny had texted that morning that he was going somewhere with his dad but that he'd be ready for the dance in plenty of time. Nothing about her birthday, of course. Maybe she should have told people. She didn't want any fuss, but she really did—at the same time. She sighed. "I wonder if I'll ever understand myself," she whispered.

Uncle Martin insisted that she eat a little something. Then she'd finish getting dressed. Her bathrobe already covered underclothes, and she was wearing the silver and garnet necklace Dad had given her for her birthday that morning. Uncle Martin had firmly closed a seldom-used room off the kitchen. "It's a birthday surprise," he said. "You'll open that door only when I say you may."

Hannah was halfway through her salad—"This is all I want, Uncle Martin"—when she received a text from Porter. "Danny is running late. He'll meet us there. My dad and I will pick you up." That was strange, although she wouldn't mind walking in with just Porter.

The dress was even more special than it had been at Christmastime—possibly it fit better. It seemed brand new—since none of her friends had seen her wearing it. She, Porter, and Danny had agreed that flowers weren't necessary. Too weird for sixth-grade boys to give girls a corsage! But not for a Dad to do so. As soon as Porter's father arrived and she'd put on her long coat, Hannah would add the gardenia wrist corsage Dad had given her at breakfast.

Would those at the dance think Porter had given it to her? Hannah shrugged. What did it matter? She wouldn't mind one bit.

Beth had just put on the pink flats when Mom and Kelly entered her bedroom. "Oh, wow!" Kelly exclaimed. "I'm going to look just like you someday. Will you save that dress for me, Beth? After you outgrow it, of course."

"Deal," Beth said. Then she smiled at her mother. "Thank you for buying it, Mom. It's the nicest dress I've ever owned. And thanks for the shoes, too. I didn't expect new ones."

"They were meant," Mom said. "How else can you explain my finding pink shoes this time of year? Oh, is that the wrap Kylie is lending you?" She pointed to the white fake fur cape. "It's just right. We'd better go. Kurt is downstairs waiting, and I'm sure Dad will want to take some photos before he and Porter leave to pick up Hannah."

Beth glanced once more into the mirror before grabbing the cape and a tiny purse. All of a sudden, she felt uncertain. Kurt had never seen her looking so grownup. Kelly raced downstairs and made a grand announcement, as if Beth were a princess.

Kurt opened his mouth but nothing came out. Kurt speechless? Well, that was different. His mom had come inside, too, and watched, amused.

"As soon as Kurt stops his fish imitations, we'll take some pictures," Dad said, holding up his new iPhone with its exceptionally fine camera.

"Right," Kurt said, coming to his senses. "Here, Beth. It's a wrist corsage, so you don't have to put a pin in your beautiful dress."

The tiny pink roses were the finishing touch.

"Text when you need me to pick you up," Dad said, "and I'll drop you off at the Rendina's house. It's going to be a mighty late night."

"I don't think it will be too late."

"Doesn't matter," Dad said. "Doesn't happen often."

"Hannah has no idea we even know it's her birthday. I made arrangements with the jazz band to play Happy Birthday right as Danny walks in with her present. She's going to remember this birthday forever!"

"Would you put my present in your car, Mr. Walters?" Kurt pointed to an oddly wrapped, oversized package near the front door.

"Uh, maybe, if you tell me what it is."

"Nothing lethal. Just a bag of Puppy Kibble—economy size."

Beth sighed. It was going to be a wonderful night. She thought it likely Kylie would invite her to stay over. Marla would be there, too. Both Kylie and Marla would be anxious to hear how Imani's and Priyanka's dates went. To throw it in Joe's face for not inviting Imani, Kylie and Marla had asked Brad and Eric to do the honors. The two boys were happy to help. And Hannah would be thrilled to have so many high school kids at her party.

As they got into his mom's car, Kurt whispered, "Won't it be amusing to see Joe's reaction when he sees Brad and Eric?"

Beth nodded, but she thought Kurt was mainly relieved not to be the only high school boy attending a middle school dance.

"And promise me, Beth, that you'll wear that dress to the dance at Crofts next month."

Beth laughed. "An easy promise to keep, considering it will be a long time before Mom will buy me a different one."

Danny held the birthday bundle, Betsy, now fast asleep after exuberant greetings and face washings. He hoped Hannah would keep the name. He grinned. The Three Musketeers—Bingo, Boots, and Betsy! They were certain to be great friends—in time.

He had waited in the car forever while Dad had taken care of things at the vet's office in Milwaukee. There was no point, Dad had said, in packing the wheelchair into the car and dragging it out more than one time in a day. Dad had carried him to the passenger seat and would carry him back inside when they reached home. With Dad's assistance, Danny could have walked, of course, but that would have meant giving away too much of the surprise. The way he was progressing, Danny was certain he—and Colin—would walk before the final curtain.

"So, Hannah's dad will help when we get home? The dance has started already."

"Or maybe Martin. One of them will hold Betsy while I get you inside and changed. Then we'll get you and the wheelchair into the car and be on our way again."

"With Betsy."

"Are you sure, Danny? You could wait and present Betsy at the party."

"No, I'm sure. The dance will be almost over by the time I get there. I didn't want to go anyway. I'm going to text Beth when we arrive, and she'll have the band play Happy Birthday, just as I roll in with Betsy on my lap. Then we'll all go to Hannah's for her party."

"Won't Hannah be mad at you? You were supposed to be one of her dates."

"Once she sees Betsy, I doubt it." Danny grinned. That was true, but it was also true that having only Porter for her date would be fine with Hannah. It was more likely that Porter would be mad at him.

Porter's dad dropped them off on the corner. "I imagine you'd rather walk in with a crowd," he'd said.

Hannah didn't care, but she could tell Porter was grateful. He seemed nervous. "Too bad Danny isn't here," she said. "I wonder what this mysterious errand is about."

"Guess we'll find out," Porter said, as they approached the school steps. "Hannah, I've got to tell you something. I—uh—I really don't know how to dance."

Hannah laughed. "You think I do? Don't worry about it, Porter. Think of it as being a party with friends. I doubt if you'll see many kids dancing. Maybe some of the eighth graders, especially ones with ninth-grade dates, like Beth. Mainly we'll just be hanging out. There might even be some games set up, and refreshments, of course. I just wanted to be a part of things and wear my dress while it still fits."

"It's very pretty," Porter said.

Hannah wondered if he meant *you're very pretty.* Whatever, it was a nice compliment. "Thanks. If we're not having a good time, we can always run lines and talk about the play."

Porter brightened. Talking about the play was always fun.

Hannah was right. Only a few of the older kids were dancing, but the band was great. She and Porter enjoyed watching Joe's reaction when Imani and Kylie's boyfriend, Brad, demonstrated the latest Hip Hop, and then encouraged everyone to try. Imani returned to her date, Eric, and Brad to Priyanka, who was almost as tall as Brad and stunning in her purple and violet sari.

Imani seemed almost grownup in her daring short dress. In fact, all of the eighth-grade girls, including Beth, in a dress as lovely as Hannah's, were starting to look as if they belonged in high school, rather than middle school. Then Brad tapped her on the shoulder. "Care to give it a try, Hannah?"

"Sure." She was surprised he even knew her name.

Beth heard a ping in her little purse. "Finally," she said to Kurt. The two of them had decided to take a break from the strenuous Hip Hop. It was more fun watching others' attempts.

"Danny?"

Beth nodded.

"I'll go out and help," Kurt said. "You warn the band."

That made sense. Either Kurt could hold the dog or help get the wheelchair out of the van. An extra pair of hands would be useful. They and their friends had alerted as many people as possible what to expect. As soon as a trumpeter played a fanfare, they would move to one side or the other, leaving room for Danny to wheel in with Hannah's present on his lap.

The dance was coming to a close. The main event for most people was to announce the results of the election for the King and Queen of Hearts. Only eighth graders were eligible. They had to be present but not necessarily a couple. Actually, Castle Bluff Middle School discouraged dating—not that the students paid much attention. Crowning the king and queen at the end of the night might not be as special as it would be at the beginning, but this gave everyone a chance to vote, and the royal couple would have their picture taken for the yearbook. Beth wasn't that interested; it was certain to go to a cheerleader and a sports jock. She'd voted for Imani and the boy playing the trumpet.

Before approaching the band, Beth caught Imani's eye and signaled that the Hip Hop demonstration must come to an end. It was time, and everyone agreed later that Alan, the trumpeter, did a marvelous job playing a fanfare.

Hannah might have had the only puzzled face in the room, Beth thought, watching Porter physically restraining her from following the crowd away from the center. Then Beth watched her blush as the band played Happy Birthday, and just about everyone began to sing.

"Come on, Danny," Beth whispered. This was way too embarrassing for Hannah. She really doesn't like being the center of attention. But just as the song came to end, in rolled Danny, straight to Hannah, with an eager, happy puppy on his lap. The little dog, with a pink bow on her head, was sitting in a red, quilted bed, made especially by Danny's mother. One paw held down a pink stuffed bone, also made by Mrs. Kennedy.

"Happy Birthday, Hannah," Danny said. "This is Betsy. She's your birthday present."

Sensibly, the crowd cheered and sang Happy Birthday again. Hannah, too, did the only sensible thing. She hugged Betsy and burst into tears.

SCENE 7 — SECRETS AND GARDENS

HANNAH WAS WIDE-AWAKE, BUT dear little Betsy, cuddled up next to her, was sound asleep. Yesterday had probably been the most exhausting day of Betsy's short life, as well as Hannah's very best. She wondered if anyone had ever had a stranger year. Her twelfth birthday had been awful, with Mother screaming, walking out, and getting a quickie divorce faster than anyone thought possible. Dad had let her have everything, except Hannah, whom Mom didn't seem to want anyway. Then Dad and Uncle Martin moved that summer to Castle Bluff, where Hannah's life changed again, this time for the better.

Carefully, Hannah reached over and grabbed her phone. Nope. Not a word. Not an email or a text—Dad had given Mom the information—so why should Hannah want to live with anyone who couldn't be bothered to remember her birthday? Probably it wouldn't even be a good idea to visit. What if her mother decided a good way to punish Dad was to not let her go home again? She'd heard of cases like that. Hannah shrugged. She'd talk to Dad about it someday. Didn't she have any legal rights?

Reacting to the movement, Betsy gave a puppy yawn and snuggled closer. "I'll have to go to the bathroom soon," Hannah whispered, "and you should, too." Good thing Betsy was housebroken, although she did not like the cold. It had started to snow just as the guests left the party at midnight.

And what a party! The only surprise party she'd ever had turned out to be the best party she'd ever had. She wasn't sure she even knew everyone who came, but all of her friends were there, except for Kammy, who sent a card and homemade cookies. "I made them," Kammy had written, "so swallow with care." Not a problem; they were delicious. Hannah guessed that Gee, who'd brought the cookies to the party, had helped. Other than introducing Betsy to Bingo and Boots, Hannah planned to spend the day writing thank you notes and cleaning the kitchen and living room. It was really too late last night to expect anyone to help.

"That's it, Betsy! Time to get up. Potty time for both of us."

"Ow!" Danny grabbed his stomach. "Honestly, you guys, stop being so hysterically funny. It hurts."

"They're certain to fall asleep soon," Hannah said.

Hannah's dad and uncle had carried Danny to the new room, created especially for the three animals. There, Danny was plunked into a chair and told to let them know when he wanted to go home again. Hannah had brought over Boots and Bingo, and then closed the door and placed another chair in front of it. "Just in case," she said. "I'll send Beth a text to tell her about the chair."

Beth, in the kitchen talking to Hannah's dad about her art portfolio, sent a quick reply. "I'll be sure to knock first, so Boots doesn't escape."

But that wasn't the reason for the chair. Danny was perfectly capable now of walking around the room, but that was top secret— from any adult who might barge in. Of course, he still couldn't handle the back porch steps on either house, so being carried was appreciated. For close to an hour, he and Hannah had been howling at the animals' antics.

The biggest surprise was Boots, who not only didn't fear Betsy, but fell in love with her. Boots spent about five minutes gazing down and hissing from the cat tower/scratching post—created by Hannah's uncle—before deciding to make a new friend. Betsy, too young to find any creature threatening, gave Boots a full-face washing before batting a tennis ball across the room. Boots promptly chased it, then batted it back to Betsy. A game, seemingly with its own special rules, ensued. The animals took turns initiating the chase.

Delighted, Danny and Hannah didn't notice at first that Bingo was cowering in a corner. "Oh, come on, you big coward," Danny scolded.

Hannah sat on the floor next to him. "That's okay, Bingo," she said, fondling an ear. "You're older and wiser. You're right to be cautious."

Danny snorted. "Let's see how he acts once the snow melts. How cautious do you think he'll be when you throw a Frisbee again?"

Hannah shuddered. "If you think I'll ever throw one again, I'll—"

"Look," Danny interrupted. "It's nap time. Betsy had curled up in a comfortable bed—the red quilted one was in Hannah's bedroom—and Boots was doing her circling and curling routine at the top of the cat tower. Bingo, seeing that he was safe for now, stood and stretched before lying down near Danny.

Hannah jumped to her feet. "I've been deserted," she said.

Danny looked at her with envy. "Gosh, I'll be glad when I can do that again."

"Do what?"

"Get off the floor without even thinking about it. In fact, do lots of things without thinking."

"You're right, Danny. It's amazing how many things we take for granted."

"I'm looking forward to that, too. Just taking things for granted. I should go home soon. I'm getting awfully stiff in this chair." Danny didn't mention that he needed to go to the bathroom. This compact room for pets had a litter box for Boots and shredded paper for the dogs, but few accommodations for humans.

"Do you need help standing up?"

"Yes! Then I'll walk around the room before I sit down again. Then you can text your dad."

"What about Boots and Bingo?"

"Bingo can go with me. I don't think he's ready to be alone with Betsy. But could Boots stay here until she wakes up?"

"Okay," Hannah agreed. "I'll take her home later, and maybe we can run lines."

"Good idea."

"These, I think, are your best," Hannah's father said, pointing to six of Beth's paintings and sketches, spread out on the kitchen table. For the last hour, Mr. Rendina and Beth had been poring over and discussing each item in Beth's portfolio, accompanied by the laughter coming from the animal playroom. Beth wanted the art teacher's advice about what to frame and submit to the school's spring art show.

"Thanks," Beth said. "I thought I'd ask Kurt if I could borrow the painting I gave him for Christmas." She showed Mr. Rendina both the sketch and photo.

"I agree. Then you'll have one oil, four watercolors, and two pen and inks—a good sampling of your work. I'm wondering, too, about this." He held up an incomplete sketch of a garden. "If this were in color, I think it would be lovely."

"Oh. That's just an idea for the garden in our play."

Hannah's dad nodded. "*The Secret Garden*. Love the stone wall. And the flowers look authentic to the location and time of year."

"Yeah, I did some research. I guess I could turn it into a painting. The play will be over before the art show, so I wouldn't be giving anything away."

"Think about it," Mr. Rendina said. "You could add some silhouettes of people."

All of a sudden, Beth saw it clearly—a beautiful garden scene, with silhouettes of a boy in a wheelchair and a girl, with a robin on her shoulder, peering down at the boy from a tall tree. "Thanks, Mr. Rendina. I know exactly what I'll do."

Both of their phones dinged. "Danny," Beth said. "He wants to go home."

Hannah's dad laughed. "I wondered how comfortable he'd be in that chair. We need to find him a better one. Beth, whenever you're ready, I'd be glad to help you frame your entries. We could do it in my studio at Community. I have plenty of materials, so it wouldn't cost you a cent."

"That would be wonderful, Mr. Rendina. Thank you so much!" Beth had been worrying about how she could ever afford to mat and frame everything. Now she almost wished Kylie hadn't invited her to dinner. She couldn't wait to go home and work on her secret garden painting.

SCENE 8 – CLOSER TO THE TRUTH

D ANNY SENT BACK A NOTE to Rob, his old Cross Country buddy, hoping neither of them would get caught. It was fun being back in school—just a regular kid again. Well, almost a regular kid. He was still in a wheelchair, and Sid thought that might be the case for the rest of the year. "Or at least with a walker," Sid had said. "Yes, you'll do a lot more walking once the play is over, but you will become tired quickly. You do not want to reinjure yourself." No, Danny did not want that.

Rob had all kinds of questions for Dan. "When will you return to school full-time?"

"Not sure."

"Can you stay for lunch?"

"Maybe soon."

"Do you think you'll be able to do sports this spring?"

"No. Maybe fall."

"Will you stay in Drama Club?"

All of a sudden, Danny noticed that his math teacher was totally aware of the note passing but was pretending not to notice. It was super nice of him, but Danny thought he'd rather get into trouble, like any normal student. He tucked the note into his math book and returned to his assignment. He already had English homework. It would be nice to be done with math. Besides, after Mom picked him up and he had lunch, he wanted to play with the animals. After he and Hannah had patiently worked with them for several weeks, Bingo and Betsy were finally at peace with each other and approaching friendship.

Besides, he didn't want to answer Rob's question. He wasn't certain the All-Sports-Always boy would understand. Yes, even when Danny could run again, he would stay in Drama Club. His theater friends had never given up on him, but his former teammates had. Sure, they would welcome him back — if he could help the team to victory. They could learn a few things about sportsmanship from Drama Club members.

Finish your math, he told himself, so Betsy can come visit while Hannah has rehearsal.

Thanks to Mr. Rendina, Beth's sketches and paintings were framed and all but two submitted. She would wait until deadline to turn in Kurt's Christmas gift, *A Midsummer Night's Dream*, and the latest, *The Secret Garden*. Kurt didn't want to take a chance on anything happening to his painting, and Beth wanted to keep her garden, well, an actual secret.

Her eighth-grade art teacher, Mrs. Snow, was okay, but Beth couldn't wait for high school, where there would be all kinds of choices, as soon as she was allowed electives. No lecture today; just an assignment on shadows and shading, which gave Beth a chance to think while doing.

She had intended to go to the rehearsal at the castle after school. She had a few questions for Miss Armstrong and also wanted to see the last scene still to be blocked — the one between Robin and Mary. But the plan changed when Beth received a text from Miss Armstrong, saying that she should not attend. The rehearsal would be for Hannah and Kamirah only. Okay, but Gabrielle received the same text. That was strange. Gabrielle was student director and stage manager and should totally be there.

Gabby didn't seem to mind, although she was surprised. Beth had sat with her in the cafe at lunchtime. "I'm way behind in school," Gabby said, "and soon rehearsals will be here on stage — almost every day. I did not expect the play to take over my life." Beth had nodded but didn't reply. Plays always took over your life. Miss Armstrong had led Gabby to believe differently, and that wasn't fair.

"How is your grandfather doing?" she'd asked, changing the subject.

"Not good. He's going to die soon. I just hope he can hold off until after the performances." Gabby flushed. "I didn't mean to sound so—"

Cold? Uncaring? But Gabby looked exhausted. "It must be hard on your whole family," Beth had said. Gabby turned away, but not before Beth had seen tears.

Beth jumped when someone touched her shoulder and brought her back into the art room. Mrs. Snow was making her way around the tables. "That's coming along fine, Beth. Maybe just a little more shading here." Mrs. Snow pointed to the tallest building in Beth's city scene.

"Thanks, Mrs. Snow. You're right."

As soon as the teacher moved on to the next table, Beth returned to thoughts about Gabby. Gabby, too, thought it weird that she wasn't included in today's rehearsal. "I mean, I should be there to write the blocking into the prompt book, even if it's only a couple of pages."

Beth nodded. "Do you have any idea what the robin is supposed to do? It's not like Kammy's robin can show the way by flying over the wall into the secret garden."

Gabby shook her head. "No idea, and Miss Armstrong has been pretty open about everything else."

"Maybe it has to do with security. Only a few people know that Kammy is living in the castle."

"If she's still in danger, she shouldn't be in the play," Gabby said. "Soon everyone will be rehearsing on stage—even Kammy and Danny."

"How is Danny working out?" Beth was anxious to change the subject.

"He's really good." Then Gabby giggled. "Not that Joe thinks so. Miss Armstrong really gave it to him."

Beth gasped. "She didn't give away the secret?"

"No, don't worry. Joe asked to speak to Miss Armstrong in private, but Miss Armstrong didn't ask me to leave. Joe started to complain that Danny shouldn't play Colin because he wouldn't be able to walk at the end. Miss Armstrong just looked at him calmly and then asked who he thought should play Colin."

"There isn't anyone, unless a girl took the part."

"And that would be awful. Joe didn't even answer Miss Armstrong. He always acts like he's an expert on everything. Fortunately, he's only in a few scenes, although they are important ones."

"But you said Miss Armstrong gave it to him. What else did she say?"

"If you could have heard her, Beth! She told him if he didn't change his attitude—make an attitude adjustment, her words—she would drop him from the play. He sputtered about performances being in only two weeks and who would replace him."

"He knows we don't have anyone."

"True, but she said she could get Brad Michaels or Eric Stein from the high school."

"Oh, either of them would be perfect! I'll bet that shut Joe up."

"Yes, he didn't have much to say after that."

Beth and Gabby didn't have much to say after that, either. Beth was thinking how different she was this year and was glad they had become friends. She wondered if Gabby was thinking something similar—about how she had been completely taken in by Jaimie and had done things she regretted. Everyone was lucky Jaimie had moved away.

The bell rang, jarring Beth out of her thoughts and back to the art assignment. She hadn't even been aware of finishing it. Mrs. Snow requested that completed work be put in her large tray and incomplete ones on the back table.

To Beth's surprise, Gabrielle was waiting outside her locker. "Beth, I was just thinking since we both thought we had rehearsal and had made arrangements, we could go to Smithy's and talk about tech stuff instead. I called my mom. We can give you a ride home."

"Great idea," Beth said. "I'll text my dad and tell him. He will be pleased."

"Sorry I'm late," Hannah said, joining Miss Armstrong in the ballroom. "I was supposed to get a ride from Beth's mom, but then Beth got a text not to come. I had to get a pass for the activity bus."

Miss Armstrong looked sheepish. "I am sorry. I got caught up in things and forgot to send a text earlier. Kammy's lawyer wants to wait until dress rehearsals are at school before other people see her."

Hannah didn't comment, but she thought that sounded crazy. Wasn't Kammy safer in the castle than she'd be at school?

Perhaps Miss Armstrong guessed Hannah's thoughts. "There will be a police presence whenever Kammy is in the building," she said. "Hopefully, the safety issue will be over for her soon."

Hannah had loads of questions but decided she had a better chance at answers from Kammy—if they were ever alone.

"I'll text Janet for both of them to join us. Janet will play the piano."

"Piano?" Hannah didn't mean to make a face, but she must have, for Miss Armstrong laughed.

"Don't worry. We'll tape Janet's music. It will seem like Martha is in the house playing while the robin is dancing outside. We found the perfect music but no recordings anywhere. Janet has the sheet music."

Well, Martha playing the piano made sense. Some of the lines had to do with her musical ability, and Laurel, as Martha, sang a lovely lullaby. So Robin must be a dancing part, not a talking one. Hannah didn't know Kammy was a dancer.

"Oh, I'm so happy you're here!"

"Kammy! I love your costume! It's perfect! You are a robin!"

Kammy wore a brown unitard with long sleeves, a red vest covered with feathers, and a feathered headpiece. "Gee made it. The ballet shoes were the hardest."

"We finally found a beige pair in a dance catalogue," Miss Armstrong said. "Expensive, but good shoes are vital for dancing."

"First time I ever had any dancing shoes, period." Kammy grinned. "I'm not really a dancer, Hannah. I never even had lessons."

"But able to do more with her body than those with years of lessons," Janet said. "Let's get started. I've got a gingerbread in the oven."

"Yummy," Hannah said.

Janet nodded. "Exactly why we're inviting you to dinner. Kammy needs someone her own age to chat with." She sat at the piano.

Hannah was certain Dad and Uncle Martin wouldn't mind. She'd text them as soon as the rehearsal was over.

Miss Armstrong opened her prompt book. "Now this scene is difficult to block, which is one of the reasons I wanted only you two to come today. The garden wall will be located Up Center. Obviously, Robin can't fly over it. However, she can lead Mary to the door, which will be covered in vines. One of the problems is that since Kammy choreographed her own dance, every time she does it, it's a bit different. Kammy, try to at least nail down your approximate locations on stage, so that Hannah will have an idea of where you'll be. It doesn't matter if you change the steps."

"What if I watch her a few times?" Hannah suggested. "I guess you'll want me to follow her, not exactly dancing, but sort of being graceful, too."

"Exactly," Miss Armstrong said, sounding relieved.

"The music is perfect," Kammy said. "Just wait until you hear it. Janet had the sheet music. It's called "The Song of the Robin.""

"The music sounds English," Janet said, "but it was written by an American composer. I played it in a recital when I was in high school. Kammy is wearing her costume today because Gee wants to know if it works."

Kammy giggled. "She wants to find out how badly I'll molt."

Janet began to play. The tinkling tune suggested a happy robin, frolicking and rejoicing over a beautiful day. Kammy turned into a bird, with fluid, ethereal movements. Her dancing wasn't ballet, exactly. It was more like the music was flowing through her. Hannah could see what Miss Armstrong meant. The dance was probably different every time. Then the music changed suddenly, and the bird became anxious, insistent. Robin had something important to tell Mary—something she must understand right now! Then the song came to an end, and Janet lifted her fingers from the keys.

Not wanting to break the mood, Hannah said softly, "Please dance again, Kammy, and I'll think about how Mary should follow you. I think I'll start by looking up at the window Stage Right and hearing Martha playing. Then I'll notice Robin."

Janet did break the mood. "Sounds like a good plan—but one that will take awhile. Let me text Leland and ask him to take the cake out of the oven."

Fortunately, the music was more than capable of recapturing the mood, and before the next hour had passed, the girls had worked out their routine.

"I'm thrilled!" Miss Armstrong said. "What a team! Both of you are splendid! I didn't need to be here at all."

Hannah was too embarrassed to say anything, but she knew Miss Armstrong had just done a fine job of directing. She got out of the way and allowed Mary and Robin to work it out. She would have told them if they were off track.

"Now to tend to the rest of dinner," Janet said. "Are you joining us, Anna? I know you have a date this evening."

"Yes, but I'll eat with you," Miss Armstrong said. "It's too soon for a dinner date. We'll probably go somewhere nearby for a drink and conversation. I should get changed, though. You should do the same, Kammy. Was the costume okay?"

"Just right," Kammy said. "I hardly molted at all."

"Then don't wear it again until dress rehearsal. Better contact your dad, Hannah."

"Okay, Miss Armstrong."

Hannah had hoped to have a long heart-to-heart talk with Kammy in private—to find out about the trial and to learn, maybe, who had killed her grandfather. She was certain Danny would demand to know. Instead, once Kammy had changed, the sound of a gong filled the castle.

"Dinner," Kammy said. "Come on, Hannah. Leland doesn't like it if we're late; he says it's disrespectful to Janet."

After a few bites of Janet's beef stew and homemade biscuits, Hannah agreed with Leland completely. Not giving immediate and complete attention to this meal would be a travesty. "This is delicious," she said. "Thank you so much for inviting me."

Leland beamed. "Just save room for the gingerbread," he said.

Miss Armstrong rose. "And save a slice for me. I'd better freshen my makeup and get my coat. Web should arrive any minute."

Kammy giggled. "His name is Web?"

Mr. Markey laughed, too. "Maybe he's Spiderman, wiry but bloodless."

"Hush up, children." But Miss Armstrong smiled. "I guess I'm glad Robbie is in New York and not here to tease me, too."

Leland stood. "I'll clear the table, Janet. You and Mr. Markey can have your cake and coffee in the kitchen. Kamirah, you and Hannah go to the parlor. I'll serve you in there. That way, you can peek out the curtains at Anna and her date. Best that Spiderman not see Kamirah. We can't be too careful, you know."

"You be careful, too, Anna," Janet said. "It's probably okay, but meeting someone on the Internet named Web is peculiar. Call if you need Leland and me to pick you up." Miss Armstrong smiled fondly but did not seem worried.

Soon, Hannah and Kammy were peeking out of the parlor drapes. Hannah thought it strange that Miss Armstrong had a date, almost like she was a teenager.

Kammy shrugged. "We just think she's old because she's a teacher. She's awfully pretty."

"I guess." Hannah had never thought about it before. "Kammy, I've been dying to ask you what's going on? I mean, about the trial and everything."

"My part is over, and I guess I can tell you that my uncle killed my grandfather. My grandfather used to brag about having a treasure, but he didn't, really — or if he did, he meant me, not money. But that's what my uncle thought."

Hannah gasped. "His own son?" She was surprised. The man driving the truck — the one she thought must be the killer — was white.

"No, my stepmom's brother. He's not really my uncle, but I used to think he was. I know what you're thinking. My stepmother is white. She married my father, but he died."

"You're a good mind reader. Did your uncle, I mean the killer, act alone? Mr. Kennedy said there was more than one person arrested."

"Right. His girlfriend was with him." Kammy became very quiet, no doubt remembering. "I saw it happen," she whispered. "I ran out the back so they wouldn't kill me, too. I was afraid they'd find me. That's why I hid out here."

Hannah had troubles in her own complicated family, but this was a totally unfamiliar world. She put a hand on Kammy's shoulder. "But it's over now, right? Soon you'll be back in school, we'll be in the play, and everything will be okay."

Kammy shook her head. "I don't know what will happen yet. And please don't tell anyone what I told you. I shouldn't have, but no one here wants to talk about it. They're so good to me, but they can't really understand. The cops and my lawyer say I'm still in danger, that there could be others involved. You and Gee are the only outsiders who know I'm here."

"And Porter and Danny and Beth," Hannah added. "Oh, and Gabby and Mr. Kennedy, too."

Kammy frowned. "I forgot. Yes, I guess too many people know."

"But won't tell," Hannah said. "You're safe now, Kammy."

"My lawyer doesn't think so. He was even angry Miss Armstrong included my name on the cast list. He doesn't think I should be in the play."

"Oh, but you must. You're wonderful!"

"Shhh," Kammy said. "Here comes lover boy. Miss Armstrong is going out to meet him. She looks beautiful, but . . ." Her voice trailed off.

But was right, Hannah thought. Miss Armstrong looked about the same as she had at dinner, but her date looked— "Unkempt" was a word she'd read recently, one she'd googled for meaning. Miss Armstrong's date was unkempt. He also seemed to be arguing with

Miss Armstrong about something. Whatever it was, Miss Armstrong won, and they got into his car and left.

"I wouldn't bet on the success of that date," Hannah said. "Kammy?" Her friend seemed awfully glum. "Are you okay?"

Kammy put her hand to her head. "A really bad headache. I'll ask Janet for a couple of Tylenol and go to bed early. I agree with you about the date, though."

Hannah hadn't had a headache in a long time. Stress, she supposed. Kammy had had plenty of it—good reason not to feel well. "I'll call Dad to come pick me up now," she said. "You don't have to wait with me."

"I'm sorry."

"No, I understand. Besides, I still have a ton of homework."

Kammy left the parlor. Hannah texted.

SCENE 9 – AN UNWELCOME MYSTERY

SOMEONE SHOOK HER GENTLY. "WHAT? What's wrong, Dad? I set my alarm." Sleepily, Hannah raised herself on an elbow to check the clock. Only six when she always got up at seven. "Dad?"

"You need to wake up, sweetheart. It could be an emergency. I just got a call from Miss Armstrong. Kammy is missing. She's probably been gone all night. Her bed hadn't been slept in. Miss Armstrong thinks you might have been the last one to see her."

"Kammy?"

"Get dressed, dear. Miss Armstrong and the Duncans are on their way over. Martin has to go to work, but I don't have classes this morning. I'll make a pot of coffee and defrost some bagels."

Hannah grabbed a pair of jeans and a sweatshirt, not even thinking about school. Kammy missing did not make sense. She was safe and happy at the castle. And why did no one check on her last night? Why had Miss Armstrong checked so early this morning? Hannah supposed those questions didn't matter as much as—where was Kammy now?

Downstairs, Dad was ready, waiting for the group from the castle, and surprisingly, so was Mr. Kennedy from next door. "I called Dan," Dad explained, "because I didn't think I'd be able to drive to school today. I called in to say you wouldn't be there."

"Thanks." Until they found Kammy, Hannah knew she'd be too nervous to concentrate on school.

"Jane will drive Danny," Mr. Kennedy said. "She'll just tell him I had a work emergency."

That was smart. No one would be able to endure Danny's questions. Mr. Kennedy said he'd called his policeman friend. Hannah didn't know whether that was smart or not.

Leland, Janet, and Miss Armstrong, in tears, arrived soon, and Hannah found herself bombarded with questions. "I . . . I don't know," she said. "I need to think." She looked helplessly at Dad.

"Hannah just woke up," Dad said. "Come sit in the kitchen. I've made coffee."

Uncle Martin handed her a mug of hot chocolate and kissed her forehead. "I'm sure you'll find her. Wish I could stay and help. I'll call later."

The chocolate brought Hannah away from dreams and to the problem at hand. "I don't know what happened," she said, "or where Kammy might be."

"Did she say anything about being unhappy with us?" Leland asked.

"No." Hannah tried remembering. Something had been strange before she texted Dad to pick her up.

Janet reached over and held her arm. "She seemed fine at dinner. But after—when the two of you were in the parlor, did anything happen? Did you notice any change?"

"Well, we were looking out the window watching Miss Armstrong and her date. Miss Armstrong looked nice, of course, but—"

"But let me say it." Miss Armstrong gave a short, bitter laugh. "My date looked awful, I know. I never should have got into the car with him, but I guess I was too embarrassed not to."

"That's why no one checked in on Kammy to say goodnight," Janet said. "We got a call from Anna to go pick her up. The date was not satisfactory."

"It certainly wasn't," Leland said, "but let's get back to Kammy. I doubt if Anna's date is connected."

Hannah wasn't sure. "It might be. I think that's when Kammy changed. She said how beautiful Miss Armstrong looked, and then she got very quiet. She said she had a bad headache and needed to go to bed. That's when I contacted Dad. Kammy didn't even wait with me." Hannah put her hand up, indicating quiet. What else did she remember? "Miss Armstrong, you and the man were arguing. What about? I was surprised. It seemed like a strange thing to do with someone you just met."

Miss Armstrong nodded. "Yes, looking back, it was. He kept asking questions about the castle—wanting to know how many rooms there were and if he could go inside. When I said maybe another time, he said maybe he would later. Then he didn't take me anyplace nice. We went to a nasty bar on the west side. I excused myself and went to the ladies' room and called Leland. And I stayed there until Janet texted that they were outside. I'm through with online dating."

"Kammy might have known who he was and thought he was looking for her." Before the others could ask why Kammy hadn't said anything to one of them, Hannah added quickly, "She's not very good at trusting people."

Everyone grew quiet. There was a likely chance Kamirah thought she had been betrayed, once again. But where could the poor girl have gone?

The doorbell rang, and Mr. Kennedy left to welcome his friend, Sergeant Dean Lodge.

"They'll probably want to talk in private," Hannah said. She looked at the clock. Still early. "I need to feed Betsy and let her out." Not giving the others a chance to reply, she dashed into Betsy's little room, where she also planned to call Porter. Porter always saw things clearly.

This was supposed to be a special day for Danny—the first time he would have lunch in school. The cafeteria was on the same floor as his morning classes, the ground floor, so he didn't need the elevator. Soon he would, of course, once his rehearsals began in the auditorium. He wheeled his way into the renovated cafeteria, which looked like a huge, sterile restaurant, perhaps in a modern hotel or an airport. Porter should have been there to help him, but Danny hadn't seen him all morning. He hadn't seen Hannah, either, although he didn't normally since they weren't in the same grade. Now what? He would not be able to handle a tray of food and his wheelchair.

"Darn it, Porter," he whispered. "You knew this was important to me."

"Danny?" It was Mrs. Hunt. "I don't think I've seen you here before. You look troubled. Need some help?"

"Thanks, Mrs. Hunt. I do. It's my first time. Porter Walters was supposed to buy lunch for me, but I don't see him anywhere."

"His name was on the absentee list this morning. Let's see who might be able to give you a hand." Mrs. Hunt, too, looked out at the students, seated around tables, engrossed in eating or in each other.

Danny noticed a few boys from his Cross Country team. They saw him but turned away. At another table, Danny saw a boy waving frantically.

"Hey, 'Colin,' want to eat with me?" It was Seth Edwards, who played Ben Weatherstaff, the gardener. Danny had had a number of rehearsals with Seth at the castle.

"Seth, I would like that. Thanks. But why are you eating with the sixth grade?"

"I've got an orthodontist appointment during seventh-grade lunch, and since I've got a study hall now, I got permission. I could use your company."

With Seth's help, Danny soon had a grilled cheese sandwich, a cup of tomato soup, and a carton of milk. Not for the first time Danny reflected that the Drama Club kids could give lessons on sportsmanship. He vowed that when next fall came, he'd outrun that table of boys who'd shunned him a few minutes ago. He'd show them!

Danny and Seth discovered they had more in common than just the play. They liked the same video games, movies and, most of all, dogs. "Maybe you can come over next Saturday and meet Bingo."

Seth said he'd check with his mom. Too soon, it was time to gobble down the remainder of their lunches before the warning bell rang. Then Seth cleared off both trays, and they went out front to meet their moms.

"Just a routine check-up," Seth said, "but the only appointment we could get."

Danny wished Seth could eat with the sixth graders every day, but at least he had a new friend. Seth was really good in the play, and the only actor Miss Armstrong was allowing to try a Yorkshire accent. Probably Seth and Hannah would be the important eighth graders in Drama Club next year. He and Porter would have to wait another year. Porter. What in the world was going on?

Beth had the same thought. What in the world was going on? Porter had been ready to leave for school when he got a text, and then Mom got a phone call. Beth was told to leave for school alone; Porter would be there later. But he wasn't. Beth discovered this when she went to the office to deliver a message to be read for afternoon announcements and saw that Porter Walters was included on the absentee list. He wasn't sick, but something was definitely wrong.

Curious—Hannah Rendina was also on the list. Good thing they don't have rehearsal today, Beth thought, but tomorrow everyone needed to be there. All-day tech this Saturday, followed by dress rehearsals next week. Opening night, a week from Friday! It was all going too fast. She remembered what Miss Armstrong said last year—"I always think I need two more weeks." Beth thought they needed two more months.

Well, she simply didn't have time to worry about it. As well as math and English tests, she had an important tech meeting after school, right there on stage. Her set builder friends from the high school were coming to help on construction, so she had to make certain they understood her design. One of the middle school custodians was driving there with the scrim, which would be hanged. "Hanged." Beth giggled. She and everyone else wanted to say hung, of course, but the high school show-offs insisted "hanged" was the correct term. And when she spoke with the costume crew, she now talked about building costumes, rather than making or sewing them. Theater had its own language. Well, so did art. She imagined every specialty did. You needed to understand and speak the language if you wanted to be "in."

As soon as Mr. Kennedy's friend, Sergeant Lodge, arrived at Hannah's house, he suggested that the first step was to make a thorough search of the castle. "I'm sure you looked in the obvious rooms, but if Kammy is hiding, she won't go for the obvious."

Hannah nodded. "And she spent so much time there alone, I'll bet she knows places that even Mr. Markey doesn't."

"Or remembers," Leland said. "I've lived there for over twenty years, but I don't know every corner. I think we've made a mistake, rushing here, leaving Mr. Markey alone. He could be in danger, whether or not Kammy is there."

Horrified, they looked at each other. They'd come to the conclusion that Miss Armstrong's "date" must have been responsible for Kammy's reaction and disappearance. "Web, or whatever his name is, could try to get into the castle," Hannah said. And, she thought, Mr. Markey could very well decide that Miss Armstrong had been mistaken about Web—that he was a friend after all.

Sergeant Lodge took charge. "Mr. and Mrs. Duncan and Miss Armstrong, you'll go to the castle; I'll join you there as soon as I check in at the station. Dan, you and Porter stay here with the Rendinas and keep on thinking."

As Miss Armstrong was about to leave, Hannah stopped her. "Miss Armstrong, would you check Kammy's clothes to see if anything is missing, especially her coat? It's too cold to go anywhere without one. And then call me, please."

Miss Armstrong nodded. "Good idea. I'll do that first thing."

Hannah's dad looked at the somber faces remaining. "I'll fix a meal we might as well call brunch."

"Protein power," Mr. Kennedy said. "I'll give you a hand. Besides, Hannah and Porter will talk more if we're not around. I don't think Porter has said a word since he got here."

Porter smiled. "Can't talk and think at the same time."

"He's right, you know," Hannah said, as soon as they were alone. "You're awfully quiet, even for you."

"Crazy day," Porter said. "Not exactly what I expected. I'm going to miss two tests and a science presentation. I guess Mom will write me an excuse, but—"

"Poor you. Dad woke me at six! Don't worry about school. Both of us are doing great. Our teachers will understand we're not blowing them off. Now, what do you think? Is Kammy hiding in the castle?"

Porter shook his head. "I doubt it. Trusting adults isn't exactly her thing. It would help to know if any of her clothes are missing."

Hannah glanced at her phone. "Ouch! I missed a text. I expected Miss Armstrong to call me. Okay, she says that Janet checked.

Kammy's coat is still there. So that means she is in the castle somewhere."

Porter frowned. "Maybe yes—maybe no. Ask her what color Kammy's coat is."

"But we already know that."

"Do we? Ask anyway."

Miss Armstrong replied immediately. "It's rose pink. Janet bought it for her a few weeks ago." The call ended quickly.

"A rose pink coat—I've never seen that one. I'll bet Janet bought her lots of new clothes. What, Porter? What are you thinking?"

"Just that if Kammy believes she's been betrayed, maybe she left the castle with her old clothes—including that jacket that looked like it was a mass of bullet holes."

Hannah's mouth dropped. "So where would she go? It's cold out there, and you, Danny, and I are her only friends. She might not trust us, either."

Porter might have answered, but Hannah's dad stuck his head out from the kitchen. "Come on, you two. Past time for some nourishment."

Waffles and bacon did make a difference, they decided, and Hannah announced that her brains had been restored. "I've got an idea, but first I'll let Betsy out, and then have her join us."

"Good idea, but I've got a better one," Mr. Kennedy said. "I'll go home and let Bingo out. Then he and Betsy can have some time together in their playroom."

"Or sleeping room. Martin's creation was inspired." Hannah's dad and Porter cleared the table while the others attended to animal duties.

No one was surprised when Boots joined the dogs. Hannah giggled. "Boots refuses to be left out of anything." As soon as they returned to the living room, she dropped her bombshell.

"Okay," Hannah said. "I've figured out where Kammy must be."

SCENE 10 — THE ROBIN WHO SHOWED THE WAY

AFTER MOM PICKED DANNY UP, they headed directly to physical therapy. "How did school go?" Mom asked, as if it were an ordinary day. He didn't tell her that he had never been so tired.

This would not do. Tomorrow, and for the rest of the week, he'd have rehearsal after school. True, he wouldn't be there for a full day, but he probably should go home before lunch, and then return for rehearsal. He'd ask Sid, who had become both confidant and co-conspirator. Sid planned to attend a few rehearsals to make sure Danny could make the transfer from his electric wheelchair to the uncomfortable wooden one without re-injuring himself. He'd already purchased tickets for both performances.

"Everything went great," Danny said, "except I don't get why Porter and Hannah weren't there. Beth doesn't know, either. I've texted them a few times, but no answer."

Mom sighed. "Something's going on, but I don't know what exactly. Your father was next door all morning when he should have gone to work. Then a few people from the castle showed up, including Miss Armstrong—"

"Beth got a text from Miss Armstrong, saying she couldn't come to rehearsal. Beth was pretty mad at having to take complete charge of set construction. Even though she's the designer, she's still a kid!

An adult should be there. Sorry for interrupting, Mom. What happened next?"

Mom shrugged. "Then Dad's friend, Dean Lodge, showed up." Mom's dislike for the policeman was apparent. "Why he always tries to involve your dad in his business is beyond me."

"Well, maybe, but if it has something to do with Hannah's family and Porter and people from the castle. . ." Danny's voice drifted off.

"You're right. I don't know for sure, but I think it has something to do with that girl, Kamirah Williams."

That's what Danny figured, but a ping on his phone kept him from coming up with a reply. "It's Porter. Oh, no, you're right, Mom. Kammy has disappeared again. Porter says he'll call me tonight."

"She's in the play, isn't she? I wonder if Miss Armstrong made a mistake in casting her."

"Maybe." But that wasn't what worried Danny. Sure, the play was important, but not as important as Kammy's safety.

Sid met them out on the sidewalk and helped Danny's mom get the wheelchair out of the van. For the next hour, Danny concentrated so hard on standing from a sitting position, without help, that he hardly had the brainpower to think about Kammy or to wonder what was happening at Hannah's house.

"I'm pleased with his progress," Sid told Mom, "and I'm sure he'll do fine in his play." Privately, Sid told Danny that this was the first time he'd ever looked forward to attending one.

Danny had grinned. "Me, too. I couldn't convince Mom and Dad to come to just the last performance, so I told Miss Armstrong I'd walk at the end of both shows. She sort of fired the boy, who would pretend to be me and walk behind the scrim. He was really happy and promised not to tell anyone about it."

"You'll be a star," Sid had said. "But afterwards, you need to take it easy. No running before the end of summer, and then, only if I okay it. You don't want to backslide."

No, Danny did not want that. However, he was so exhausted right that minute, he couldn't imagine what he'd be like when the show was over.

Beth was no longer angry with Miss Armstrong. Porter had texted that Kammy was missing and that Miss Armstrong was involved in finding her. Then Miss Armstrong texted again to say that a teacher from the high school would accompany the techie kids planning to help. Fingers crossed for Kammy, of course, but Beth thought the high school teacher, Mr. Fielding, who knew tons about building and lighting sets, would be a huge improvement over Miss Armstrong.

No Kammy could mean no Robin, but Beth thought they'd figure a way around that. Maybe they could play bird trills that Hannah could pretend to follow. "Beth, this is not your problem," she whispered.

Mr. Fielding greeted her with a big smile and a firm handshake. He and Beth had been mutual fans since she had helped with the park district/high school play last summer.

"I'm really glad you could come, Mr. Fielding."

"And I'm glad I was available. Miss Armstrong shot me an emergency text this morning. Hope your missing actor turns up soon."

Beth nodded. "Me, too, but the play will be fine. We're mainly hoping she's safe."

"If your set design is any indication, the play will be wonderful. Technically, this may be the most difficult play your school has ever attempted, but your renovated theater is up to the challenge. I think it could compete with every middle school in the state—and some high schools."

"I'm so happy we can borrow a scrim."

"Not a problem, Beth, but it couldn't achieve the effect you need if the school hadn't installed a whole new lighting system. Oh, good, the boys are here. Ask the custodian to pull up to the loading dock, fellas, and then bring in the scrim, backdrop, and trees."

The secret garden would be placed behind the scrim and fairly simple — borrowed fake trees from the high school, plus real plants and flowers that florists from a few towns had agreed to donate in return for full-page ads in the program. The stage would be spike taped, showing where the live plants would be placed and delivered on the morning of the first performance. When the stage was lit from the front, the scrim would look like a solid piece of material. When the lighting came from the back, it would seem to be semi-transparent at first, showing everything in silhouette, creating the appearance of a dead garden. During intermission, the live plants would be added. In Act Two, lights would come from the front, and the scrim would open from the center. Finally, actors would be seen in the actual garden. It really wasn't as complicated as it sounded, as long as they had the right equipment. Beth decided that the delayed start of school, giving time for everything to be completed, had been worth the wait, after all.

It took several hours for the high school boys and a few middle school volunteers to set up the sky backdrop and the scrim. Beth had told her parents she would be super late, so that was one less worry. But all of the workers were becoming very hungry.

"Tell you what, Beth," Mr. Fielding said. "I'll send out for pizza."

"Oh, thank you! I'll ask Miss Armstrong to pay you back. Thanks to what you've loaned us, we've got plenty left in our budget."

"I'm not worried, but you should let Miss Armstrong know that your set won't be ready for two more days, at least. A lot of painting is still needed, and, as you know, paint takes awhile to dry. You've done a wonderful job, but your director and stage manager needed to be here today. If I hadn't been able to come, I wouldn't have allowed my crew to help. No adult supervisor would have been against both schools' rules."

"I'll text Miss Armstrong," Beth said. "Do you think we'll be ready for tech on Saturday?"

"If you can work for the rest of the week. I can't be here tomorrow, but Friday is possible. I'll definitely come Saturday morning and bring whatever crew is available. But you need to supply more workers, too."

That was the problem. Their best techies had gone on to high school. Well, the whole cast needed to help. Beth explained everything in a text to Miss Armstrong, but she added a heart emoji and said she hoped everything was okay. To her surprise, Miss Armstrong got right back to her. "Everyone is planning to come for a rehearsal tomorrow, anyway. You may put them to work. Just decide on the jobs that need doing, and who might do them." That could take hours! Thank goodness her homework was done! Cheers interrupted her thoughts. The pizza had arrived.

Once they were energized from the hasty meal, they tackled the rest of the garden. At least morning art classes would sketch the stones needed on the wall, now only a plain flat. Not everyone could paint stones. Beth would need to teach the few cast members she thought might learn quickly and find easy jobs for the rest. At least no other flats were needed. An ornate bed frame, to be delivered from the castle, and a simple twin mattress that the props chair's mom was about to throw out, were all that was needed for Colin's room. The bed could be wheeled in and out quickly. All other scenes took place on the apron or in front of the scrim. Beth's design made the garden the main event.

Finally at 8:00, Beth thanked everyone. Surprisingly, the high school students thanked her. "We needed the Thespian points," one boy said.

Mr. Fielding offered her a lift home. "Text your parents and say you're on your way," he said.

To her relief, Beth had received another text—from Porter, mostly written in emojis. But the symbols meant, "Found her. Am beat, but wake me when you get home."

They should return to the West Village Flats, Hannah had told them. "We must talk to the mother and children Porter and I met when we went looking for Kammy before. The children said Kammy sometimes played with them. The mother wasn't friendly, exactly, but she wasn't unfriendly, either."

"That's right, Hannah. And remember, the little boy, Alec, said Kammy knew great places to hide when they played Hide and Seek."

"Yes!" Then she thought it over. "But would those hiding places be someplace warm?" That was, Hannah had learned, a rhetorical question. No answer was possible or expected.

Dad reached for his coat. "Guess we'd better take a drive."

"Wait," Mr. Kennedy cautioned. "Shouldn't we call for backup?"

Hannah shook her head. "The police would scare that family. Then they might not tell us anything."

"You're right. In fact, Uncle Dan, you and Mr. Rendina should wait in the car. Hannah and I should be the only ones going to the door. They'll remember us. I think they could tell we cared about Kammy."

"Unit 22," Hannah said, as they pulled into the lot. "Maybe don't park right in front of it."

"Just close enough in case you need us," Mr. Kennedy said. He didn't like the idea of letting Hannah and Porter go alone.

"We won't take our eyes off you for a second," Dad said.

"Brrr," Porter said, as they walked to the door. "Kammy better be dressed warmly if she's hiding outside somewhere."

Crossing her fingers first, Hannah rang the doorbell. She sensed, rather than saw, someone peeking out from the curtain. Then she heard scrambling sounds coming from inside, and then someone stage whispering, "Please don't open it."

"Porter, I think she's in there, but she won't be for long. Go tell Mr. Kennedy to call his policeman friend. Just him. See if he can bring over the key to Unit 26."

"Got it." Porter dashed back to the car, just as the door opened.

"Hello," Hannah said to the same woman they'd met before. "Do you remember me?"

"Can't say I do."

Hannah pretended not to notice the woman's unpleasantness. She also pretended not to hear a backdoor slam. "I met you when I was looking for my friend, Kammy. Your son Alec said that she played Hide and Seek with your children. I found her, but she's disappeared again. It's all a big misunderstanding, and it's important that I find her again. Could you help, please?"

"Sorry. Haven't seen her. Please go. I have work to do, and my husband will be home soon for lunch. He doesn't like strangers coming here."

"Sorry to have bothered you," Hannah said. She'd managed to see enough. Flung over a living room chair was Kammy's old jacket, dirty white with large black spots, some worn through, looking like bullet holes.

Hannah returned to the car. "I might have changed my mind about backup," she said. "But we do need Sergeant Lodge."

"He's coming with the key," Mr. Kennedy said. "Leland and Janet are coming, too. Anna—that is, Miss Armstrong—is staying with Mr. Markey. Obviously, they didn't find anything."

"What happened after I left, Hannah? Did she let you in?"

"Nope. But I heard the backdoor slam and also saw Hannah's jacket in the living room. It's too cold for her to go far without it."

"Not that it would do her much good. So you're thinking she's hiding in her old house?"

"Makes sense, I guess. The robin showed me the way."

Porter nodded. "Or at least her jacket did."

They didn't have long to wait before two cars arrived—Leland's and a police car. Hannah was surprised to see Janet in tears. Leland looked as if he were barely controlling his anger. She and Porter were told to wait in the car while Sergeant Lodge, Janet, and Leland went to the front door, and Mr. Kennedy and Hannah's dad went to the back.

"Porter, I can understand why Janet is crying, but why is Leland so mad?"

"I noticed that, too. He's very protective of Janet and doesn't like to see her unhappy. The thing is, Kammy came here to people who don't even care about her. Okay, the children like her, but just as someone fun to play with. I think Leland is angry because Kammy didn't trust the people, especially Janet, who have given her protection and love. She didn't trust you to help her when she saw the man Miss Armstrong was dating."

"And Kammy ran away before she could find out that Miss Armstrong had called Leland to rescue her. I guess I should be mad, too, but I'm not. Mainly I just feel sorry for her."

"Maybe it will be like my parents. If Beth or I are late and they don't know where we are, first they're scared, and then when we turn up, they get mad. Then, boy, are we in trouble! I bet most parents are like that. Of course, the people at the castle aren't her parents."

"Here they come now. Yes, Kammy is with them."

Hannah squeezed over to make room, hoping Kammy would drive with them, even though it made more sense for her to go in Leland's car. But both sides of her thoughts were wrong. Instead, she saw the officer lead Kammy to the police car, and Mr. Kennedy climbed in next to her. "I don't understand," she said, when Dad returned.

"They're going to the police station to sort things out. I'm not certain Leland wants Kammy to return to the castle, at least not until they learn why she left."

Porter was right about Leland, Hannah thought, but decided to talk to Dad about it later. "I wonder what's going to happen to the play," she said. The show must go on, of course, but would Kammy be a part of it?

SCENE 11 – IN THE GARDEN

THE HOUSELIGHTS DIMMED. THE AUDIENCE grew quiet. In the lights booth, operators said a silent prayer to Thespis, while those on sound assured each other that cues had been checked and double-checked. Backstage, actors waited, concentrating on their first lines, trying to ignore their jittery stomachs. In the Green Room, Danny sat in his motorized wheelchair — he wouldn't transfer himself to the bed until the last minute — and wondered what would happen if he threw up on stage. Thinking about how Hannah (Mary) and Imani (Mrs. Medlock) could possibly cover for him made him grin, snicker, and finally laugh out loud.

"Shhh," warned others in the Green Room, staring at the monitor, waiting for the house to go dark and for Priyanka, the narrator and Mary Lennox's Ayah, to step into a single spotlight and give the opening line. Hannah was backstage already, waiting for her first entrance.

Oddly, Hannah was not nervous. It seemed strange, though, feeling like two people. She was Mary Lennox but controlled by Hannah Rendina. Mary was about to be a sad little brat in Misselthwaite Manor, but she was also Hannah, whose two dads were in the audience proudly watching.

Neither Mary nor Hannah had a mother in their lives, but at least Hannah's was living. Playing a girl who had lost her mother had helped Hannah decide to reach out and visit hers next summer. It was time to attempt to repair her family.

Mary was about to help Colin walk again while Hannah was one of the few people who knew a grand secret that would be revealed tonight. After many months, Danny Kennedy would also walk again.

Mary's best friends were Dickon and Colin. Danny was still Hannah's best friend, of course, but Porter might become her boyfriend someday. At least that's what she hoped.

Perhaps Mary's best girlfriend was Martha. Hannah was starting to make girlfriends, too. Sometimes she and Laurel went to Smithy's for shakes and to run lines. She'd thought Kammy would be her best friend at school. It was no longer likely. Surprisingly, this did not make Hannah sad. She had accepted that she didn't really know Kammy. Mainly, she had liked the idea of her. It was thrilling to have such a mysterious friend. She was glad she'd been able to help, and she did feel sorry for her, but they hadn't been together enough to establish a strong, true friendship.

So much had happened since the police car left West Village Flats—so many decisions had been made. As soon as the play was over, Kammy would leave Castle Bluff and go to another state where she would live in a children's home, similar to the one in Castle Bluff, but far from where dangers might still lurk. She'd recognized Miss Armstrong's date, who'd called himself Web, as a close friend of her uncle's, but the police had been unable to trace him. Perhaps he'd meant Kammy harm, or maybe he was just curious about the castle. Kammy's lawyer and the police were not willing to take a chance. Her taped testimony was all that was needed for a court case that could drag on for some time. Mr. Markey said she could come back for holidays, that the castle would always be her home. Hannah wasn't sure. Mr. Markey loved and forgave everyone, but could Leland, Janet, and Miss Armstrong? The robin would dance tonight and tomorrow night. After that, it would fly away. Hannah might never see Kammy again. If she did, she'd figure it out then.

Oh, her cue! She ran onto the stage. *Where is my Ayah? I want her right now!*

It was time to be Mary for the next ninety minutes.

Imani, always a fine actor, was splendid as Mrs. Medlock, the frustrated housekeeper. She managed to keep Medlock always on the verge of being mean. She never crossed the line. Instead, she played the part in such a way that the audience understood why she was impatient with Mary. After all, she had to deal with the sickly Colin, manage the huge estate and its staff, while worrying about what the Master might think when or if he returned. Medlock didn't have time to concern herself with a spoiled child who refused to dress herself.

She's that contrary, Medlock told Martha, the pretty housemaid, played by Laurel Mullen.

Martha giggled. *And her name is Mary?* Then she started singing, loudly enough for the strange girl from India to hear. *Mistress Mary, quite contrary, how does your garden grow? With silver bells and cockleshells and pretty maids all in a row.*

Don't you dare sing that! I am not contrary! Don't you ever sing that again!

Mrs. Medlock gave a tired smile before bustling off to her many duties.

Martha entered Mary's room. *I will stop if you stop being contrary. Everyone in this household is too busy to put up with another spoiled child.*

Mary opened her mouth to complain again—*I'm not a—* but stopped suddenly. *I—I think you're lucky. You're busy. You don't have to stay in this room all day with nothing to do.*

Nothing to do but play. I would change places with you if I could— A look of panic came into Laurel's eyes, as she dropped character. She was supposed to say more, but what?"

Fortunately, Hannah noticed her distress and was able to cover. *I would rather learn to polish the brasses and silver than be here alone.*

Laurel picked up the cue and became Martha again. *It is pretty when it's all shiny, but my hands are rough and tired, and more chores await me at home. It is growing late. Soon, Cook will come with your tea, and then you will go to sleep.*

I can't sleep unless my Ayah sings to me. I will lie awake and cry, and then I will be contrary all tomorrow.

Martha smiled. *I must go home to help my mother, but I will sing the lullaby she sings to me — if you promise to sleep tonight.*

I'll try. Then came one of Hannah's favorite parts of the show — Martha's lullaby. Laurel truly had a beautiful voice.

Mother of mine, where go the stars, go the stars, go the stars?
Mother of mine, where go the stars, the moment the night is over?

They put out their lights and close their eyes, close their eyes, close their
    eyes. And rest far above the sunlit skies, until the day is over.

Mother of mine, where goes the moon, goes the moon, goes the moon?
Mother of mine, where goes the moon, the moment the night is over?

It lowers its lamp and sails away, sails away, sails away
To far and beyond where it will stay, until the day is over.

Then the child asks her mother where the sun goes at night, and Mother answers:

It goes to its home beneath the sky, 'neath the sky, 'neath the sky.
And there it will sleep like you and I, until the night is over.

Laurel thought the audience would grow tired of hearing all the verses, but no one else agreed. On stage, Mary didn't cry, but Hannah had to force herself not to.

Tomorrow, I'll return, Mistress Mary, and teach you to dress yourself. Then you may go into the garden and play. Ben Weatherstaff will give you a trowel and seeds, and you can start your own garden.

The scene ended, as the stage grew dark. Laurel and Hannah exited. "Thanks, Hannah. Thank you for covering," Laurel whispered, before returning to the Green Room. Hannah remained backstage. Mary Lennox was about to meet Colin Craven.

Stagehands had rolled the bed with him in it onto the stage, but Danny still waited for his backstage cue from tonight's stage manager, Gabrielle. His signal to howl would come even before the lights came up. During this part of the show, his role was easier than Hannah's. He didn't have to be both irritating and endearing. The audience didn't have to like him. He just had to be unpleasant. Later, his part was harder when Colin needed to change inside and out.

"Go!" Gabrielle whispered.

Ow! My back! I have a lump. I'm going to die! The lights were brought up to half. It was late at night; Colin was in bed.

Mary entered. *I knew it wasn't the wind I heard. Everyone keeps lying to me.*

Who are you?

I was going to ask you the same question. I'm Mary Lennox, and I've come from India to live.

India? You don't look Indian.

I'm not. Different kinds of people live in India. Like many places, I suppose. But who are you?

Colin Craven. You shouldn't be here. I'm sick. I'm dying. Maybe you'll die, too. I hope you do!

That's not very nice of you. Did you say Craven? That's my uncle's name.

He's my father, but I hardly ever see him. He doesn't like looking at me. It makes him sad.

My parents didn't like looking at me, either. My mother was beautiful. I liked looking at her, but now my parents are dead. Everyone is gone.

I'm still here, even though everyone wishes I weren't. We must be cousins. I never knew I had a cousin before. But it's no use. I have a big lump on my back. I'll be dead soon. Probably by morning.

Let me see that lump! Why, there's nothing there at all. You don't have a lump, any more than I do. You're just a big baby, trying to get attention.

I do have a lump. You don't know anything. Go away!

Mrs. Medlock rushed into the room. *Mary, you have no business in here! The idea — wandering about late at night! Colin, you must have your tonic and go back to sleep. Mary, return to your room at once!*

Gladly! You couldn't pay me to be around this whining child!

The scene was over. Danny was grateful to be wheeled off stage and helped into his own wheelchair. The mattress was uncomfortable, and the wooden wheelchair killed his back. No wonder Colin howled. But Danny was determined to make it through the show. So many people were counting on him. Heck, *he* was counting on him!

In the next scene, Ben Weatherstaff gives Mary some seeds and a trowel and shows her where she might plant a garden. Mary glimpses a robin, flying over a stone wall. At this point in the play, it's only a pretend robin. She asks Ben what's on the other side of the wall, and Ben tells her it's a secret garden. The key to it is lost, but no one is allowed inside, anyway.

One more scene to go, and the first act would be over. "It's going splendidly," Marla, seated on one side of Beth, whispered. "I can't wait to see your garden."

Most of the second act was set in the garden. Beth and Miss Armstrong purposely planned it that way. The audience would have grown tired of constant scenery changes. They could do a lot on their remodeled stage, but it was still a middle school auditorium, not meant for lavish productions. "Dickon is next," Beth whispered. "Wait until you see Porter!"

Hannah's scene, alone with Porter, was her favorite in the whole play, and it wasn't because she liked him so much. Actually, she forgot he was Porter. The other actors were good, but she was always aware they were her friends playing roles. Dickon was Dickon—not in the least like Porter, except for the times he was quiet and gentle, holding an animal. Other times, he was Porter's opposite. Dickon romped and played, pulled tricks and told jokes—almost like a mythical creature of the forest.

Mr. Chippy, this is my friend, Mary Lennox. Dickon petted one of the many realistic-looking stuffed animals they used in his scenes. *What did you say, Mr. Chippy? No, I guarantee she won't hurt you.*

Mary quickly agreed. *I promise, Mr. Chippy Chipmunk. I'll even help you find food, if you tell me what you like and where to look.*

Dickon shook his head. *Mr. Chippy believes you won't hurt him, but he doesn't trust that you won't steal his food. He thanks you very much indeed but says he will take care of high tea himself.*

Mary laughed, and then shivered. *Dickon, someone is watching us. That is Mrs. Fox. She often comes to visit when her four kits are asleep. Will you ask her to come closer? I've never met a fox before. And she's never met a girl. Perhaps someday she will, and that girl will be you.*

Their scene ended with Dickon's promise to help Mary with her garden and to introduce her to more animals. It was the only scene in the act that did not have an element of sadness. But Colin forced a return.

I want to see Dickon. Bring him to me now!

I won't, you horrid boy! I won't let you ruin my day! Mary flounced out of the room.

But I want to play and have fun, too! Colin's plaintive wail ended Act One.

Beth rushed backstage during intermission, even though Marla and Kurt were anxious to talk about Porter's performance. She just had to tell the cast how wonderful they were. And not just the cast; lights, sound, run crew—every single cue had been handled to perfection, and everyone deserved her praise.

Beth peered into a classroom, occupied solely by Kamirah Williams and her police officer guard. She would like to wish Kammy luck—perhaps Break-a-wing, rather than leg—but she knew the officer would not allow it. Miss Armstrong had told Beth that the police, the school administration, and Kammy's lawyer had decided that Kammy would be allowed to dance both nights, but that was it. She would arrive at school during intermission and leave directly after her dance. Later, she would receive a link to the video of tonight's performance, and Beth had purchased a friendship card for those who wished to sign. Beth gave a little wave through the window, but if Kammy saw her, she did not respond.

Once in the Green Room, Hannah grabbed her arm. "Beth, is Kammy here?"

Beth nodded.

"Can I talk to her?"

Beth shook her head.

"Well, maybe after the show."

"Sorry, Hannah. She won't be allowed to stay tonight or tomorrow, either—not even for Curtain Call. I know it's hard, but that's the only way the school would agree to having her in the building." Beth didn't mention what a time Miss Armstrong had had getting the administration to agree. "But Kammy will get the video link, and you can sign the card I bought. Now I need to talk to a few other people before intermission is over. You're doing a super job."

"Thanks. I thought the scene with Porter was great, but I can't get him to talk to me. He's just sitting in a corner, staring into space."

Beth looked to where Hannah was pointing and smiled knowingly. "That's what Kurt does, once a show begins. Porter is a true actor; he's staying in character until the play is over, and he won't let anyone disturb him."

Hannah looked puzzled. "Well, okay. I guess I'll talk to Danny."

Beth saw Danny fooling around with the boy who played the doctor. Danny was doing fine, but no one would accuse him of being a true actor. "You could do that, Hannah, or maybe you could follow Porter's lead and think about Act Two. Gotta go." Beth hoped Kurt would save her a few cookies.

For some reason, Hannah was nervous waiting for Act Two to begin. It might have something to do with Kammy, or maybe because the big secret would soon be no more. Everyone would learn the truth about Danny. This was the most exciting, thrilling night of her life. Nothing else came close, not even the Valentine's Day dance, except for getting Betsy.

The houselights went down, and the stage lights came up. All that could be seen on stage was the wall and the ancient door to the secret garden. Then bird trills, followed by the robin's song, as recorded by Janet—softly at first, then louder as Kammy appeared on stage. Then Mary entered and gazed at the window as if hearing Martha play the piano. Then, turning, she saw the robin.

Little robin, wait for me! Show me the way, please!

The dance, rehearsed only that one time at the castle, began. Hannah wondered if she was Mary, pursuing the robin, or Hannah, anxious to communicate with Kammy. Both goals were urgent, but at the moment, the second seemed more so. A friendship card, signed by many, was not good enough. Suddenly, Hannah knew exactly what to do. She hoped Miss Armstrong would forgive her for adding a short line—especially since she'd never done it before and never would again. The dance came to an end when the robin reached down next to the door, revealing a key.

Thank you, Robin! You are my friend. I will never forget you.

Startled, Kammy's eyes met Hannah's, and the two girls smiled at each other. An inspired sound operator added bird trills as the robin exited.

A few people in the audience, who knew exactly what had just taken place, felt their eyes well up.

Mary inserted the large key into the keyhole and turned. A grating sound played, the stone wall was rolled off, and lights backlit the scrim. Mary heard the audience gasp as they finally saw Beth's creation, the running-wild Secret Garden. The main curtain closed, and the audience applauded. Danny had said that an audience applauding a set meant it was a bad set. Hannah didn't believe that for one minute, and she didn't care. Beth deserved the applause — and the applause that would soon follow.

Wait until the next time they saw the garden, Hannah thought, blooming and tidy after only one short scene. Originally, as written, the dance had come at the end of Act One, giving the crew all intermission to "restore" the garden to glory. The change came because of safety concerns for Kammy and others.

Because of last-minute changes and problems, the director and stage managers were not able to determine accurate playing times for each act. They were not able to say how much time would go by until the dance scene meant to end Act One. Thus, the administration was not willing for Kammy to sit through Act One until the last scene was reached. She must dance right after intermission, or not at all.

Miss Armstrong, Beth, and crews were forced to make drastic changes on the actual day of the performance. The run crew had gone to school early that morning and had had one chance only to practice the impossible set change. Hannah thought they deserved a curtain call all to themselves.

But everyone connected with the show had become flexible. Right before the first dress rehearsal, Gabrielle had to quit her part as Susan Sowerberry because of almost intolerable conditions at home. She was allowed to stage manage tonight, but Priyanka would take charge tomorrow. Fortunately, the part was small, and Miss Armstrong was able to cut it. That was an advantage in having the script writer on hand.

The program, revised once again and run off again at lunchtime, spelled out the scenes and the times, so the audience wouldn't become confused.

The next scene in Act Two took place three months later and was performed on the apron. Mrs. Medlock and the doctor were in the very short scene, with the main curtain closed, while the crew behind the scrim hustled to put live flowers and plants in the correct places. Miss Armstrong had given Imani and Tim extra business in an attempt to stall the scene. Mrs. Medlock folded laundry on a table, and the doctor rummaged through his medicine bag. They were told to ad lib as much as they could, and then to strike the table and props when the scene ended. All available crew was needed to create the garden.

He is outside all day, Doctor, with the girl. They refuse to tell me where they go. You remember how poor their appetites were. Now both of them eat every morsel put in front of them, and then demand more. You've seen for yourself how they have changed in appearance.

They have changed on the inside as well. Both have gained weight. They are almost glowing with good health. Perhaps, Mrs. Medlock, they are the correct medicine for each other. I was not pleased when the girl arrived, but it seems I was wrong. Sunshine and each other are their cure. There will be no more talk of dying in this household.

Colin still acts the Lord of the Manor, but he doesn't howl anymore. Mary no longer talks back or demands to be waited upon. She has become

Martha's best helper, and I swear she is almost pretty. I wonder, Doctor, do you think we should ask the Master to come home? What's happening here could be of help to him, too.

That's a wise thought, Mrs. Medlock. I shall send him a telegram. I won't mention Colin but will advise him that his own physical exam is long overdue.

Let us hope he cares, Doctor.

What a team, Danny thought. He knew that Imani and Tim had added lines, but he wasn't sure which lines they were. He saw them shake hands as soon as they set down the table backstage. He thought he had just witnessed a brand new friendship forming. Yes, theater was definitely a team sport.

The rest of the play took place in the garden and was demanding—physically, of course, but in other ways, too. He had to step up to the plate, not to play ball, but act. He had very few lines, which somehow made it harder. Miss Armstrong was right. If you had lines to say, the acting was easier. If you had to keep quiet and react to everything, you really had to stay focused. It was time to forget about Danny and concentrate on Colin, soon to walk again.

Backstage, Danny lifted himself into the wooden wheelchair. Hannah and Porter wheeled him onto the stage behind the scrim and waited in the secret garden. The main curtain opened, the scrim was backlit, and the children were seen as silhouettes. Then the scrim opened from the center, and the lights came full up. The audience cheered.

Beth crossed her fingers. "Hold for applause, guys," she whispered. "Wait for it to die down. Please remember." They did, and the scene began.

Mary and Dickon helped Colin up from the wheelchair. Standing on either side of him, they helped him take tentative steps, and then a few more. Before sitting back down, with Dickon holding the chair steady, Colin took two steps on his own.

Danny had done that much at physical therapy, so his mom and dad would be pleased, but not surprised — yet.

Next, Dickon brought over animals, one by one, and introduced them. Mary, herself, brought Mrs. Fox over. She and the shy fox had become friends.

Then Colin rose, unassisted, to his feet and began to chant. *The sun is shining. That is the Magic. The flowers are growing — the roots are stirring. That is the Magic. Being alive is the Magic — being strong is the Magic. The Magic is in me!*

Now, you must say it, too, Mary and Dickon. Let's say it together!

Mary and Dickon joined hands and danced in a circle while chanting. *The sun is shining. That is the Magic. The flowers are growing — the roots are stirring. That is the Magic. Being alive is the Magic — being strong is the Magic. The Magic is in me!*

Then, carefully, they took Colin's hands and walked slowly in a circle with him.

The children didn't notice that they were no longer alone in the garden. Mr. Craven (Joe) entered. Children trespassing in his deceased, beloved wife's garden? Furious, Mr. Craven watched the children's circle game. Then the pretend fury turned to actual amazement as Joe realized that one of the actors was not a stand-in but Danny himself. Mr. Craven's lower lip quivered before his eyes filled with tears. Colin walked the full width of the garden to him. *Father, don't you recognize me? It's I — Colin.* Tears coursed down Mr. Craven's cheeks, and he made no effort to stop them.

Kurt, who was in on the surprise and knew Danny could walk, nudged Beth. "Wow," he whispered, "Joe is some actor!"

Beth didn't respond. Yes, Joe was good, but he wasn't capable of giving Mr. Craven sudden real tears. Joe was so moved by the sight of Danny Kennedy walking again that he was crying for joy. Could they be seeing the real Joe, or the Joe he could be? In so many ways, a play was an outline, she thought, or maybe a shell. In truth, there were many plays within this play: Danny's story of recovery, Porter discovering his strengths and talent, Hannah learning to give and trust friendships. Beth wasn't sure about herself. Maybe it had to do with what Mom had told her the night before. "Beth, you have grown so much this year. I couldn't be prouder of you."

Finally, Priyanka gave the closing line, as Mary, Dickon, Mr. Craven, and Colin, joined from both sides by the entire cast, crossed down to the apron: *Across the lawn came the Master of Misselthwaite, and he looked as many of them had never seen him. And by his side, with his head up in the air and his eyes full of laughter, walked as strongly and steadily as any boy in Yorkshire – Master Colin!*

The audience went wild as the cast came together and, breaking tradition, first acknowledged the crews by holding up their hands toward the lights booth and applauding. Then they held hands and bowed. They were an ensemble cast. One bow together was all that was needed. As loud as the crowd was, Beth could hear clearly, "Oh, my boy!" Danny's mother and Beth's, best friends, said the same thing at the same time. Danny could walk again, and Porter, Mom told Beth later, could out-act everyone else on that stage!

SCENE 12 – THAT IS THE MAGIC

THE PLAY WAS MAGIC, BETH THOUGHT, late the next night. The whole process—from Miss Armstrong's writing dream and the cast being chosen, all the way through the final performance—was even more magical than the story of *The Secret Garden* itself. No matter what came along before eighth-grade graduation, this was the highlight of her year.

So much magic in one middle school play!

Kylie embracing and thanking Miss Armstrong—that was special. Surely whatever had gone wrong between them was over—and almost magical. What else was magic?

Was it her parents' wonder when they discovered how talented Porter was? Or Uncle Dan and Aunt Jane's stunned amazement, seeing their son walk, realizing that he'd kept it as a grand surprise for them? No one present would ever forget Danny moving across the stage, or crossing down to join the cast in taking a bow. He was not ready to run a race—yet—but it was only a matter of time.

Potentially, Kammy's robin was magical, as it showed her the way to a future, where she must learn to lean on those worthy of trust—and herself.

Hannah no longer looked down with haughty disdain from the branch of a tree. Instead, her magic happened when she embraced her friends and family—finally taking a chance on happiness. And also having a monumental crush on Beth's brother!

These were all grand, beautiful events that should be announced full blast over the intercom, except for the magic Beth would remember most. That was quiet. It was Joe MacCracken, tears rolling down his face when he saw Danny Kennedy walk again.

In her two years at middle school, she'd seen so many people grow and change, in small and major ways: Mateo – Marla – Leland – Gabby – Kurt – Hannah – Danny – her own family. If she continued to observe, she'd see more this year and in the years ahead. The magic was growing and changing—and being alive. She thought of Colin's chant. *The sun is shining. That is the Magic. The flowers are growing—the roots are stirring. That is the Magic. Being alive is the Magic—being strong is the Magic. The Magic is in me.*

"The Magic is in me," Beth whispered.

ABOUT THE AUTHOR

Just A Stage, a continuation of *No Small Parts*, is Marilyn Ludwig's eleventh novel. She was pleased to return to the imaginary village of Castle Bluff, with its striking gingerbread castle and its active theater program at the middle school. During these pandemic times in which real friends aren't often seen, it's been comforting to visit old friends from *No Small Parts*, as well as making new ones. Marilyn is a theater director and a member of the Society of Children's Book Writers and Illustrators (SCBWI). Special thanks to Sarah and Tammy Fantinel, for allowing excerpts from their award-winning play, *Bob's Woodland Adventure*, to be used in this novel.